THE
GRYPHON
HEIST

"Mitch Rapp and Sydney Bristow have nothing on Talia Inger—CIA rookie spy. James Hannibal has crafted a story slam full of mystery, danger, twists, and turns. Breathless with anticipation, I couldn't flip the pages fast enough—or bother to stop to breathe. You don't want to miss this one!"

Lynette Eason, bestselling, award-winning author
of the Blue Justice series

"A movie-worthy tale of espionage and intrigue. Hannibal has done it again."

Steven James, national bestselling author
of *Every Wicked Man*

"Cutting-edge technology and age-old cons collide in this high-stakes thriller from James R. Hannibal. *The Gryphon Heist* plunges readers into a world where no one can be trusted, nothing is as it seems, and choosing the wrong side could be catastrophic."

Lynn H. Blackburn, award-winning and bestselling author
of the Dive Team Investigations series

"Leap on board *The Gryphon Heist* and ride the whirlwind of suspense. Don't let go!"

DiAnn Mills, author of *Burden of Proof*,
www.DiAnnMills.com

THE
GRYPHON
HEIST

JAMES R. HANNIBAL

Revell
a division of Baker Publishing Group
Grand Rapids, Michigan

Published by Revell
a division of Baker Publishing Group
PO Box 6287, Grand Rapids, MI 49516-6287
www.revellbooks.com

Printed in the United States of America

Library of Congress Cataloging-in-Publication Data
Names: Hannibal, James R., author.
Title: The gryphon heist / James R. Hannibal.
Description: Grand Rapids, MI : Revell, a division of Baker Publishing Group,
    [2019]
Identifiers: LCCN 2019013790 | ISBN 9780800735777 (paper)
Subjects: | GSAFD: Christian fiction. | Adventure fiction.
Classification: LCC PS3608.A71576 G79 2019 | DDC 813/.6—dc23
LC record available at https://lccn.loc.gov/2019013790

ISBN 978-0-8007-3713-9 (casebound)

19 20 21 22 23 24 25   7 6 5 4 3 2 1

CHAPTER ONE

PRESENT DAY
UNDISCLOSED LOCATION

TALIA INGER CLUTCHED HER SIDE, letting her shoulder fall against the alley wall. The pain had been growing for the last half hour, threatening to overtake her as it had in Windsor.

Eddie Gupta, her team specialized skills officer, sat cross-legged on the asphalt beside her, hidden from the street by a dumpster defaced with Cyrillic graffiti. He looked up with concern, fingers hovering over a tablet computer. "Are you all right?"

"I'm fine." Talia shoved the pain to the back of her mind. She wouldn't fail—not again. "Bring up Whisper One. Show me the square."

An app expanded to show infrared video of a small city square. A few gray, lukewarm figures drifted across the cold black of the cobblestones. A white heat source flared near the center, blocking out a good bit of the image for a moment before the filters kicked in. The flash subsided to reveal a single individual seated on the edge of a fountain. The hot spot remained where his hand should be for several seconds, then dropped to the ground and was snuffed out, crushed under his heel.

"There's Borov." A hint of British Indian colored Eddie's accent. "He's giving us the all-clear signal. Do you remember his code name?"

7

Talia shot him a look, and he answered with a sly smile. She remembered everything. Always. Eddie knew that. Her eyes returned to the drone feed. "Escort, Siphon is ready. Move in."

"On it, Control," a young woman replied through Talia's earpiece. "Moving now."

The infrared camera on Eddie's Whisper nano-drone picked up another gray figure entering the square from the west, moving toward the fountain at a brisk pace. Even from behind the alley dumpster, two streets away, Talia could hear the echoing *clop* of the linguist's designer heels on the stones. "Take it easy, Kayla," she said, using the girl's name instead of her call sign to be sure she caught her attention. Kayla hated the handle *Escort*, anyway. "Slow is fast, remember?"

The linguist slowed her pace to an exaggerated stroll. Talia closed her eyes and shook her head. She should have kept her mouth shut. The abrupt change looked out of place in the quiet square—enough to draw the attention of any local opposition. She held her breath. The pain in her side flared. But no enemy forces stormed in to grab Kayla.

Alexi Borov's deep grumble came to her through the comm link—a low, intense string of Belarusian. When he moved to stand, Kayla touched his arm and sat beside him, offering what Talia hoped were whispered assurances of his safety. After a few tense seconds, he nodded. More grumbles. Kayla switched to English. "Two, six, nine, seven."

A third player read back the sequence. "Two, six, nine, seven. Black Bag copies. Stand by."

In the silence that followed, Eddie glanced up at Talia. She gave him a smile, made thin by her pain. "We'll make it. It's been a year. We can last another twenty minutes."

One year.

One year of academics, field craft, and mock missions, knowing everything—fake embassy balls, live-fire exercises, chance meetings with undercover agents in Chestertown—everything was a test. Talia's only break had been the TGT—the Trainee Grand Tour—which had taken her across four continents in two months, sampling every menial, low-risk job the Agency could offer. And even that had ended in a twenty-page evaluation from six different supervisors. One year of weeding out the chaff.

Only five candidates remained. Tonight was their final exam.

Success hinged on two interconnected objectives: extract a Belarusian scientist from an urban environment and use his access code to steal a device from a corporate lab. They had Siphon in hand. Once Black Bag recovered the device and Talia got them all to the extraction point, the rest was pomp and paperwork. She would pass through the black curtain into the CIA's Directorate of Operations, better known as the Clandestine Service.

Scott, the candidate who had read back the numeric sequence, broke the silence on the comms. "Green light, Control. Code one was solid. Black Bag is inside the compound."

"Copy." Talia widened her eyes at Eddie in a *here we go* look. "Escort, Siphon's info is genuine. Get him to the bridge."

Eddie tapped the screen again. The first window shrank to half its size and a second window labeled WHISPER TWO opened beside it, giving them a bird's-eye view of a walled compound. Four L-shaped office buildings surrounded a flat bunker. Two gray figures, her teammates Hannah and Scott acting together as Black Bag, slipped through a gate in the south wall and crouch-ran to the shadows of the nearest structure. Another pair casually strolled in their direction, leaving the central bunker. None of the candidates knew what waited inside that bunker, the infamous Sanctum. No graduate had ever revealed the answer. They were spies, after all, and what good were spies who couldn't keep secrets?

"Black Bag, two guards are headed your way. Use the eastern approach."

"Copy. Black Bag is moving east. We'll be at the door in minutes, Control. We need the second code."

Talia gave Kayla a chance to reply, but the linguist was busy. She and Borov had stopped at the exit from the square, arguing in whispered Belarusian.

"Escort?"

"Siphon says the western street will be watched." Kayla turned north, letting the mock scientist take the lead. "He knows a better route, to the south."

Eddie opened his mouth to protest, but Talia held up a hand to quiet him. She called up a map of the city in her head and looked for a route to the bridge. It would work. "That's fine, Escort. Tell him we need the second code, though."

"He says we'll get it when we're out of danger."

"Great." Scott's usual pessimism came in loud and clear. "So we play hide-and-seek with armed guards until Siphon gets a warm, fuzzy feeling inside? Escort, shove your gun in his ear and see if that changes his mind."

"Negative, Black Bag," Talia said. "That's not how we do business."

"Right. I forgot who was running this op. Miss Everything by the Book."

Strange motion on the video feed cut the argument short. Talia watched as the roof of the Sanctum expanded to fill the frame. "Eddie, check Whisper Two. You've got a runaway zoom."

The SSO tapped the screen, frowned, and tapped harder as granules of cinder on the roof rushed toward the lens. The feed went black.

Scott's voice grew tense on the audio link. "We heard a *crunch* from the Sanctum. The guards are moving that way."

Eddie locked eyes with Talia. "That was not a zoom issue."

"I know. Redirect Whisper One. We need to get eyes on our team."

Kayla and Borov moved out of frame as the drone left them behind. Through the SATCOM, Talia distinctly heard the scientist say *"Prabaččie."* With his sorrowful tone and inflection, it sounded so similar to a phrase she knew in Russian. *"Prostitye."*

Forgive me.

She heard a metallic *sptt.* Kayla let out a muffled cry. At the same time Whisper One dropped out of the sky and crashed into the Sanctum roof beside the first.

"Escort, check in!"

Nothing but static.

"Kayla? Kayla, respond!" Talia clenched her fist, pounding the brick wall behind her, and then doubled over to stop the needles shooting through her midsection.

The pain had been with her for years, most of her life. But it had not become crippling until the previous spring, at Windsor, in the middle of the national rowing championships. It had cost Talia the gold medal. The team doctors at Georgetown had found nothing. The specialists had checked her kidneys, her liver, her blood-work. Nothing. Now with her career—her future—on the line, it was back.

"You are *not* fine." Eddie stood, taking her elbow to support her.

She pushed him back. "Doesn't matter. Black Bag, Siphon sold us out. You're walking into an ambush."

Scott didn't answer. They had no visuals and no comms. They would have to breach the Sanctum both deaf and blind.

CHAPTER
TWO

EDDIE SLAPPED THE TABLET down into his lap. "I have heard rumors about this. Whole classes wash out on Sanctum night. This is the Kobayashi Maru."

Talia gave him a blank stare.

He spread his hands. "The Kobayashi Maru. *Star Trek*? How is it possible you don't know this?"

She jerked him out of the alley.

With their SIG Sauer P226s drawn, Talia and Eddie hurried across the square. She kept her weapon down, reminding herself to aim chest level if she encountered a threat. The Farm's Simunition paint rounds looked and fired like real bullets, carrying enough velocity to make a head shot deadly.

"I can hack the instructor cameras," Eddie said, puffing hard and pushing his glasses into place as the two threw their backs against the compound wall.

She made no answer, leaning forward just enough to look up and down the perimeter.

"Hacking the system is exactly what they want us to do—thinking outside the box and all that." Eddie nudged her with an elbow. "We are spies now. Sometimes spies break the rules. Besides, it worked for James T. Kirk."

Spies played dirty. Talia understood. At the Farm, there had been plenty of morality discussions. The book was for the über-nerds at the FBI. But how quickly would good guys cease to be good when they crossed every line? "We're not hacking the instructor cams. That's cheating. And since you went there, Kirk slept with every green alien girl who crossed his path. Maybe you should find a new role model."

Eddie stomped his foot. "You *do* know *Star Trek*."

Siphon's code still worked on the southern door to the compound. Talia and Eddie ran to the shelter of a colonnade of trees bordering the same building where they had last seen their teammates. "Black Bag, say your status."

Nothing.

"Hannah? Scott?"

White static filled the comms. In the darkness beyond the trees, there were muted flashes, accompanied by four rapid spits. The two crept to the edge and found Hannah and Scott lying motionless on the cobblestones. Red blotches marked their tactical vests. There was no sign of the shooter.

Eddie poked Scott with the toe of his boot. "So much for Black Bag."

This earned him a glower from below. Scott bared his teeth, but he remained silent. The rules were clear.

Meanwhile, Talia grabbed the collar of Hannah's vest and dragged her back into the enclave of trees. She thrust a chin at Scott. "Grab him, Eddie. We have to get them out of sight."

"Why bother? We're blown."

"We're not blown. We're betrayed. Where are the guards? The sirens?" Talia reached the bushes and lowered Hannah to the grass. "Borov must have doubled back. He got the Agency's money. Now he wants his corporate payday, but he'll have to silence us first. That has to be the scenario we're facing."

When Eddie failed to move Scott, Talia did the job herself, grunting against the phantom pain in her side. "I saw a jeep . . . outside . . . the compound. We retrieve the device, drag the bodies out . . . and drive to the bridge." She didn't have enough strength left to lower Scott gently to the grass. She dropped him.

Scott let out an involuntary "*Oomph!*"

"Shhh!" Talia gave him a stern frown, then pointed at Eddie. "I am *not losing this*. Got it? Get the charges. Hannah has them."

Eddie folded his arms. "We don't have the second code. How are we supposed to enter the Sanctum?"

"Hannah. Has. *The charges.*"

"Oh, right." As Eddie squatted next to his teammate, Hannah opened one eye and stared at him hard. He pulled his hands back. "Um. Where *exactly* did she put them?"

"Now, Eddie."

"Okay. Not a problem." The SSO winced as he patted the pockets on Hannah's thighs and midsection. "Sorry. So sorry."

"Eddie," Talia hissed at him, "what are the two keys to infiltration?"

"Uh . . . Shut up and hurry up."

She gave him a *you're not doing either* glare.

"Found them." He held up two black discs, the size of hockey pucks, and followed her up the lane leading to the Sanctum.

The bunker looked unguarded, but that was too much to hope for. Talia and Eddie were halfway to the Sanctum's steel door when two silhouettes wandered into the orange circle of light spilling from the lamp above.

Talia pressed Eddie back against the wall, her side throbbing.

The guards looked their way and started down the lane.

An alcove a few feet away offered the only shelter. She pulled Eddie into it. He sniffled, and she dug her fingernails into his arm in the universal signal for *Don't you dare sneeze.*

The guards walked past.

When Talia and Eddie reached the circle of light, she held an explosive disc close to the door and let its magnetic backing do the rest. The disc jumped from her hand and clamped itself to the metal with a soft *clink*. She glanced at Eddie. "Backpack."

"What about it?"

"Give it to me."

"Uh . . . This is my *personal* gear, Talia. This bag is a Givenchy."

"You bought a designer bag? This is why you haven't had a date since our junior year." Talia glanced up and down the intersecting street. They couldn't stay in the light, exposed, for much longer. "I'll need your tactical vest too. And your sweatshirt. Hurry up."

A knife through the strap, wedged into the doorframe, held the pack in place over the charge, and Talia stuffed it near to bursting with the vest and sweatshirt. She dialed the charge to its lowest setting and started the timer, and the two retreated to a safe distance.

There was a light *pop* and a muted flash. White smoke rose from behind the Givenchy bag.

Eddie let out a quiet whimper. "Twelve hundred dollars."

"For a backpack?"

"It's *real* leather."

Somewhere, watching through the instructor feed, a judge must have decided the mock explosive had done its job. The steel door swung inward with a long, awkward *creak*. The two crossed the circle of light and pushed inside.

"Whoa," Eddie said, smoking backpack hanging from his right hand.

The Sanctum.

Weapon ready, Talia peered over a polished green rail. Five levels of arched mahogany galleries and light green pillars descended below them, all the way to a bottom floor made of the same stone. The balcony walkways each formed a different shape—hexagon, pentagon, square, and triangle.

Eddie slipped his tactical vest over his head. "If we were in a video game, this would be the palace of the final boss. Is that ... jade?"

"Someone at the CIA has a flare for the dramatic." Talia shook her head. "And no regard for the taxpayers." On the floor at the bottom of the chamber, she saw an old, worn briefcase with the letters CEMP painted sloppily on the side. "The target is down there. Out in the open."

"Then let's grab it." Eddie made for the nearest stairwell.

Talia caught his arm. "Wait. This is too easy."

"Tell that to Scott, Hannah, and Kayla."

"Think about it. The case *must* be guarded. Maybe they're hiding beneath the balcony."

Eddie produced the second charge. "So drop this baby down the disturbing green well. Boom. Problem solved."

"We can't. Those guards are just doing their job. No collateral damage, Eddie." Talia's pain flared again. She winced, but she gritted her teeth and waved off the offered explosive, starting toward the stairs.

She expected a surprise around every corner, but found none. The jade floor at the bottom level remained quiet and empty. The briefcase called to her from the center.

"Perhaps that's it." Eddie panned his SIG from left to right. "Inside the case we'll find a message. 'Congratulations. You win.'"

His suggestion didn't sound right. Talia still had to get her team, bodies and all, to the bridge. But in the moment, she saw no obstacles. She walked out across the floor, reaching for the briefcase.

Thunk.

Talia heard the spit of the suppressor and wheeled in time to see Eddie drop to the floor, a red blotch on his chest.

No. No, no, no. She dodged the bullet she knew was coming and made a grab for the case, but her hand fell short.

Thunk.

The impact of a Simunition round slamming into the small of her back only added to the pain. Talia spun. The room around her spun as well.

Amid the slow pitch and tilt of the jade floor and the mahogany arches, the fake Borov grinned, covering her with a silenced Stechkin pistol. "It appears I've caught intruders within the Sanctum."

He wasn't talking to Talia.

Mary Jordan, chief of the CIA's Russian Eastern European Division and the woman who had recruited Talia two years before, walked deliberately to the center of the room and picked up the case. She wore a submachine gun slung at her side, a twin to those carried by the guards. "You're tenacious, Talia. But you still failed." She cocked her head, squinting a little. "And by the way, when the opposing force shoots you, you're supposed to fall. Rules are rules."

She raised the gun and opened fire.

CHAPTER THREE

THE POTOMAC RIVER
EAST OF THE GEORGETOWN BOATHOUSE

DO YOU WANT to change the world, Miss Inger?

Sweat beaded on Talia's forehead. A drop of it trickled down her neck behind dark hair threaded into a tight ponytail. With rhythmic cadence, she lifted her oars out of the water, compressed her body against the stop, and dropped them in again for one angry pull after another. The racing shell surged against the current.

After the humiliation of the exercise, sleep had not been an option. Talia had retreated to the Potomac. Most of her classmates at Georgetown had been transplants, but Washington, DC, was Talia's home, and when the world turned against her, she always ran to the river.

Talia closed her eyes, trying and failing to block out overlapping visions of Mary Jordan. One moment the CIA officer was standing over her with a Kalashnikov. The next, she was seated on a sunlit bench on Georgetown University's Healy Lawn the day the two had met, smiling and looking so much like the woman Talia had always wanted to be—fierce, in command, unstoppable. Talia saw every detail of both moments, the curse of an eidetic memory.

Another pull against the current. Another breath.

"Do you want to change the world, Miss Inger?" Jordan, the picture of power chic in an Armani skirt suit, had laid a file between them on the wooden bench. "We've had our eye on you, a scholarship kid rising out of the foster care system to the top of her class, a force to be reckoned with in women's crew." The CIA officer had lifted her Wayfarers, concern clouding her eyes. "Your file says you submitted an application to the FBI—that you want to make a difference. You can do that at the CIA, Talia, on a global scale."

A force to be reckoned with. Jordan had honed in on the one thing Talia wanted—needed—to be after a life in foster care. And from that moment, Talia became her disciple. Jordan guided her course selections and placed her in the intern program at the State Department. But there was a catch. Talia had to withdraw her application to the FBI. She also had to turn down several lucrative corporate offers. They didn't matter. The Agency became her only goal.

The sweat came in rivulets, gliding down the back of Talia's neck. Her breathing grew more labored, but she kept up her rhythm—compress, drive, compress, drive—approaching the twenty-degree bend at the Three Sisters islands. Her quads and shoulders burned. Her chest and back ached. The phantom pain in her side had subsided, making room for the bruises left by Jordan's Simunition rounds.

"You gave up the high ground." Jordan had pulled Talia up from the Sanctum floor and walked her to an elevator. The green fluorescents gave both their faces a sickly hue. "You broke the cardinal rule," she said as the doors closed. "What were you thinking? I taught you better."

The scull dug a shallow curve through the water as Talia made the quarter turn at the Three Sisters. Another half mile to go. Her paddles left a pair of swirling circles each time she pulled them from the water. Talia broke her rhythm to wipe her eyes, blurry from sweat and tears.

"The high ground is everything." Jordan pounded her fist into her hand. "When you run an operation, you do whatever it takes to maintain the advantage. You mine every resource until you hit bedrock. You leverage your tech. You get an edge and you *keep* it."

"The instructors failed our tech. We had no options."

"Don't give me that. Gupta offered you *two* options, upstaging you on the review tapes. You could have hacked the compound network or dropped the charge into the Sanctum and killed everyone on the bottom floor."

"But killing innocent guards wasn't the job."

"The *job* was to complete the *mission*." Jordan looked her in the eyes. "We serve a greater good. And sometimes that responsibility mandates a broken rule. Sometimes it demands a sacrifice."

Talia had seen a coldness in her gaze then—a coldness she didn't know if she could emulate. Maybe she wasn't a young Jordan after all.

When the elevator doors opened, Jordan had walked briskly out onto the empty streets, leaving Talia behind. "You failed, sweetie. I was wrong about you, and you're out. Tough luck."

The two-mile marker at Windy Run flashed by, and Talia let up, allowing her blades to skim the surface for balance. Her legs and arms shook. She had poured everything, all the anger and fear, into the river. Dipping an oar, she brought the shell about for the drift back to the boathouse and then dropped her head to her knees and sobbed.

A dog tag slipped from Talia's shirt, hanging from her neck by a silver chain. She clutched it to her chest. In her memories of her father, there had been a second tag and a cross made of bronze nails as well, but they had been lost by the mortuary after the accident. At least, that's what Talia assumed. She had been only seven years old.

He was the reason she always came back to the river. Looking up through her tears, Talia could see him there, at the shore, with a little girl standing next to him in red rubber galoshes. He whispered in the little girl's ear. *So this line came up empty, Natalia. Cast another and things will look better. Remember who is in control.*

She let out a bitter laugh. The *one in control* had stolen him from her. Now Jordan had betrayed her too.

Talia caught movement at the boathouse and dried her eyes. The last thing she needed was for a stranger to see her crying. But the waiting figure was no stranger. As Talia guided the shell alongside the dock, Mary Jordan reached down to help her out of the boat.

"Good morning. Let's talk."

FOUR

THE POTOMAC RIVER
GEORGETOWN BOATHOUSE

TALIA SWUNG AN OAR onto the dock, forcing Jordan back. "I don't need your help."

The CIA officer nodded as Talia pressed herself up to a crouch in the boat, perfectly balanced, and stepped onto the dock. "No, I guess you don't. Not with this, anyway."

The statement was obvious bait, but Talia made no retort. Her patience for games had run out. She had failed. She didn't have to play anymore. She hauled the thirty-pound shell out of the water and again forced Jordan to hop out of the way, swinging the boat around to lay it on the wash rack.

"Do you know the problem with winners?" Jordan dodged a ribbon of soapy water as Talia slapped a sponge against the hull. "The team captains and the valedictorians, the state champions and the triple threats—that's what we get at the Farm. That's what I was, and that's what you were."

That's what you were. Past tense. Talia dipped the sponge into the bucket and drew it out, slinging the water. She didn't take precise aim at the Armani skirt, but she made no effort to avoid it, either.

"Failure," Jordan said, once Talia had made it clear she would not be goaded into conversation. "Failure is what's missing from a winner's résumé, and the need for failure is the reason I had the Farm pull out all the stops for your final exam. I created a Kobayashi Maru, as Gupta so elegantly noted."

The shock of her blatant admission shook Talia out of her silence. "So you set us up." She wrung out the sponge, wishing it was Jordan's neck. "You had no right."

"Oh, Talia. You and I and all the other alphas who find their way to the Farm spend so much time at the top that we forget what failure feels like." She removed her sunglasses and wiped off the mist from Talia's passive-aggressive cleaning. "What kind of operative does that produce?"

"You're forgetting Windsor—my silver at nationals."

Jordan took on a look of mock sympathy. "Oh no. *Boo-hoo Barbie* got second place." She frowned. "I'm talking about the instructive power of a gut-wrenching, life-altering defeat. Total failure, Talia. That's what every upcoming officer needs." Jordan stopped the sponge with a hand on Talia's. "And that's exactly what I told the review board an hour ago, while I was fighting for your future."

"My . . . future?" Hope bloomed.

"I'm here with an opportunity."

Hope faded. An opportunity—not a graduation certificate. Jordan had brought her a consolation prize.

Talia yanked her hand away and carried her bucket into the boathouse to exchange it for a hose and sprayer.

Jordan called to her from the dock. "Ask yourself why I came down on you so hard. Maybe I care. Maybe I've learned over the years that a blade reforged from broken pieces is always stronger than the original."

Talia stopped, listening.

"When you're ready to talk, you know where to find me." Jordan's voice grew distant. "But don't wait too long. Some doors don't stay open forever."

By the time Talia emerged into sunlight again, dragging the hose, her mentor had gone.

TALIA'S SHOWER STARTED SLOW and finished quickly as the steam carried off some of the bitterness, leaving room for reflection. Jordan had promised an opportunity. She had spoken of Talia's future. What if the door to the CIA remained open?

She hurried across the road to the campus with hair still damp from the shower, feeling the coolness of the April morning. Her phone buzzed as she approached Healy Lawn. Talia frowned at the caller ID and, with a quick tap, rejected the call.

"What part of my speech brought you back?" Jordan sat with her legs crossed on the same bench where the two had met three years earlier.

"The part you left out." Talia slid a strand of wet hair back over her ear as she sat beside her. "You said you fought for me with the board. How did they answer?"

"Kayla's in." Jordan managed to avoid the question. "Linguists with her level of skill are hard to come by. Scott and Hannah"—she winced—"they were already low on points. To be honest, Hannah was always destined for the analysts' floor, and Scott was always destined to be the assistant manager at Joe's Burgers in Chestertown."

"And Eddie?"

Jordan smiled. "Don't you want to know your own status?"

How could this woman manipulate her so easily? "Yes."

"Okay then." Jordan laid a manila folder down on the bench. "Here it is."

"Is that—?"

"Your first posting."

Moscow Station. Talia reached for the folder. She deserved Moscow. She had fought for every point at the Farm to earn Moscow.

Jordan dropped a knuckle to keep her from picking it up. "It's not Moscow."

"But—"

Jordan cocked her head.

"I failed the final. I gave up the high ground."

Once Jordan removed her knuckle, Talia was slow in picking up the folder. A part of her didn't want to face it. If not Moscow, where? Greenland? The Sudan? Or worse. Cleveland. She opened the folder and read the heading. "This is . . . here, in Washington." She looked up at Jordan. "I've been assigned to your division."

A positive amid all the disappointment. Under Jordan's leadership, the Russian Eastern European Division of the Directorate of Operations had built a sterling reputation. Jordan had a flare for getting REED's people to the right locations at the right time with all the right information. "You won't be working directly under me." Jordan rested an elbow on the back of the bench. "Not yet. But REED is a great place to cut your teeth. It's not Moscow, but it's a foot in the door."

The two stood. Jordan glanced at Talia's purse. "You rejected a call as you were walking up. Who was it?"

"No one. No one important."

"This is a critical year for you. You don't have time for relationships."

"I know. It wasn't a guy."

"Good." Jordan inclined her head in the general direction of Langley. "Now get over there. Getting riddled with bullets doesn't buy you a day off, not in my house. And, Talia"—Jordan lowered the Wayfarers to the bridge of her nose—"welcome to the Clandestine Service."

CHAPTER FIVE

A WELL-DRESSED GENTLEMAN sat in the refined comfort of a nineteenth-century town house near the Georgetown campus, gazing out through its third-floor windows and sipping his favorite tea—Earl Gray with a dash of milk.

He watched the young woman walk away from her rendezvous with Mary Jordan. A camera, rotating on an automated gimbal, tracked the subject's progress until she passed beyond the weathered concrete blocks of the university library. With its track lost, the camera stopped rotating and bowed its lens, defeated.

"Don't worry, my friend." The man lifted the device and laid it in the custom foam cutout of a carrying case. "You did your job well, as always."

After securing the camera, he pressed a laser microphone into the foam beside it, chuckling to himself. Both tools fit into a case smaller than a child's lunch box, but the gentleman remembered a time when a listening device alone required a backpack worthy of an Everest Sherpa. Those were the days of parabolic microphones.

Today he had shone a pen-size laser beam on the iron leg of a park bench to capture the voices of the two women. Vibrations imperceptible to the human eye returned to the transmitter-receiver, where a tablet computer transformed them into crystal-clear, real-time playback. Easy and inexpensive.

The gentleman made a *tsk* noise with his tongue and unfolded the tablet's detachable keyboard. The girl was new to the game, but Jordan should have been more cautious. Then again, for this meet, the CIA officer had chosen a noisy closed campus with brick buildings on three sides. How could she have anticipated an adversary willing to take out a quarter-of-a-million-dollar lease on a nearby residence in hopes of catching a single conversation?

The well-dressed gentleman allowed himself a grin.

Sipping his tea, he selected three segments of video and dropped them into a shared folder for his employer to review, then folded up the keyboard. Before he could shut off the tablet, a chat window popped open. A line of text appeared under the username ICRON11.

Files received. Your analysis?

What did his employer expect him to say? The man closed his eyes for a heartbeat, took an additional fifteen to pour his third cup of tea, adding the milk first, and typed an answer.

She is in. Just as you desired.

The reply came back sharp and quick.

I desired none of this.

The gentleman had touched a nerve, as intended. Despite more than one heated discussion, he still felt his employer was rushing into this. He frowned at the screen.

Are you certain you are ready for her?

The chat window closed on its own, ending the conversation.

CHAPTER SIX

TALIA MADE TWO STOPS on her way to the Directorate of Operations, deep in the bowels of the New Headquarters Building at Langley. The first was not by choice. A set of turnstiles straight out of a New York subway barred her entry. She scanned a temporary ID card across a black panel on the center turnstile. It answered with a sharp buzz and a red octagon.

Before Talia could try the turnstile next door, a contract guard in a black uniform pushed out through a panel in the wall, one hand on the 9mm at his side. The safety was off. "Good morning, Miss Inger. I'll take that temp from you. Turn and face the camera, please."

She handed over her badge, looking in the direction he indicated. "What cam—"

A bulb flashed.

"That'll do. Wait here."

The security protective officer, known as a SPO, vanished into the wall and returned moments later with a new badge. He also brought out a stack of forms big enough to put all other stacks of forms everywhere to shame. "First-day paperwork. Tax forms, emergency contact, living will."

"I don't want a living will."

"Take it up with legal." The SPO swiped the new badge on the turnstile, slapped it down on top of the forms, and waved her through. "Ops. Sublevel 3."

The conversation was over.

She walked on, reading the top form through the curled purple ribbon of the lanyard. The second line listed her supervisor.

FRANK BRENNAN, DIRECTORATE OF OPERATIONS,
RUSSIAN EASTERN EUROPEAN DIVISION.

Talia's second stop fulfilled a minor fantasy. Farm students, with their futures still in question, had no access to the New Headquarters Building. They could only gaze up at its impenetrable green glass walls from the garden of the Old Headquarters Building, wondering what treasures lay inside. Talia had seen evidence of one such treasure in the hands of officers and analysts wandering the grounds. Now, having entered Aladdin's Cave, she could smell it.

Passing beneath a model of the A-12 OXCART, the forerunner to the SR-71 Blackbird, she followed the scent of roasted coffee beans to a sun-filled atrium. There, surrounded by storefront café tables, she found the CIA compound's most infamous and alluring feature—its very own top-secret Starbucks.

"One venti white chocolate mocha, please."

"Skinny?" The barista, a black woman with the name LU-ANNE printed on an extra-large green apron, looked Talia up and down and added just enough inflection to the word to leave Talia wondering whether it was a question or an indictment.

Talia took it as a challenge. She dropped her stack of forms on the counter with a heavy *thwap*. "No." She checked herself a moment later. "But no whip."

Luanne turned her body toward the coffeemakers, letting her head follow half a second later. "Your funeral. First day, honey?"

"Come again?"

"Those forms you so loudly dropped on my counter. I seen 'em a thousand times if I seen 'em once, along with that deer-in-the-headlights look in your badge photo." She placed a hand on her hip, glancing over her shoulder. "You have any idea where you're goin', rookie?"

Agency employees were never supposed to talk about their positions, even on campus, unless the other party had a need to know. Exactly what sort of background check did a CIA barista get? "I can figure it out."

Luanne returned to her work, lowering a steamer into a steel cup. "Aright."

The coffee took far longer in coming than Talia anticipated, and by the time she had paid for and accepted the overlarge cup, she felt the morning closing in on her. She swept up her stack and walked off.

Luanne whistled. "Nope." She pointed the opposite direction, toward a passage intersecting the main hallway.

"How do you—"

"Your badge. That purple outline around your photo tells me you belong to Ops."

Talia nodded and reversed course.

"And you'll want a lid for that coffee."

"I'm fine, thanks."

Luanne did her little turn—body first, then head, raising a hand. "Like I said, rookie. Your funeral."

The doors in the hallway to which Luanne directed Talia had numbers but no labels, and each was painted a solid color. Most were single or double doors, but in one alcove was a set of elevator doors—painted purple, the color Luanne had noted on Talia's badge.

The elevator, of course, required a swipe of her card for access, and two failed attempts loosened her tenuous hold on her forms. The third swipe succeeded, and in her hurry to step inside, Talia caught the corner of her stack on an opening door, ripping the whole mess from her arms.

Papers flew.

Hot, sugary mocha splashed on her wrist, soaking her cuff.

Somehow this was all Luanne's doing.

Half of the forms fell inside the elevator and half out. Talia knelt and gathered what she could, but a small platoon of drenched papers clung to the floor. The elevator let out a ding. It wanted to leave, with or without her. She stood and stomped on the stragglers, dragging them across the threshold as the doors slid closed. Another patron with a purple lanyard hurried toward her, hand outstretched, but she gave him a helpless shrug. "Sorry!"

Could her first day get any worse?

Dumb question.

Sublevel 3, that's what the guard had said. She hit the button, and thankfully the elevator did not stop at any other levels on the way down. She passed six in total. Thanks to the varied terrain of the hilltop compound, the main entrance was on Level 4. The long descent allowed Talia to regain some dignity. By the time the doors opened, she had picked up the rest of her papers and assembled them into a semi-chaotic pile.

She ventured out into an incongruous blend of black marble columns and acrylic offices. A sign hanging from the ceiling read RUSSIAN EASTERN EUROPEAN DIVISION. "Frank Brennan?" Talia directed her gaze at a passerby wearing a black far-too-tight-for-arms-like-that golf shirt. "I'm looking for Frank Brennan."

Tight-Shirt Guy looked sidelong at her coffee-stained forms and walked on.

Talia tried again, calling after him and reaching out with the now half-empty coffee cup. "Excuse me. Where can I fi—"

He disappeared behind a marble wall.

She lowered the cup. "Never mind."

Brass plates identified the first few acrylic-walled branches as BALTIC STATES, FORMER YUGOSLAVIA, UKRAINE, and RUSSIA. Each plate also identified the branch chief—none of whom were Frank Brennan.

The denizens of Sublevel 3 drew diagrams on their clear walls, tapped at computer keyboards, and argued across conference tables. Not one soul made eye contact with Talia, and she wasn't about to go around reading ID badges to find her boss. She took a deep breath, marched to what she decided was the intersection of the two main aisles, and raised her voice. "Does *anyone* know where I can find Frank Brennan?"

The buzz of conversation slackened. A few dozen eyes turned her way. Then they all went back to work.

"Talia?" Eddie Gupta popped his head out from behind a column. "Together again, huh? I've been waiting for you. Our section is this way."

He walked past her, heading the way she'd come, and Talia assumed she'd simply missed the correct office. She was wrong. The buzz of activity fell behind. The two walked past the elevator and down a dimly lit hallway to a dented gray door.

Eddie bowed, gesturing with both hands. "After you, m'lady."

"Here?" She couldn't keep her expression from falling. "This looks like a utility closet." The door had its own brass plate, like the acrylic partitions. But while those plates were bolted in place, this one was pasted on, one corner a nanometer south of level, and it listed no region name or branch chief.

The brass plate simply read OTHER.

CHAPTER
SEVEN

OTHER BRANCH'S UTILITY-CLOSET feel did not improve when Talia opened the door. She had suspected it wouldn't. Walking down the dark hallway, the same pit had opened in her stomach she'd often felt as a foster child arriving at a new home. Plastic furniture on the lawn, a garden with more weeds than flowers, siding hanging loose between the windows—the inside of a house like that was never going to look like a palace. Its occupants would never be royalty ready to adopt her as a princess.

The sole occupant of Other was no exception.

"Good. You're here. It's about time." Frank Brennan swiveled to face them in his desk chair, but did not bother getting up.

Talia was not entirely certain he *could* get up. Like his tiny section, with its water-stained walls and chipped Formica workstations, Frank Brennan had seen better days.

A corded phone rested on his shoulder, mercilessly trapped between the lower of his two chins and a plaid button-down marred by pit stains. "Good start, by the way." With a shrug, Brennan dropped the phone into his hand and hung it up. "That was my esteemed colleague from Ukraine Branch, filing the first

33

of what I can only imagine will be many complaints." The chair squeaked forward. He rested his elbows on the table. "For future reference, Miss Inger, please refrain from shouting my name in these hallowed halls. It won't win you any friends."

"The shouting?" Talia set her forms and coffee down on a rare patch of uncluttered Formica. "Or your name?"

"Both." Brennan lifted one elbow to point at a red-and-white box teetering atop a stack of three-ring binders. "Donuts are over there."

"Nobody eats donuts anymore."

"More for me then." For emphasis, he sat back and peeled a white-powdered blob off a napkin. He took a gratuitous bite, leaving a good bit of it on his mustache.

Eddie raised a hesitant finger, circling near his own lip. "You've got something—"

"Got what?" Brennan asked, pressing bushy eyebrows together.

"Nothing."

"Relax, kid. I'm just messing with ya." Brennan wiped the powder away, transferring it from his mustache to the hair of his arm. He caught Talia's disapproving scowl and nodded at the coffee-stained cuff peeking out from her cardigan sleeve. "Oh, like you're the Queen of Clean?"

Talia pulled the sleeve down to cover it and, remembering the lanyard she had hastily thrown over her head, she untucked her hair from its hold and smoothed out the strays.

Brennan looked bemused by her discomfort. "Welcome to Other, children. You now have the privilege of working for this sublevel's longest continuous resident. Read into that what you will."

Talia would. She already had, and it was nothing good. "I'm . . . happy to be here." Her eyes dropped to a file on the edge of Brennan's desk. The sooner she got to work, the sooner she could claw her way out to a real branch. "So what does Other have in the way of current ops?" she asked, reaching for the file.

The donut fell to its napkin, sending up a cloud of white as Brennan slapped down a paw and dragged the file from under her hand. "We should establish some rules. Rule One: files on my desk are for my eyes only. You don't mess with need-to-know around here. Got it?"

Talia took a step back. "Okay . . . what's Rule Two?"

"I'll let you know when I think of it."

The new tension in the room triggered Eddie's shy-geek defenses. Talia heard the familiar whir of a five-bladed fidget spinner. Eddie had made it while they were at Georgetown together, out of copper and cobalt. He claimed the toy was so perfectly balanced it would spin forever, but his fingers worked the blades with steady rhythm when he was nervous. She cringed at the look on Brennan's face.

"What is he doing?"

"It helps me focus," Eddie said, answering for himself between spins.

Talia reached back and covered the thing with her hand, pressing it down toward Eddie's pocket. "No, it doesn't. Put it away."

Whatever she thought of the habit, Eddie's spinner tamed the bear she had drawn out of Brennan by going for the file. Brennan tucked the file into a locking drawer and thrust the upper of his two chins at some dusty three-ring binders piled on a workstation. "We'll make this Rule Two. Before you even think about current ops, commit every detail of the illustrious territories of Other to memory."

It was a dumb rule, but Talia did not argue. She picked up a binder marked ABKHAZIA, pretending to read but wondering about the mystery file. Brennan had gone from eccentric uncle to raging überboss in less than a heartbeat. Could mere concern for need-to-know cause such a reaction? What was he hiding?

CHAPTER
EIGHT

MERIDIAN HILL PARK
WASHINGTON, DC

FRANK BRENNAN LEFT HIS CAR in the visitors' lot of his DC apartment complex and walked through the adjacent park on the way to his condo. He had a garage. He was *paying* for a garage. But an Agency doctor had ordered him to walk the half mile between the open lot and his front door twice a day. All that exercise had not made a dent in his weight. A daily mile was no match for equally frequent helpings of steak and jelly-filled pastries.

The unfairness of it disrupted his thoughts so much he almost missed the signal beside the path. Not that it was easy to see in the first place. The rock, set at the eight o'clock position in the shadow of an oversize flowerpot, was nearly invisible to his aging, borderline-diabetic eyes.

Brennan kicked the rock into the foliage and checked his watch as he turned back toward the car, doubling his pace. Eight o'clock. He had less than thirty minutes to cover the distance. What were they trying to do? Kill him?

Frank's collar was still wet with sweat when he pulled up to the little Armenian restaurant off Route 1. The location had been his choice when these meetings started, close enough to drive from the condo, far enough from the city centers around DC that he wasn't likely to run into anyone he knew. The two-star Yelp rating didn't hurt either.

He found his contact seated in a corner booth with his face shrouded in shadow. Frank slid in across from him, squeezing his gut past the table. "You know how I hate being summoned."

The gentleman, overdressed, twisted a silver cuff link at his wrist and folded his hands. "Do not think of it as a summons. Think of it as a request for an audience—a meeting between colleagues."

"I said the same thing to an agent I was cultivating in Belarus once." Frank drew a laminated menu from its holder. "The GRU shot him a week later. Don't manage me. Just get to the point."

"As you wish." The contact lifted the menu from his fingers. "And you won't be needing that. I've already taken the liberty."

"Of course you have."

A waiter brought the overdressed gentleman a plate of lamb kebabs and slid a hollowed-out pumpkin in front of Frank, sides blackened and curling. Frank poked at the stringy orange noodles inside. "I suppose you think this is funny?"

"Not at all." The gentleman dragged a cube of lamb off a skewer with the tines of his fork. "My employer has legitimate concerns about your"—he cleared his throat—"lifestyle. He wants to ensure you live to see this effort through."

Frank shoved a forkful of the concoction into his mouth and snorted. "He'll have to do better than this." He swallowed the pumpkin-noodle-whatever, blanched, and pushed the rest away.

"How is our subject?"

"Feisty. Her ego's too big for her size 2 britches. You should have seen the death stare I got when she saw the office for the first time."

"My employer advised you to clean up before her arrival." The gentleman arranged his lamb cubes into a row on his plate. He hadn't yet taken a bite.

"And, if you remember, I told you exactly what he could do with his advice. Doesn't matter. She's in my branch whether she likes it or not."

"True. When will she be ready? We are on a strict timetable."

"That's not my problem." The noodles had left an unpleasant aftertaste. Brennan took a swig of gritty water from a plastic tumbler and wiped his mustache. "New ops officers have a strict adjustment period. If I send her out too soon, red flags will go up." He pushed the cup over beside the pumpkin bowl. "Tell your boss I like my condo—and my pension. The girl heads out when I say so. Not a moment before."

"As you wish. I am only the messenger." The gentleman signaled for the check.

**CIA HEADQUARTERS
LANGLEY, VIRGINIA**

"DONE," TALIA SAID, first thing on Monday.

Brennan pushed past her and sat at his desk, rooting through the remains of Friday's donuts. "Context, please."

"The binders." Talia drew the donut box out from under her boss's face to get his full attention. She should have thrown it away when she had come in alone on Saturday. "Every country report, every ops cable, every archived intelligence update—I read them all."

Twice, she didn't say.

In the space of four days, Talia had been through every document Other Branch had to offer. Brennan had made her take Sunday off, but a ten-kilometer row on the Potomac had barely put a dent in her morning, so she had signed the binders out and read through them all again. Her phone had rung all afternoon—about once an hour. Each time she had let it ring out and kept on reading. Talia knew who was calling. She didn't want to talk.

She had finished that night, and after staring at the empty walls of her apartment until morning, she had hurried in to ambush her boss.

"How is that possible?" Brennan pulled the donuts back to his side of the desk. "No one's that fast."

"You said if I read them all, I could start working on current ops. Remember?"

"I say a lot of things." He stood and ambled out from behind the desk, pushing past her. "I'm heading across the river. I'll be out for most of the day."

"But you promised. You said if I—"

With a *click* of the office door, Brennan was gone.

"Transnistria," Talia grumbled several hours later, having been reduced to re-covering what was now very old ground. "What possible interest could the Agency have in Transnistria?"

The workstation shook with a *thump* and a muted "Ow!" Eddie appeared beside her right knee, a rainbow of data cords resting on his shoulders. Brennan had him upgrading Other's data systems. "Transistor-what?"

"Not transistor. Transnistria, a disputed territory in Moldova."

"Oh. Don't know. Don't care." Eddie crawled out from under the desk and stood, brushing the dust off his chinos. "Need a break? There's someone I want you to meet, one of my peeps."

At the Directorate, paramilitary officers were the jocks, specialized skills officers were the geeks, and ops officers were the cool kids—except Talia, of course. Cool kids did not spill coffee all over themselves on day one. In any case, at the Directorate, as in high school, Talia had observed the geeks forming faster and tighter bonds than the other groups. She and Eddie had been CIA officers for barely four days and a wake-up, and Eddie already had *peeps*.

"You'll love this guy," he said once they were in the elevator, watching the numbers count down to Sublevel 6. "He's brilliant. And he's got the coolest office in the building."

The doors opened onto a hallway made of some black-and-blue crosshatched material. Talia let her fingers graze the wall. It was warm to the touch. "Is this—?"

"Carbon fiber, fused with a polymer matrix for hardcore EM shielding. There are a lot of signals running around down here. We wouldn't want them running into each other." Eddie turned, walking backward and spreading his arms. "Welcome to Tech Ops, also known as the Caves."

The angle of the intersecting hallways gave Talia the sense that the sublevel was laid out like a spiderweb. She couldn't decide whether to be awed or creeped out, particularly since they were heading for the center.

"All roads lead to Franklin," Eddie said.

"Franklin?"

"Franklin Perez, the chief of the Caves—the head goblin."

The goblin's den leaned far more toward a mad scientist's lab than an *office*, as Eddie had put it. Partitions of semitranslucent glass created a small labyrinth of stark white equipment, bubbling chemicals, and the occasional homey touch like a tank shell etched with the motto SEMPER FI or a legion of orc figurines surrounding a dashboard hula girl.

"Franklin?" Eddie called, leading the way into the maze.

"Over here, *mano*. What'd you bring me?"

Out from behind a big robotic arm rolled a Latino man in a gray electric wheelchair. He wore a Hawaiian shirt and khakis tied off where his thighs should have been. He saw Talia and his eyes lit up. "Oh." Franklin rolled right past Eddie, the seat of his chair rising to put him closer to Talia's eye level. He took her hand with the grace of a Don Juan. "Franklin Perez. Pleased to meet you."

"Talia Inger. I . . . Uh . . ." She tried and failed to avoid looking down at his stumps.

Franklin tapped a control pad on his armrest and sank down again, laughing. "That's all right, *chica*. You go ahead and look. I spent a few years in the Marines before science caught my

41

eye. Left a piece of myself behind with the Corps." He winked. "Two pieces."

She coughed, resolving to regain an equal footing in the conversation. "Actually I was going to ask about your shirt. Not exactly regulation."

His eyes flashed, as if recognizing a sparring match had begun, and he pulled the faded flower shirt away from his chest. "You like it? We're a little loosey-goosey with the dress code down here." Franklin turned his attention to Eddie. "Hey, kid. You do the homework I gave you?"

"Most of it. I binge-watched two of the three original seasons. I'll concede they have a certain conceptual purity. And they have Captain Kirk, of course, but neither makes up for the qualitative failures."

"Qualitative failures? Are you out of your mind?" The chair spun, and Franklin motored toward the other side of his lab with Eddie right behind. "Don't insult the artistry, kid. We're talking real visual effects and modeling versus what? CGI?"

"CGI *is* artistry, *old man.*"

Talia followed, marveling at the unifying power of geekery. Here was a millennial, the child of Indian immigrants, arguing with a Hispanic double amputee–slash–war veteran two decades his senior. And the two were speaking precisely the same cultural language.

Her awe must have shown on her face, because as the two reached a bank of keyboards and looked back at her, they stopped. Each pushed his glasses up the bridge of his nose. "What?"

"Nothing."

Franklin began working one of his keyboards. A digital chart appeared in the glass wall above the desk. Smart glass. Talia had read about the tech, but never experienced it in person. She glanced around the lab, noting a similar translucent look in all the partitions. In effect, Franklin's entire lab was a computer.

"Inger. Inger." A magenta line rolled down the chart until it highlighted Talia's name. "There you are. I have you scheduled for equipment checks tomorrow, but since you're here . . ." He spun the chair around and held out a palm, snapping his fingers. "Phone, please."

"Why?"

"Security protocols."

"My phone was checked, logged, and modified at the Farm, just like everyone else's."

"Your phone is obsolete, chica." Franklin glanced at Eddie with a look that said Talia was trying his patience, possibly. "Phone, please."

Talia slapped the device into his hand. He laid it down on a black rubber pad and set another phone beside it. Both screens came to life.

"Wait. What are you—?" She watched all her apps appear on the other device, one by one. Franklin had cloned her phone in a matter of seconds.

He dropped her original phone in a drawer on top of a pile of others and handed her the new one. "Sorry about the color. We only do slate gray. Government contracts. Bulk orders." He slid the drawer closed.

Talia watched her phone disappear. "My whole life was on that thing."

"And now it's on your new one. Along with a few bonuses. Everything the modern spy needs—camera, maps, voice recorder, sat phone, translator—"

"Can I shoot someone with it?" Talia's patience with his quirkiness had run out, double-amputee or not. Eddie should have warned her that Franklin would confiscate her phone.

"No, but you can blind an attacker. The flashlight produces over ten thousand lumens. Here, let me show you." Franklin made a grab for the device.

Eddie caught his arm. "Maybe . . . show her something less weaponish."

"Sure. Let's start with encrypted mode." Franklin guided Talia through a few security steps, and black icons appeared on the screen—a compass, a drone, and others. At the bottom was a hideous face and the words BROUGHT TO YOU BY THE GOBLIN KING.

"Seriously?" Talia pointed to the text.

"Hey, folks give you a weird name, your best defense is to own it like you love it."

Once Talia had gotten her primer on the phone's features, the two returned to Sublevel 3. On the way, Eddie revised his previous assessment of the Tech Ops chief. "Franklin is . . . an acquired taste."

"He stole my phone."

"And gave you a new and better one." Eddie hesitated on the elevator. "I need some of Luanne's coffee. Want one?"

"No." She waved him away.

Even after their little break, Talia could not look at the Transnistria binder for one more second. Her gaze drifted over to Brennan's desk, as it had on several occasions since her first day. Nothing stood between her and the file he had so savagely protected but a 1980s drawer lock—child's play for a Farm-trained ops officer. The file called to her like Poe's telltale heart.

"I can't," she said to the empty room. Need-to-know was need-to-know, and Talia always strove to do the right thing, ever since the night her father was taken. It had become a compulsion as much as an ethical code.

The curse of an eidetic memory had left Talia with an image of every word and deed in her life—everything except that night. Crammed like a tumor between perfectly recalled pictures of homework pages and soggy fishing trips, the accident that had killed her father left her with nothing more than scant images. The memory was gone. And no therapy session, no breathing exercise—no midnight scream at a bewildered foster mother—could ever bring it back.

Yet some piece of seven-year-old Talia had scrawled an idea on the brick wall her mind had built around the memory—the idea that she had done something wrong. Little Talia had committed some sin, and God's uncompromising punishment had been to take away her dad. So Talia had become uncompromising as well. She lived a moral life and stayed out of God's way, hoping he would stay out of hers.

She rolled her chair back. Brennan had promised she could work on something real once she read the branch's literature, but he had violated his promise. What was it he didn't want her to see?

She let her eyes linger on the drawer's pointless lock for a few seconds longer, then shook her head. Talia couldn't bring herself to cross that line. But perhaps there was another path.

CHAPTER TEN

TALIA LEFT THE CALL of the mystery file behind and wandered out into the acrylic jungle of REED. At the far end of Russian Ops, the largest of the branches, stood a two-story wall of black marble, veined with rivers of white and silver. Beside its carved wooden door hung a silver plaque.

MARY JORDAN
SENIOR CHIEF
RUSSIAN EASTERN EUROPEAN DIVISION

Talia raised a hand to knock.

"Looking for me?" Jordan called to her from a dark oak conference table. Talia had been so intent on her task she hadn't noticed her mentor standing there. Jordan held up a finger for her to wait and returned to a conversation with a young man. "Get the new intel to me by tomorrow afternoon. If a high-tech weapon is entering the black market, I want to know the who, what, and where."

"Yes, ma'am." The young man shot a glance at Talia, and she

recognized him as the guy who had tried to join her in the elevator on day one. Talia lowered her eyes as he walked off.

Jordan seemed to catch the exchange. "You know Terrance?" she asked, sweeping up a pair of files as she left the table.

"Uh . . . We kind of met earlier."

"I see. Come on in." Jordan pushed open the door and nodded for Talia to go first. "In the future, look for me on the floor. I don't spend much time in here."

"You like to be in the action. I get it." Talia's eyes passed over the molded oak walls and leather chairs of the office—so masculine and old school—she half expected to see a box of Cuban cigars on the desk.

The division chief motioned her over to a couch, and the two sat down together. "So, what brings you to my humble office?"

"A hunch." Talia relayed the whole story of Savage Brennan and the Mystery File. "I don't have any proof, but . . . it feels like he's hiding something."

"Have you confronted him?"

"No."

"Instead, you want me to do some digging behind his back."

She nodded.

Jordan held her poker face, one Talia had never learned to read. "Okay. I'll look into it."

"Really?"

"You have good instincts. But I don't expect to find anything." Jordan stood, leading Talia to the door. "To tell you the truth, this is fairly common. A good many ops officers spend their first year paranoid—a side effect of Farm training, where everything is a test. Chances are this is all in your head."

It didn't feel like this was all in her head. But Jordan had agreed to look into Brennan's actions, so Talia didn't press her any further. "Thank you," she said, and opened the door.

Frank Brennan was standing on the other side.

"Inger? What are you two conspiring about?"

Talia was too stunned to answer.

Jordan covered for her. "Can't I take a few minutes to catch up with one of my recruits?"

"You can." The gap between Brennan's bushy eyebrows closed. "But you usually don't."

Rather than let the moment go on, Talia inched past him. "I'll get back to work."

"Don't bother."

"Um . . . I'm sorry?"

"I saw you checked out those binders on Sunday, despite my orders to take the day off. I don't want you burning yourself out in the first two weeks." Brennan thrust a thumb toward the back hallway. "Go find your nerd friend and get out of here, both of you. Knock off early."

Talia glanced at Jordan, who gave her a single nod. "You heard the man. Get out of here."

"Right. Sure." Talia could do nothing else but turn and walk away. She made it to the other side of Russian Ops before Brennan called after her.

"And, Inger . . ."

She cringed. "Yes?"

"Stay safe out there."

STAY SAFE OUT THERE. In four days, Brennan had never advised Talia to stay safe, keep safe, drive safe, or be safe in any form or fashion. The phrase ground at her so much as she drove home that she nearly ran a red light. A guy in a crossing Range Rover laid on his horn as she skidded to a stop. She gave him an apologetic wave. He yelled something she couldn't hear and steered around her.

When the light finally changed, Talia's phone rang. She gave the caller ID a cursory glance, unwilling to take her eyes off the road for more than an instant. It was a number, not a name. She raised it to her ear. "Yes?"

"Talia? Hey, I finally caught you."

She winced. "Jenni?" Why hadn't the caller ID caught the number? The answer came to her before her mind had finished the question. *Franklin.* This wasn't her real phone. Had the Goblin King inadvertently deleted her contacts during the cloning process? She would kill him.

"Are you still there?"

She could pretend to lose the signal, but that was probably going too far. "Yeah. I'm still here."

"Good. Good. Listen . . ." There was a long silence, as if Jenni had not expected to catch her and so did not know what to say.

"I'm not dodging you. I swear."

"Yes. You are. I don't know if you've seen a calendar lately, but it's been, like, a year."

She could hear the hurt. Talia bit her lip. "I'm sorry."

"It's okay. I get it." Another pause. A sigh. "This isn't working over the phone. Can we meet? Say . . . dinner . . . tonight?"

Talia could not survive the awkwardness of a full meal. There was so much of the last year of her life she couldn't talk about. "Tonight's no good. I probably won't even eat. I'm hitting the water for a workout, and then it's straight to bed."

"Perfect. I haven't rowed in forever. I'll go with you."

CHAPTER
ELEVEN

POTOMAC RIVER
GEORGETOWN BOATHOUSE

TALIA ARRIVED AT THE BOATHOUSE early and tugged at the strap of a single-person shell, not so much hatching a plan as posing a what-if.

What if Talia was out on the water when Jenni arrived? Jenni might give up and leave. *Oops. I assumed we'd use two singles. You mean after five years of no rowing, you couldn't drag a shell out of the boathouse on your own?* It could work. She unfastened the strap and moved on to the next.

"Hey."

Talia's hurrying fingers froze. She turned to find her former foster sister, Jenni Lewis, standing there. "Hey. You came."

"Don't sound so excited." Jenni, taller than Talia and blonde with the infuriating Michigan-slash-Scandinavian heritage of her family, eyed the boat. "You're taking out a single? Why can't we row together?"

"We could." Talia turned back to the shell, re-threading the first strap. "I mean, we will."

"I'm not late, am I?"

"Nope. You're not late. Not *one* second late." Talia laid her hands on the fiberglass hull, took a breath, and moved to the two-person boat on the rack above. "Come on. Help me with this one."

"But that's a pair."

As if Talia didn't know that. The *pair* was arguably the most difficult boat in the sport—two rowers, one behind the other, each with one big oar, naturally unbalanced. It never left much room for conversation. "The double has a broken oarlock." Talia took a step back and crossed her arms. "It's the pair or nothing. What's wrong? Can't handle it?"

"Oh, I can handle it. I wasn't sure if you could." Jenni stepped up beside her and began working the buckle of a strap.

She might not have rowed in college, but Jenni had rowed all seven years of middle school and high school, starting two years earlier than Talia. Jenni's father, Bill, had goaded Talia into joining the team when she came to live with them, and she had excelled. Both girls went to Georgetown. Talia rowed. Jenni didn't. But by the way Jenni moved around the boathouse, it looked like she hadn't forgotten much.

Evening sunlight danced on the ridges of the river's chop—more chop than Talia had seen in a while. The spring current was running stronger than usual. On the water, she kept Jenni busy with instructions, receiving a series of *I knows* and *I've got its* in response.

The boat dipped left. "Watch it. You're digging in again."

"I know. I've got it."

On the next stroke the shell ran true again, and Talia had no instruction to give. Jenni didn't waste the opportunity. "I . . . I miss you. You know that, right? Mom and Dad too."

Talia didn't answer.

"I haven't seen you since you left school."

Two strokes went by. "I'm busy, Jenni."

"I get that. Working at Foggy Bottom is no joke." She used the DC slang for the State Department. "I'm there too, now. I've told you in about a dozen texts."

Jenni was at State? "Right. Sure. Which department was that?"

"Public Affairs. But I stop by the Foreign Service wing all the time. I never see you there."

Now they were encroaching on dangerous ground. What would happen if Jenni guessed that Talia worked for the CIA? "I . . . travel a lot."

"And those places don't have Facetime? Twitter?" The boat dipped left again and Jenni let out a labored huff. "This isn't working. I feel like I'm talking to your ponytail. I want to talk to my sister."

Another two strokes went by. When Talia spoke, her voice was quiet, barely louder than the slosh of the oars. "I'm not your sister, Jenni. I never was."

"Could've fooled me. We shared a room for half of high school and all of college, not to mention a set of parents."

The boat wobbled a little more with each stroke. Talia could feel their rhythm failing. "Focus, Jenni. You're going to flip us."

"Like I care. And speaking of *our* parents, Dad knows you blocked his number. He doesn't understand why you're so mad."

There it was. Had Bill sent Jenni to force a meeting? "Yes. He does."

He hadn't been the worst of Talia's foster fathers—far from it. Most foster kids would say she'd hit the jackpot. Bill had treated her with respect, even love. And he had worked from home, so he had been there for Talia—a lot and in the best ways.

Right up until the day he wasn't.

"He didn't come, Jenni. The one day in six years I really needed him, he didn't come."

"This is about nationals?" The boat dipped way left as Jenni dug in with her oar. "Dad had to travel for work. You're looking for an excuse to be angry. Can't you see that?"

"He didn't have to work. He wanted to. And he never told me he was going. He just . . . wasn't there. Bill shouldn't have tried to be my dad if he never planned on following through."

The moment he had come home, Talia and Bill had a knock-down, drag-out, fight—and not only about nationals. His absence there had been a symptom of a much larger issue. After six years, a lot of foster kids with a lot less attentive caregivers would have been adopted. He had made excuses. She had moved out the next morning. She hadn't spoken to him since.

"He made it to our graduation a week later." Jenni had missed the fight, and she was still missing the point.

"For you, not me. He had to see the return on the four years of Ivy League tuition and books he shelled out for his real daughter."

Talia heard a sniffle from behind. "That's not fair. You had a scholarship."

Waves sloshed over the side. The boat shimmied, as if the oars were moving in opposite directions, attempting to rip the hull in two. Talia knew what was coming next.

They flipped.

Talia had expected Jenni to flip them early, before they left the shallows, not a mile upstream in the Three Sisters channel. The water there in late spring was eighty feet deep.

Talia surfaced with one hand on the upturned shell. "Jenni!"

She heard a sputtering cry. Jenni popped up near the center, where the current was strongest, waving an arm and moving away. "Talia, hel—" She sank, and the river closed over her.

CHAPTER
TWELVE

TALIA PUSHED THE BOAT to her front, oars dragging in their locks, and kicked with all her might. She had to catch the same current as her sister.

Jenni popped up again, closer now, gasping for breath.

"Grab the bow!"

She tried. She missed. She went down again.

Momentum threatened to carry Talia past. But with a heavy kick, she changed her vector and caught Jenni's arm. She pulled her up to the hull.

Jenni threw both arms over the top, coughing. "Thank you."

They made several attempts to right the pair on the way in. None were successful, and both girls were laughing by the time they dragged the shell up onto the dock—the hysterical relief following a trauma. They dropped the boat into the slings and collapsed cross-legged under the boathouse lights.

Jenni looked up at a rack of life vests hanging just inside. "Where were those an hour ago?"

She was kidding, but Talia understood what scheming to avoid a conversation had almost caused, and it hit her hard. "I . . . I didn't . . ."

Jenni met her eyes, held Talia's worried stare for a long moment, and then burst out laughing. Talia laughed with her—the way the two had laughed on so many nights in high school, until Bill had to march up the stairs and tell them both to go to sleep.

Once the laughter subsided, Talia nodded. "I'll call more. I promise."

"Dad too?"

Talia looked away to the trees.

Jenni touched her knee. "I get it. Too much, too soon." She pushed herself to her feet, searching out the wash bucket. "But we could hang out more often than once a year. With other people if you want. Our Young Grads group from church eats at the Tombs all the time, right there on campus. And we're restoring a place in the Heights for a new campus." She slapped a sponge into Talia's hand, holding it there. "The guys in the group are nice. No . . . expectations."

No expectations. That didn't sound too bad. Talia's entire year had been filled with expectations. But group settings meant meeting people. Questions. A CIA officer could handle questions anywhere in the world except Washington, DC, where everyone was only two steps away from guessing the truth. "I'll . . . think about it."

Jenni hadn't brought a change of clothes. "I didn't know we were going swimming," she said, smirking at Talia as they walked to the parking lot.

There was a Taurus at the far end, the only vehicle besides theirs. Talia squinted at the windshield, trying to see if anyone was behind the wheel.

"Thank you." Jenni gave her a wet hug.

"For meeting up, or for saving your life?"

The hug got a little tighter. "For both." Jenni leaned back. "You'll call. Right?"

"I will. Count on it." Talia truly hoped it wasn't a lie.

NIGHT HAD REACHED FULL BLOOM by the time Talia came out of the showers. The Taurus was still there. With the change of light, she could see past the reflections on the windshield. Movement. Someone *was* behind the wheel—a man, she thought.

"Speaking of guys and expectations," Talia said under her breath as she half walked, half jogged to her Civic. She tried to write the guy off as an everyday creep, but the instincts she had developed at the Farm were on fire.

After turning the corner onto Prospect Street, Talia lingered. She didn't have to wait long. The black Taurus rounded the corner behind her.

Her heart began to pound. Talia fought to settle it down, taking 34th toward the Francis Scott Key Bridge. The whole episode could be a matter of coincidence, but Talia couldn't shake the image of Brennan standing outside Jordan's office. And she couldn't shake his strange goodbye.

"Stay safe out there."

"Okay." Talia glanced in the mirror, watching the Taurus follow her across the bridge, three cars back. "Let's see if you're a bona fide tail."

She picked one of three SDRs— surveillance detection routes—she had developed specifically for travel between Georgetown and her apartment as part of a Farm exercise. Making precisely four superfluous turns, Talia moved south through the mini skyscrapers of Rosslyn and then took the Roosevelt Bridge back across the river. Any driver that stayed behind her through that mess was either a tail or lost.

Talia glanced in the mirror as she pulled off the bridge, a block away from the Lincoln Memorial.

No Taurus.

Jordan had warned Talia about the common paranoia of new ops officers. And here she was, four days in, informing on her boss and seeing killers in the night. She pulled into an empty space by the curb, put the Civic in park, and dropped her head to the steering wheel in a mixture of laughter and sobs.

Talia sat motionless, head on the wheel, for a long time, and then took a deep breath. She fixed her hair in the rearview mirror, and then took the Roosevelt Bridge back across the Potomac. The streets of Rosslyn were empty, the office buildings and medical suites dark for the night. But when Talia turned down a one-way street, headlights swept across her mirror.

The Taurus.

"How?" she asked out loud, but she already knew. The Taurus had goaded her into using an SDR, designed around strange pathways through less traveled areas, and then waited for her to let her guard down and double back. The driver wasn't tailing Talia. He was corralling her.

She stepped on the gas, but a white delivery truck lurched backward into the next intersection, blocking her path. Talia slammed on her brakes, skidding sideways.

Two men stepped out of the sedan. Two more jumped down from the back of the delivery truck, one the size of a house, the other small and wiry. All four carried submachine guns, raised and ready.

Instinct told Talia to go for the 9mm she kept in a special holster under the Civic's front passenger seat, but the wiry guy's submachine gun had a cylinder mounted beneath the barrel. He tilted it up a few inches and fired.

The smoke of the oncoming grenade traced an arc through the air. Talia dove from the car and hit the ground shoulder first in a half somersault. The canister clinked on the pavement. She heard it roll under the car. Slow. Lazy. Maybe she had a chance. Her feet found purchase, and then she was up, sprinting for the granite pillars of an office building.

She never made it.

Talia's world vanished in a dazzling white blur. A thunderous *bang* ripped through her brain.

Her senses spun. She couldn't keep her feet. Dark figures in ski masks—balaclavas—converged. Talia swung wildly and her right fist connected with a jaw. Her victim let out a surprised grunt. Her knuckles stung, but she kept swinging until strong hands caught hold of her arms. She kicked, bucked, fought, screamed, but within moments they had her lying in the back of the truck, hands and feet zip-tied.

The biggest of the four dropped his shin onto her thighs, pinning her legs. He yanked a black cloth bag down over her head and cinched it tight.

Talia heard the ratchet and creak of the door coming down. Someone outside pounded on the side of the cargo bay and shouted, *"Poyekhali!" Let's go* in Russian.

LOCATION UNKNOWN

A HAND WHISKED THE BAG from Talia's head perhaps thirty minutes later, exchanging one darkness for another. Wherever they had taken her, the lights were off. Talia breathed deep. Increasing her oxygen intake would aid her night vision, another trick from the Farm. Her eyes adjusted and she became aware of a silhouette beside her, seated in a chair, hands behind his back. Talia couldn't see enough to be sure, but the shape of his glasses looked familiar.

"Eddie?"

"Talia?" The other prisoner half turned his head. "What's happening? Who are these guys?"

Riding helpless in the back of that truck had given Talia time to think. A suspicion had been growing in her mind, a new and simpler answer to the same questions Eddie had just posed. She had counted turns and stops, counted the minutes on the highway. She had listened to the accents of the two men who rode with her, naming them Thing One and Thing Two after a pair of characters in her favorite Dr. Seuss story. She had taken note of the way they handled her as they dragged her out of the truck.

Talia dropped her voice to an urgent whisper. "Don't tell them anything."

"Yeah. No kidding."

Thing Two's gravelly voice came out of the darkness before them. By his silhouette, she pegged him as the wiry guy—the one who had launched the flash bang. "Oh, you *will* tell me what I want to know."

With an electric *clang*, blinding white work lights flashed on, smashing into Talia's senses. Through the spots in her eyes, she watched Thing Two bring a short rod close to her face. An electric arc crackled at its end. "You will tell me everything."

Thing One was there as well. He began the interrogation, leaning down between Talia and Eddie from behind their chairs, still wearing the balaclava. "Who do you work for?"

Neither answered.

A heavy foot kicked Talia's chair. "I ask you question!"

"And I hear question." Talia mimicked his poor English. "But I'm not in a talkative mood."

Anger. Frustration. Talia had always kept plenty of each in reserve, and at the Farm she had learned to channel both to suppress panic. She could have descended into tears, but most thugs and terrorists were sociopaths. They lacked the mental wiring for sympathy. Tears might buy her a bullet—though she suspected not.

"Who do you work for?" The cattle prod advanced toward Talia's nose, then shifted. Thing Two brought it close enough to Eddie's side to make him squirm in his chair. "Tell me now, or I make Four-Eyes suffer."

"All right. Take it easy." Talia played along, allowing the guy a small victory for his efforts. "I work for the US State Department."

"Liar."

The prod dug into Eddie's side. He let out a constrained cry, body convulsing.

Talia's eyes widened as her friend slumped in his chair. She hadn't expected them to escalate so quickly. Every candidate for the Clandestine Service had been tased, flash-banged, shot with Simunition, and given a drug that inflamed the nervous system, so she knew Eddie could take the abuse. That didn't make watching it any easier. "I'm *not* lying. I'm sure your friends pulled my backpack from the car. Look inside, you'll find a State Department ID."

"Yes, we have bag. And we found ID. It is prop. A fake." The prod crackled. Eddie convulsed again. When it was over, his breathing grew labored.

Talia strained against her bonds. "Stop that!"

Thing One intervened. The big guy gently pushed Thing Two aside and stepped around Talia's chair, crouching down in front of her. "You want us to stop, yes? Then talk."

Thing Two paced behind him. "Our people watch you drive onto the same compound day in and day out, *Agent* Inger. We *know* answer to question already, so why not tell us?"

"I'm a low-level State Department employee, a nobody who works in a cubicle on a joint government compound."

"Have it your way, *Agent* Inger." Thing Two pressed the prod toward Eddie's neck.

Thing One caught his wrist with millimeters to spare. "Please, Miss Inger. My friend, he is . . . touchy, yes? Do not press him."

What choice did she have? "I work for State. Take it or leave it."

"Enough lies!" Thing Two shoved the barrel of his submachine gun up under Eddie's chin. "Answer question or your friend dies. Who do you work for?"

"You! All right?" Talia refused to play any longer. Either she was right, or she and Eddie were dead. "I work for the same organization as you."

Thing Two cocked his head and lowered his weapon. Thing One let out a relieved breath. Both straightened and looked back through the lights, as if waiting for instructions.

With another electric *clang*, the bright lights shut down. Softer overheads came on in their place. Talia blinked, willing her eyes to adjust for the third time. Etched into the opposite wall was a Bible quote. AND YE SHALL KNOW THE TRUTH, AND THE TRUTH SHALL MAKE YOU FREE.

Mary Jordan strode into view, clapping, with Brennan at her shoulder.

CHAPTER
FOURTEEN

JORDAN'S ASSAULT TEAM had planted Talia and Eddie at the dead center of the CIA seal in the Old Headquarters Building. Five paramilitary officers from the Directorate's Special Activities Division—knuckle-draggers and throat-slitters as the operations officers liked to say—stood off to one side of the work lights, pulling off their balaclavas and muttering to one another.

Other Directorate personnel loitered at the periphery, watching the show. Talia recognized several faces from REED. She frowned at Brennan. "I thought we were done with tests."

"Consider this more of an initiation." He opened a folding chair and sat down in front of her. "And it isn't over. How did you know you were at the Agency?"

"How about we cut these zip ties first?" Talia glanced at Eddie, whose forehead had gone clammy. Sweat colored the neck and armpits of his I Heart Wookies T-shirt. "And maybe get Eddie a soda?"

Jordan folded her arms, cocking a hip. "You're stalling, Inger."

"Not in the slightest." Talia leaned forward and stretched her arms high behind her back as Thing One drew a stiletto from his boot. He had a kind face for a gorilla. Thing Two, however, reminded her of a weasel. "It started with him," she said, tilting her head back to indicate Thing One. "He dropped his knee on my thighs to pin me down—the standard alternative to straddling a woman during a violent exercise." The zip ties snapped and she brought her hands around in front of her, rubbing the marks on her wrists. "And then there was the placement of his hands."

Thing One had moved on to Eddie. He looked up in shock. "My hands? But . . . I was careful."

"Exactly." Talia gave him a wry smile. "Too careful. I doubt any girl has ever been manhandled in so gentlemanly a fashion."

The big guy looked away, bending down to shove the knife back into his boot. Talia thought she caught a hint of red in his cheeks.

Thing Two laughed, twirling his cattle prod. "Way to go, Tom."

"And you." Talia shot him a scowl that burned the smirk right off his face. "Your Russian accent is all over the place—Moscow, Vladivostok, Siberia. Pick one and stick with it."

An ops officer brought Eddie a cola and handed a bottle of water to Talia. She twisted off the cap. "And what was up with the whole 'Agent Inger' thing?" The wannabes from Homeland and the FBI loved the agent title, but the CIA reserved the term for the foreigners they recruited to steal intelligence. Most Russian organizations understood that. "Did you steal that villain persona from a B spy movie? They teach acting at Georgetown. Audit a class or two and get back to me."

There were several giggles from both groups, the ops officers, and the paramilitary team. Thing Two gripped his cattle prod and glared. Talia had not made a friend.

"Thin." Brennan looked unimpressed. "If that's all you had, then you took an unacceptable risk just now."

Talia uncrossed her legs and sat forward, locking eyes with her boss. "Oh, I had more. To be honest, I got everything I needed from the drive to the Compound. Speaking of which, what happened to my car?"

Brennan frowned at her attempt to change the subject. "It's fine, being detailed as we speak."

Jordan waved him off. "Are you telling us that you mapped the route in your head?" She glanced at one of the paramilitary officers, most likely the driver.

He swallowed and dropped his gaze to his boots.

"Don't blame him." Sugar and caffeine had brought Eddie back to life. "Talia is ridiculously good at that sort of thing. This one time, our class tried to stump her with a multidimensional blind man's bluff involving four Metro trains, three Ubers, and a cat we—"

Brennan glared.

Eddie sheepishly returned to his drink. "I guess you had to be there."

That seemed good enough for Jordan. "Stand, please." She placed a hand on each of their shoulders. "Talia Inger. Eddie Gupta. You have walked through the fire and entered the circle." She gestured at the seal beneath their feet. "It is time to swear you in."

The entire episode—the kidnapping, the interrogation, the shocking of poor Eddie with a low-voltage cattle prod—had all been part of a mystery play created for their swearing-in ceremony.

"What if we *had* cracked?" Eddie asked.

Brennan slapped his knees and heaved himself up, allowing Thing One to take his chair. "Then we'd have kicked you to the curb. More cake for me."

He wasn't joking. Two of the knuckle-draggers brought in a table with an elaborate American flag cake. Brennan loudly declared that it had to be eaten in its entirety before the end of the night, for the sake of national security.

So that was Talia's final induction into Directorate of Operations—the Clandestine Service. She'd been kidnapped by assassins, delivered to the Agency hog-tied in the back of a truck, and sworn in by a man she had betrayed only hours before.

But when she looked for him after the ceremony, Brennan had disappeared.

TALIA FOUND HER BOSS on Sublevel 3. Brennan waited at the door to their broom-closet office, holding a piece of cake so big it threatened the integrity of his paper plate.

"Took you a while," he said, checking his watch. "But I knew you'd come looking for me. Got something to say?"

Talia chose her steps carefully as she stepped into the office. "Jordan told you."

"She didn't have to. I saw it plain as day on your face when I found you in her office, and I put the rest together when she questioned me about my files." Brennan gestured at her workstation chair, strategically placed in front of his desk. "Come in. Sit down."

Talia did as she was told. "Are you mad?" Dumb question. "You're mad."

Brennan put his plate down and sat as well, looking tired. "I'm not much to look at, Talia. But I'm no traitor. However"— he sighed, pulling the file from its drawer and laying it down next to the cake—"I *did* overreact when you tried to take this file. And that made it look like I was hiding something."

"You *were* hiding something." Of that, Talia was certain. Microexpressions did not lie.

"Correct. The swearing-in ceremony." Brennan dug a plastic fork into his cake. "Or hadn't you figured that out yet? I couldn't let you in on current ops because we hadn't sworn you in, and I couldn't tell you the time or nature of the ceremony because of our traditions."

His argument made sense. Brennan's story met all the points of logic required to explain his behavior. So why were her instincts still crying foul? Maybe she was worn out, frazzled by the night's events. "Okay. What now?"

"We move on." Brennan's expression shifted. He picked at his frosting. "This is good cake, isn't it? Nothing but the best for our new operatives." With his other hand, he pushed the file across the desk. "Our new *field* operatives."

Field operatives. Brennan wasn't simply sharing current ops. He was sending her out into the wild. Talia hesitated and then snatched up the mystery file. A smile spread across her lips, until she scanned the first few lines.

NEW INTELLIGENCE: MOLDOVA/TRANSNISTRIA, OTHER BRANCH

SOURCE: MR. ADAM TYLER; REGIONAL BUSINESSMAN; IMPORT-EXPORT

SOURCE RATING: CREDIBLE

FREE TEXT: MR. TYLER REPORTS RUMORS FROM HIS TIRASPOL BUSINESS CONTACTS OF A POTENTIAL ATTEMPT TO STEAL TECHNOLOGY FROM AVANTEC, A MOLDOVAN AEROSPACE CORPORATION WITH US DEFENSE CONTRACTS.

It went on, but the file was nothing—a basic RIR, a raw intelligence report, covering a minor theft threat against some backwater Moldovan tech firm based in the unrecognized territory of Transnistria.

"You and Gupta will go in undercover to assess Avantec's security protocols." Brennan looked up from his cake. "Your job is to ensure the safety of US-related projects."

Talia flipped back and forth between the two scant pages, searching every line for signs of something truly sinister, or at least interesting. She found none. "This is rent-a-cop stuff." And then Talia understood. "No. This is a punishment. I read the country profile. Moldova is the moldiest, sweatiest armpit of Eastern Europe." She closed the file. "You *are* mad about my thing with Jordan. You said I was forgiven."

"I said we were moving on. Besides, even when we're forgiven, there are often consequences for our actions." Brennan's mustache could not hide his smirk. "Take it on the chin, Inger. You're going."

Worst Monday ever.

CHAPTER

FIFTEEN

CIA HEADQUARTERS
LANGLEY, VIRGINIA

AFTER SOME ADDITIONAL PUSHBACK from Talia, Brennan had added a coffee to her penance. She picked it up on the way in on Tuesday morning.

"Skinny?" Luanne asked when Talia ordered a tall white mocha.

Talia lowered her eyes. "Yes. And add Frank's usual. On me."

Luanne typed the order into the register. "One skinny white mocha for the rookie, and one Frank special: a venti half-sugar, half-fat combo with a little coffee thrown in." She stuffed Talia's cash into the drawer and went to work adding milk from two separate jugs to a pair of steel cups. Talia expected her to use whole milk for Frank's, but the jug read, HALF AND HALF. Luanne shook her head. "One day, Frank Brennan is gonna keel over, and the po-lice gonna haul me in for the world's slowest murder."

When Talia didn't laugh at her joke, Luanne glanced up from the cups. "Who kicked your cat today?"

"It's nothing."

"Girl, please." She left the two milk cups to froth and returned to the counter. "You in trouble with the boss. If I seen that look once, I seen it a thousand times."

Talia lifted her eyes. "You already used the 'thousand times' line with my badge picture."

The barista dropped a shoulder. "Then how 'bout this, rookie. If I had a *dollar*"— she cast a pointed look at the tip jar—"for every time I seen a downcast face on a new recruit, I'd be a wealthy woman. What'd you do, lose some classified file?"

Talia *wished* she could lose that file. She slipped a bill into the jar. "I had a rough night. That's all."

"*Mm*-hmm. Sure. That's *all*." Luanne finished Frank's dessert and Talia's worthless diet caffeine concoction and set both cups on the counter. Talia tried to take them, but Luanne held on, forcing Talia to meet her eyes. "Here's the thing, girl. Pretty soon, you gonna head out into that great big, messed-up world, and life is gonna come at you hard. *Death* too. And you gonna wish for the good ol' days when all you had to worry about was an overbearing boss." She wheeled around in her signature Luanne turn—hips first, head later. "That's my two cents, anyhow."

Pretty soon. Talia walked away with her coffees.

Down on Sublevel 3, she set Brennan's mocha on his desk. "Your fat bomb, sir."

In return, Brennan held out a scarred leather portfolio. "Your tickets."

"That was fast." She opened the portfolio, scanning the documents. Air travel, hotel, rental car. She scrunched up her brow as she read. "What's Tram Air?"

"Your only option for getting into Tiraspol." Brennan handed her an additional folder. "Read this before you leave, but don't take it with you. You're going in as Natalia Wright from Wright Way Security Consultants. Your job is to gain the principal's trust and evaluate his security."

The principal was a Dr. Pavel Ivanov, a young engineer and the CEO of Avantec Industries. The photo clipped to page one showed a confident man in his late twenties with an olive complexion and an expensive suit. The man had coin and connections, with a state-of-the-art compound near Tiraspol and investments all over the European Union.

"Once you have the layout," Brennan continued, "report back."

"To what end?"

Brennan gave the answer she was hoping for. "If"—he frowned, gesturing at her with his coffee—"*If* you can convince me that US interests in Avantec are well protected, I'll bring you home. We'll get started on something with better surroundings. Like Bucharest."

"Deal." Talia would be out of there in a week, maybe less. She turned to go. "I'll find Eddie and get him prepped."

"Wait." The word was muffled, as Brennan was halfway through a gulp of mocha cream. "You'll have some additional help. Remember the source that brought us this intel?"

The name appeared in Talia's head, unbidden. "Adam Tyler. Businessman."

"He has ties in the area. I'm sending him in with you to grease the skids. Don't worry. He's worked with the Agency before."

A civilian? More babysitting. Talia forced a smile. "No problem." She would do with Tyler what she had done when foster parents brought her in as a nanny instead of daughter—ignore her charge from the moment she arrived. Let him run wild. What did she care?

"You're meeting him at the Jefferson Memorial this afternoon. Details are in that folder I gave you." Brennan narrowed his eyes, clearly reading her microexpressions. "Play nice."

"WHAT DID YOU DO, TALIA?" She and Eddie were in the elevator, headed down to Franklin's goblin cave. Eddie untucked his pink button-down and showed her the red marks on his side. "Last night I was tortured. Now we're heading to Transnistria, Eastern Europe's Wild West." He stuffed his shirt back into his pants and began idly playing with his fidget spinner. "I looked it up. Did you know their hospitals have tiny ants that infest closed wounds by hiding in the surgical instruments? Their ants, Talia. They infest people." Eddie stopped the spinner and frowned. "We're suffering more than your average rookies. What aren't you telling me?"

She watched the numbers tick by above the elevator doors, counting up even though they were heading down. It felt weird. "This is a little setback, that's all."

Franklin reversed his chair into view as they entered his lab. "Ah, here you are. Heroes of the Directorate's latest swearing-in. Last night, you passed a trial by fire. Today you venture deep into the dark cave to receive boons from the Goblin King."

Talia hung back. "Boons? Last time you stole my phone and deleted my contacts."

"Did I? That was an accident."

"Not the stealing the phone part."

"But I gave you a new one."

"With no contacts."

Franklin's bright expression dimmed. He shifted his gaze to Eddie. "You said she was cool. This"—he gestured at Talia as if she were an inanimate object—"is not cool."

Eddie gave him an apologetic head tilt. "She's kind of intense sometimes, but she'll grow on you. Give her time."

"Time is all I've got." Franklin's grin returned and he looked Talia up and down. "You look like an Oakleys girl," he said, and drove back to his keyboard.

"Ray-Bans, actually."

"Bup, bup, beh. I'm working here." Franklin waved away her input, typing with the other hand, and then snapped his fingers. "Phone."

With a glance at Eddie that said, *I will kill him if I lose my contacts again*, Talia handed it over.

"Bueno." Franklin opened a standing cabinet, drew out a pair of Oakleys, and passed them to Talia over his shoulder.

The lenses were a little large for her taste, but otherwise they looked normal. "Shades?" she asked, turning them over and back in her hand.

"Because your future's so bright. Try them on." Franklin pressed a key, and the dark lenses faded to a light, translucent blue.

The moment she had the glasses in place, the word READY appeared in bold green letters, hovering before her. Talia whipped them off again and checked the lenses, but could see no word from the front side. She put them back on. "Okay, that's pretty cool."

Franklin snapped the fingers of both hands. "She likes 'em. Now. Watch this." He toyed with her phone and the word hovering in front of Talia changed to PAIRED. An instant later, Eddie and Franklin—the whole lab—grew sharper, as if Talia's already-perfect vison had improved. "What is this?"

"CLEO. Color Light Enhanced Optics—a perfect storm of sensors. Your phone acts as the CPU, optimizing the image from the cameras in the bridge and sending it back to the lenses."

"So it's Bluetooth," Talia said.

"Whoa." Franklin gave Eddie another *What's wrong with her?* look. "Don't make 'em sound so cheap." He handed over an Oakley case, along with her phone. "Eddie can link up via SATCOM and send videos, images, documents—whatever— straight to your eyes."

"Um . . ." Eddie patted his own chest. "I like shades too."

"Sorry. Ops Os only. Budget cuts." Franklin led them across the lab to a pedestal with two handguns and four small magazines. "But you can have one of these."

"Those are Glocks," Talia said. "I carry a SIG."

The chair slowly rotated. Franklin sighed and let his head loll to one side to look up at her. "You ever see the movie *Frozen*?"

"Are you saying I should let it go?"

"Hey, the girl shows promise." He raised his hands, waggling

them in the air. "All good things. All good things." Then he passed
them each a weapon. "These are Agency-customized Glock 42s.
Zero metal parts. The rounds are high-density ceramic. Use them
wisely, you've got six each. Standard .380 ammo will work for
reloads."

TALIA SPENT THE REST OF THE DAY memorizing Ivanov's
file and prepping for her meeting with Adam Tyler, her civilian
deadweight. Brennan gave her very little background on the
American-born businessman. He was nearly twenty years her
senior, with his financial fingers in several sketchy fly-by-night
companies. The file focused more on Tyler's intel. His contacts
in Moldova had told him of a small weapons deal and a dis-
pute among local thugs. The rumors spoke of an outsider, an
underworld boss called Lukon, planning a move to steal some
of Avantec's technology—although the rumors did not specify
the nature of that technology.

In the parking garage, on her way out to the meeting, Talia
ran into Mary Jordan. They chatted in cryptic terms about the
previous night's adventure, and then Talia broached the subject
of her mission. "You did sign off on this, right?"

Jordan read the not-so-subtle *Are you really going to make
me do this?* and nodded. "I like the idea of getting you out in
the field early, gaining experience."

"On a glorified rent-a-cop security job?"

"Don't sell this mission short, Talia." Jordan cracked a smile.
"Dr. Ivanov and Avantec give America a firm footing in the
Eastern European defense sector. It's important to protect our
interests there."

"Right." Talia hadn't looked at the op from that point of view.
"But what about this source, Adam Tyler? I'll be working with
him on location." A flash of the eyes told Talia Jordan hadn't
heard about Tyler's involvement. "You didn't know?"

Jordan regained her usual unreadable expression. "I gave Brennan free rein on the logistics. And Tyler has a . . . history . . . with the Directorate." She narrowed her eyes. "But watch him carefully."

"Why? Tyler's the one who brought us this intelligence in the first place."

"True." Jordan turned and walked away, clicking a remote to unlock a nearby Mercedes. "But when the devil brings a gift to your doorstep, he's usually coming after your soul."

SIXTEEN

NATIONAL MALL
WASHINGTON, DC

ARM'S LENGTH. Maybe a ten-foot pole.

Talia resolved to keep Tyler well out on the periphery of the mission. Her cryptic conversation with Jordan had not inspired confidence.

A late cold front whipped the last of the cherry blossom petals into swirls above the gently curving sidewalks of the National Mall. Passing the reflecting pool, she drew her new shades from her peacoat and slipped them on. "Let's give the Faux-kleys a test run, shall we?" The lenses darkened with the sunlight.

A discreet earpiece connected her to Eddie's workstation back at the compound. His voice came through crystal clear. "I'm sending you Tyler's description now. Stand by."

Height, weight, age, complexion—the data from Tyler's file floated in space to the left of the path, close enough to read but far enough it wouldn't block Talia's vision. Six foot two, one hundred ninety pounds, dark brown hair. To the right, Tyler's photo appeared, rendered in three dimensions by predictive software, slowly rotating back and forth. "Wow. I'm impressed."

An extra voice came over the comms, distant but readable. "Ha. I told you she liked 'em."

Talia frowned, glancing left and right before quickstepping across Independence Avenue. "Eddie, are you in Franklin's lab?"

No answer.

"Eddie, I did not authorize you to include Franklin in this meet."

"But Franklin's desk is *so* much cooler than mine."

She sighed. *Boys.*

Brennan had staged the rendezvous beneath the great marble portico of the Jefferson Memorial. A red triangle appeared over the dome, along with green arrows showing her the best route. They appeared flat on the sidewalk, as if painted on the concrete. She didn't need them, but it was a good test. "Not bad."

Franklin's voice came over the comms again. "The word you're looking for is incredible, chica."

"Franklin, get off my comms. You're not part of this op."

"But it's my lab."

"Rules are rules. I'm already on thin ice with Brennan, don't make it worse."

The towering bronze statue of Jefferson, shaded by a dome more than a hundred feet high, rose into view as Talia climbed the steps. The Jefferson Memorial was one of the most beautiful and impressive monuments in DC, but it was also one of the least visited, making it an ideal choice for meeting an unfamiliar contact. He stood close to one of the four engraved walls, staring up at a passage that began with "Almighty God."

Tyler wore a burgundy scarf and a gray Armani overcoat that reached to his calves. Neither was distinctive, but the patchwork flatcap on his head matched the one in his file picture. After counting to sixty, pretending to read the quotes and marvel at the statue, Talia picked an exit path that took her straight past her target. A casual observer, perhaps even a focused observer, would never have noticed her touch Tyler's elbow.

She was waiting at a bench beside the Tidal Basin, shaded by the quivering branches of a cherry tree, when Tyler came strolling down the path. He sat at the opposite end, folded his hands on his knee, and looked directly at her.

Where had Brennan found this guy? Didn't he say Tyler had worked with the Agency before? "Don't speak and don't look in my direction." Talia kept her gaze focused ahead. "You don't know me. We're just two people out for some late afternoon air who happen to be sharing a bench."

"Right." Instead of looking away, Tyler leaned over and nudged her arm. "Spy stuff. Tradecraft. Say no more." He sat back and looked out across the water.

Talia rolled her eyes behind the Faux-kleys. "This is my op. We do things my way. You're just along for the ride." She took a breath, but before she could launch into the rest of the *I'm in charge* spiel she had prepared on the way over, Tyler interrupted.

"I know but one code of morality for men whether acting singly or collectively."

This time, it was Talia who violated tradecraft, glancing at him. She kicked herself mentally and dropped her gaze to her peacoat, brushing away a scattering of cherry blossom petals. "What are you talking about?"

"Jefferson's quote. From the northwest wall of the portico." Tyler laid an arm across the back of the bench. "He was writing about the dark side of foreign policy—spies and assassins. Jefferson believed in one code of morality, whether for a man or for a nation."

"Okay." Talia would bite. "And what do you believe, Mr. Tyler?"

"Does it matter? This is your mission. I'm just along for the ride."

Inside, she screamed. Was he going to be like this every day? Talia kept her eyes moving, watchful for lingering gazes. The menial nature of her mission didn't absolve her from the duty of caution. A couple walked beside the basin on the other side, fingers intertwined. A little boy knelt at the edge thirty meters away, feeding the ducks. "You are my local expert," she said, keeping her voice even. "You are not a spy"—she glanced at him sideways—"or an assassin. If I need information, I'll find you. Otherwise, make no contact. Remember that if you happen to see me at the airport this evening."

"Don't worry about the airport." Tyler stood to leave, straightening his scarf and overcoat. "I'm flying out of Teterboro on my private jet." He looked right at her and raised his voice so much the little boy looked up from his ducks. "The Gulfstream can fly straight to Tiraspol. You want a ride?"

Blatant. Exasperating.

Talia fought the urge to stare daggers at him as he strode away, and then waited an extra five minutes before starting off in the opposite direction. A new data stream flowed into her lenses, a picture of a Honda Civic and green arrows directing her to her car—Eddie's idea of a joke.

She heard a voice in her earpiece. "So that went well, eh, chica?"

Talia jerked the glasses off and stuffed them in her pocket. "Shut up, Franklin."

CHAPTER
SEVENTEEN

BY 4:00 P.M., TALIA AND EDDIE had completed all their pre-mission arrangements. The Directorate's Print and Copy Division, known for generations as the *boffins*, had established their cover IDs, creating and then distressing freshly minted drivers' licenses and passports for both. They had also created a web presence for Talia's fake security firm.

With a half hour of dead time before she had to leave for Dulles, Talia picked up her phone, let her thumb hover over the screen for a moment, then dialed Jenni.

"Hey. It's Talia . . . Yeah . . . You too. Listen. I have to go away for a while."

Talia couldn't explain the compulsion to call her foster sister. Maybe it was as simple as doing the right thing—her standard policy of steering clear of a vengeful God. She had told Jenni she would do better. So she would. Simple.

"You're telling me this because you don't plan on calling for a while," Jenni said after Talia explained she would be in places where she really wouldn't have easy access to social media or messaging systems.

"I'm telling you because it's true."

She could hear Jenni mulling over this information. Given

her State Department knowledge, Jenni would be inches from guessing Talia's true line of work. After a while she sighed into the phone. "That bad, huh?"

"You have no idea."

"In that case, you'll be in my prayers."

Talia cringed. Thoughts and prayers. Great. "Yeah . . . Thanks."

THE FLIGHT TO FRANKFURT left the gate at 6:00 p.m. for the first leg of the journey. "Eddie Pandey," Eddie grumbled through his teeth, scrunching his body down into a steerage-class center seat. "What a stupid name. Why couldn't they give me Eddie Brock or Edward Nygma?"

"Quiet." Talia bumped his elbow hard enough to knock it off the armrest between them. She dropped her voice to a whisper. "That's your cover. Deal with it. Pandey is an Indian name."

"So?"

"Your real name is Gupta. *You* are Indian."

"And that means I can't be Eddie Brock?" He leaned forward enough to glare at her. "That's racist."

"Don't be a snowflake."

"You're the snowflake."

They both grinned as Eddie fell back into his seat. It had been their private joke since Georgetown.

Unfortunately, Talia's good humor did not survive the first hour of the flight. The turbulence came too soon and lasted too long, leaving her tense and white-knuckled. She hated flying. How could there be speed bumps in empty *air*? To make matters worse, her seat did not recline, and a constant line of bladder-conscious passengers laid hands and arms on her headrest while waiting for the lavatory, which could have used a better air freshener. After a few hours, though, exhaustion overcame fear and discomfort, and Talia descended into a protracted delirium of head nods and nightmarish flashes.

A windshield appeared, blurry at first, but sharpening, so close to her eyes. Light rain pelted the glass. Mist hung over the road. Talia flew through the gray wisps like a superhero.

A voice called to her. "No, *puiule Natalia*. Don't!"

Puiule Natalia. Little Natalia. That's what her father had called her.

Headlights flashed. A horn blared.

Puiule Natalia.

A bang. The road and the trees spun together. The windshield shattered around her. Blood tinted the shards.

Puiule Natalia. Puiule Natalia. Her father's voice was unrelenting in the chaos.

"Talia!"

Her head snapped upright. She breathed, eyes finding focus. "Eddie?"

Concern darkened the eyes behind those thick glasses. Nearby passengers cast subtle glances her way. A heavyset man waiting for the lavatory stared outright.

Eddie lowered his chin. "Are you . . . back?"

Her fingers hurt. She had a death grip on the armrest. Eddie had a hand on her forearm. Slowly, he released her, and Talia released the armrest.

"I'm fine." She wanted to escape, but to where? "I . . . need something to drink." Talia unbuckled her seat belt and half rose only to find a flight attendant waiting in the aisle with a plastic cup of water.

"You want this, sweetie?"

"Yes. Thank you." The humiliation of being the center of attention washed into Talia's cheeks as she sank down into her seat again.

The flight attendant wasn't finished. "Anything else I can get you? We have ibuprofen."

"No. Thank you. I'm fine."

"You sure, sweetie? It's no trouble."

Humiliation gave way to anger. The old pain in Talia's hip began to throb. "I said, 'I'm fine.'" She looked around at the other passengers. "Did you all hear? *I'm fine.*"

They all looked away. Blushing, the heavyset man crammed himself into the lavatory.

Eddie gave the flight attendant a grateful nod and eased Talia back against her seat rest. "Hey. Calm down. Is this what you call maintaining a low profile?"

"I'm sorry." She took another drink and scrunched up her face as she swallowed. "Did I cry out in my sleep?"

"Like a wounded mongoose." Eddie fished a pair of ibuprofen from his backpack and pressed them into her hand. "That must have been a serious bad dream."

"It was . . . an old one."

The nightmares had persisted into Talia's teens—snippets of the accident, rarely in the correct order. Unable to retrieve the rest, her last government therapist had taught her to suppress the memory instead. Using guided meditation and soothing string music, she had strengthened the wall Talia's mind had built, finally hemming the nightmare in for good.

Or so Talia had thought.

What sort of trigger had released the nightmare from its pen? Talia let the events of the last few days roll through her mind. The mock kidnapping seemed the most likely culprit, especially with the jolt of the flash grenade. But Talia had experienced similar scenarios at the Farm.

Maybe this slip was a one-off, a symptom of a major shift in her life, entering the real Clandestine Service. Maybe.

"You good?" Eddie asked, still worried.

Talia pressed her earbuds into place and selected a string quartet by Mozart. She leaned her head back and closed her eyes. "Yeah. I'm good."

CHAPTER
EIGHTEEN

A STEADY RAIN drummed against the flat tin roof of Tira-spol's open airport terminal—so loud Talia could barely hear the girl behind the rental counter. She and Eddie had been in transit more than fifteen hours, including a two-hour layover in Frankfurt followed by a mad sprint from one end of Belgrade International to the other. And from the girl's shouted, broken English and insistent pointing, Talia gathered the actual rental facility was off-site, a block away.

In the movies, spies travel light. Together, however, Talia and Eddie dragged a total of six bags down the sidewalk. Their roller bags clacked as Eddie tried to squeeze under Talia's umbrella. He had failed to bring one.

An A-frame shed with the sign DA! AUTO and a gravel lot full of beaters appeared to hold a local monopoly on the rental market. A line of soaked customers started twenty yards short of the awning. As Talia and Eddie huddled together, shuffling an inch or two every few minutes, a black Mercedes G-Wagon rolled by. The look of it set off all kinds of alarms in Talia's brain.

"Eddie, get ready to bolt."

"What? Why?"

She didn't answer. Squinting through the droplets on her eyelashes, Talia watched the overpriced SUV make a three-point turn to head back their way. Maybe the driver was lost.

Maybe not.

The G-Wagon slowed to a stop with Talia's warped reflection squarely framed in its tinted rear passenger window. She held her ground, fingers tightening into a fist. And then the window motored down.

"Tyler."

"Well, hello there. Fancy meeting you here."

"Yeah. What a coincidence."

"I came because I thought you might like a ride, so I think the phrase you're looking for is 'thank you.' Do you want to soak in Tiraspol drop by drop, or would you like to get in?" Tyler looked her up and down as if assessing the state of a muddy child. "Your choice, but the wet-cat look doesn't suit you."

The others in line watched the conversation with mild curiosity. Most seemed more interested in the Mercedes than its occupant. A man near the hood reached out to touch the paint job, and the Moldovan at the wheel, wearing a driver's cap and sunglasses, pounded the horn. The man jumped back and shook his fist, shouting at him in dialectic Romanian.

Talia stepped off the curb, closer to the window. "What happened to 'we don't know each other'?"

"I filed it away with 'You're just along for the ride.'"

The line hadn't moved the entire time they'd been talking. The offer was tempting, but Talia couldn't just leave. "We need our rental."

"No. You don't. Not right this minute, anyway. Get in and I'll explain."

Tyler had crossed the line when he spoke to her in front of all those people. What did it matter now if she accepted the ride? Talia looked to Eddie. The SSO was already loading his bags into the back of the G-Wagon.

"What?" he asked in answer to her openmouthed stare. "We both knew where this was headed."

As he steered the G-Wagon away from the curb, the driver passed each of his new passengers a spotless white towel. Tyler intercepted Talia's and wiped the spatter from the inside of his door before passing it along. "Make sure to get the seat around you too. I can't handle the feel of wet leather."

She pursed her lips. "Thanks."

"Don't mention it. Your accommodations?"

"The Best Choice Motel." Talia handed him a card.

"I know it. Not the most apt name." He passed the card to the driver.

The man checked the address, then offered a salute. "Yeah. Okay. No problem."

"Now," Tyler said. "About your rental. With my resources, your mission—"

"Ahem." Eddie interrupted him with a cough from the front passenger seat. He made a subtle head tilt toward the driver.

"Oh, don't worry about Davian. He doesn't speak a lick of English." Tyler patted the man's shoulder. "Do you, Davian?"

Davian gave him another salute. "Yeah. Okay. No problem."

"Look." Talia slapped the towel into his hand, blackened by her running mascara. "I know you think this is all some kind of game. You think it's fun to poke at my boundaries. But I put those boundaries in place for your protection, as well as for mine and Eddie's."

Tyler answered with a sage nod. "I understand."

"Then what possessed you to swing by and pick us up?"

"Look around you." He gestured at the people dotting the sidewalk, shoulders hunched against the rain. Hardly any carried umbrellas. "This is Moldova, Europe's poorest country and at the same time its largest per-capita consumer of hard liquor.

Think about that. These people are too miserable to care one whit about a couple of Americans meeting in the street."

The G-Wagon turned down the first tree-lined lane they had seen since leaving the airport. An alabaster building topped with bloodred tiles rose from the greenery, an oasis amid the urban sprawl. Talia had studied maps of Tiraspol. That building was nowhere near the route to the Best Choice Motel. She touched the driver's shoulder. "Hey, where are you taking us?"

Davian smiled at her in the mirror. "Yeah. Okay. No problem."

"Relax," Tyler said. "He's taking the scenic route."

"Tiraspol doesn't *have* a scenic route."

"Touché."

The G-wagon wound its way through the trees until it passed the alabaster building. The red-tiled roof pierced the rain clouds twelve stories up. At its base, a gatehouse kept unwanteds away from a circular drive and a covered entry with gold-painted columns.

Eddie pressed his face against his window, fingers caressing the glass. "That's the Mandarin, the only five-star hotel within a hundred miles."

"Meh." Tyler bobbled his head. "Five stars is a stretch. The Ming vases are fake, but the marble counters are real enough." He cast Talia what she took as a creepy, *I'm not too old for you* gaze. "Did I mention I have a standing hold on the presidential suite? Plenty of space if you prefer Egyptian cotton and silk carpet to that moth-eaten roach-fest Brennan booked for you."

"You want us to stay with you?"

Tyler shrugged. "It makes the logistics easier. No need for a rental."

Eddie's eyes pleaded for her to say yes like the sad eyes of a bespectacled basset hound.

Twenty minutes later the two trudged a wet outdoor staircase at the Best Choice Motel.

"I can't believe you said no." Eddie hauled his bags over a lip of rusted steel as he reached the concrete walkway on the third level.

"Operational. Boundaries." Talia walked ahead of him. One of her bags lolled sideways and she kicked it to keep it rolling straight. "I'm not going off book at the start of my first mission."

Eddie mimicked her in a childish voice. *"I'm not going off book."* The door to his room, bloated from the rain, got stuck in its frame. With a thrust of his shoulder, he forced it open, and a musty blend of mold and smoker's carpet smell blew out to meet them both. "The man said Egyptian cotton, Talia." He tossed and kicked his bags over the threshold. "Egyptian cotton."

The door slammed shut.

TYLER WATCHED, hands in the pockets of his overcoat, from the railing of a parking structure two streets over. The overhang of the level above kept him dry and kept the G-Wagon well hidden. He didn't speak for a long time after Eddie and Talia disappeared into their rooms.

The driver stuck his head out the window and removed his sunglasses. "Shall we go, then?" he asked in perfect English.

Tyler held up a finger. "Wait for it."

"Wait for wh—?"

Before Davian could finish the question, Talia emerged from her room and opened her umbrella against the rain. She hurried down the stairs.

"She's headed back to the rental place." Tyler returned to the SUV and got in. "I could have taken her myself, but she's not ready to ask for my help—nor anyone else's."

Down below, Talia hailed a cab, shaking out the umbrella as she ducked inside.

The driver cranked up the Mercedes. "You want me to follow?"

"No. Miss Inger can take care of herself." He settled back and drew a smartphone from his inside pocket, unlocking the screen. "Head back to the Mandarin. I have other business."

CHAPTER
NINETEEN

TALIA AND EDDIE DROVE EAST of Tiraspol in a mid-nineties Opel Astra with a tree-shaped air freshener dangling from the mirror. Its weak pine scent wasn't fooling anyone. Talia had picked up the rental from Da! Autos the night before, getting soaked to the bone and fleeced by her cabdriver in the process. But she had done it her way, not Tyler's.

"This is nice." Eddie poked at a water-stained dip in the fabric above his head. "Way better than the Mercedes."

"This is a victory."

"If you say so. Are you okay? You've got some . . ." Eddie's voice faded and he pointed to the region beneath his eyes.

"Bags?"

"Yeah."

"Thanks." Talia cranked the wheel hard, turning south between a pair of tobacco fields guarded by the region's ever-present barbed-wire fences.

After drying her hair, Talia had curled up on her musty sheets with a Dr. Seuss book, a tradition she observed every time she found herself in a strange bed. That happened a lot for foster kids. Usually it helped her sleep—not the story, but the feel

90

of that well-worn copy of *The Cat in the Hat*. The book hadn't helped this time. All night, Talia had suffered through cold sweats and nightmare images. She kept those details to herself. "My bed was like a slab of concrete."

"Mine too. We'll be out of the motel soon, though, right? We're making quick progress."

"Right." Talia's answer did not mirror his optimistic tone.

Their *quick progress* didn't sit well with her. It should have taken days to set up a meeting with Ivanov's people. But that morning, when Talia had made her first attempt to establish contact, it seemed as if the receptionist at Avantec had been expecting her call.

"Yes, Ms. Wright of Wright Way Security," the woman had said in crisp, almost British, English. "Dr. Ivanov will see you at nine thirty. Do you know where to find us?"

All the lines Talia had rehearsed before dialing were suddenly useless. "Uh . . . Yes. I do."

"Excellent. Please arrive promptly at nine fifteen and present identification at the gate."

Talia let out an involuntary growl at the memory.

The Avantec research compound stood on a grassy plateau near the Ukrainian border. Eddie glanced over at her as the gatehouse came into view, three-quarters of the way up the hill. "You still think Tyler set up this meeting?"

"Who else."

"And that makes you angry."

"Yes."

"Because . . . he got us exactly what we wanted?"

She glared at him, bringing the Opel to a halt an inch from the wrought-iron gate. "Just make sure you have your Glock. You're going to need it."

The guard checked their IDs against a list and waved them onward, and when they crested the hill, Eddie caught his breath. "Whoa. That's a horse of a different color."

By their surroundings, Talia and Eddie might have been driving onto the campus of a Silicon Valley tech giant, despite having left one of the poorest cities in Eastern Europe less than an hour before. She steered the Opel along a smooth asphalt lane that curved its way between S-shaped buildings of black-tinted glass.

Eddie admired the manicured lawns and brick paths surrounding the guest lot. "I could work here." He nodded at a man-made lake between their parking spot and the main building. Water poured from a shining aluminum sculpture at the center—three stylized rockets in flight. "I wonder if Dr. Ivanov is hiring."

"Don't count on a big paycheck." Talia locked the car and the two started up the path. "Labor and materials here cost a tenth of what they do in the States. Ivanov can undercut US companies by half and still—" The next word caught in her throat. A G-Wagon was parked near the entrance, in one of the executive spaces. Talia shook her head. "It can't be."

"It is." Eddie nudged her with an elbow. "He's *heeeerrre*."

"MISS NATALIA!" Tyler leaped up from his place at the sixth-floor conference table. Two men stood with him, one whom Talia recognized as Pavel Ivanov, though he looked younger—and perhaps handsomer—than the man from her file photos. Ivanov and the other remained in place, but Tyler walked the length of the onyx table, arms spread wide as if greeting a favorite niece. He squeezed her arm, propelling her toward the CEO. "Come. Meet Pavel. Pavel, this is Natalia Wright, security expert extraordinaire. Your secrets are safer simply by having her in the room."

"Ms. Wright." Ivanov's low-key, even cold tone was a welcome relief after Tyler's greeting. He took her hand. "I am afraid my friend has been overselling you all morning. I suspect he is trying to run up your consulting fee."

Tyler clapped him on the shoulder. "From which I would take only a tiny percentage."

"Your friend?" Talia asked as Ivanov moved on and greeted Eddie.

Tyler pulled two additional chairs back from the table. "Pavel and I have known each other for more than a year now. He allows me to use Avantec's private runway, along with some hangar space for my Gulfstream."

"And Mr. Tyler . . . facilitates . . . my American business dealings." Ivanov gestured at the leather chairs, indicating they should all sit down. "But I am afraid you've wasted a trip, Miss Wright. I already have excellent security, overseen by Mr. Bazin." His steel-gray eyes shifted to his comrade, a bulky man with the bulge of a sizable weapon beneath his suit jacket.

Talia took the seat Tyler had pulled out for her, swatting his hand as he tried to help her into it. She had to follow his script, but she didn't have to let him paw at her. "I admire your confidence, Dr. Ivanov. But my associate and I have a track record that speaks for itself." *A false track record created by the Agency boffins*, she thought, holding an equally false smile. "If it helps, we're willing to make an initial assessment free of charge."

"How kind of you." Ivanov matched her plastic smile with one of his own. "But your services are not necessary."

"Oh"—Talia laid her Glock on the table—"I think they are."

Bazin came out of his chair, body half covering Ivanov's. At the same time, he leveled a .50-caliber hand cannon at Talia. "Do not move!"

She didn't flinch. Talia held his gaze for a count of two and then eased her hand away from her weapon. It had been a calculated risk, but with it, Talia had purchased valuable insight. Bazin's quickness told her he had training, and the rigid position of his rear thumb, straight up on the side of his nickel-plated Desert Eagle, screamed Spetsnaz. Ivanov had the wisdom and resources to hire security from outside the local thuggery—a good sign.

However, working with a former Spetsnaz meant contending with a serious ego. Talia began by tossing out a backhanded compliment. "You have excellent reflexes, Mr. Bazin, but I should never have gotten a gun this close to your boss—not to mention *two* guns."

Eddie held up a cautioning hand and laid his own Glock next to Talia's. He pushed them both to the center of the table. "We slipped these past your gate, your metal detectors, and your lobby guards." He raised an eyebrow at Ivanov. "How many other holes might we find in *Mr. Bazin's* security?"

The Russian held the Desert Eagle steady, seething. "I am within right to shoot." Apparently his Spetsnaz training did not include English grammar.

"Sit down, Alexi." Ivanov laid a gentle hand on the bear's shoulder. "Our new friends were merely making a point."

"*Scoring* a point would be more accurate," Tyler interjected.

"Quite." Ivanov pushed back from the table. "I think they have earned a tour of the facility, at the very least." He stood, beckoning for Talia to follow, and together they walked to a window that looked out over a three-story clean room. Men and women in white coveralls tinkered with metal cylinders and pored over machines with flickering digital displays.

Talia understood none of it. "To be honest, Dr. Ivanov, Mr. Tyler mentioned your Defense Department connections, but he never told me precisely what you do here."

"Rocketry." Ivanov folded his arms and watched his workers with pride, the way a coach watches a champion Little League team. "Avantec supplies your government with parts for missiles."

CHAPTER
TWENTY

"SO, MISS WRIGHT," IVANOV SAID as the four strolled through a hallway of aluminum and glass. He had dismissed Bazin to other duties, despite the Russian's strenuous objections, another point for Talia against the big guy's ego.

"Please, call me Talia."

"Miss Talia." The Moldovan nodded, not quite letting go of his formality. "You give credence to Mr. Tyler's worries of an impending theft?"

"You don't?"

Ivanov shrugged, and then broke from the conversation to greet a lab tech hurrying past in the direction they were headed. On the wall behind the two, a sixty-inch OLED screen showed a digital animation of a black, angular airship hovering in a constantly flowing aurora. The caption at the bottom read GRY-PHON: THE FUTURE OF ATMOSPHERIC SATELLITES.

After a brief exchange in Romanian, the woman rushed ahead and Ivanov returned his attention to his guests. Before he could speak, Eddie interrupted, pointing past him to the display. "What is that?"

"Ah." Ivanov smiled. "That is Gryphon, our newest initiative—

a mesospheric airship. I will personally introduce the concept next week at EAE, the European Aerospace Expo. An airship is far more cost effective than a communications satellite, with many other uses as well."

"What sort of uses?" Eddie held his glasses in place and craned his neck toward the image. "This material reminds me of a stealth bomber. It's—"

Talia kicked the back of his heel to shut him up. Geeking out on airships was not part of the mission. "Is Gryphon's technology the type Lukon might come after?"

Ivanov chuckled, continuing their walk down the hallway. "I think Mr. Lukon is more myth than man. To be honest, I am afraid you and I have been drawn in by Adam's propensity for melodrama." He glanced over his shoulder at Tyler. "No offense."

"None taken." Tyler clapped him on the back—a gesture Ivanov did not seem to appreciate. "I like melodrama. Keeps things interesting. But Lukon is real enough. My sources tell me he started as an MI-6 assassin, now in business for himself—mostly high-level heists, some of them violent. Over the last decade and a half, a lot of weapons and drugs have gone missing, along with a few CEOs and crime bosses."

"He's eliminating competition," Ivanov said with a grim smile. "And absorbing their operations. Now this legend has found his way into Eastern Europe, is that it?"

Tyler shrugged. "So I hear. Two months ago, someone hit the biggest weapons operation in the Czech Republic—a semi-legitimate manufacturer. A team moved in like ghosts and took every gun, bullet, and grenade in a single night. The boss vanished as well, but—"

"Lukon hit an arms dealer?" Talia stopped, bringing the whole group to a halt.

Tyler touched his nose. "And what do you call a legal arms dealer, Miss Wright?"

"A defense contractor." Talia's rent-a-cop assignment was rapidly turning into something more serious. She glanced at Ivanov. "If these rumors are true, then Mr. Tyler's fears for Avantec are well-founded. Mr. Lukon may see you as competition in the regional arms trade."

Tyler pushed his head between them. "*Lukon.*"

Talia gave him a *What are you talking about?* squint.

"It's not *Mr.* Lukon. It's just Lukon."

Eddie nodded his agreement.

Armed guards met them at a pair of heavy vault doors. Ivanov lifted one of several garment bags from a hook on the wall. "As you can see, we keep our main laboratory well protected"—he unzipped the bag and showed Talia a set of white coveralls—"from dust as well as thieves."

As the four entered the clean room, dressed in their coveralls, Talia noticed a second set of doors closing at the back. The woman Ivanov had spoken to in the hallway—a strawberry blonde in her late thirties or early forties—met them at the door and ushered the group to a white, powder-coated workbench.

"May I present Dr. Ella Visser." Ivanov thrust a gloved hand toward the woman as she placed what amounted to a faceted titanium egg on a miniature tripod. "Our top researcher in guidance systems."

Dr. Visser fixed a cable to a connector at the bottom of the egg, more intent on the delicate task than bothering with introductions.

"Visser," Eddie offered. "Is that Dutch?"

This earned him a nervous smile. "Yes. Very good. Dr. Ivanov and I met while I was a visiting professor at Cambridge." Her eyes flitted to Ivanov, as if seeking approval. He remained placid, and she plugged the cable into a laptop. A window opened depicting a three-dimensional gyro. "Ah. We are ready."

Ivanov positioned the laptop for them all to see. "This is Dr. Visser's pride and joy," he said. "And mine. What may look to you like an egg sculpture is actually a GPS-integrated inertial guidance system—one I hope will one day steer America's long-range cruise missiles."

Talia did not see anything incredibly special about the egg, but the phrases *cruise missile* and *guidance system* were both red flags. Something at Avantec was worth stealing, and thus worth protecting.

The group bid farewell to Dr. Visser and her wondrous egg, and after viewing a couple of miniaturized rocket engines, Talia finally convinced Ivanov to discuss his security measures. She handed her coveralls to an attendant outside the lab as she gave the CEO a serious look. "We can't rule out the possibility of a kidnapping, with your technology as the ransom. Talk to me about transportation. How do you get to and from the compound?"

"On most days, I walk." Ivanov chuckled at her confused expression and explained. "I live here, on the compound"—he gestured at a gaggle of technicians in the hallway—"as do many of my scientists. There are dormitories on the grounds."

Eddie looked up, still fighting to remove one of his booties. "You keep your employees on the property?"

"We do not *keep* anyone. We *offer* our top employees a higher standard of living than most ever dreamed possible."

Eddie finished his battle with the bootie, and Ivanov led them back toward the lobby. "To answer your original question, Miss Talia, I do not leave the compound often, but when I do, I am accompanied by Mr. Bazin, and we are both well protected in an armored vehicle."

Talia slipped behind the lobby counter, motioning for a confused guard to stay seated as she inspected his video monitors. "I'll need to see that vehicle. And my associate will need to see your server rooms."

"Fine. I will hire Wright Way and allow you to continue this assessment on two conditions."

Talia didn't like conditions. She came out from behind the counter. "Which are?"

"A 20 percent reduction on your standard fee and dinner—tomorrow night, my treat—so you can *assess* my transportation arrangements."

"Done," Eddie said without so much as glancing at Talia for confirmation. "But we don't come cheap. We're talking six courses minimum, with steak *and* lobster."

She slapped his arm with the back of her hand. "Dr. Ivanov means me, Eddie." She had read the look in the CEO's eyes. "Just me."

"Oh." Eddie dropped his gaze to his sneakers. "Well, that's disappointing."

CHAPTER
TWENTY-ONE

"THIS IS SOOO A DATE." Eddie stood in the doorway between their adjoining motel rooms, arms crossed.

"Business meeting." Talia bent close to the bathroom mirror, trying to even out her eye shadow.

"Nope. It's a date."

They had been jabbing at each other like that since the previous afternoon. Their second day at Avantec had been more productive than Talia could have hoped, with Ivanov allowing her access to Bazin's security staff and the compound's utility grid. The day had also given her a reprieve from Tyler, who had chosen to follow Eddie when he split off with Bazin to get a look at the server farm and the perimeter surveillance system.

If all went well that evening, Talia could wrap things up the following day. Ivanov had blocked off his afternoon to let her make a few final assessments and present her findings. She had a growing list, but nothing Ivanov couldn't handle with his resources. Avantec's US interests were safe. With any luck, she and Eddie would catch the first flight out of there on Monday.

Talia stepped back from the counter and assessed her makeup. "For the last time, Eddie, this is a business meeting."

This was so totally a date. It was also a key component of a business transaction, and Tyler was getting a cut. What did that say about their professional relationship? Talia cringed and stepped up to the counter again to remove some of the eye shadow.

"Well," she said, emerging from the bathroom a few minutes later. She did a quick twirl for Eddie. The LBD, or little black dress, was considered mandatory equipment for a CIA officer. Embassy parties and fancy dinners were a common hazard in the field. "How do I look?"

"I always said you clean up nice." Eddie leaned a shoulder against the doorframe. "Where's your Glock?"

"Thigh holster."

His shoulder slipped and he dropped an arm to catch himself. "Uh . . . right."

THE MANDARIN BOASTED the only restaurant in Tiraspol worthy of a man like Ivanov—the Red Dragon. Talia arrived separately, and the valet accepted the keys to the Opel as if they were a used banana peel. A sad knowing darkened his features. The tip later that night would likely match the car.

Talia had come early to scope out the place. A pair of Chinese lions greeted her at the door, and again in the Mandarin's main lobby, where black and gold banners of serpentine dragons hung from marble arches. The restaurant stood to her left, a darkened space lit by red silk lanterns. She saw no threats among the patrons, until her eyes found the bar.

"Mr. Tyler," she said with a sigh, taking the stool next to him. "What are you doing here?"

Tyler sipped a white, frothy drink through a tiny straw, smacked his lips, and gave her a sardonic look. "I live here."

"I mean what are you doing *here*, in the Red Dragon? You know this is where I'm meeting Dr. Ivanov."

"I'm having a drink, Miss *Wright*. Is that a crime?" Tyler shifted his eyes to the great brass gong hanging behind the bar and took another drink, wincing. "Did you know many Eastern European bars use vodka instead of rum in their piña coladas? They say you can taste the difference."

"Okay. I'll bite. Which did they use in yours?"

"Neither. I'm not much of a drinker." He took another sip and winced again. "But this one is *remarkably* cold."

One day Talia would make Brennan suffer for forcing her to work with this guy. She checked her watch, then checked the door. Ivanov could arrive at any second. "Please go away."

"Not until I finish my drink. I'm taking it slow. I can't handle brain freeze."

"Ugh." Talia spun on her stool and laid her elbows on the bar. At the far end, a young woman sat alone, dressed to kill in a red sequined dress.

"Look." Talia nudged Tyler. "That girl down there is practically screaming for a sugar daddy to pick her up. Why don't you take her and the drink upstairs? Isn't that what rich guys do?"

Tyler kept working on his icy virgin piña colada. His eyes darkened. "That's not who I am."

"I guess that's the point. I don't know who you are, Mr. Tyler. And I don't want to know."

"Then what do you want?"

"For you. To go. *Away!*" She pounded the bar with each phrase.

The girl in the red dress gave her an accusing look that said, *You must be sooo desperate for attention.* Talia dropped her forehead into her hand.

The slurping sound of the last few drops of a cold virgin piña colada roused her from her frustration. Tyler set down his glass with an exaggerated "Ahhh" and patted her bare shoulder. "That's it for me." He slid off the stool and tossed a pair of bills onto the bar. "And don't look now, but your date's here."

Two bellhops opened a pair of the Mandarin's glass doors as Ivanov strolled through, a black SUV pulling away in his wake. Talia ditched Tyler without another word. She walked out to her date, doing her best to banish a sudden fear of stumbling in the unfamiliar heels.

"Where's your Russian friend?" she asked as Ivanov shifted course to meet her.

"I left Mr. Bazin with the car. After all, I have you to protect me." He bowed to kiss her hand, but stopped halfway, eyes shifting to the front desk, where Tyler had conveniently stopped to chat with the clerk. "Is that—?"

"Yes. He's staying at this hotel."

"And are you two—?"

"*No.*" She might have placed more emphasis on the word than necessary. Talia tugged Ivanov toward the restaurant, having never received that hand kiss. "Shall we sit down?"

Ivanov had the menu memorized. He ordered for them both, advising Talia that Nicolai, the not-so-Chinese chef of the Red Dragon, made only one dish well. He also inquired about a bottle of wine, but Talia refused. She was there on business, no matter how dashing her Moldovan date.

A rehash of her suggestions for Avantec's security kept the business barrier raised through the first two courses. The more she interviewed Ivanov, the more Talia worried a kidnapping might be Lukon's best option. And here she was, drawing the target out of his compound.

Her eyes flitted to the entrance and windows during transition movements—a bite of duck or a sip of water—whenever she managed to tear her gaze from his. Ivanov's gray eyes were at once brilliant, passionate, and playful, especially when he spoke of the lab and his work there.

"I do my best work in my home lab," he said, handing his plate to the waiter when he had finished. "That place is like a manifestation of my own mind."

Talia had noticed. She had inspected his residence, across the lake from the main building. In some ways, Ivanov's personal lab was more impressive than the clean room, and yet more overtly masculine, with polished concrete furnishings and random bundles of wire and steel.

"Are you sure you don't want another look at it?" he asked, folding his arms on the table. "The house and the lab, I mean. We could go this evening." There was that playfulness again.

Talia swallowed the boulder forming in her throat. "No. I don't think that's a good idea. Not tonight." She couldn't believe she had added that last bit. To redirect the conversation, she broached new ground. "What about family, Dr. Ivanov?"

"Pavel."

"Right." She felt herself blush. "Pavel. Lukon could use your loved ones against you." It occurred to Talia as she broached the subject that Ivanov's file had not mentioned a marital status. Neither had he, as yet. A part of her cringed, waiting for his reply.

"Family is no issue." Ivanov raised a hand, and the waiter rushed over with a dessert card. "I have no wife, and I no longer have ties with the children's home that raised me."

She nearly choked on the water she was drinking. "You're an orphan?"

His eyes narrowed. "As . . . are you."

"I . . ." What was she supposed to say? From one slip of genuine surprise, Ivanov had read her past. Talia kicked herself, dabbing the dribble from her chin. She had let her guard down too far. Now she had to own it. A lie would never work. "Yes. My mother died in childbirth. I lost my father at a young age."

"I never knew my parents at all. I have always been an outsider. I suppose that is the reason I am so desperate for acceptance into the European aerospace community, not easy for any CEO from a city east of Vienna." Ivanov eased his chair around to her side of the table. "In many ways next week's expo is my coming-out party in polite society. Natalia," he said, dropping the "Miss" for the first time and laying a hand on her wrist, "we have much in common. Perhaps this is why I asked you to dinner." He raised his eyes to hers. "I hope you can forgive the impertinence, but—"

Glass shattered behind them.

Talia spun out of her chair, Glock up and ready, and a waitress backed away with hands raised, abandoning a pile of broken glasses and a fallen tray. The girl in the red dress, now seated with her young date, glanced at Talia and just shook her head.

Talia grabbed Ivanov's wrist and dragged him to the doors. "I'm getting you out of here."

"It was only a few glasses, Natalia." Ivanov signaled the waiter over her shoulder, rubbing his fingers together in the cash sign.

The waiter answered with a *we'll take care of it later* nod.

"For now, yes. But I drew my weapon, so if a real threat is out there, I've just shown my hand." She let go of him out on the drive. "Call Bazin."

Ivanov didn't have to. The Russian pulled up as she spoke, looking none too pleased at their sudden appearance. Ivanov's eyes turned playful again. "Does this mean you are coming with me? The night is young. There are still places in Tiraspol I could show you."

"No." Talia gave the valet the ticket for her Opel, ignoring the roll of the young man's eyes. "You're going home. Alone."

CHAPTER
TWENTY-TWO

TALIA AND EDDIE LEFT THE MOTEL for their final day at Avantec late in the afternoon. After she rejected his offer of an extended date, Ivanov had given her some line about an all-day project. He had asked her to meet him the following evening at the compound's private airfield, the only section she hadn't inspected yet. Talia suspected his true motivation was to shorten the goodbye.

She didn't blame him.

As they got in the car, Eddie asked how the dinner had gone. The tone behind Talia's "Fine" shut him down.

What had she been thinking, showing romantic interest in the subject of her mission? The guy didn't even know her real name. To take things further would only punish them both. An abrupt end to their relationship, professional or otherwise, was the right play.

Eddie was staring, and Talia realized she had the Opel's gas pedal pinned to the floor. She let up and glanced at him. "What?"

"Nothing."

Bazin met them at guest parking and crammed his oversize form into the driver's seat of a golf cart. "I take you to airfield."

A twelve-foot fence topped with concertina wire surrounded the airfield and its hangars. As Bazin drove down the perimeter road, Eddie leaned forward from the rear seat and nodded at the gauges. "So what kind of mileage does this thing get?"

The big bear hit him with a scowl.

Eddie raised his hands. "Never mind. Forget I asked."

Bazin drove them down a row of flat offices and in through the back of a sparkling-clean hangar. No grease stains marred the polished floor. Complex machinery manned by a small army of engineers left no stretch of wall uncovered. The Russian walked Talia and Eddie to the open doors at the front, facing the runway, and tucked his hands behind him in a military stance.

All three stood there for a long while. Eddie clearly could not handle the silence. "So," he asked, fidget spinner twirling in his fingers, "where's your boss?"

"Dr. Ivanov arrive soon."

Talia was intrigued. "With Mr. Tyler, I presume? On his Gulfstream?"

Bazin shook his head. "No Mr. Tyler." A deep chuckle rumbled in the bear's chest. "I think he bored with whole business."

"That sounds about right." Talia shifted her gaze out to the runway. Bad grammar or not, Bazin could be fairly insightful.

A few seconds later, the Russian pointed high above the orange glow of the setting sun. "Dr. Ivanov."

The aircraft began as a black wedge, falling out of the sky like an elevator, with no sound at all. Talia could make out four massive engines with cowlings that swiveled within the hull. Their fans kicked up to a whine and then a roar, rapidly slowing the craft to a hover five feet over the runway. The cowlings tilted forward, and the craft floated along a short network of taxiways until it reached the apron, where tricycle gear extended to cushion its final touchdown. A hatch with built-in stairs extended from the side, and a pilot in a gray, form-fitting flight suit sauntered down the steps.

Talia knew him by his walk before he pulled off his helmet. "Pavel?" She used his first name without thinking.

Ivanov lobbed the helmet to Eddie and grinned. "What do you think?"

"I think you set up this whole scenario to impress me."

EDDIE WAVED THE HELMET AT HIM. "I might have gone with a dramatic head toss when you pulled this off, but I'm not sure you have the hair for it. So good call."

Ivanov ignored him, giving Talia a bow. "You read me so well. But did it work?"

"Yes." A smile forced its way past the poker face she was fighting to hold. "Yes, it did."

"Excellent. I like hearing you say that word."

"You mean, 'Yes'?"

"Exactly." Ivanov accepted a tablet from one of his engineers and used it to gesture at the craft. "I give you the Mark Seven, Avantec's prototype free-flying lift."

"Soo, it's a helicopter." Eddie passed the helmet off to another engineer.

Talia stifled a laugh. "It is impressive. But I'm afraid I'm not one for heights."

"That is too bad." Pavel began typing on his tablet. "I would love to give you a ride. As for your comment," he said, glancing at Eddie, "the Mark Seven's performance reaches far beyond any helicopter. It is a hybrid rocket-jet that can reach the highest suborbital altitude."

"Suborbital?" Eddie's sarcasm faded and the tech geek emerged. "To what purpose?"

"Any purpose I desire." Ivanov offered Eddie a congenial smile, but Talia felt a sense of barely contained power behind the statement. "Mostly it will service Gryphon, as a towing and maintenance vehicle." He led them into the hangar. "Let me get changed. I want to show you the airfield, but not in this pressure suit. You have no idea how much it itches."

TALIA FOUND THE AIRFIELD surprisingly well defended, with an armed patrol in a HiLux pickup, motion sensors, and cameras. She could understand the security hardware for a tech company, but the armed patrol seemed excessive.

Ivanov read her mind, nodding at the pickup as they passed. "See, I have already taken your concerns to heart—extra men to stop Mr. Lukon."

Night had fallen by the time the four reached the conference room. From her portfolio, Talia removed a set of papers. "Here are our recommendations, all the changes and additions you need to make to protect yourself. And Wright Way will continue to employ our intelligence resources to look into Lukon. If we find out more, you'll hear from me."

"In that case I hope you do find more." Ivanov laid a hand on top of hers, stopping the papers, that playful glint in his eyes. "Perhaps I should be the one to call on you. In case I have questions."

There it was. Talia resolved to manage his expectations, right there and then. She started by drawing her hand out from under his. "Dr. Ivanov, my life is fluid. I'll be halfway across Europe tomorrow."

His eyes went from playful to mystified at the emphasis she put on *Dr. Ivanov*. And then he stiffened. He slid the papers over to Bazin. "I see. Then your report is for my head of security, not me. I will leave you with him to discuss the details. Thank you for your time." He pushed back from the table and left the room.

Bazin watched him go, then folded his hands on top of the papers. "Glad that over. I feel like fourth wheel all week."

"Third wheel," Eddie said, correcting the idiom.

Bazin furrowed his brow.

Talia touched Eddie's arm. "Don't. Don't even try."

The language barrier did not help the review of Talia's security suggestions. She and Bazin conducted most of it in Russian, stopping occasionally to include Eddie, and by the time the three walked off the elevator and into the lobby, only a few lights were lit. The beat-up Opel sat alone in the parking lot. There was no Mercedes G-Wagon, and Ivanov made no appearance for a final goodbye.

Talia said little on the drive to the gatehouse and would have remained silent all the way to the motel if the guard had been awake to open the gate for her. Not a good sign. She would have to call Bazin in the morning to report the infraction, and Bazin would likely throttle the man for sleeping on the job. She honked the horn and rolled down the window. "Hey! A little help here!"

No response.

A breath of wind and a soft *creak* shifted Talia's attention to the gate. It hung loose on its hinges—not quite closed. She shut off the engine and drew her Glock.

"Whoa," Eddie said. "I know you're in a bad mood, but you can't shoot the guy for slacking off."

Talia scanned the scene outside, watching the periphery of the gate's spotlights for movement. Nothing. She cracked her door. "Stay here."

Moving in an arc with her weapon up, Talia shouldered her way through the door and found the guard facedown at his station. She checked his pulse. Faint, but present. He was still breathing.

A shadow moved in the monitors, and she spun.

"Easy. *Easy*. It's just me." Eddie came through the door, frowning at her Glock.

"I told you to stay in the car."

"Bad call. Which of us can tell if someone's messed with the gatehouse computer, hmm?" He walked past.

She lowered the Glock and watched him work the keyboard. On a hunch, Talia picked up the guard's coffee. She lifted the lid and gave it a sniff. She handed him the cup. "Smell this."

He grimaced. "Smells like the milk went bad."

"Valerian oil. Heavy sedative. This guy was drugged."

"They hacked his computer too." Eddie turned back to the keyboard and typed some more. "Specifically . . . the motion detectors on a section of the outer fence."

A dark well opened in Talia's stomach. "Which section?"

"Southwest section, near the—"

Talia was already running for the car. "Near the residence!"

She and Eddie had the Opel speeding around the lake less than a minute later. Talia had her phone to her ear. "Come on, Pavel. Pick up the—" She didn't finish. A massive explosion lit up the water.

CHAPTER
TWENTY-THREE

THE OPEL SKIDDED TO A STOP fifty yards from the burning residence. Eddie opened an aluminum case in his lap, body swaying with the motion of the car. He offered Talia an earbud. "Take this and go long."

"What?"

He nodded toward the building. "Just go. I'll have comms up in under a minute."

Steel beams groaned. Melting glass popped and crackled as Talia raced up the lawn, making for the cover of a smaller version of the lake fountain. Where was the HiLux full of armed guards? She felt exposed, running blind into a potential gunfight, but Ivanov's life was at stake. Assuming he was still alive.

As she peered out from behind the fountain to scan for threats, Eddie's voice came through the earpiece. "Comms are up. Watch out. Here comes Sibby."

"Sibby?" Talia glanced back in time to see him chuck a black ball her way.

Eddie didn't have much of an arm, but the ball never fell. Rotors sprang out at the apex of the throw, transforming it into a mini-drone. "Sibby," he said, ducking down behind the car.

"That's short for Surveillance Intelligence Ball. She's—" Eddie stopped, and the drone shot up twenty feet in the air. "Check your northeast quarter. I have a moving heat signature."

Methodically, Talia pivoted in her crouch and moved to the opposite edge of the fountain. She lowered her weapon. A uniformed guard was running away from the fire. Coward. Bazin had some housecleaning to do.

The *rat-a-tat* of a three-round burst and the answering *boom* of a heavy-caliber weapon drew her attention back to the building. The *boom* sounded a lot like a .50-cal Desert Eagle. Bazin must already be inside. Talia had to get in there and help.

"Talia," Eddie said. "I have two more bogeys, fleeing through the fence line. Should Sibby follow?"

Her first inclination was yes, but Talia's training—and her failure at the Sanctum—had taught her better. "Negative. I need her eyes with me."

"Copy."

She watched Sibby zip through a shattered window, waited for an unbearable ten count, and followed. The explosion had come from the second floor, but it had shattered most of the first-floor windows as well, making entry a nonissue. Talia used her elbow to knock out a triangle of glass and ducked inside. Blue flame tinged with yellow snaked across the ceiling. The smoke threatened to swallow her whole. Talia coughed and shouted. "Pavel!"

Boom, rat-a-tat, boom. Somewhere ahead a gun battle raged. One or more of the attackers were still in the building. She followed the sounds as best she could. Where was that drone? "Talk to me, Eddie."

"The heat is killing my infrared. Optical is not much better. Too much smoke."

"What about acoustics?" Talia buried her face in the crook of her elbow to shield her lungs from the smoke. "Can Sibby follow sounds?"

"Ooh. Good . . . idea." Eddie's answer was stilted, as if he were typing on his tablet as he spoke. "Switching now. Check your phone for her video."

Talia advanced from one hallway corner to the next and unlocked her screen the way Franklin had taught her. Sibby's app came up automatically. Smoke passed across the video feed. She could make out a tile floor and a section of wall, but nothing useful. Before she could ask how to find the drone, Eddie gave her the answer.

"Glasses."

"Right." Talia put them on and slipped the phone in her pocket. Through the blue tint of the lenses she saw green arrows pointing her toward the drone. Sibby's video ran in her right peripheral, still nothing but smoke and walls. "Find Ivanov, Eddie."

"What sounds am I looking for?"

Talia answered between coughs. "*Gunfire.*"

"Oh. Yeah. No need to get snappy."

The video in Talia's peripheral came alive with blue and red lines. The drone was reading the acoustics of its surroundings. Talia heard another burst from the machine gun, closer now, and corresponding green circles appeared like ripples in a pond. The video moved. Sibby shifted to bring the ripples to the center of her forward camera. A polished concrete counter materialized through the smoke.

"The lab!" Talia broke into a sprint, still coughing. "They're . . . in the lab!"

Steel doors appeared in front of her, one standing ajar. Talia placed a hand against one of them. Warm, but not hot.

Sibby had already flown through the gap. In the video, Talia saw Ivanov, hiding behind a lab counter with Bazin crouched beside him. The Russian shifted out into the open and squeezed off two ear-splitting rounds. A burst of machine gun fire answered, and the drone rotated to locate the source. The camera settled on a man in a hard face mask of black composite. The intruder had taken cover behind a heavy-duty 3D printer. A woman with strawberry-blonde hair lay motionless beside him.

"That's Visser," Eddie said. The video zoomed in on a dark pool. "She's bleeding out. Talia, get in there."

"Working on it. Bring Sibby higher. I need an overview."

Eddie complied. Talia took a last look to gauge the layout of the fight, then kicked open the door.

The intruder saw her coming and shifted to the other side of the machinery. He couldn't last there. The new position left him no angle to keep Bazin pinned down, and the Russian knew it.

Bazin advanced.

Talia advanced as well. "Give it up! Drop your weapon and show me your hands!" Bazin repeated the command in Russian, and the man tossed something at the opposite wall. It stuck there—a glob of white, not a machine gun.

"Bomb!" Talia turned and dove for the floor.

The explosion rocked her brain, but she forced her body to stay in the fight. Looking up, she saw the intruder pushing his way through the billowing smoke. How had he survived so close to the blast? *A directional charge.* The smoke dissipated to reveal a jagged hole in the wall, exposing the lab to the night air. The intruder ran through. Talia fired one, two, three rounds. She heard a grunt, but the man kept running and vanished into the dark.

"Eddie, follow him!" She watched her video feed as Sibby zipped out through the same hole, camera frantically shifting left and right. Even with the infrared, she found no trace of the thief.

CHAPTER
TWENTY-FOUR

HORNS BLARED amid the roar of the flames, more present in Talia's earpiece than in her surroundings.

"Talia, the cavalry is here, such as it is. The HiLux and Ivanov's miniature fire brigade are both on scene."

"Better late than never." Talia glanced toward the lab exit, now completely obscured by smoke. There was no way she would risk dragging Ivanov back through the burning building. "I'm bringing our boy out through the hole the intruder blew in the wall. Is our path clear?"

"Clear. Sibby can't see any threats."

"Doesn't mean they're not out there." Talia retreated to Visser's body and checked for a pulse. Nothing. But Talia wouldn't leave her there—just in case. "Bazin!" She waved to get his attention, pointed to the downed scientist, and then thrust a flat hand toward the hole.

The big bear nodded in understanding.

As he did, the building groaned. They couldn't stay much longer. "Are you sure the area behind the structure is clear, Eddie?"

"Positive. Get out of there!"

Talia kept one hand on Ivanov's shoulder as she propelled

him through the rear gardens. Bazin followed, Desert Eagle at the ready despite the extra burden of a limp scientist draped over his shoulders. Two paramedics rolled a gurney to meet them as they came around the house.

"Careful. Careful," Talia said as Bazin laid Dr. Visser down. It didn't matter. The older paramedic checked Visser's vitals and shook his head. He pulled a sheet over her forehead.

While Talia gazed at the face beneath the cloth, Ivanov stumbled away into the open, dazed. Men and women in a variety of uniforms swirled around him—too many people Talia did not recognize. On a gut reaction she rushed him, grabbed him with both hands, and pushed him back against the fire truck.

"What are you doing?" Bazin strode up beside her.

Talia caught the bear by his lapel and dragged his snout down to her level. "Your boss is too exposed out here. Take him to the dormitories. Clean him up and lock it down."

"And what are you going to do?"

"What I do best. Gather intelligence."

The duties of an intelligence officer and a detective were not mutually exclusive either, no matter what the gumshoes at the FBI said. Often, generating actionable intelligence had as much to do with following crime scene evidence as any murder investigation.

The fire brigade, however, was fighting a losing battle. Talia's crime scene continued to burn, so she turned to her witnesses. A hostile expression, a commanding voice, and perhaps some terrifyingly bedraggled hair netted her and Eddie a line of subjects to interview.

None of them had seen a thing. No one even knew where to find the guard that had run away.

Frustrated. Empty-handed. Talia and Eddie found Ivanov in a room at the dormitories. Bazin had blocked off the whole floor, and his boss offered rooms for Talia and Eddie, giving her the one next door to his own. Talia asked Bazin to retrieve any security video he could find and pass it to Eddie, then dismissed them both. The bear didn't like taking more of her orders, but a hard look from Ivanov sent him on his way.

"I can't believe Ella is gone. Murdered, and for what?"

His lament brought a lingering question to the forefront of Talia's mind. "What was Dr. Visser doing at your residence so late in the first place?" She made no attempt to mask the accusation in her tone. But her jealousy rang hollow the moment she gave it voice. Visser had been in Ivanov's lab, not his bedroom—not that Talia had any right to care either way.

Ivanov looked stricken.

She didn't wait for his response. "I'm sorry."

"It is all right. Ella was a treasured colleague, nothing more. We were working on . . ." Ivanov's voice faded, and he offered her a weak smile. "A pet project of mine." The smile dropped away. "Now she is gone, a victim of a failed robbery."

"Failed?"

"Yes. Lukon's thieves took nothing of value."

Talia didn't understand. If they ran away with nothing, then why the explosion? Why the gun battle? "How can you be sure?"

Ivanov poured himself a drink in the room's kitchenette. "Because there was nothing of value to steal." He lifted an empty glass, offering to pour Talia a drink as well, but she refused. Ivanov nodded and went on. "If Mr. Lukon is after weaponry, as you and Mr. Tyler suggest, then his team hit my residence because of the data servers on the second floor."

"The explosion?" A chill swept through Talia as the image of the blast returned to her.

"Just so. It would seem Mr. Lukon knew I use those servers for my most high-level projects. And he likely emptied the hard drives." Ivanov downed his drink in one gulp and began pouring another. His smile returned. "What Mr. Lukon does *not* know, and what he will certainly discover when he tries to view them, is the files he stole are only shells—encryption nodes. My data is routed through them and immediately transferred to a secure, off-site vault."

Talia studied his microexpressions. True or not, Ivanov was convinced of his story. For now, his weapon designs were safe. "Pavel, what was Lukon after?"

"That, I cannot tell you."

Can't or won't? she wondered. "What about this data vault? Where is it?"

He took another drink, expression turning serious. "I cannot tell that either. Only Bazin and I know its current location. And few, even within Avantec, know of its existence. After tonight, I prefer to keep it this way."

Talia didn't press. They said good night in the hall. "Try and get some sleep." She touched his shoulders—the same place she had grabbed him when she shoved him back into the fire truck—and then she retreated to her room.

CHAPTER
TWENTY-FIVE

NO AMOUNT OF SHOWERING could banish the smell of smoke from Talia's skin. And no amount of scrubbing could remove Dr. Visser's blood from her blouse. As she fought with the stain, dressed in a set of Avantec sweats, Talia felt the scientist's death resting squarely on her shoulders. When had this assignment made the leap from a rent-a-cop security job to a life-and-death battle over unknown weapon designs? Talia paused in her scrubbing and looked in the mirror, anger tightening her features. Visser's death was *not* her fault.

That blame belonged with Brennan.

Barefoot, she padded the twelve or so feet to the next room over, and quietly knocked.

After a long wait, the door opened. Eddie rubbed his eyes. "What's wrong? Can't sleep?"

Talia pushed past him and took command of his bed, leaving Eddie the small table in the kitchenette.

He flopped down in a wooden chair. "You know. Because I *can* sleep. But hey, come on in."

"This doesn't make any sense, Eddie." Talia sat cross-legged at the center of the mattress.

"A pretty girl on my bed and me nodding off ten feet away at the kitchen table?" Eddie rolled his eyes. "No. That makes perfect sense."

She pursed her lips at him.

"Sorry. Go on."

"Brennan played this assignment off as small potatoes—a way to get our feet wet. Now we're dealing with blown-up buildings and murdered scientists." She crossed her arms. "I want to talk to him. Get him up on SATCOM."

Eddie picked up a tablet from his table. "You want to see the security video first?"

"Bazin came through?"

"If you can call it that." Eddie began working the screen. "The files he gave me were ugly, corrupted by the software Lukon's people uploaded at the gatehouse. I spent the last half hour running enhancement algorithms." He looked up at her, eyelids drooping. "I had just gotten to sleep when you knocked."

"I get it. I interrupted your beauty sleep." Talia held out a hand, curling and uncurling her fingers. "Bring it here, snow-flake."

"You're the snowflake." Eddie got up to bring her the tablet, then sat down again, cheeks flushing. "Um . . . Why don't *you* come *here* . . . to the table?"

She had forgotten who she was dealing with. Eddie took chivalry and virtue as seriously as one of Arthur's knights. Sitting on a bed with a girl made him uncomfortable. Talia bounced herself up and walked over. "Yeah. Okay."

Two open windows on the tablet showed varying levels of grainy, wavy video. Eddie started the playback in both simultaneously. "These come from the residence. I matched up the times."

Talia held a finger close to the second window. Amid the flickers and distortion, she could make out two standing racks of black boxes, all with green, blue, and red LEDs flashing at random. "That's Ivanov's personal server room."

"Correct. Second floor of the residence. I was in there yesterday, checking it out with Bazin while your boyfriend gave you a personal tour of his six-thousand-square-foot living quarters."

"You mean while I was checking *Dr. Ivanov's* motion detectors."

"That's what I said, right?" Eddie glanced down at his tablet. "Oops. Here they come."

Three figures moved through the first video window, all in black, making their way down a long hall toward the camera. The largest of them looked up at the camera as they passed. The prickling sensation in Talia's neck told her it was the same man she had faced in the lab, and he wore the same rigid mask. The eyes were covered by tinted glass.

"We're looking at the main hallway." Eddie pointed out the spot on a rough diagram he had drawn on a notepad. "They entered through the front door. Brash."

"Probably let in by our mystery guard. He wasn't running away. He was on their team."

"I'll have Bazin check his rosters."

"Good call, but I'm betting Lukon is too good to leave that kind of trail behind."

Seconds after the three intruders passed the hallway camera, two of them appeared in the server room feed, blinking in and out of view like ghosts in the distorted playback. Talia watched for several seconds, then touched Eddie's arm. "Whoa. Go back."

He rewound the footage and played it frame by frame. Between the flashes of digital snow, the two figures moved within the server stacks, placing white globs.

"There," she said, lifting his hand away to keep him from advancing further.

"Those are the bombs." Eddie shrugged. "Can't tell much about them from the video. Could be C4, but we can't be sure."

"Actually"—Talia used her thumb and forefinger to zoom in on a black box fixed to one of the figure's belts—"I was looking at that. What would you say it is?"

Eddie held his glasses steady as he looked closer. "Portable hard drive. Ten petabytes, maybe more. The blue LED tells me there's data on board." Realization hit, and he let the tablet slap down on the table. "So Lukon got what he came for. We lost."

"No. We didn't." Talia got up and started pacing. "I'll explain later. For now, get me Brennan."

BRENNAN HAD NOT GIVEN Talia the full story on Ivanov, Lukon, and Avantec. He couldn't have. Talia wanted to throttle him, and the cumbersome nature of a secure call into a monster system like the CIA's didn't help. Satellite to hard line. Digital to analog. Multiplexing, scrubbing, encryption, decryption. Talia understood the process, but the pregnant pauses it caused before Brennan's every answer still gave her the feeling he was hiding something.

"Stop," she said when Brennan tried to explain away the explosives and the shoot-out as pointless violence from an over-zealous thief. "Just stop. Lukon is a serious player, former CIA if Tyler is right. The stakes here are higher than a simple rent-a-cop security job. What is Ivanov working on? What type of weapon was I sent here to protect?"

Halfway through the encryption-decryption pause, Talia added, "And so help me, if the phrase 'need-to-know' comes out of your mouth, I'll fly home right now and choke you with your own donuts."

When Brennan spoke again, Talia could hear the resigned sigh in his tinny, overprocessed voice. "Tyler."

Talia exchanged a look with Eddie, then frowned at the tablet's blank screen. "Tyler is not a weapon, Frank."

"No, but Tyler has the answers you're looking for. Go talk to him." The secure line went dead.

CHAPTER
TWENTY-SIX

TYLER DIDN'T ANSWER TALIA'S CALLS until the following morning, and added a little too much shock and dismay to his voice when she finally reached him. "Oh *no*! Is Pavel all right?"

"Save it." Talia had no time for his games. "Warm up the G-Wagon and get out here. We need to talk."

As she hung up, a porter appeared at the door with breakfast and three boxes of clothes and shoes.

"I sent into town for them," Ivanov said when he dropped by a short time later. "To my favorite tailor's." He gestured up and down Talia's form, smiling at the outfit she had chosen. "The man deserves a commendation."

Talia blushed. She had on a set of gray slacks, a black blouse, and a pair of flats. Nothing fancy, but Ivanov was right. They fit her remarkably well. "Thank you," she said, setting down the remainder of her coffee. "This was kind. But I'm afraid I have to get them dirty."

"THE GROUND IS STILL WARM," Eddie said as he and Talia picked their way through the tangle of aluminum beams at the edge of Ivanov's ruined residence. One skeletal corner of the second floor remained, but the rest of it had collapsed into the first.

Talia steadied her partner and then moved on, careful not to touch any standing beams, lest they collapse as well. "Step carefully. Some of it will still be oven hot. Punch through the wrong bit of crust and you'll melt your shoes."

"So you're saying I should watch out for hot pockets?"

Talia glanced over her shoulder with a frown.

He shrugged. "What? We can't laugh in the face of tragedy? Don't be such a curmudgeon."

"Don't be such a clown."

They stared each other down for a long moment and then both said at once, "Snowflake."

Ivanov had not come with them, and she understood. He had a great deal of work to do in the wake of the attack, but mostly he wasn't ready to stand in the ashes of his former home.

For the most part, the building was a loss, but portions of the lab, with all its concrete, had survived. Talia focused her efforts there.

"What are we looking for?" Eddie asked.

"Slugs. Jacket fragments. Brass." Talia used a pen to stir the ashes near the counter where Bazin and Pavel had taken cover. "Anything that tells us about the composition of Lukon's bullets. Our shooter, maybe Lukon himself, fired a lot of rounds. If we can determine their makeup, Franklin can trace them to a dealer."

It sounded good. Except Talia could find no slugs or fragments.

"Maybe they melted." Eddie crouched beside her.

"Yeah, but we should still see *something*."

Talia used the high-powered light on her phone to wash away the morning shadows masking the counter's front. No slugs were embedded in the concrete. There were, however, several gray-brown marks, roundish, almost like paint-gun splatter. "Are you carrying your pocketknife?"

"Always." Eddie slapped a Smith & Wesson pocketknife into her open palm, and Talia scraped at the markings. She held the blade up to her nose, scrunched up her brow, and handed the knife back to Eddie. He gave it a sniff and frowned. "Smells like clay."

"I know. Weird, right?"

A glint of brass caught Talia's eye, and she used the tip of her pen to lift it out of the ashes. Finally, something made sense. "This is one of Bazin's .50-caliber shell casings," she said, rising and showing it to Eddie. "And if Bazin's brass survived, then . . ." She let the statement hang and picked her way through the wreckage to the charred lump of plastic and aluminum that had once been Pavel's oversize 3D printing machine—the one the intruder had used for cover.

Again, Talia dug around in the ashes. No brass. She stood, looking out toward the trees where the shooter had fled. "I hate this guy."

Tyler never showed. And once the local constabulary appeared, Talia and Eddie vacated the crime scene. She didn't feel like answering questions—only asking them.

Eddie could barely keep up as she headed down the brick path to the Opel. "Where are we going?"

"Tiraspol. If Tyler won't come to us, we'll go to him."

NEARLY AN HOUR LATER, with Talia *in a mood*—as Eddie liked to call it—the Mandarin's express elevator bumped to a stop at the top-floor penthouse, announcing its arrival with a light *ding*. The clerk at the front desk had not been cooperative. Mr. Tyler was not to be disturbed.

Talia had called in the manager, who regarded the ash marks on her blouse and slacks with open disdain, and the two had argued in both English and Russian. Muttering to himself in Romanian, the man had called up to Tyler's room. After listening for several seconds, and with a sullen *I can't believe I lost this argument* look at Talia, he had finally handed over the express elevator's key.

The elevator doors opened onto an opulent suite. White marble steps, peppered with gold flake, led down to a sunken living room with silk furniture right out of Victorian Hong Kong.

"About time you got here." The voice came from behind a chrome-plated espresso machine in the kitchen. Tyler leaned out so they could see him. He had traded his business suit for a loose white shirt and cotton pajama pants. "Want some coffee? We have lots to discuss."

Of course Talia wanted coffee. In her state, she *needed* coffee. "No thanks. I'm good."

"Does that thing do mocha?" Eddie abandoned her at a pace just short of a jog.

So much for loyalty.

After showing Eddie the controls, Tyler met Talia in the living room with the cappuccino she hadn't asked him for. "Two sugars, right?"

He had nailed it. That wasn't creepy at all. "It'll have to do." She took the cup, glancing down at his bare feet, man-toes drowning in gold shag carpet. "So you ignore my summons and force me to come to you, and my visit doesn't even merit footwear?"

"Apologies. I was . . . otherwise engaged all morning. Do I detect hostility?"

"Disgust. There's a reason five-star hotels give you free slippers."

Tyler let the insult hang there over the shag and walked up the steps to the open balcony. "Hypersonics."

"I'm sorry?"

"You're here because you want to know what this is all about, and the answer is hypersonics. A new weapon of mass destruction. That's what Ivanov is hiding."

The word *hiding* didn't sit well with Talia. "Pavel isn't hiding anything. He's protecting trade secrets."

Tyler turned, leaning the small of his back against the balcony rail and raising an eyebrow. "Pavel?"

"Dr. Ivanov."

He smiled. "Call him whatever you want. Either way, Brennan and I think he's cracked the Holy Grail of weapons technology—combining a plasma-breathing scramjet with flight controls that can handle speeds north of Mach 80."

"Mach 80?" Eddie came down into the sunken living room carrying a cup that looked more like a soup bowl with a handle. "The best hypersonic weapons so far are tungsten glide bombs that reach Mach 20, enough kinetic energy to create the blast equivalent of a small tactical nuke. A Mach 80 impact would be like—"

"Hiroshima." Tyler let the name sink in as he picked a strawberry from a fruit plate on the balcony table. He dipped it in some cream and took a bite. "Plus, a scramjet gives off no launch signature, and anything traveling through the atmosphere above Mach 10 creates a sheath of burning plasma that can't be penetrated by radar."

Talia sat down in a claw-foot chair with her cappuccino. "Stealth missiles."

"*Devastating* stealth missiles. Any entity with this technology can launch untraceable, nuke-level attacks, shaping the world from the shadows." Tyler picked up the plate of fruit and cream and returned to the sitting area. "That's the power Lukon is after. And it gets worse."

"Worse?" Eddie lowered his bowl of mocha halfway through a sip, leaving a wet mustache on his upper lip. "How can it get worse?"

"We think Ivanov built a prototype."

"Oh." Eddie wiped his lips with his sleeve. "Yeah. That's worse."

"I've been watching him for weeks. He hasn't led me to it. But someone, either Ivanov or Lukon, is planning to use it."

Talia set her cappuccino on the coffee table next to Tyler's fruit plate. "Explain."

Tyler sat down across from her on the room's orange corduroy couch, showing unusual strain on his face as he did. Was he injured? Talia didn't get the chance to ask. He picked up a remote and pressed a button. "Read this."

A marble wall panel moved inward and motored down to reveal a television. As the display warmed up, an image appeared—a screenshot from some corner of the Dark Web, evidenced by the unsavory artwork in the margins. White Cyrillic text filled a black field. Ukrainian. Close enough to Russian for Talia to translate. An unnamed party was advertising an auction of hypersonic technology, obliquely referring interested buyers to a contact listed only as *the Englishman*.

"This has to be Lukon," Talia said, reading further. "He showed his hand by coming after the designs, and he—" She stopped arguing as her eyes reached the last line. The party advertising the auction had promised a demonstration of the weapon.

Watch the news, the post said. *Watch Washington, DC, and you will know the power of this technology.* And then it listed a time and date less than a week away.

TWENTY-SEVEN

THE MANDARIN OF TIRASPOL
TRANSNISTRIA UNRECOGNIZED TERRITORY

TALIA POINTED AT THE TEXT, glaring at Tyler. "This mission now has a deadline. I assume you know what that says."

"Yes."

"Then you'll agree we have to talk to Ivanov *immediately*."

"No."

She fell back in her chair. "Aaaggh!" Then she pulled out her phone. "I don't need your permission. This is my op. I'm in charge. I'm calling him."

"Eddie"—Tyler held up a hand for Talia to wait—"check for a recent communiqué from your boss."

Eddie set down his bowl of coffee and opened the secure communications software on his tablet. He fiddled with it for several seconds, then made an apologetic face at Talia and turned the screen so she could see. There was a message from Brennan, way too pointed and simple to be coincidental.

DON'T TALK TO IVANOV.

"You went over my head," Talia said.

"I had a conversation with an old friend. That's all."

"You're insane." Talia shoved her phone back in her pocket and folded her arms. "You think Ivanov would blow up his own house?"

Tyler picked up a wedge of pineapple from his fruit plate and dipped it in cream. "No." He put the whole thing in his mouth, licking his fingers. "I think Ivanov hid his new tech from his DoD contacts, put it out there for a black-market auction, and inadvertently drew Lukon's attention. So now we have two problems to solve."

Talia didn't buy it. She had looked into Ivanov's eyes after the attack. Tyler hadn't. Tyler hadn't even bothered to come out to the compound. Ivanov was a genius, not a criminal. Lukon must have discovered Ivanov's secret some other way.

"Look." Tyler wiped his hands on a napkin and softened his expression. "I know you're fond of the guy, but the date of the demonstration promised in that Dark Web post is also the day Ivanov plans to unveil the Gryphon concept in Milan next week."

"Coincidence," Talia said.

"Manufactured alibi," Tyler countered.

Eddie clapped his hands. "This is all about Gryphon."

The other two stopped arguing and looked at the geek. "What?"

Eddie pointed both index fingers at Talia. "Ivanov has a secret off-site data vault, right? Only he and Bazin know its current location."

She nodded. "That's what he told me. So?"

"So data vaults are pretty common in big business." Eddie sat forward, resetting his glasses. "Major corporations dodge corporate espionage with software that automatically deletes working files, maintaining the originals through an encrypted link at an off-site, high-security vault." He spread his hands. "They get so serious about it that some of these vault companies rent space on military bases."

Tyler seemed to regard the geek with more interest than before. "The files Lukon missed. You think Ivanov sent them to a military base?"

"No." Eddie picked up his tablet again. "Ivanov said he and Bazin know the *current location*. That implies mobility. He also said the Gryphon concept has uses beyond replacing expensive satellites."

"Ivanov built Gryphon," Talia said, nodding. "He created his own roving data vault."

"Not just roving." Eddie's fingers worked his tablet screen. "The most high-security data vault ever conceived. It's brilliant." He glanced at Tyler and gestured at the television. "Do you mind?"

"Mind what?"

Eddie didn't answer. A moment later, the television blinked, showing static at first and then the looped CGI of Gryphon they had seen at Avantec. Colorful clouds of light rushed past its angular black hull.

Tyler looked to Talia with surprise. "How did he—"

"I don't know. It's what he does."

"I might have borrowed a few files on Gryphon from Avantec's servers." Eddie put down the tablet and recovered his giant mug. "Lightweight rigid composites, and a reaction control system with monopropellant jets for positioning. All hovering in the netherworld of the mesosphere." He paused to draw a slice of melon from the fruit plate.

"So it's a blimp." Tyler put his bare man-feet up on the coffee table, within inches of Talia's cappuccino.

"Airship," Eddie countered.

Talia made a show of sliding her cup to the other end of the table, next to a leather-bound book, a Bible—worn and weathered, certainly no hotel copy. The sight of it gave her pause. What was a scoundrel like Tyler doing with a Bible? She sat back again. "Blimp. Airship. Neither sounds too secure. Couldn't Lukon just fly up there and download the files?"

"Just fly up there?" Eddie held up the melon slice in a *one does not simply walk into Mordor* gesture. "We're talking about the *mesosphere*, Talia—one of the most hostile environments known to science. Freezing temperatures. Blood-boiling pressure."

"Toxic clouds left by vaporized meteors." Tyler pumped his eyebrows at Talia. He seemed to know a little on the topic. "Random electrical fireworks with fantastic names."

This kicked off an animated back-and-forth between geek and scoundrel.

"Blue sprites."

"Golden halos."

"Green pixies."

"And purple horseshoes, I suppose," Talia said, stopping them.

Eddie scrunched up his nose. "No. None of those." He popped the melon wedge into his mouth and continued as he chewed. "But what you really have to watch out for are the red elves— disc-shaped lightning a hundred miles wide. It's like Ivanov is storing his data at the center of a giant three-dimensional minefield." In his excitement over the idea, he let his giant mocha tilt to a precarious degree.

Tyler leaned over and gently brought it to level. "Eddie's right. Ivanov's mystery vault has to be Gryphon."

"Which means the hypersonic designs are safe from Lukon." Talia added a strong note of finality. She retrieved her cappuccino. "Good job, Eddie. Report our findings to the home office."

"Ooh." Tyler puckered his lips. "Risky. Do you really want to sit on your hands and *hope* Ivanov is the good guy in all this? And what about Lukon? If we know about Gryphon, chances are, so does he. I understand Lukon is a master at building one-off specialized teams. Mesosphere or not, he'll go after the hypersonic designs."

She pursed her lips at him over her cup. "So what's the play?"

Tyler only shrugged. "That's your call. It's your op. Remember? But from where I'm sitting, there's only one option."

At the other end of the couch, Eddie slapped the cushion. "I've got it. We build our own team. We steal the designs first."

CHAPTER
TWENTY-EIGHT

THE MANDARIN OF TIRASPOL
TRANSNISTRIA UNRECOGNIZED TERRITORY

"WE'RE TALKING THE MOTHER of all heists." Eddie was up from the couch and pacing the marble floor above the sitting room. The fidget spinner had come out, so Talia knew there was no stopping him.

Tyler egged him on. "With a highly specialized team, right? Elite."

"*Elite.*" Eddie repeated the word as if hypnotized. His pacing led him into the kitchen. He pulled open the refrigerator and disappeared behind the door. "I saw Avantec's security programs. They're state of the art. Only a few hackers in the world can handle that kind of architecture."

"And even fewer cat burglars would even consider hitting a target in the mesosphere," Tyler added. "One, maybe two."

Eddie popped into view again with half a lobster roll in his formerly free hand. He gave Tyler a questioning look and received a *knock yourself out* wave. "So we're not just stealing the hypersonic designs. If we move fast, we'll be hijacking Lukon's team before he can hire them." He closed the refrigerator with a hip check and waggled the lobster roll in the air. "This is good.

This is good. We jump ahead in the race and hamstring Lukon on our way past."

"Eddie." Talia held out a hand. "You're not thinking this through. We can't hire high-class thieves."

To her surprise, Tyler backed her up. "Thieves at this level won't surface for a job unless the employer has name recognition and offers a serious cash deposit. Talia's right. We can't steal Lukon's team."

"We can't." Eddie moved the lobster roll back and forth between himself and Talia. "But *you* can." He crossed the floor and stood behind the couch, painting the air around Tyler with his fidget spinner. "You've already got this dark, mysterious aura. Put it to good use."

"You want me to *be* Lukon?" Tyler laughed.

Talia did not see the humor. "No way, Eddie. Brennan will never go for it."

"Yes. He will."

The argument had come from Tyler, voice distant.

"Tyler, be serious."

"I am serious." The cocky, scoundrel persona had dropped away. "Brennan is always telling me to put my money where my mouth is. Now's my chance." The gears turned behind his eyes for a few heartbeats, and then the scoundrel was back, smiling. "I like it. But if we're going to sell this—if I'm going to play Lukon the criminal mastermind—I need a backdrop worthy of his legend." Tyler chuckled to himself. "And I know just the place." He snapped his fingers and held out an open palm toward Talia. "Tablet, please."

The tablet stayed exactly where it was, lying on the coffee table. Talia had no intention of jumping every time Tyler snapped his fingers.

Eddie, however, seemed perfectly happy to do so. He stuffed the remains of the lobster roll in his cheeks like a squirrel, jogged around the couch, unlocked the tablet, and handed it over.

Tyler played with the screen for a few seconds, then turned the tablet around, showing them a timber chateau resting on a valley hillside. The lake beyond its raw stone balconies was all aflame with the oranges and golds of a perfect sunset.

Eddie drew in a breath, almost choking on the remnant of his lobster roll.

Talia pressed her lips together. "That's your place, isn't it?"

"Guilty. Five floors and ten bedrooms in the Swiss-Italian lake region of Lugano." Tyler handed the tablet back to Eddie. "It's an ideal base for recruiting elite thieves. And I had planned to stop by this week anyway. My personal chef, Conrad, misses me when I'm away."

Eddie used the tablet to shield his face from Tyler's view and mouthed the words "personal chef" at Talia. He lowered it and walked around the table to stand next to him. "Please, Talia. Let the man do his patriotic duty."

She was going to regret this. Letting a civilian pretend to be a master criminal. Conning an elite team of thieves. At some point, this plan would go horribly wrong. Her voice seemed to detach itself from the rational portion of her brain and to speak on its own. "Fine."

"Yes!" Eddie almost knocked her over with a hug.

THE LUKON DECEPTION, as Eddie immediately named their plan, left Talia with a prickling sense of unease. For as long as she'd known him, Eddie had lived with one foot in a fantasy realm—orcs and magic rings, robots molding empires. Talia, however, remained firmly grounded in reality. Life in the foster care system had made certain of that. The balance between the two was a reason they worked so well together. But Tyler, with his money, his plane, and his ridiculous chateau, had upended the scales.

Reality should have kicked in with a vengeance when Talia

and Eddie returned to the motel and contacted Brennan for permission. No senior operations officer in his right mind would sign off on such a plan.

Brennan, it seemed, was not in his right mind.

"If Tyler is on board, then so am I," he said over the tinny, encrypted line. "I'll settle things on this end—get the boffins to restructure your aliases, run interference with national police forces, that sort of thing." The line went quiet for several seconds and then he added, "Tyler's chateau is less than an hour from the aerospace expo in Milan, isn't it? That's a stroke of good luck."

"Right." Talia dropped her head into her hands while Eddie danced a jig behind her. "How fortuitous."

They took the Gulfstream that night, taking off from the Avantec runway. Ivanov saw them off, which bolstered Talia's faith in his innocence. He took Talia's hand as the others packed their luggage into the jet. "I am sorry to see you go. But I think you know this."

She squeezed his fingers, cautioning herself against showing any more emotion than that. All she wanted was to tell him the truth about what they knew. She went with a different truth. "I don't consider my work here finished. I will do my utmost to protect you."

"You will stop Lukon from stealing my life's work."

"Yes." *But I mean so much more.* Talia glanced over her shoulder as the Gulfstream hummed to life. "I have to go."

When she boarded the aircraft, she found Eddie reclining in a leather seat, sipping a Perrier. Otherwise the cabin was empty.

"Where's Tyler?"

He nodded at the open flight deck door. "Where do you think?"

"You're kidding me. He doesn't have a pilot?"

"He *is* the pilot."

Talia hurried through the door and squeezed herself into the right seat as Tyler taxied onto the runway.

"Good thinking," he said, flipping a toggle that did who knows what. He pushed up the throttles and raised his voice over the noise of the engines. "I'm technically required to have a copilot."

"But I'm not a pilot. I'm a passenger"—Talia gripped the armrests—"who hates to fly!"

"Potato-potahto." Tyler released the brakes, and the acceleration pushed her back into her seat. A few seconds later he looked over, taking his eyes completely off the runway, and thrust his chin at the straps dangling from the sides of Talia's seat. "But you might want to buckle up."

Tyler clearly had some skills. He handled the controls with ease, and a diplomatic clearance that Brennan had supplied got them across Romania and into European Union airspace without trouble. Despite Tyler's seat-belt joke, Talia did not feel like she needed the seat's five-point harness until they reached the Swiss-Italian Alps, where he clicked off the autopilot and pushed the nose abruptly down.

"Oh!" she said with surprise as the Gulfstream punched into the misty gray of a midnight cloud deck. Talia watched Tyler flip several toggles. The flashing lights on the wingtips went dark. "Wait. Don't we need those?"

"Not in the clouds. Saves electricity. Smaller carbon footprint." He furrowed his brow at her. "I thought you millennials liked that kind of thing."

"But there are mountains below us."

"And lights won't move them out of the way." Tyler coughed into his fist and frowned. "I'm thirsty. Are you thirsty? Hey! Eddie!"

The endless clouds whipped past the windshield. The altitude readout rolled past twenty-five thousand feet as Eddie's answer drifted in from the cabin. "Yeah, boss?"

"Grab me a Perrier, will you? Watch the walnut facing on

the fridge, though. It's new." He glanced at Talia. "Ginger ale for you, right?"

Talia always drank ginger ale when she flew. Did he know that, or was it a guess? Either way, she didn't answer. Her eyes were glued to the altimeter. Twenty thousand and still falling.

Tyler shouted over his shoulder. "Bring a Socata too, Eddie!" He lowered his voice and leaned across the cockpit. "It's kind of like ginger ale. Best I can do in this region. Smuggling weapons into Switzerland? No problem. Ginger ale?" Tyler shook his head. "Uh-uh."

The geek brought a pair of fizzing glasses through the flight deck door and offered Tyler's first. "Here you go, boss."

Talia pried her not-a-ginger-ale out of his other hand. "Stop calling him boss."

"Can't. He's Lukon, remember? I'm getting into character."

The aircraft jumped, forcing Eddie to grab the doorframe for balance on his way out.

"What was that?" Talia grabbed her armrest with her free hand. It dawned on her she was holding a soda in the other while they were plunging to their deaths. How had Tyler gotten her to that point?

The control column between her knees made tiny movements in all directions, mirroring Tyler's movements with his own column. "Mountain wave."

Talia still saw nothing but clouds outside. "And that means mountains, right?"

"It *is* the Alps." He rolled his head over to look at her. "Did you know the mountains of the Swiss-Italian border claim nine of the ten highest peaks in Europe? Most of them reach close to fifteen thousand feet."

"Fifteen thousand?" Talia checked the altimeter. They had just passed fourteen thousand.

"Tighten that belt of yours," Tyler said. "This is where the fun begins."

CHAPTER
TWENTY-NINE

A SHORT *WHOOP, WHOOP* ALARM sounded and Tyler punched it off.

"What was that?" asked Talia.

"Proximity alert."

"Proximity with what?"

"Nothing important."

She was done with his cavalier attitude. "Tyler, we can't see the mountains in these clouds."

"Maybe you can't. I can see fine. Instrument flying is all about knowing where to look." He pointed with two fingers at his displays. "I'll give you a hint. It's not outside."

Talia tore her eyes from the windscreen and focused on the displays, a pair of monitors in front of her control column matching those in front of Tyler. The left screen resembled a cartoonish video game, with animated mountains flying past and a blue river below. Talia recognized the display to the right as a blend of optical, infrared, and radar similar to drone feeds she had used at the Farm. The infrared gave definition to the clouds, showing the breaks between them. The radar outlined the terrain behind them in ghostly blue.

"Synthetic vision." Tyler tapped his videogame screen. "Shows me the mountains and other obstacles."

"Obstacles? Besides the mountains, what kind of obstacles are there?"

"That kind." As Tyler banked the jet to follow the curvature of a descending valley, a computer-generated cell tower came into view, approaching fast. As it grew nearer, the blue outline expanded to include a set of razor-thin guy wires ready to slice off their wings.

Tyler shifted to the other side of the valley to give it a wide berth. "I hate guy wires."

"Me too." Talia unconsciously leaned to one side as she watched the glowing blue cables of death fly past. "I never hated them before, but I do now."

After the guy-wire discussion, Tyler stopped speaking altogether. His control movements remained subtle and confident, but there was an added tension in his arms, a tautness in his jaw. Talia had been frustrated by his flippant tone, but that same tone had given her some comfort. Now, with Tyler no longer speaking, her comfort evaporated.

When he spoke again, it didn't help. "Flaps coming out," he said, moving a lever beside the throttles.

Talia knew enough to understand that flaps meant they were landing soon. But where? She saw no runways on the displays.

The clouds dissipated, and she looked out through the windscreen to see a faint string of lights ahead. They matched up with one of the animations on her digital display—a curving gray ribbon with dashed lines down the center. She grabbed Tyler's arm. "That's a road."

"Please don't touch the pilot." He banked the Gulfstream and dropped the gear.

She jerked her hand away. "Right. Sorry. But by 'That's a road,' I mean it's not a runway."

The gray line straightened, growing larger. Outside, street-lamps and a speed limit sign flew past.

"Tyler!"

"A little busy here."

With a soft *thump*, the main wheels touched down, and Tyler brought the nose down a moment later, right on the road's dashed centerline. He pulled up the flaps and applied enough brakes to turn right onto a near-invisible stretch of black pavement, heading straight for the valley wall.

Spotlights flashed on, illuminating huge doors covered in dirt and brush, already swinging open. In seconds, they were through. The doors closed. Halogens flickered to life.

"This is a hangar," Talia said as Tyler shut down the engines.

"Nothing gets by you, Miss CIA Officer." Tyler sat back from the controls and let out a breath. A hint of sweat glistened on his brow. "A few Swiss roads double as landing strips—holdovers from the Cold War. There are entire squadrons of Swiss fighters still residing beneath the Alps." With a flick of his thumb and forefinger, he released his harness and stood. "They're a bit of a financial drain on the state, so most were shut down."

"And what?" Talia pressed close to the windshield, tilting her head to see the rock ceiling and the old iron beams far above. "The Swiss government decided to give you one?"

"Something like that."

Three men and a woman hurried out to bed down the aircraft as Tyler dropped the Gulfstream's stairs. Eddie's jaw dropped when he stepped out through the hatch. "We have an underground lair."

"It's a hangar," Talia countered.

Tyler patted her shoulder. "I like lair. To be honest, it came with the house. The Ticino family that owned the chalet had leased this land to the Swiss government for generations. They wanted to downsize. The Swiss wanted to unload the hangar. I happened to have cash on hand. It was a win-win-win."

Two of his workers brought the luggage over. Tyler greeted them in Italian, and the woman gave him a hug and a basket of bread. After a short exchange, the man touched the woman's arm and the pair walked back to the jet, close and familiar. The other two, an older man and a younger, cracked open a toolbox and began pulling panels off the engine housings. They shared several features—same nose, same chin.

Talia quietly turned to Tyler. "You employ whole families here?"

"I offer some part-time work to the locals. Luciano and his son are mechanics, quite well known in Formula One racing. They've turned high-performance aircraft into a bit of a hobby."

"Formula One. Sure. And I suppose the married couple unloading your cargo bay are both executives with Lamborghini Corporation."

"You mean Carmine and Sofia?" Tyler walked away, heading for a glass-walled elevator. "Don't be absurd. They run the local bakery."

The glass elevator carried the trio up along the rock wall of the cavern. As they ascended, Talia noticed Luciano and Carmine pulling a green heavy-duty crate out of the cargo bay. It looked almost military. "What's in the crate?" she asked as the cavern swallowed them, blocking her view. Wet rock, spotted with lichen, passed by the glass doors.

"Import-export, remember? Did you think I spent all my time in Moldova doing charity work for the CIA?"

The elevator brought them up to a limestone grotto in the valley wall. The open portion looked out over a dark lake streaked with the yellow-gold of the village lights. The reflection of a church steeple, lit with spotlights, seemed to reach across the water to touch the far shore.

The grotto extended to an entry on the chalet's third level, where an older gentleman met them at the door, smartly dressed in slacks and a cable-knit sweater. He bowed, waving them through into the foyer. "Welcome to Switzerland's Campione d'Italia, an independent enclave with the world's most liberal tax laws and most questionable residents." His gaze strayed to Tyler at the words "questionable residents." He gave Talia a grandfatherly smile. "You may call me Conrad. I look after Chateau Ticino and all its guests. May I take your bag?"

Talia consented, as did Eddie, and Conrad set their luggage aside long enough to shake Tyler's hand. "Glad to have you home, sir."

"Glad to *be* home." The way the two clasped hands spoke to Talia of brothers in arms rather than cook and master.

Talia and Eddie followed Tyler into a rustic great room backed by a two-story fireplace. Flying in on the Gulfstream, she had pictured a place like the penthouse at the Mandarin, which screamed *man* and *money*. But the chateau had an unassuming feel—no gaudy artwork, only a few icons and paintings in the Eastern Orthodox style, adding color to the corners and alcoves.

Tyler walked backward along a wall of windows that looked out over the lake. "You want the grand tour?"

"Yes," Eddie said.

"No," Talia said at the same time. "I need rest. So do you, Eddie. Tomorrow's a busy day."

"At least let me show you the kitchen." Tyler took a left past the windows and descended a short stair behind the fireplace into a kitchen with granite counters and blond wood cabinets. He gestured at a platter with enough sandwiches to feed a small army. "Conrad always makes my favorite snack when I fly in."

Eddie began building himself a pile.

Tyler snapped his fingers and pointed. "You. Leave some for the folks down in the hangar. Luciano's kid can eat his own weight in these things."

After Talia had eaten a tuna sandwich to satisfy Tyler, Conrad led her to a room on the fifth floor. The religious artwork continued in the upper hall with a collection of decorative crosses in a host of materials and styles. Conrad paused to let her admire them and then pushed open a door on the lake side of the hallway. "In here, miss."

Her bags were waiting inside, with the largest suitcase laid out on a folding rack near the bed, a tall queen with a silk burgundy duvet. A candle was lit on the nightstand. A small tea service sat beside it, warmed and ready. Talia smiled at the cook. "Sandwiches?"

"A delay tactic. I put them out to tempt guests while I set up the rooms just so. It makes me look a bit like a magician."

She touched his hand as she stepped inside. "Thank you. It's lovely."

"You're quite welcome, miss. Have a good rest." He bowed good night and closed her door without making a sound.

Talia began moving her clothes from the suitcase to a dresser beside the door, but stopped when she noticed the framed picture resting on top. She let out a quiet laugh. The photo, with two signatures at the bottom, showed Luciano and his son, posing between a pair of Formula One race cars.

CHAPTER
THIRTY

CHATEAU TICINO
CAMPIONE D'ITALIA, SWITZERLAND

TALIA AWOKE LATE IN THE MORNING to the scent of bacon and waffles.

Conrad.

She knew how to read people—more from her years in the foster care system than from her Farm training. A young girl had to anticipate the need to hide from an older foster sister or recognize the signs of an alcoholic. She had to know when to hunker down or make a run for it the moment the lights went out. Whatever Talia thought of Tyler, she liked Conrad.

He made her feel safe.

She found him in the kitchen, drizzling maple syrup over a pan of bacon, wearing a tweed waistcoat and slacks and an apron with lips on it that said *Kiss the cook*.

"Tyler gave you that apron, didn't he?"

Conrad pulled the bacon off the stove and slid the strips out of the pan onto a clay platter. He shot a look at Tyler, who was seated at the counter, already working on an egg white omelet. "You see? No one believes I would wear this voluntarily." He pulled out a stool for Talia. "I only put it on because the man who bought it writes my paychecks."

The heated buffet on the counter held a spread from Talia's innermost culinary desires—waffles, maple bacon, scrambled eggs with a sprinkling of Swiss cheese. A silver carafe of coffee at the end was surrounded by cream, brown sugar, nutmeg, and white chocolate shavings.

Talia had outrun the famous freshman fifteen well past her senior year. But if she stayed in that chateau too long, those pounds would finally catch up. She ignored the warnings in her head and dropped two spoonfuls of shavings into a mug. "Where's Eddie? The smell of bacon alone should have brought him down."

"He isn't coming." Tyler set his fork down, omelet finished. "He asked if you'd bring him a tray."

Talia's spoon hovered over her coffee. "Eddie wants me to bring him breakfast in bed?"

"Not to his bedroom." Conrad took the liberty of sliding a pair of waffles onto Talia's plate. "To the chateau's media room. He's been in there since before sunup, and I do believe wild horses could not drag him out again." He pointed his spatula at a small porcelain pitcher. "Try the blueberry syrup. I made it from scratch."

"I love blueberry syrup."

"Really?" Conrad rounded the end of the island on his way to the sink, collecting Tyler's plate as he passed. "What a surprise."

The media room, as Conrad called it, took up half the fourth floor. Talia had pictured a few comfortable seats and a projector. What she found was a high-tech operations center that blended gadgetry and processing power with the chateau's alpine decor.

"I'm home," Eddie said as Talia and Tyler came through the door. He sat on a stool at a counter-height conference table glowing with internal monitors and scattered with keyboards and devices. "I'm calling it Mission Control." He nodded at a giant parabolic screen dominating the far wall. "How big is that thing, Mr. Tyler? A hundred and eighty inches?"

"Two-ten." Tyler set a tray of waffles, eggs, and bacon on the table. "Anything less than one-ninety-five and the holographic mode won't look right."

"It has a holographic mode?" Eddie blindly stabbed at a waffle and missed, clicking the fork against the plate. "I'm never leaving this house."

"Sorry," Tyler said. "You can't afford the rent."

"Then adopt me."

"O-*kay* . . ." Talia snatched up a piece of bacon from the breakfast tray Tyler had brought up for Eddie. "Back to the mission."

She walked over to the main screen. A wire-frame diagram of the Gryphon swiveled between top-down and profile views with blue lines running to rolling data points. Beside it were cut-outs of the interior and a blueprint of the Avantec compound. "You've been busy."

"Actually"—Eddie gave her a wink—"I've been a little naughty. I used the access codes we gained during the security assessment to bypass Avantec's firewalls. We were right. Gryphon is alive and kicking, and now I know her secrets."

Tyler slipped his hands into his pockets, resting his back against a timber pillar. "If you're inside the system, can you access the airship's data vault?"

"Negative."

"What about the location of the prototype?" Talia asked.

"Also negative. I think that information is on Gryphon's servers, which currently cannot be accessed from the ground." Eddie zoomed in on the compound blueprint. "Dr. Ivanov kept a single direct-access terminal with biometric locks here, in his residence—which Lukon blew up."

Tyler left his pillar to join the others. "So my thieves will have to breach the airship itself."

Talia didn't like his phrasing. "You mean *our* thieves."

"*My* thieves." Command darkened his tone. "I have to become Lukon. *Speak* as Lukon. Buy into that now, or put a bullet between my eyes, because that's exactly what the thieves will do if they sense a double cross. Got it?"

She stared at him, mouth slightly open. Talia had been liberal with harsh tones, but Tyler had never returned them, not until that moment. "Yeah. I've got it." She turned around, hips falling against the conference table, red rushing into her cheeks.

"Eddie," Tyler said. Talia could feel him staring at the back of her head. "Tell us what else you've learned."

"I've *learned* this heist is impossible." Eddie rotated the blueprints of the Avantec compound, shifting the view from Ivanov's residence to the airfield. "For starters, only one aircraft in existence is capable of docking with Gryphon—her maintenance and tow vehicle."

Talia recognized the hangar under his cursor. "You mean the Mark Seven."

"Bingo. This is two jobs in one. First, we have to steal the Mark Seven—"

"And then fly it up to Gryphon to steal the plans," Tyler said, finishing the thought.

"Oh, it's nowhere near that simple." Eddie pointed a stick of bacon at him and then bit off a piece, chewing as he explained. "Ivanov is bringing the Mark Seven with him to the Milan aerospace expo."

"That's good," Talia said.

"Is it? Assuming our hypothetical team of elite criminals can break in, sneak past all those pesky defense contractors, and steal it, they'll still have to fly this one-of-a-kind hybrid rocket-jet well enough to navigate a hostile environment worthy of a sci-fi horror flick." Eddie tapped a key and the blueprints faded, allowing Gryphon's to fill the screen. "Then they'll have to execute a docking procedure none of us knows, bypass a ten-digit cypher lock on the high-pressure seal, and access an on-site terminal using—"

"Ivanov's biometrics," Talia said, "like the remote terminal Lukon destroyed."

Eddie zoomed in on Gryphon's flight deck, where the outline of a control panel started flashing. "To be specific, a voiceprint ID. We get two tries. Use the wrong phrase or wrong voice more than twice and Gryphon will delete all her data. No weapon plans. No prototype location."

During the final portion of Eddie's doom-and-gloom explanation, Tyler had gone silent. Talia watched him in the reflection on the screen and saw him jotting down a list on a notepad. He ripped off the page and handed it to Eddie.

"What's this?"

"Think of those as job listings—for which you just listed the requirements. Tap into the Dark Web and identify the experts we need before the real Lukon finds them."

Eddie examined the scribblings. "Chemist, hacker, wheelman, cat burglar." He held up the sheet and pointed. "What about this last one? Valkyrie. What's that?"

"Not what. Who. Valkyrie is a specialist whom I believe Lukon will try to hire for this job."

"So hire Valkyrie first." Talia tried to regain some feeling of control over the operation. "You know, speak as Lukon." She gave Tyler a flat look. "Like you said."

"Can't. The two of us have a mutual acquaintance."

"Valkyrie knows you?"

"You could say that."

Eddie looked from one to the other, as if waiting for the exchange to continue. He lost patience. "So bring this specialist of yours in on the plan. Use your connection."

"It's a little more complicated." Tyler started for the door.

Talia walked to the end of the table and stopped. She could sense he didn't want to be followed. "Where are you going?"

"To set up a meeting."

CHAPTER THIRTY-ONE

CHATEAU TICINO
CAMPIONE D'ITALIA, SWITZERLAND

TYLER'S TESLA MODEL X peeled off down the ridge before Talia even managed to locate the garage. She vowed he would never slip away from her again and used the next hour or so to familiarize herself with the chateau's layout—five floors, ten bedrooms, every one of them a suite.

The Eastern Orthodox iconography she had noticed the night before made up the bulk of his art collection, along with a few scriptures. Talia had little trouble translating one faded tapestry inscribed with calligraphic Cyrillic. *Ask, and it shall be given you. Seek, and ye shall find. Knock, and it shall be opened unto you.* She almost laughed. Talia planned to do some seeking of her own, into Tyler's past. And what would she find? Nothing holy, she was sure.

Tyler returned shortly after noon, but said nothing. Talia left him alone while she and Eddie worked on their list of thieves. Their options were narrow—a wheelman who could fly a hybrid rocket-jet, a cat burglar, and a chemist with the knowledge and experience necessary to work on the edge of space. When she could no longer stomach the images floating through the Dark

Web, she went downstairs. The scent of rosemary and juniper drew her into the kitchen.

"Mr. Tyler was in here ten minutes ago." Conrad held a copper pot over the flames of the stove. Talia hadn't asked the question, but it had been on the tip of her tongue. Conrad dialed back the heat and let the pot simmer. "He asked me to save him a plate for a late supper. I haven't heard from him since."

"He didn't mention a meeting of some kind?"

"I am afraid not, miss."

Talia dropped her arms. "Right. Why would he talk to either of us about a key step in our life-and-death mission? That would be silly."

"You'll have to forgive him, miss. Mr. Tyler makes a good show of things, but he spent a large portion of his life alone. There are times when the nuances of person-to-person interactions elude him."

Talia could relate, but Conrad's choice of words struck her. "I'll *have* to forgive him?"

"Well you should." Raising an eyebrow, Conrad gestured with a wooden spoon toward a painting on the wall behind her, one of Tyler's scriptures. She recognized the text as the Lord's Prayer, but it did not end with the bit about forgiving debts. There were two more verses.

FOR IF YOU FORGIVE OTHERS WHEN THEY SIN AGAINST YOU, YOUR HEAVENLY FATHER WILL ALSO FORGIVE YOU.

BUT IF YOU DO NOT FORGIVE OTHERS THEIR SINS, YOUR FATHER WILL NOT FORGIVE YOURS.

Talia had never known that such sentiments followed the famous prayer. She frowned, reading the last verse out loud.

"Sounds a little harsh for your loving God," she said, turning back to Conrad. "What happened to all the grace?"

"Oh, grace abounds." Conrad shifted his pot again, stirring with a deliberate hand as if the wooden spoon were his brush and the sauce his masterpiece. "But I think those verses remind us that clinging to unforgiveness is the same as clinging to any other habitual sin."

Unforgiveness? As Talia opened her mouth to respond, she heard the garage door opening. "Tyler," she said to herself. She had told herself she wouldn't let him slip away again. "Save me some dinner, Conrad. I have to go."

"I thought you might. I'll set a plate aside for both of you. Because nothing adds to the full flavor of a homemade cacciatore like the radiological bombardment only a microwave can provide."

"Thanks." She pecked his cheek on her way to the back stair.

"Take the Alfa," he called after her. "Seeing you arrive in it will annoy him to no end. Keys are on the wall behind the door!"

None of the specialized vehicles Talia had encountered during her time at the Farm compared to the Alfa in terms of sheer brute power. She nearly drove it off a cliff thirty seconds after she left the garage. With the lightest touch of the gas pedal, the thing lurched like a bulldog at the end of its leash. But thanks to that power, she caught up to the Tesla in short order. Talia killed her lights and let Tyler lead her around the lake. He parked a short way down a grassy hill from San Pietro, the village church.

Talia watched as he made his way up the hill, coasted the Alfa in behind the Tesla, and then got out and followed.

The spotlights illuminating the church steeple did little for the graveyard behind, where she was certain Tyler had gone. He and his mystery date might have easily hidden behind any of the statues and weathered monuments—mere silhouettes in the night—but that did not strike Talia as Tyler's style. And as she explored, she found a stone path that brought her through the graves to a little round structure set into the rear wall. An iron gate barred the entrance. She gave it a tug. Locked.

In a moment of uncertainty, Talia wondered if she had gone the wrong way, but a faint orange glow illuminating a spiral staircase beyond the gate told her different. She dropped to a knee and pulled a flat pouch from the rear pocket of her slacks. Lock-picking had been a mandatory class at the Farm. She hadn't been the best in her class. But she had been close.

The lock clicked. With a quiet *creak* of the gate, Talia slipped through, hunching under the uncomfortable gaze of a chipped and scarred Virgin Mary.

No one challenged her in the stairwell. And she found no guards waiting in the narrow passage at the bottom—only a single lantern and jumbled bones crammed into niches too small for any full-grown human. Groundwater seeped in, falling with an echoing *drip drip* into scattered puddles on the floor. Twenty meters to her right, a few of these reflected the light of another lantern hanging in an intersecting passage. She pulled her Glock and kept moving.

One by one, like bread crumbs, the lanterns led her deeper into the labyrinth. The passages branched and split at random, filled to capacity with the dead. Around one corner she might find a row of crumbling stone coffins, lids broken as if the occupants were trying to escape; around the next, a shiny new granite monolith adorned with fresh flowers. At each turn, though, another flicker led her onward.

At any moment, Talia expected to hear Tyler's voice or footfalls. But the minutes passed in silence. She rested her back against the wall to think. Something cold and wet had pressed into her shoulder. Talia lurched away from it and spun, only to see human heads pushing out of the stone, faces contorted in pain. Red rivulets ran down their cheeks like tears of blood.

It took all her self-control not to scream.

"Stone," she whispered to herself. "They're made of stone."

The groundwater, tinted by minerals as it passed through the hill, dripped onto the faces, bringing them to life. The pounding of Talia's heartbeat settled, and she turned to put her eyes on the passage where they belonged. What would drive anyone to leave such terrifying markers? Sixteenth-century Catholics were messed up.

She had hardly finished the thought when a shadow flitted through her peripheral vision, sending her heart rate up again. Something had run across the passage at the next intersection, and she couldn't write it off as macabre artwork. Sculptures didn't move.

Following that ghost would lead her away from the nearest lantern.

Glasses, a voice that seemed set apart from her own subconscious told her.

She felt for her pocket and found them. Without a connection to Eddie, the Faux-kleys had no guidance arrows or video, but the enhanced optics still worked. The blue lenses did not banish the shadows entirely, but they pushed them back, giving her an edge, confidence.

She hurried to the corner where she had seen the figure and listened, and was rewarded with the gentle splash of a sole touching down in a puddle.

Talia rushed after the sound, and at the next turn, she caught a glimpse of a black suit. She was catching up. She risked a whispered call. "Tyler!"

Her quarry abandoned stealth and ducked into a branching passage.

Talia ran after him, barely keeping him in sight, even with the glasses.

The light in the passage dimmed to near black and then grew again, rapidly. Seconds later both raced out into an underground cathedral with a domed ceiling. Lanterns hung from carved pillars at one end, illuminating a crucifix bounded by weeping cherubs. A broken sarcophagus lay at the foot of the cross. The man ahead of her broke into a sprint, making a bid for one of the many tunnels leading away.

She couldn't let him return to the maze. "Tyler, stop!"

The man jogged to a halt and turned.

Talia stopped too, several meters away, and raised her Glock. "You're . . . not Tyler."

He was young, much younger than Tyler—almost a boy. The boy raised his hands, but he did not look scared, nor even concerned. He smiled and said something in Italian, tilting his head to Talia's right. At the same time, she heard the ratcheting *click* of a handgun being cocked.

Another young man in a matching black suit emerged from one of the tunnels, leveling a Beretta. A third came in from her left, also armed. And slow, deliberate footsteps at her back told Talia a fourth had entered from the same tunnel she had run through moments before.

The voice of the fourth, however, was not that of a young man. "Lower your weapon, *signorina*," he said in a heavy Italian accent, "before someone gets hurt."

THIRTY-TWO

SAN PIETRO CATACOMBS
CAMPIONE D'ITALIA, SWITZERLAND

TALIA HAD NO INTENTION of lowering her Glock. The young man she had chased into the cathedral reached down and opened his jacket, revealing a shoulder holster, but he didn't bother drawing the Beretta secured there. If she fired at him, the other two would gun her down. She would duck and turn, firing at those two first, and then make for the cover of the nearest tunnel. She gave herself a seventy-thirty chance, unless the guy behind her was armed as well. In that case, her odds of survival dropped to nil.

"*Signorina*, please. Lower the gun."

She was out of time. Talia's finger tightened around her trigger.

"Don Marco, what is happening in here?" Tyler came walking in through an arch beside the altar, hands spread wide. "I send my protégé in ahead of me, and you greet her with a firing squad?"

"Your protégé?" The older Italian walked past Talia as if she wasn't there. "My boys caught her sneaking through the *labirinto*, and you know how cautious they are." Broad in both the chest and waist, he clapped Tyler hard on the shoulders, kissed him on both cheeks, and wrapped him in a crushing bear hug. "Adam, *il mio angelo custode*, my guardian angel, where have you been these last few months, eh?"

Grunting under the constriction of the hug, Tyler shot Talia a look that said, *Put your gun away.*

She hesitated, then made a show of tucking the Glock into the holster at the small of her back. Once her hands were empty, the men to her left and right lowered their Berettas. The one she had chased said something obviously snide in Italian and let his jacket fall closed.

Talia answered with a frown and a chin lift. "Right. You got me. Good for you."

"Please forgive her, Don Marco." Tyler smoothed out his sport jacket as the Italian released him. "Natalia is often . . . overzealous in her efforts to keep me safe."

You wish. Talia didn't say it out loud, however much she wanted to. She played along with Tyler's protégé story and positioned herself at his shoulder.

Don Marco assessed her, raising one half of a snow-white unibrow. "I still struggle to believe that this little *topolina* is your protégé."

Talia didn't know what *topolina* meant, but she didn't take it as a compliment.

Tyler held out a hand for her to let it go. "She may be small in stature, Don Marco, but she is highly capable."

"And yet you and the highly capable mouse have come to me for help." Don Marco strolled along the pillars, examining their spiraling Latin inscriptions.

Tyler followed, with Talia keeping pace a step behind. "I need to contact Valkyrie."

The don stopped beside the last of the pillars, and Talia thought she caught a tensing of his great shoulders.

He snapped his fingers.

The security detail faded back into the tunnels, out of sight.

Once the three young men were gone, Don Marco spoke, but he kept his eyes on the pillar. "I have kept you two apart for a reason."

"I know," Tyler said, lowering his gaze in a respectful manner Talia had never observed him use before. "But lives are at stake."

"How many lives?"

"Thousands."

Finally Don Marco turned. "And so Valkyrie's life, too, will be at risk. Do you understand what you are asking?"

Talia opened her mouth to speak, but Tyler touched her arm to quiet her. "I do. And I cannot guarantee Valkyrie's safety."

"I saw you coming. Can you believe that?" Don Marco started walking again, hands clasped behind his back. "This morning in my meditations, I saw you walking toward me out of the shadows with hand outstretched like a begging child. And I swore I would grant whatever you asked."

"So you'll do it? You'll pass the message, offer Valkyrie the job?"

Tyler's question went unanswered for a long while. The don reached the altar and bowed his head. After a time, he raised his eyes to the crucifix and then turned to face the other two. "No message. You want Valkyrie's help? Then you must ask for it in person."

Tyler took a step forward, hand coming out like the begging child the Italian had described. "Don Marco, I have much to do, I can't—"

"Those are my terms, Adam."

Talia studied the faces of both men, wheels turning. Their whole conversation felt strangely familial.

"All right," Tyler said. "Give me a location."

"No location. Only a name—Khafra. If that is not enough, then you are not worthy of Valkyrie in the first place."

"It is enough." Tyler squared his shoulders and spoke the words with confidence.

Talia caught herself chuckling inside. *Like he gave you a choice.* Despite the eerie setting and the armed men lurking nearby, she was starting to enjoy herself. She liked watching this old gentleman put Tyler in his place.

Don Marco crossed the chamber to clasp Tyler's hand. "And you understand that when this is over, you and Valkyrie will come and see me. Together." He held the hand fast, squeezing a little tighter. "For dinner, of course."

Talia watched Tyler swallow. It seemed his throat had gone dry. "Of course."

After a long hard look, the don released him. "Good." He snapped his fingers, and the three young men returned. "Then I believe this meeting is over."

TALIA AND TYLER WALKED down the grassy hill from the churchyard together. "So . . ." she asked. "Are we going to talk about the fact that we just had a meeting with a mafia don?"

Tyler was playing on his phone, only half paying attention. "Don Marco is a term of endearment used by the locals, because they often see him praying."

"Praying?"

He sighed and lowered the phone. "This is Il Campione, not Hollywood. Here the term *don* is used for nobility and priests. In the eyes of his friends, Don Marco is a little of both."

A holy man with an armed escort. Right. Talia didn't press. She had other bones to pick. "You ran off to this meeting without me, Tyler. Why didn't you want me along?"

"So you wouldn't get shot."

"By the holy noble's armed escort?"

"Correct." Tyler returned to his phone and kept walking.

She stopped, dropping her arms and watching him go. "No. It's more than that. I was getting a family vibe down there, like a father-son thing."

Talia didn't get an answer. Tyler held out an open palm. "Give me the keys to the Alfa. If it has so much as a hairline scratch, I'll send Brennan a bill, and you can explain what it's for."

She caught up to him and handed over the keys, and he gave her the Tesla keys in exchange.

"So . . . I can't touch the Alfa, but I can drive the Tesla home?"

"No, the Tesla is driving *you* home."

They reached the bottom of the hill, and the Tesla's door opened of its own accord. Tyler pointed at the flawless white leather. "Sit there. Keep your hands off the wheel, they're filthy."

As she dropped into the driver's seat, Talia stole a glance at Tyler's phone. She expected to see the controls for the Tesla. Instead, she saw he'd been running a search for the name Don Marco had given him. "Khafra," she read out loud. "Sounds Egyptian."

"It is."

"Okay. Does that mean we're flying to Cairo to find this Valkyrie?"

"Nope." Tyler clicked a link in the search engine and held the phone low so Talia could see what came up—an advertisement for an exhibition at a museum called the Gallerie dell'Accademia. "We're flying to Venice."

CHAPTER THIRTY-THREE

AFTER THE MEETING in the catacombs, Talia and Tyler found Eddie asleep in Mission Control, facedown on the couch with a list of names and faces on the screen—the job listings he and Talia had been working on earlier.

Tyler woke him with a kick to the cushions. "Hey. Where's my hacker? I don't see a hacker here."

"You're . . ." Eddie sat up, yawning and stretching. "You're looking at him."

"How's that, exactly?" Talia asked.

The geek rubbed the sleep from his eyes and reseated his glasses. "I've been *inside* Avantec's server rooms—*touched* the hardware. I know their infrastructure. I'm your guy."

"No. You're not." Tyler swatted Eddie's legs out of the way and sat down beside him on the couch. "You have no criminal history. You have no rep. How can I convince our thieves to trust you with their lives when no one's ever heard of you?"

"Oh, but they have. Look."

Eddie pulled a keyboard from under a couch pillow and police mug shot—Eddie doing his best smolder—came up on the big screen, followed by rap sheets in four languages and a series

164

of articles covering unsolved cybercrimes. He zoomed in on an alias in the English rap sheet and deepened his voice. "I'm *Red Leader*."

Tyler dropped his head into his hands. "And I'm a dead man."

"I think Eddie's right." Talia scanned the articles on the screen. Her instincts had cringed at Eddie's fake handle, but using him as the hacker would limit the number of real thieves she and Tyler would have to con. "I vote yes. You're bringing in Valkyrie. I get Eddie."

Tyler lifted his head from his hands and gave her an incredulous look. "We're not picking kickball teams on a playground."

"Take it or leave it."

He gritted his teeth and growled, "Fine. Eddie, you're in. Show me the others."

There were four—two options for the high-flying cat burglar, one demolitions expert, and a Scottish pilot built like a professional wrestler. Tyler thrust his chin at the second face in the cat burglar column. "We'll go with the Australian, Finn."

"Ehhhh." Eddie bobbled his head. "Finn's okay, but he's a loner. The other guy, Garrett Mason, works with crews. He'll be Lukon's first choice, so he should be ours."

"Wrong. Lukon and Mason have a history. Put those two in a room together, only one will walk out alive."

This was news to Talia. "Our file on Lukon doesn't mention Mason."

"Then your file is incomplete." Tyler offered no further explanation. "We grab Finn, leaving the real Lukon no option." He gave Eddie a commanding nod. "Send Finn a message. Wow him with a dollar figure."

"I can't." Eddie's cursor jumped to an empty black space beside CONTACT in the information column. "Like I said, Finn only works for himself, so he doesn't bother hanging out a digital shingle."

Tyler sat back against the couch cushions, crossing his arms. "What about a location?"

"All I have are rumors."

"Good enough."

TALIA AND TYLER flew out early the next morning, leaving Eddie to continue his work in Mission Control. His rumors concerning Finn's location came with a narrow time window, so Venice would have to wait. "Welcome to St. Moritz," Tyler said, taxiing the Gulfstream clear of a snow-dusted runway, "the highest commercial airfield in Europe."

They bought clothing appropriate for the cold at the airport shops and rented a car with studded snow tires. Tyler insisted the vehicle be a BMW, citing no reason for the excess, and paid in cash, promising to send the Agency a bill. Talia answered him with a flat laugh. Brennan would never sign off on the charges.

After a breakfast in a local café, they drove up into a high-mountain valley on the Swiss-Italian border, well above the last of the misty green pines. Tyler parked on a field of white among a hundred Porsches, Jags, and Aston Martins.

Talia pulled herself up from the BMW's passenger seat and looked around at all the extravagant cars. "This is why you wanted a Beamer."

"It's important to blend in, right?"

A pair of thirteen-thousand-foot peaks rose into the deep blue on either side of them, and light aircraft buzzed overhead. A banner stretching across a makeshift exit from the parking area welcomed them to the Bellavista Glacier Airshow.

"And speaking of blending in." Tyler frowned at the snowsuit Talia had chosen from the airport shops. "Why did you have to pick black?"

"I like black." Talia let the Beamer's door fall shut. "And it was cheap."

"You look like a cop."

Out on the glacier, small packs of wealthy tourists gathered around exotic snow trucks and propeller-driven sleds, and bought hot chocolate from roving vendors. The whole crowd let out a prolonged *Oohhh!* as Talia and Tyler passed under the welcome banner. She shielded her eyes and looked toward the grandstand to see a pair of biplanes flying low, one inverted above the other, along a runway carved into the top of the glacier. They split up, circled, and touched down, bouncing on oversize tires.

Tyler whooped and applauded with the rest of the crowd. When Talia did not, he nudged her. "Come on. It's okay to be impressed. And not just with the aerobatics." He pointed at the taxiing biplanes with his program. "Those aircraft are feats of mechanical brilliance, highly modified to perform in thin air. Did you know most aerobatic shows take place a thousand feet or more *below* the altitude of the ice you're standing on?"

"And that's why we're here, right?" Talia eyed the expensive toys and experimental planes on display. "High-altitude heists are Finn's specialty. You and Eddie think he's planning to swipe some special aircraft?"

"Who said anything about a heist?"

Tyler raised his eyes to the sky, and Talia followed his gaze, slipping on her special sunglasses to fight off the glare. She saw a glint of silver above the western peak. "Is that . . . a weather balloon?"

Metal music drowned out Tyler's answer, blaring from the loudspeakers bracketing the grandstand. Thumping bass and whining electric guitars joined in crescendo while the announcer shouted an introduction.

"*Ladies annnd gentlemen. Like the arctic snow fox, our next guest appears without warning. We hoped he would show, and now he has. I give you . . . Michaelllll . . . Fiiiinnnnn!*"

The crescendo ended with a thundering downbeat that threatened to knock the snow from the valley walls.

The weather balloon exploded.

Sparks flew from the fireball, and one large piece fell away, trailing red smoke. Fearing it might fall on the spectators, Talia touched her glasses to zoom in. The falling object was no piece of wreckage. It was a man in a silver wingsuit, diving toward the peak. The crowd roared with delight.

"Finn," she said under her breath.

Tyler slapped the rolled-up program against his leg. "You have to give the kid credit. He knows how to make an entrance."

The red smoke traced an arc down the snowy face of the mountain. Talia zoomed out again to keep it all in view. "Are you seeing this, Eddie?"

"I am," he said through her earpiece. "Hold still. I'm taking a screenshot."

"For reference?"

"No. So I can use it as my wallpaper."

The red streak drew closer and closer to the glacier, and still Talia saw no parachute. The crowd let out a collective gasp. At the last possible second, the thief flared his body and threw out a drogue. With a *swack*, a blue parasail snapped open behind him and he flew down the runway, touching down on short skis and skidding to a stop in a shower of glistening white. The crowd went wild.

Talia felt bad for the sad little gyrocopter act that followed, because it seemed as if half the grandstand had emptied to get Finn's autograph—the female half. Getting close to the rock-star jumper was no easy task. She and Tyler worked their way along the rope line, pushing through a mass of pink-and-white snow-bunny suits.

"Let me do the talking," Tyler said as they neared the center. "I'm supposed to be Lukon. He has to think I'm in charge."

Talia frowned up at him. "Right. Whatever."

Maybe it was Talia's smaller size—or maybe she had fewer qualms about shoving giggly rich girls out of her way than Tyler—but she reached Finn first. There he was, at the corner of the grandstand, signing some blonde's arm with a permanent marker. The ski goggles strapped to his forehead sent his bangs off in wild directions, but that did nothing to detract from his good looks. He had them—Talia couldn't deny it. And from the way he handled that blonde, she half expected him to unzip the wingsuit and step out wearing a full tuxedo. *Finn. Michael Finn.*

Exhausting.

Talia glanced over her shoulder. Where was Tyler? She wouldn't wait. Talia put her hands to her mouth and shouted over the giggling and squawking girls. "Hey! Finn!"

The thief took one look at her and bolted.

CHAPTER
THIRTY-FOUR

FINN'S SILVER WINGSUIT evaporated into the forest of steel and aluminum beneath the stands while screaming girls in pink and white converged to block Talia's view.

Tyler strolled up beside her, shaking his head. "I told you to stop looking like a cop."

"I don't look like a cop."

"Could've fooled him." Tyler helped Talia duck under the rope and the two jogged along the front of the grandstand. "Finn's not going anywhere. He can't run in that wingsuit."

Finn, it turned out, was well aware of this. He crawled out through the fabric skirt, wearing jeans, a T-shirt, and ridiculous toe shoes and took off at a sprint toward a cordoned-off arena. Three stuntmen on motorcycles with skis for front tires weaved in and out of one another, entertaining the crowd in the dead time between aerial acts. The leader was flying a big French flag. Finn vaulted over the fence and tackled him off his bike.

The crowd let out a pained *Ohh!*

More confident on the ice than Talia, Tyler spit out ahead. He jumped the fence just as Finn got a hand on the empty bike, hooked the thief under the arm, and spun. Finn's feet went fully skyward before Tyler slammed him down. The crowd reacted with an even bigger *Ohhhh!*

All three Frenchmen joined in the scuffle, slipping, sliding, and falling over one another. The people in the stands loved it. They answered every punch and tackle with laughter and moans. Finn was the first to break free. He mounted the leader's bike, gunned the engine, and plowed through the temporary fence, French flag whipping behind. Talia caught up a moment later. She mounted a second bike and gave chase. The lead Frenchman tried to block her path, but she held the throttle down, and he dove out of the way.

Finn drove straight down the center of the runway, and Talia followed, wind stinging her cheeks and threatening to tear Franklin's sunglasses from her face. Tears blurred her vision, but she saw Finn glance back and wave. He pointed ahead.

Talia shifted her gaze and saw biplanes. Two of them. Side by side. The aerial team that was performing when she first arrived now barreled down the runway, heading straight for her.

"Turn, Talia," Eddie said through the headset, as if a crash might get him killed as well. "Turn now."

"Only if Finn turns first."

He didn't. Finn hunched his body down and sped between the biplanes, inches from the wings on either side of him. Talia gritted her teeth, planning to do the same, but the pilots had a different plan. They pulled up. The engines growled as they passed overhead, and the prop wash hit her like a cold ocean wave. The bike fishtailed, but Talia kept it upright.

She was gaining.

Everything Talia had learned about Finn in the last few minutes told her he had another trick up his sleeve. He did. The thief slowed, drifting toward the edge of the runway, dropped a foot, and skidded through a U-turn. Another aircraft taxied by and Finn throttled after it. He pulled alongside, ditched the bike, and leaped onto the wing, locking an arm through a rail fixed to the fuselage. The aircraft lifted off. Finn popped a red smoke flare and held it up into the wind.

"There he goes, ladies and gentlemen," the announcer shouted, "*Michaellll . . . Fiiinnnn!* And let's have a round of applause for his stunt-woman partner. Isn't she a looker?"

"That's you," Eddie whispered through Talia's earpiece. "Take a bow."

The crowd applauded, as prompted.

Talia turned and stomped through the crunching snow toward the stands. "Not a chance."

After only a few steps a dune buggy rolled up, driven by a woman in a high-visibility vest. Tyler and the leader of the French stuntmen climbed out of the back. Talia shook her head. "It's like Finn planned the whole thing."

"He did," Tyler said as the Frenchman ran off to fuss over his bike. "Finn bought off the biker team before the show. Tackling their leader was all part of the act. The others came after me because they thought I was a confused member of show security, spoiling everything." He watched Finn's ride bank its wings and descend beyond the ridgeline. "You have to give the kid credit—"

"If you say 'He knows how to make an exit,' I will slap you." Talia climbed into the dune buggy and tapped the driver on the shoulder. "Excuse me, but Mr. Finn can't stay on that wing for long. Where will the aircraft land?"

When the driver tried to answer, Tyler waved her off. "Doesn't matter." He dropped into the front passenger seat. "Finn has a giant head start and we don't have time to track him down. Right now, we have to go to Venice. We have a date with Valkyrie."

THE SUN WAS SETTING over the Laguna Veneta as Tyler brought the Gulfstream into Marco Polo Airport. They left their earpieces in the jet, giving Eddie a little time off, and took a water taxi across the lagoon to the Piazza San Marco. From there, a gondolier brought them into the city. Darkness fell quickly in the narrow waterways between the houses and churches. Young men, standing balanced in their boats, used long poles to light gas lanterns along the canals.

Tyler conversed with their boatman in Italian, and Talia poked him with a finger. "Would you mind switching to English? Where exactly are we going?"

"I showed you last night." Tyler signaled left with the flat of his hand, and the gondolier turned onto a new canal. "The Gallerie dell'Accademia. Tonight, they're having a gala to celebrate the unveiling of the Khafra collection. Invitation only."

"We don't *have* invitations."

"Eddie took care of that. Check your email."

Talia pulled out her phone and opened her secure email. She scowled at the screen. "Signore and Signora Rosiello. A married couple? Are you insane?" She glanced over at Tyler. "You're, like . . . twenty years older than me."

"Fifteen, and you know it. And it could be fifty for all these people care. Welcome to Italy." Tyler looked her up and down, assessing her clothes. "I hope you still have your government credit card. We need to do some more shopping."

Despite the crack about her credit card, Tyler insisted on paying. And Talia was glad. Any dress in any shop on Rio de San Moisè would have put her over her limit. She chose a silk number, emerald green with a low V back. And then she wore her purchase out of the store, something she'd sworn she'd never do again after she left the foster care system.

The boatman gave a low whistle as he helped her down the steps into the gondola. He smirked and said something in Italian. Talia heard *bambolina*. It sounded a lot like Don Marco's *topolina*, only this guy's tone was much worse. She looked him straight in the eye. "Say that again and I'll knock you overboard."

The four wings of the Gallerie dell'Accademia formed a perfect square. The gala was set in the open plaza at the middle, with candlelit tables and live music. Talia bristled at the centerpiece, an ice sculpture of the Sphinx lit from beneath with blue LEDs. She had seen enough ice for one lifetime earlier in the day.

Tyler looked the part of rich-older-husband-with-trophy-wife in a double-breasted tux paired with a vintage cravat tie in jewel-tone green to match her dress. He bent close to Talia's ear as the viola player plucked the first bars of a minuet. "Watch out. Heads are turning. You look like a princess at the ball."

"Perhaps a princess forced to marry the villain of the story, the wart-faced king of a dark and distant land."

The rest of the quartet joined the viola. Miniature forks clinked down on half-empty dessert plates as several couples left their tables to dance. Talia set off toward an open table, but Tyler caught her fingers and pulled her back to face him. He placed a hand on her waist and guided her into the flow of dancers. "I've never had a wart a day in my life."

"But you *are* playing the evil king."

"Not in my version of the story."

Talia imagined him delivering that last counter with a grin, but she couldn't be sure. She was too busy watching her own feet, struggling to find the rhythm. Her heel caught in the grout between the pavers. She stumbled.

Tyler's hand tightened around her waist to keep her upright. "You know, this will go a lot smoother if you let me lead."

"Or maybe it would go smoother if you learned to treat me like a partner, instead of dragging me blind through every step."

"I'm dragging you because you don't *know* the steps, and I don't have time to explain them."

The violins pushed the pace. The viola answered an octave above, and the cello countered with a deep vibrato. Tyler spun Talia to dodge a couple that could not keep up. "I'm putting my life on the line to help you and the Agency. What more do you want?"

They drew closer to the stage in the turn around the ice sculpture, and she raised her voice over the music so he could hear the anger. "How about a little honesty?"

"Fine. No problem. What do you want to know?"

Another couple dropped out, laughing and breathing heavy. Only four pairs remained. Onlookers toasted Tyler and Talia as they passed, oblivious to her frustration.

"I want to know who you really are."

She felt Tyler's hold loosen. He had expected a question about the mission, not his past. Now he was the one off balance, and Talia pressed her advantage. "I can read between the lines. You were CIA once. What division? Ops? Paramilitary? Why doesn't Mary Jordan trust you?"

"Mary Jordan doesn't trust anyone. And I was never attached to a division. I was an asset." He pushed against her palm, pressing her onward as the violins took up a staccato beat.

"Meaning what?"

"You *know* what."

"I want to hear you say it." She wrapped her fingers around his, pulling and turning to keep pace with the quartet. "Tell me what you were before you became Adam Tyler."

The turn around the ice sculpture brought his whole face into shadow. Tyler growled out his answer. "An assassin, Talia. Is that what you wanted to hear? I killed people for a living."

She let go.

With two short beats and a long victorious chord, the quartet finished. The people at the tables, the dancing couples, everyone but Talia and Tyler applauded.

CHAPTER
THIRTY-FIVE

GALLERIE DELL'ACCADEMIA
VENICE, ITALY

TALIA RETREATED TO A QUIET CORNER, away from the tables. She had suspected Tyler's secret, yet she had not been prepared to hear it. How could Brennan have assigned her to work with a killer? And what did it say about the Agency—her Agency—that they employed his services at all, then or now?

Tyler appeared at her side a few moments later and handed her a drink. "Ginger ale, or as close as I could get. I got the sense your stomach had turned."

"You sensed right." Talia sipped the soda, some not-quite-sweet-enough citrus drink, and let the coolness of it calm her anger.

"Talia, I—"

"Forget it. Tell me about Valkyrie." She scanned the party-goers, not quite sure what she was looking for. "How can you be certain he'll show?"

"You mean 'she.'" Tyler nodded at a banner stretched across the stage, hanging above the quartet. Beside golden calligraphy that read *I TESORI DI KHAFRA* was a grainy headshot of a mousy woman in Coke-bottle glasses, black hair not quite contained by her librarian bun. "And 'she' is the guest of honor."

They found her haunting the buffet table. The photo did not do justice to her Mediterranean complexion, but the bad hair and thick glasses were a match. She wore an ankle-length frock barely suitable for a 1950s house party, let alone a ritzy museum gala.

"Look," Tyler said, watching her from a few steps away, "Valkyrie has a gift for reading people. She'll intuit half your life story the moment you open your mouth, so don't."

"Don't what?"

"Speak. Let's not have a repeat of your mistake with Finn, hmm?"

Talia looked daggers at the back of Tyler's head and then followed as he sidled up beside their target. Up on the stage, an exuberant balding gentleman took the microphone and introduced himself as the museum's director.

Valkyrie spoke first, keeping her voice low as the director rambled in a mix of Italian and English. The donors answered with snippets of laughter and applause. "Hello, Tyler. Marco said you might drop in. Nice dancing." She glanced past him to Talia. "Though I can't say the same for your little friend. She seems a little . . . inexperienced."

Talia read the subtext in Valkyrie's flat expression. "You mean too young for him. And you're right."

"It's not like that," Tyler said, backing her up. "This is Talia. We're working together. And we need your—"

"No."

"Valkyrie, at least let me—"

"No."

Tyler shifted his weight, tapping a finger against his leg. Talia wanted to dislike the woman, especially after the *inexperienced* remark, but she had to admire the way Valkyrie had shut Tyler down.

Valkyrie took her glasses off and polished the lenses with the hem of her dress. "Stay out of my way. Tonight is the culmination of three months' work."

As if on cue, the director gestured in Valkyrie's direction. "And finally I must thank our American colleague, Dr. Amelia Cartwright, one of the world's foremost experts in Near Eastern antiquities. She spent years in the field on the hunt for the lost treasures of the pharaoh Khafra." He gave Valkyrie a nod, and she answered with a humble wave of her glasses. "Without Dr. Cartwright's selfless request that we cover the cost of her expedition only, with no honorarium, and without your generous donations, our humble museum could never have acquired such a remarkable collection."

The director droned on, and Talia leaned close to Tyler. "I'm sorry, but this is your specialist? Why do we need an expert in Near Eastern antiquities for a high-altitude robbery?"

"You're missing the point. Valkyrie is *not* an expert in Near Eastern antiquities."

At this, Valkyrie cleared her throat, looking seriously offended.

Tyler rolled his eyes. "Okay, she *is* an expert in Near Eastern antiquities. But she is also an expert in Qin artifacts, a real estate lawyer versed in the obscurities of Myanmar property law, and—if I'm not mistaken—a superintendent in the national police force of Lichtenstein."

"*Chief* superintendent," Valkyrie countered through a frozen smile, slipping her glasses back on.

Up on the stage, the museum director reached the climax of his speech. "My dear, distinguished donors, I give you . . . the lost treasures of Khafra!" He pulled a cord, and a curtain fell. Precious artifacts glittered on a tiered display of black velvet boxes. On a pedestal at the center stood a golden pharaoh set with bands of lapis. The director held his microphone out to Valkyrie. "Dr. Cartwright, please say a few words."

"You mean she's a con woman," Talia hissed, mindful of all the eyes looking at the three of them. "And she's conning these poor donors right now."

"Oh, darling." Valkyrie set off to take the microphone. "They're anything but poor."

Tyler gave her a golf clap as she walked away. "For future reference, Talia, the proper term is *grifter*."

"We have to stop her."

"I know." He took a deep breath and smoothed his lapels. "Watch this."

Tyler passed Valkyrie on the way up the stage steps and swiped the microphone out of the museum director's hand. "Good evening, folks. I am Dr. Cartwright's assistant, Joe Bagdun. I always handle her introductions."

"He's really not." Valkyrie grabbed for the mic. "And he really doesn't. Can I get some security up here, please?"

Tyler sidestepped her grabs and bumped into the golden pharaoh's pedestal. All the donors held their breath as the statue teetered and fell, but with lightning quickness, he dropped to a knee and caught it. "Whew," he said, standing and setting it on the pedestal once more. "Close one."

Valkyrie stood off to one side, giving up on her efforts to recover the microphone. "Security? Anyone? Do the guards here speak English?"

Undaunted, Tyler placed a hand on the pharaoh's scepter and shot her a glance. "Say, Dr. Cartwright, does this look crooked to you?"

"Don't!" She lurched for him, horrified, but Tyler cranked down on the scepter anyway. The hand that held it snapped off at the wrist.

An older woman in the front row swooned.

Valkyrie closed her eyes and lowered her head.

"Oh," Tyler said in mock surprise. He turned to the museum director, showing him the broken piece. "I didn't realize gold was so brittle."

"It . . . isn't." The director approached for a closer look.

"Weird. And why is the entire cross-section black, I wonder?"

Tyler sniffed the broken section. "Smells like . . . graphite." He offered the hand and scepter to Valkyrie. "Your thoughts, Dr. Cartwright?"

"I hate you." Valkyrie ignored the scepter and stormed off the stage.

Tyler pressed the broken piece into the director's hands and followed.

Talia met them both at the bottom of the steps, but the grifter pushed past her, and the two watched her march up the aisle between the tables of murmuring donors. A pair of guards, finally mobilized by the breaking of the statue, rushed up to her, but stopped in their tracks when she held up a warning hand. They let her pass.

"The moment she reaches the plaza gate, she'll run for it," Talia said. "You know that, right?"

"Let her run. I know her playbook."

They left through the back gate of the plaza, and Tyler shifted into tour guide mode, as if they were out for a leisurely night-time stroll. "At the end of this lane," he said, pointing down a broad pedestrian thoroughfare, "you can see the dome of the Church of Santa Maria del Rosario. And that"—he shifted his aim—"is the Gesuati Monastery."

"Tyler, we don't have time for a tour. We—"

As Talia spoke, he shifted his aim again. "And that building over there is the local constabulary. They should be getting a call about . . . now."

A commotion of shouts erupted within the police station. Silhouettes moved across the windows. The door opened. Before Talia could see who came out, Tyler pulled her down an alley-way. He made two turns and then stopped at an intersection, looking down at her shoes. "I think you should ditch those heels."

He offered an arm for balance, but Talia chose instead to use the alley wall. "Are you saying it's time to run?"

"I'm saying it's time to jump." The grumbling hum of an outboard motor drifted in from a canal at the end of the cross street. "And soon. Hurry!"

The moment Talia had her second shoe off, he pulled her into a run. They sprinted down the cobblestone lane and leaped out over the water. She landed in a heap on a plush white seat at the back of a motorboat. Tyler landed on the fiberglass bow. He grabbed the windscreen and pulled himself up to the driver— Valkyrie. "Would you mind slowing down?"

"Yes, I mind." She palmed his face, squishing his nose. "Why don't you shove off?"

Try as Valkyrie might to dislodge him from her windscreen, Tyler held on, so she veered the boat left and right. His legs careened side to side. "Don Marco . . . never told me . . . you had a mean streak."

"Marco should never have sent you." Valkyrie turned the wheel even more, and the chrome gunwales bounced off the canal walls, sending up sparks.

The whole episode was more than Talia could take. She hiked up her dress and drew her Glock, bracing one foot against the passenger seat for stability. "Stop the boat!"

It was enough distraction to let Tyler scramble over the windscreen. "Belay that," he said. "Keep going."

"Why?" Talia asked.

Red and blue lights lit up the canal. A police boat turned the corner behind them.

"Oh. That."

Talia lowered the gun and Valkyrie pushed the throttle to the max, looking sideways at Tyler. "'Belay that'? Really?"

"Nautical term. And for the record, you started it with 'Shove off.'"

A second police boat joined the chase, cutting off the first from an intersecting canal. The cop in the passenger seat shouted through a megaphone. "*Fermati! Spegnere il motore!*"

Tyler shouted back, gesturing emphatically at Valkyrie. "*Mi scuso! Lei è una donna demente!*"

"That was uncalled for," Valkyrie said. "You're the one who's demented."

They crossed a waterway, jumping the wake of a passing boat before plunging through a narrow opening into the next section of canals. Tyler pointed at an upcoming intersection. "Turn right."

"I don't think so."

"I know what I'm doing. Turn right."

"No."

The intersecting canal came and went as they argued, but another lay ahead. Tyler reached over and cranked the wheel. The boat swung around the corner, and a wall of spray slammed into a passing gondolier, knocking him overboard.

Valkyrie punched him in the arm. "I was heading for open water."

"Where more cops will be waiting. We have to lose them in the canals."

A T-intersection came up, and Valkyrie turned the boat hard, backing off the throttle just enough to avoid slamming into the centuries-old bricks. "Fine. But we can't drive around all night. Where are we supposed to hide?"

Images from earlier in the night rolled through Talia's memory. She saw the shop on Rio de San Moisè with its stone stairway leading up into an Aladdin's cave of silk and chiffon. She saw the gas lamps on the canal behind the Piazza San Marco. Before Tyler could answer Valkyrie's question, Talia pushed out a hand. "Left! Take the next left!"

The other two looked back at her, like parents looking back at a child from the front seat of the station wagon.

Talia stomped a foot. "I'm telling you. I know where to go. Take the next left."

Rebuilding a map of the canals from memory, Talia talked

Valkyrie through the turns. And the grifter took them as fast as she dared. In minutes, their lead had increased so much the cop boats fell out of view. Yet the sound of the motors still buzzed behind them.

"They're following our wake," Tyler said. "We need more distance to let it settle."

"Three more turns." Talia had seen several boat garages on the canals, and all had been blocked by painted iron gates that dipped down into the water—all except one. Near the piazza was a garage with its gate being refinished. The two halves were leaning against the rail of a nearby walkway. Halfway through the final turn, Talia saw it, a black hole slightly left of a three-way intersection. "There!"

Valkyrie hit the garage at an angle, cranked the wheel, and cut the engine, and the boat spun into a one-eighty, drifting backward into the shadows. The water calmed. The sirens of the two police boats grew loud and then softened again as they sped past. They didn't even look.

As soon as they were gone, Valkyrie shoved Tyler toward the loading dock. "Get out. I never want to see you again. The museum hadn't transferred the money yet. You cost me more than a quarter million euros."

"And I'll pay it," Tyler said. He waved off a look from Talia. "Plus a bonus, but only if you help us."

"You trashed my con so you could blackmail me?" Valkyrie shook her head. "That's low, Tyler, even for a man of your reputation."

As the two argued, Talia listened to the sounds from the canals. The police sirens were still distant, but they weren't getting softer anymore. "Can we do this later? The *polizia* are coming back."

CHAPTER THIRTY-SIX

THE THREE CLIMBED A LADDER to the piazza. In the better light, Talia could hardly believe Valkyrie, who asked that they call her Val, was the same woman she had met at the gala. The grifter had tossed her Coke-bottle glasses into the water, yanked out the rubber band holding her bun in check, and shed her frumpy dress, revealing slacks and a sleeveless tank top. The mousy academian was gone.

A stop at a tourist trap bought Talia a new look as well—in ill-fitting shorts, a T-shirt, and flip-flops. She also bought a backpack. No way was she leaving that dress behind.

Tyler simply stripped away the jacket, waistcoat, and tie, and stuffed them into a trash bin.

A small troop of *polizia* were trolling the ferry line, so the three split for boarding. They reconvened at a table on the lower deck, well away from the other passengers.

"So," Val said, resting her chin on her fingers and looking up at Talia, "tell me how you steered us to that loading dock. Are you some kind of Rainman?"

"Eidetic memory. I built a map in my head. And no, I'm not"—Talia made air quotes—"some kind of Rainman. You can't use that term anymore. It's offensive."

Val shot an *Is she serious?* glance at Tyler.

He nodded. "A lot of terms are offensive now. Ask any millennial. They'll make you a list."

The pretense of civility dropped from Val's expression. "I suspected the eidetic memory. Thanks for confirming it. I didn't get the rest until now." She frowned at Tyler, lowering her voice. "Well done. Not only did you spoil my payday, you also led a CIA officer straight to me. You know the Agency works with Interpol these days."

"How . . ." Talia looked wide-eyed at Tyler. "How did she figure out I was CIA?"

"I warned you. She reads people. I told you not to speak." Before Talia could challenge the absurdity of that last bit, Tyler laid his palms on the table in the international sign for *Everybody simmer down*. "Talia, we were going to tell her about your Agency affiliation anyway. Val, Talia won't give you up—not if you help us."

Val gave Talia the evil eye. "Oh good. More blackmail." After a long look at both of them, she flopped back in her seat. "Fine. I'm in. It's not like I have a choice."

BACK AT THE CHATEAU, Val and Conrad became fast friends on the common ground of bashing Tyler.

"Oh, I admit Adam *is* trying at times," Conrad told her, leading them all to a table laid out with an assortment of dumplings and sauces. "Did he do that thing in which he leaps into your path like a child shouting '*Boo!*'?"

"Yes!"

"Maddening."

"I hate to interrupt." Tyler glanced around the dining room.

"But where's Eddie? I would expect him to be hovering over these dumplings like a vulture."

Conrad nodded toward the stairs. "He took a tray up to Mission Control, as he calls it. You should go up as well. He has something for you."

As promised, Eddie had turned the image of Finn proximity flying down the mountainside into a screen saver for the room's giant display.

"Talk to me." Tyler added more dumplings to his tray as if adding a coin to a street performer's hat.

"I have a bead on our next two candidates." Eddie punched his keyboard, and Finn's action shot dematerialized, leaving two photos complete with profiles—an attractive young black woman walking across a university campus, and a pro-wrestler-size Scotsman posing in front of a space plane. "Meet our chemist, Darcy Emile," he said, making the young woman's profile expand to block out the pilot's. "A brilliant young woman who wrote a treatise on demolition operations in the vacuum of space during her undergrad years. Since then she has claimed three master's degrees, two doctorates, and my heart."

Talia squinted at him, a dumpling hovering at her lips. "Wait. What was that last one?"

"What? Hmm?" Eddie feigned confusion. He waved his hands. "Not important. Not important. As the youngest chemistry professor at Paris Polytech, Miss Emile once spent half a lecture arguing that explosions constitute a form of art. The university challenged this assertion in a press release, and Darcy doubled down by blowing up the planetary sciences lab." A video played. In a shaky nighttime scene, a bio-dome vanished in a pillar of flame. Screams could be heard near the camera. Eddie bobbled his head. "She no longer works there."

Tyler held up a hand to stop Talia from arguing against bringing a pyromaniac terrorist into the chateau. "Where is she now?"

"Unknown." Eddie brought up a map of Europe with points marked by animated miniature explosions. "Her most recent jobs were banks, usually with sketchy political connections. No wounded. She's been dark for six months, but I've identified a bitcoin account. Give me some time. I'll find her."

"I'll bet you will," Val said.

Tyler set his dumplings on the conference table and turned to the screen. "What about our wheelman?"

Darcy's profile shrank away and the second profile came up. "Macauley Plucket. Formerly a test pilot in the RAF, Mr. Plucket spent two years in the EU space program, including multiple mesospheric excursions in hybrid aircraft. He's smart for such a big guy, but he has a gambling problem." A video of fighters in an octagonal ring came up. The larger man smashed a heavy fist into the other's jaw and dropped him like a rock.

"Betting on fights?" asked Talia.

"Betting on his *own* fights." Eddie paused the video. "Just so we're clear, Mac is the one still standing. Two weeks before his first mission, the European Space Agency gave him the boot for misconduct. Now he makes bank doing odd flying and enforcement jobs."

Talia had a hard time swallowing her dumplings. They were about to hire and con two criminal sociopaths. When the house of cards fell, one would smash their heads in and the other would blow up the chateau. "And have you located our big Scottish friend?"

"Roussillon," Eddie said. "He's working off a debt to a French bookie as part of an intimidation gang. The French call it *une escouade brute*, a brute squad." A black-and-white security photo grew to fill most of the screen. Mac and two other beefy men were hovering over a frightened shop owner. The Scotsman was hanging back. "He prefers to fight in the ring, not pick on shopkeeps. Chances are, he'll bail on the bookie if we cover his debt."

Tyler studied the face in the black-and-white photo. After a while he nodded. "I don't like the look of this guy, but we need him." He thrust his chin at Eddie. "Send the payment tonight. Get him here tomorrow, if you can. The flight is less than an hour. Meanwhile, Talia and I will put Val in play. Her part in this is critical."

Val raised her eyebrows. "And what part is that, might I ask?"

"You'll see."

THIRTY-SEVEN

TALIA HAD ALMOST FORGOTTEN about the European Aerospace Expo—the conference at which Ivanov intended to unveil his Mark Seven and the Gryphon concept. "We're already lying to a pack of thieves," she said from the back seat of Tyler's Model X. An hour before, when they had left the chateau for the drive south, Val had demanded the front passenger seat, citing back issues. Talia did not believe her. "Do we have to lie to Ivanov too? Can't we bring him in?"

"No. For two reasons." Tyler pulled to a stop at the periphery of the airport's unique parking complex—linked circles of pavement with grassy mounds at the centers. The Alps stood in the distance, capped with snow. "First, assuming Ivanov is innocent in all this, he is still unlikely to give us the information we need—access codes and a voiceprint ID for Gryphon. Second, taking Val off the market might have slowed Lukon's play, but it won't stop him. He'll regroup and send someone else after the same information."

Val climbed out and bent sideways to look in at Talia as the Tesla's outlandish gull-wing door swung upward. "And I'll be there to spot that someone else."

The three walked out of the lot, leaving the Model X to find its own parking spot. Talia caught up to Val. "You'll be there to keep Ivanov safe as well, right? Lukon's grifter might be dangerous."

Val pulled her hair back, tying it with a band. "I'm not going to take a bullet for him, if that's what you're asking."

Talia scowled at her.

"What?" She donned a stylish set of glasses and shrugged. "I won't. Not my job."

Inside the terminal, Talia and Tyler found a table at its only restaurant, La Mela d'Oro, and watched through partially frosted windows as Valkyrie approached her first mark of the job.

Like Val, the woman wore a skirt suit and glasses with her hair tied back. The mark's suit was gray, Val's was a darker charcoal, but otherwise the two looked like members of the same team. Their understated name tags from Milan's Hotel Excelsior might as well have been matching jerseys.

"She certainly looks the part," Talia said as Val tapped the woman on the shoulder.

Tyler signaled the waiter for a menu. "She studied up. Always does. The Excelsior always hosts this conference. As part of the deal, they provide an executive assistant to their visiting CEOs—usually a very attractive woman." He raised his hands in answer to Talia's disapproving look. "Again, welcome to Italy. Like it or not, that's the playing field, and we just sent our new ringer in to remove and replace the girl assigned to Ivanov."

At the rope line on the edge of the customs area, Val and the mark exchanged pleasantries. The woman took on a mildly surprised and somewhat skeptical expression, dug her phone out of her purse, and checked the screen. A few seconds later, not only did she hand her iPad and key fob over to Val, she pulled the grifter into an embrace. The two held each other by the shoulders and jumped up and down together, and then, after a second hug, the girl kissed Val on both cheeks and speed-walked away.

Talia looked to Tyler, widened eyes demanding an explanation.

He obliged. "The assistant, Giovanna Alfonsi, is an aspiring cover girl. Thanks to a photo ad she did for her uncle's gelato shop and a little prod from Eddie, she has now been discovered by a makeup brand in Hong Kong. Her flight leaves in"—he checked his watch—"Ooh! Twenty minutes." Tyler watched the girl run across the terminal to the ticket counter. "Val promised to pack up her things and mail them tomorrow."

Talia shifted her gaze back to the rope line in time to see Val flash her a smile and brandish the girl's ID badge. With a quick dip of a hand into her purse and a rub of her thumb across the badge, Val covered the assistant's photo with her own. Then she held the iPad at her waist—with DR. PAVEL IVANOV printed on the screen—as if she had always been the one standing there.

The waiter brought a glass of tea and a plate of bruschetta for Tyler. He turned to Talia, but she waved him away. When he had gone, she stole a couple of bruschetta from Tyler and laid them on a napkin. "You think Ivanov will go for it?"

"God willing," Tyler said.

The casual nature of his response, spoken while stirring a packet of sweetener into his tea, hit Talia hard. *God willing.* Did a man like Tyler have the right to say such a thing? Their dance in Venice had left her with a lot of questions. Talia couldn't hold them in any longer. "What you said at the Gala—about your past."

She didn't need to elaborate. Tyler understood. "The Agency recruited me out of Delta. I spent all of ten seconds in Paramilitary Ops before the higher-ups realized I was different. I had a knack for . . ."

"Wet work." The word felt disgusting on Talia's lips, like a curse.

Tyler seemed to feel the same. He couldn't even say it—just

nodded. "They wiped my past and set me up with a flat near Heathrow and a lump sum of close to a million US to get me started."

"And then?" Talia asked.

"And then I waited for a contract." Tyler looked her in the eye. "I'm not a psychopath. I never enjoyed the work. But I was good." He went back to stirring his tea. The undissolved sweetener swirled up from the bottom in a miniature whirlwind. "I took care of the names the Agency sent me. I accepted their payments. And in between, I built a network of contacts."

Talia cast a glance toward their new team member. "Like Don Marco."

"Don Marco came later. That's a story for another day. But I met Conrad in those days. There were many others, far less close. For them, I did odd jobs—grifting, recovery, demolition— any noise I could find to drown out the names and faces from the CIA dossiers."

Talia could feel the excuse coming, some life-altering event that justified his past in the twisted logic of a professional killer. She pressed him toward it. "But something changed."

"My final contract. At least, the last contract I completed. The dossier told me he was a traitor, selling secrets. It blamed him for the death of three Americans operating in Eastern Europe. Normally I would have set it up within days, gotten it over with, and moved on."

"Except . . ."

"Except I couldn't see a solid trail of evidence. I followed the target for weeks, at work, with his family. There were suspicious behaviors. Nothing definitive. Eventually my handler demanded action. My job was not to act as jury, nor judge. I was the executioner." Tyler looked down at his hands, turning them over as if searching for something he expected to see there. "So I got the job done. There were . . . complications. And afterward, I couldn't let it go."

Talia heard palpable remorse in his tone, and she knew what he would say next. "The target was innocent."

"I don't know who sold out the officers in Eastern Europe, but it wasn't him. I poured myself into his life, searching for proof at first, later searching for redemption. What I found was a man who loved his country, his family, and above all his God." Tyler looked at her with soft and sorrowful eyes. "The more I dug into his faith, the more it became mine—a faith founded on forgiveness like none I ever expected to find. Talia, I had killed this man. And by his death, he saved me."

In retrospect, Talia should have put it all together earlier, especially with Tyler's fixation on religion, the obsession with crosses and orthodox art. But the whole *faith and forgiveness* angle had surprised her. Still, she wasn't buying it. How could a heartless God, the same God who had stolen her father away, forgive a professional assassin? "I don't want to poke holes in your delusion, but I'm not sure that's how God works."

The harshness of her response did not seem to faze Tyler. "Then you should look into a man named Saul of Tarsus. He was the one looking after the coats." He looked out through the frosted glass to check on Val. "Oops. Here we go."

Ivanov walked straight to Val once he emerged from the customs station, and Talia did not appreciate the way he took her hand when she greeted him. Val made a gesture toward the parking lot doors, and the two set off with Bazin trailing behind, handling the luggage.

"That's it?" Talia asked.

Tyler stood, laying a few euros on the table. "That's it. She's in."

"What now?"

His phone buzzed, and he checked the screen. "Now we head back to the chateau. It looks like your hacker is in a bit of a tizzy." He showed her a text from Eddie.

GET BACK HERE. URGENT.

CHAPTER THIRTY-EIGHT

TYLER DIDN'T WAIT until they had reached the chateau to find out what had Eddie all riled up. As soon as he was clear of the airport, speeding toward the Alps, he used the Tesla's seventeen-inch display to initiate a call. The chateau's great room appeared, with Eddie in the extreme foreground.

"Is that your iPad?" Talia asked.

"What else would it be?"

She didn't answer.

Eddie tilted his head to one side. "You have no idea how huge your head and shoulders are right now. It's like I'm Jack, looking up the giant's nose from the palm of his hand."

"Focus, Eddie," Tyler said, stealing a glance at the display. "What's going on?"

The geek winced. "I'm . . . having trouble locating Finn, our Aussie cat burglar. There are no extreme air shows in the near future and no rumors of his whereabouts. He's vanished."

"Auction houses." Tyler steered the Tesla around a slow-moving semitruck.

"I'm sorry?"

"Look into the big auction houses, Europe only. Cross-

194

reference big-ticket items smaller than a bread box with buyers who own penthouses in the big skyscrapers." Tyler left it at that.

Eddie blinked. "Okay."

"You'll figure out the rest. Is that why you texted me? You needed help with Finn, that's what was so urgent?"

"Uh . . . negative." Suddenly the geek was whispering. He tilted the iPad so they could see over his shoulder. A giant Scotsman with close-cropped red hair and a skintight Bad Boy MMA shirt was seated in one of Tyler's oversize chairs, making it look less oversize than normal. He was devouring a plate full of leftover dumplings. The iPad centered on Eddie again. "He's here. He's big. He's scary. And he's eating everything in the house. I don't know what to do."

"Got it. That makes a lot more sense." Tyler pressed down the accelerator, engaging the instant response of the dual electric motors. "We'll be there in thirty-five minutes."

THIRTY-FIVE MINUTES was not fast enough for Eddie. When Talia and Tyler came through the door, they found Macauley Plucket in the big chair closest to the fireside, surrounded by empty plates. He was picking his teeth with a toothpick, gaze fixed on Eddie, who was huddled up at the far end of the couch across the room like a hunted rabbit holed up in a hedge.

"How is our newest team member?" Tyler asked as Conrad took their coats.

"Demanding, sir, with an appetite to rival a horde of locusts." Conrad looked over his shoulder with a worried smile. "Your *Red Leader* will need some coaching as to how one behaves around hardened criminals, or he may soon be gobbled up as well."

As Tyler walked down the short stair to meet his guest, Talia whispered in his ear. "Remember, you're Lukon."

He cast her a sideways glance. "Thanks. I know who I am."

Tyler handled the introductions while Conrad collected the dishes surrounding the chair.

"Call me Mac, lass." The Scotsman took Talia's hand, then snapped his fingers before Conrad could escape to the kitchen. "Oi, Gran'pa. I'll take more o' them dumplins if you got 'em." He thrust an elbow toward Eddie. "And bring somethin' for Wee Man too. He's lookin' a bit malnourished."

The room turned cold.

The smile on Tyler's face turned deadly. "I'm glad you're with us, Mr. Plucket, but in the future, you will refer to our cook as 'Conrad' or 'sir.' And if you ever snap your fingers at him again, I'll remove your hand and let him serve it back to you as an appetizer."

Mac took a step back. "Yeah. All right. I was just gettin' a feel for the peckin' order."

"And I'm Red Leader," Eddie added, standing up behind Tyler with clenched fists. A hard look from Mac forced his eyes to the floor. "Or whatever." Instead of returning to the couch, Eddie fled upstairs.

Tyler's instant transformation left Talia wondering how much of the former contract killer was still in there. Enough, it seemed, to cow a bruiser three times his size. His smile shifted from deadly to warm again, and he reclined in a high-backed chair. Conrad stoked the fire, and the group chatted. Talia noted the easy way Tyler lured Mac into sharing details of his enforcement jobs—employers, dates, locations. Then their discussion turned toward the heist.

"I get Wee Man," Mac said. "He's yer hacker. I get this Valkyrie woman, yer grifter. An' I'm yer pilot, one of four men in a thousand-mile radius that can handle this Mark Seven o' yours, and the only one o' the lot with a criminal hist'ry." He nodded at Talia. "But I don' get her—sittin' over there all prim and proper like she's better'n the rest of us. What's her part in all this?"

He had her. Talia had forgotten. The Scotsman was not your

average bruiser, all brawn and no brains. He was smart—astronaut smart. She had that sinking feeling that comes from not studying for a pop quiz. "I—"

Tyler cut her off, utterly relaxed, crossing his legs and folding his hands on his knee. "She's CIA."

Talia glared. Had Tyler just sold her out?

Mac glared as well, starting to come out of his chair. "She's what?"

"CIA. Which, as you know, translates to a little corrupt and grossly underpaid. Who do you think brought me the details for this heist? Relax, Mr. Plucket"—he gave Talia a sharp *play along if you want to live* glance—"Talia is no threat. She's the source of your future payday."

Mac was too smart to take his line at face value. He sat back down, narrowing one eye at Talia. "Who's to say she's not playin' us?"

"No one." Talia forced herself to look calm under his stare. She glanced toward Tyler, remembering the part he was playing—a part it seemed he had played before. "But I am certain you're familiar with Lukon's own history with the Agency. When I brought him this opportunity, he assured me of the consequences should I betray him. That's not a risk I plan to take."

Mac did not get the chance to push the argument.

Eddie came down the stairs, peeking around the fireplace at Tyler. "I've got him."

"Got who?" Talia asked.

"Finn. I know where he'll pop up next."

CHAPTER
THIRTY-NINE

CHATEAU TICINO
CAMPIONE D'ITALIA, SWITZERLAND

"I LOOKED INTO THE CURRENT LISTINGS at the big auction houses," Eddie said as the other three joined him in Mission Control. "Like you said—Phillips, Sotheby's, Christie's. And I cross-referenced the priciest small pieces with buyers who own ultra-high penthouses." He let the statement hang, making no move toward his remote keyboard. Eddie knew how to string out a moment.

Talia rolled a finger in the air. "*Annd* you found Finn's next target, correct?"

"It's epic." Eddie threw both hands up toward the rafters. "Epic, I tell you." He brought his fingers down on the keyboard, and the white glowing lines of a holographic blueprint appeared, looking as if they were suspended a foot in front of the center of the parabolic screen.

"You figured out the holographic mode." Tyler folded his arms, chuckling.

"Oh yes." Eddie looked back with a smile. "Yes I did." The holographic blueprints rotated, scrolling up from the base of a narrow, pyramid-shaped skyscraper all the way to its jagged top. "Meet the Shard, in London, the tallest building in Western Europe."

The faint grin on Tyler's lips dropped into a frown. "Eddie, there are no residential tenants in the Shard. All the penthouses are empty."

"Correction. The penthouses *were* empty." The blueprint shifted to a top-down view, looking down through the space between the massive glass panels that served as the Shard's spires. "The four facets of the Shard are triangular panels built to look like uneven shards of glass leaning together. They don't meet at the edges, though, leaving all four corners of the main building open to the air, along with the top fifteen floors."

Talia didn't need a lecture on the building's architecture. Standing there in close proximity to Mac made her uncomfortable, as if by breathing the same air, the Scotsman would realize she was planning to betray him. "Get to the point, Eddie."

"Enter Livingston Boyd." On the screen, left of the hologram, an article covering a wealthy Londoner came up. "Oil and gas magnate in his twenties. Wildly influential. The Shard developers have been unable to fill the top-floor penthouses, but Boyd and one of his sheik buddies cut a secret deal to build three new penthouses suspended in the upper deck." Animated lines appeared within the hologram, forming new structures between the glass spires. "Construction began last year under the guise of utility work."

As usual, Eddie had fallen short of reaching the full point, thanks to the roundabout, level-by-level thinking of a gamer. He preferred to let his audience come up with the solution to beat the final boss. Talia put the last two pieces into place. "And now Boyd is furnishing his new home in the sky with expensive trinkets, one of which Finn will attempt to steal."

"Nailed it." Eddie set the keyboard down, giving her a near-silent round of applause. "Boyd purchased a jeweled Fabergé carriage from an auction at Sotheby's two days ago. Armored transport brought it to the penthouse yesterday."

Mac walked around the table to paw at the hologram. His hand passed right through. "If he wants the prize so much, why wouldn't this Finn character hit the armored transport?"

"What would be the fun in that?" Tyler asked. He turned to leave. "Finn will go in tonight. We need to get to London."

ON TYLER'S INSTRUCTIONS, Mac landed the Gulfstream at an uncontrolled airfield south of London. He was not happy about being left behind to guard it. "Oi, Lukon." The Scotsman poked his great noggin out of the hatch as Tyler and Talia walked across the open apron. "I'm not a one-trick wonder, ya know. I have other skills."

"I know all about your other skills." Tyler turned, walking backward. "But tonight I want you keeping the jet safe and warm. And Mr. Plucket"—he pointed two fingers at his eyes, then directed them at the green hills beyond the runway—"keep a sharp eye. There are thieves about."

Talia suspected Tyler had ulterior motives for making Mac do all the piloting that night. He had closed himself off in the jet's rear bedroom for most of the flight. "What were you doing back there?" she asked as the two boarded a late-night bus into the city.

"Napping." Tyler pulled a pair of Oyster public transport cards from a satchel and swiped them across the reader next to the driver. He handed one to Talia. "I'm old. Remember?"

"Ha-ha." The bus lurched into motion, and Talia grabbed a yellow bar to steady herself as she followed him down the aisle. "I heard voices through the door. I guess you do a pretty good impression of Eddie for someone talking in their sleep."

They sat across from each other, on seats upholstered with riotous pink-and-blue confetti. "You're right," Tyler said. "Eddie did call. He thinks our chemist is also in London."

"And . . ."

"And I told him to get ahold of her."

The bus let them off at the south end of the London Bridge and they strolled down Bridge Street to the base of the Shard. Talia had to tilt her head way back to see the point where the skyscraper's four jagged panels pierced the London clouds, more than a thousand feet above the Thames. It made her dizzy.

She swallowed. "Uh . . . How do we know Finn is up there?"

"He isn't. Not yet." Tyler nodded at a stock ticker, visible through the windows of the adjacent building. The clock below read three minutes to midnight. "Think of the Shard as a vertical city with a late curfew. The city closes its gates at midnight, and reopens them at 4:00 a.m."

"So Finn has a four-hour window to steal the Fabergé."

A street vendor in the corner of the Shard's small square was packing up his cart for the night. Four pounds and a tip of his flatcap bought Tyler two steaming cups of candied nuts. He gave one to Talia. "We may have a long wait ahead."

She didn't get the chance to ask how Tyler planned to get to the top of the vertical city. She didn't need to. The answer came sauntering across the square—a man dressed in the high-visibility coveralls of a window washer. Talia popped a candied nut into her mouth. "You did more than nap and talk to Eddie on the plane, didn't you?"

"Follow my lead. He thinks I'm just a rich guy looking for a thrill."

Talia snorted. "Aren't you?"

CHAPTER FORTY

TYLER TOOK ON A LIMP as they walked out to meet the man, who introduced himself as Bert, and passed him a thick envelope.

Bert tucked it into his coveralls and bid them follow him up an escalator to an open garden on the northwest corner of the structure. The escalator had been shut down for the night. "Six hundred thousand square foot o' glass," Bert said as they climbed the steps, taking it slow in deference to Tyler's fake limp. "Includin' the main panels and the open nooks at each corner—them nooks is the 'ard part. And who do ya think cleans 'em all, eh?"

"You?" Talia gave him her best, brainless *Oh my!* face.

"Correct, miss. Me and my boys." They came to a steel service door. Bert opened it with a simple key. With Tyler's skills—and hers—Talia wasn't quite sure why they needed the window washer. At least he was courteous. He opened the door for her. "After you, miss."

"Bert is the *chief* window cleaner and bottle washer here at the Shard," Tyler interjected. They entered a small locker room filled with gear and overalls. "Right, Bert?"

"That's the size of it, gov. Twelve of us in all. We do the insies, outsies, squeegin', an' repairs." He laid a hand on the door at the opposite end of the locker room. "But we don't do floors, yeah?" Bert laughed. "That's a window washer joke, it is. You know. 'Cause most 'ousemaids don't do—"

"We get it." Tyler pointed at the door. "Is that the way to the box?"

"Yeah. Sure, gov. Follow ol' Bert." As Tyler limped past, the window washer gave him a nudge and a wink, whispering a little too loud. "Lucky man, gov. That un's a beaut, she is."

Talia did her best not to wonder what he meant by it.

Beyond the second door was a glass chamber with a window washer's basket inside, cables running up into darkness. The chamber doors were reinforced with steel ribs and protected by numeric keypads.

Bert swiped a card and entered his code, and the door popped open. He bowed and motioned Talia through. "Your chariot awaits, miss. Green arrow for up. Red for down. Don't touch anythin' else. And don't get any fingerprints on my glass, yeah?" He helped Tyler up into the carbon fiber basket second, catching him as Tyler stumbled. "Easy does it, gov."

Talia caught another wink as Bert closed the glass door. She waited until the basket had risen two floors before asking Tyler about it. "Okay, what was up with all the nudging and winking?"

"Bert thinks I'm about to propose."

She closed her eyes. "Of course he does." After a long pause she added, "When we get back to the chateau, you and I are going to sit down and brainstorm some new cover stories that don't involve marriage or engagements."

The night air grew colder as the basket rose past the third floor in one of the open nooks running all the way to the top. Bert had placed them in the northwestern corner, which had the best view of London proper. The lights of the Tower Bridge and St. Paul's came into view. Talia turned away. The higher they went, the less she wanted to look.

Tyler rested his hips against the basket rail next to the controls, settling in for the climb. "Tiffany's, Mac Jazeera, a dozen major banks, and global investment groups—they're all here. Lexan glass, biometric locks on the office doors, a small army of security in the lobby and on the fifty-fourth floor. But the service entrance and elevators for the window washers?" He chuckled. "It's the same all over London. You want quiet access to a high-security building, you talk to the Washers Guild. They're the chimney sweeps of the twenty-first century."

The basket moved upward at a crawl. Talia felt like pacing, but she had nowhere to go. "Eighty floors. We'll miss Finn at this rate."

"Let's see if we can speed things up." Tyler pushed an earpiece into place and signaled for her to do the same. "Eddie, we're up on comms."

"Welcome to the Matrix," the geek said from his Mission Control room at the chateau. "Call me Red Leader."

"No," Talia said.

"And Mac will be Wheels."

"Not on your life, Wee Man."

Talia heard a sigh through her earpiece. "You people are no fun. Did you get what I asked for?"

"Coming to you now." Tyler removed Bert-the-window-washer's key card from his breast pocket and swiped it through a handheld reader. That explained the limp, which set the stage for the feigned stumble while getting into the basket. He had picked Bert's pocket. He held the card under the glow from his phone and squinted at the small print. "You're looking for Digby . . . Bert. The code he typed in was four-five-seven-one-three-six." Tyler lowered the card and looked out at the night. "Can you speed us up?"

"Working on it now."

The basket jolted to a stop. Talia grabbed the railing to keep from pitching over the side. "Eddie!"

"Still Red Leader, thank you. Patience please. I'm typing in raw code, here. It's not an exact science."

"Actually, it is."

"Yeah. Okay. Good point." The basket started moving again, at twice its original speed. "Three meters per second," Eddie said. "That's as fast as she goes—up, anyway. Going down is an entirely different story."

Down did not make Talia feel any better.

At its new speed, the basket passed the viewing platform on the seventy-second floor less than a minute later. Above that, the main structure gave way to an open cloud deck where glass walkways and styled metal scaffolding joined the three penthouses to the spires. The middle penthouse boasted an in-finity pool on its upper balcony, already filled even though the apartment was not yet finished. Sporadic rainfall filtered down through the spires above to disturb the waters, and Talia won-dered if the shower had started during their ascent, or if they had simply climbed high enough to meet it.

The basket stopped at the roof of a glass walkway connecting an elevator shaft to the top penthouse—the new London home of Livingston Boyd.

"Keep a firm grip and don't look down," Tyler said and helped her climb out of the basket past an ankle-high rail designed for the clips and tackle of the window washers.

"Don't look down." Talia latched a hand onto Tyler's belt, wobbling on the edge of vertigo as they walked. "Everyone says that, but it never helps."

The walkway ended at a small lobby, little more than a throw rug and a pair of potted trees. They dropped in through a wash-er's access panel and stepped up to a twelve-foot bronze door.

Tyler gave it a perfunctory knock. "Red Leader, we're at the penthouse."

"Copy. Stand by."

The door beeped and then clicked. Tyler gave it a tug and it swung wide on brand-new hinges. He grinned at Talia. "Knock and the door—"

"Will be opened." She walked past him. "Yeah. I get it. I went to Sunday school every week until I was seven."

The Fabergé carriage had found a prominent place among the pricey knickknacks Boyd had used to furnish his new place. It sat on the recessed mantel of a marble fireplace, surrounded by other Fabergé artifacts—eggs, a castle, a spherical clock. Talia cringed as Tyler used his pinky to open the carriage door, but no alarms sounded. Tinkling music played. The six miniature horses reared their heads one after the other.

"The genius of Fabergé is not merely in the application of jewels or scrollwork"—Tyler stepped back to admire the piece— "but in the intermingling of motion, beauty, and sound, inspired by the ballets of his time."

Talia knew all about the excesses of the nineteenth-century Romanov jeweler, and at that moment she didn't care. They had bigger concerns. "What about our cat burglar? The chief window washer let us inside. Who will Finn use? The deputy?"

"Not Finn's style." Tyler crossed the open great room to a wall of windows looking out through the Shard's spires to the city beyond. He drew a short scope from his satchel and scanned the night sky. "He's a preening egoist in the tradition of the old swashbucklers. Common sense takes a back seat to feats of derring-do."

Tyler held the scope still and motioned for Talia to take a look. The rain clouds parted like curtains, revealing a field of stars, brilliant in the blue-green of the light-enhanced display. At the dead center was a weather balloon.

"That's him," Talia said. "Not exactly original. He's using the same entrance he used at Bellavista."

"Don't be so sure."

Tyler was right. Talia took control of the scope, watching as Finn's dark form dropped from his launching platform. There were no sparks and no ball of flame. Whatever material he had used for the balloon burned up with barely a flicker in the scope—invisible to the naked eye.

The dark form rocketed down through the gap between the spires and then jerked as a black chute opened, with mere inches of clearance. Finn leveled out and sailed along a glass walkway exactly as he had sailed down the glacier runway.

Talia backed away from the window and placed the scope in Tyler's waiting hand. "We should hide."

"No need."

After a jogging landing on the walkway roof, Finn cut his chute loose and aimed a bulky pistol at some unseen target above the penthouse. He fired a hook and cable, clipped the gun to his harness, and leaped into space, swinging over to the windows.

He hit the glass with a *thump* right in front of Tyler, and began fishing around in a pouch dangling from his belt.

"Mirrored glass." Tyler exchanged his scope for a flashlight. "He can't see me. Yet. Watch this."

Tyler waited until Finn had affixed a large suction cup to the window, then put his nose to the glass directly opposite the thief's face and flipped on his light.

With a muted shout, Finn kicked away, arms flailing. He recovered quickly, though, and swung back to the same spot. He pressed his eyes close.

Tyler gave him a finger-wiggling wave.

Finn rolled his eyes and laid his head against the glass.

CHAPTER FORTY-ONE

WEARING A *WHAT IS YOUR PROBLEM?* FACE, the Australian cat burglar motioned Tyler back and drew what might have been a toothpaste tube from his pouch. He drew a wide circle of white goo around the suction cup, slipped the tube back into the pouch, and held on to the suction cup's handle.

Vapors rose from the goo. Talia heard a distinctive *crack*, and Finn pushed the circle of glass inside. He ducked his head in and held the circle out to Tyler. "As long as you're here, you might as well make yourself useful, yeah?"

Tyler obliged him, taking the circle and setting it on the floor.

One limb at a time, Finn entered the penthouse, unclipped his line, and walked past the other two. He turned to face them, rubbing his arms with gloved hands. "Whew. Cold out there. Hope you enjoyed the show. No autographs tonight. I forgot my special pen."

"Funny." Tyler made no move to grab the thief or block the door. "Sorry about the light. I didn't think you'd scare so easily."

"Surprised, mate. The word you're looking for is surprised."

"Could've fooled me." Tyler took a seat on Livingston Boyd's brand-new velvet couch. "You used a complicated ingress. Showy, but not very elegant."

"Not elegant? I dropped in from three thousand feet and threaded the needle between the spires."

"You left your chute behind. And you broke a window."

"And I suppose you bribed a window washer, who could testify against you in court."

Tyler shrugged.

"Typical." Finn wandered over to the mantel. "I see you haven't nicked the carriage yet. I'd say that makes it fair game." He gestured at the hole in the window. "Exit's over there."

Talia couldn't take much more of Finn's cockiness. The snow-bunnies might have melted at his accent, but she found it abrasive. "We didn't come for the Fabergé. We came for you."

"Bellavista, right? The motorbike? I shoulda recognized you earlier, but—to be fair—women chase me all the time."

Talia's hand went to her Glock.

"We're here to offer you a job." Tyler shot her a glance that said, *Let it go.*

"You're Mr. Lukon, right?" Finn walked into the kitchen and cracked open Boyd's fridge. "I heard through the vine you were looking for me."

"Lukon. Just Lukon. The payout is good."

"Don't need a payout—not from you." Finn drew a water bottle from the fridge, looking disappointed he had found nothing else, and pointed it at the mantel. "I'm about to score a million and a half."

Talia was no thief, but she knew Finn was overstating his take. She called him out. "That's what it sold for at auction. You'll never get the same on the street."

"Really, sweetums. What do you know about it?"

"Sweetums?"

"Don't do it for the money, then," Tyler interjected. "Do it for the challenge. I'm talking about a target in the mesosphere, literally the mesosphere. Record-breaking. You'll be a legend."

"I already am a legend."

Talia let go of the Glock, raising her hand. "I'd never heard of you until three days ago."

Finn gave her a half grin. "Not interested. Now, if you'll both excuse me, I'll take my treasure and go. Feel free to help yourself to the egg. It'll probably fetch a hundred K or so."

He took a step toward the mantel and Tyler shook his head. "I wouldn't do that."

"Why not, Mr. Lukon?"

"Just Lukon. Do you know what this is?" Tyler lifted a small silver remote from the burl-wood coffee table.

Finn stiffened. "That's a panic system."

"Correct. Rich people are so paranoid. This one is brand new. Perhaps we should test it out for Mr. Boyd."

Finn raised his hands, lips parting in genuine surprise. "Okay, mate. You have my attention. No need to be rash."

"Sorry. We've already started down this path. Might as well see where it leads." Tyler mashed down the button.

Alarms sounded. Strobe lights flashed. Finn made a grab for the carriage, but a steel gate dropped down over the recessed mantel, nearly crushing his fingers. He growled at Tyler. "You're insane."

"And now you need me."

"What's happening?" Eddie asked through the comms. "I'm reading an alarm in the building."

"Ty—" Talia cringed inside at the blunder she'd almost made. "*Lukon* pressed Boyd's panic button. Can you shut it down?"

The alarm went silent. The flashing stopped. "Done. But the system alerted a guard station twenty floors down. They'll be entering a high-speed elevator any moment now. You have thirty seconds."

"Can you stop the elevator?"

"Don't." Tyler squared his shoulders, standing between Finn and his hole in the glass. "What'll it be? A payday with us or prison? You may never reach the prison. This building is owned by Qataris. They don't always play by the rules."

The two stared each other down.

Tyler's fingers tapped against the side of his leg. "The guards are coming, Finn."

"I'm in."

"Good. Eddie, stop the elevator."

"I stopped it twenty seconds ago, but it's moving again. They must have a manual override. I can't get control."

As if to punctuate the fear in Eddie's voice, the bronze door burst open. Two men in cheap black suits barged in with guns extended. The first locked his aim on Talia. "Freeze!"

As Talia went for her Glock, Finn dropped the guy from behind with a flying elbow.

The guard stumbled unconscious into his partner and both of their guns slid across the floor. Finn and the second guard dove after them. The guard got there first, shoved Finn away with a wild kick, and scooped up a weapon. Rolling over again, he pointed the gun at Talia—the only one of his intruders holding a weapon. He pulled the trigger.

"No!" Tyler threw his body in front of Talia's as the guard cracked off three rounds. The window shattered. Talia and Tyler crashed through into empty space.

FORTY-TWO

THE SHARD
LONDON, UNITED KINGDOM

THE GLITTER OF BROKEN GLASS.

The strange pelting of raindrops falling only a little faster than she.

Talia had felt that weightless, tumbling sensation once before, in a place she could only recall in her nightmares. Water rushed up at her, littered with the tiny ringlets from the rain shower. Was it water in that ditch beside the road? Was she back again?

A jarring impact.

She sank into darkness.

"Talia!" the voice was close, but faint, as if calling to her through a brick wall.

"Talia. Can you hear me?"

She couldn't answer. She forced her eyes open and saw her father's face, scruffy and smiling, hovering above her.

"*Puiule Natalia,* do you hear me? It is time to wake up."

Talia rubbed her eyes and looked around at her bedroom. *The Cat in the Hat* still lay atop the covers from when he had read her to sleep the night before. She pushed it aside and sat up against her pillow. "It's still dark outside."

"That is the point, is it not?" His Romanian accent had never left him, even after a decade in the United States. "Did you forget what day it is?"

She had forgotten. She had forgotten so many things about that day. It took Talia a moment as the fog of sleep cleared. Then a smile spread across her seven-year-old lips. "My birthday."

"Yes! Get dressed. I will get the tackle and the poles."

Not many of the girls in Talia's class loved fishing. But they had mothers, aunts, and sisters. Talia had her father. No one else. And fishing in the Potomac was their thing.

A light shower wet the roads as they pulled out of the driveway of their little Virginia duplex. No big deal. Talia had packed her red galoshes, and a little rain would give her a reason to cuddle close to her father on the riverbank, sheltering beneath his umbrella.

But even as the thought occurred to her, Talia knew they would never reach the river.

Time shot forward through rain and mist down the gray ribbon of the road, halted by a flash of headlights and the blaring of a horn. Her father muttered as the other driver whipped past in fog so thick it gave Talia the sensation of flying through clouds. Little Talia loved the idea of flying.

As if in a trance, the seven-year-old pulled her shoulder harness out of the way and pressed her eyes closer to the windshield.

"*Natalia*, not a good idea." Her father reached over to push her back again, swerving in the process.

Bang.

A flash of yellow.

Talia screamed in surprise and confusion, but the grown-up inside her knew the front right tire had burst, cut by a two-inch drop at the shoulder of the new asphalt. The accident report she had read a hundred times told her as much.

Her father fought the skid, but physics outmatched him and the car rolled. The trees spun. The fog that had so fascinated

Talia churned and swirled until the car smashed down into a half-filled ditch. The glass shattered. Water rushed in.

"Daddy?" Talia hung upside down from her lap belt. "Daddy?"

"*Puiule Natalia.*" His voice was a whisper—constrained, weak. Blood tinted the broken glass beneath him.

"*Puiule Na . . .*" His eyes closed.

"Daddy!"

With a *smash*, the remains of Talia's window came flying in. A black knife, exactly like one she had seen on her father's bookshelf, sliced past her eyes and cut her lap belt. Strong arms pulled her free.

"No! Daddy!"

"Don't kick, honey. The glass. Don't kick."

She didn't care. Talia kicked and thrashed all the more, cutting both legs, but the strong arms were relentless. They tore her away from her father. His form faded and disappeared among the twisted aluminum.

Talia's thrashing made her slip down, but not enough to escape her captor's grasp. The strong arms did not bother pulling her into the air again. They dragged her, pink, flowery Keds leaving tracks of mud across the asphalt. She came to a stop on a grassy bank, and the strong arms took the form of a broad-shouldered silhouette. Her captor positioned himself between her and the car. Talia scrambled to rise. The man pinned her down with one hand, looking back. He watched, but he made no move toward the car.

"Help him! Help my daddy!"

"Close your eyes, honey. Please, close your eyes. Don't look."

She did look.

The car exploded. A fireball lit up the trees.

"Daddy!"

In the sudden light, Talia saw the man's eyes—green, rimmed with gold. He closed them for a moment, and she thought she saw a tear. "Natalia. That's your name, right? Are you Natalia?"

Talia woke with a start, feeling the strong arms around her once again. They dragged her over the rough concrete at the edge of a swimming pool. Fighting a dull pain in her neck, she tilted her head back to look up, and found the same green eyes.

"Talia, are you all right?"

Tyler. It was Tyler standing over her. Boyd's penthouse, with its broken window, lay two stories above him.

"Wha . . . I . . ." Talia blinked. They were on the open deck of the unfinished penthouse below Boyd's. The pool had saved them, and Tyler had pulled her out—the way he had pulled her out of the wreck years before.

Was that right?

Talia looked at him hard. Those green eyes. Pupils rimmed with gold. Those were the eyes from her memory. Had Tyler been present at her father's death, or was trauma of the present inserting itself into the muddled memory of a trauma long past?

As soon as Tyler had her on her feet, Talia backed away from him.

"What is it? You look terrified."

"It's nothing. I'm . . . okay. Sore, but okay."

Chlorinated water showered them both as Finn dropped to the pool in a cannonball dive. "Couldn't let you two have all the fun," he said, pushing himself up onto the deck. He strolled over to Tyler, reaching behind his back and producing two handguns. "Both guards are out cold. I borrowed these. You're welcome."

"Thanks." Tyler took the weapons and threw them into the pool. He winced at the motion, stumbling sideways.

Talia caught his arm, letting go of her trust issues for the moment. "What's wrong?"

"He took two bullets in the back on your account," Finn said, wringing out his shirt. "That's what."

Tyler pulled off his black sweater. He wore a bulletproof vest beneath. When he unstrapped it and lifted his T-shirt, Talia saw two big welts between his shoulder blades. She touched them. He drew in a sharp breath. "You'll have some serious bruises," she said, "but you'll live." She moved her hand a little higher. There was a third bruise, far more developed, on his right shoulder. "What's this?"

"A bruise. I get them all the time. Must have happened in Venice." Tyler pulled the shirt back into place. He found Talia's Glock lying on the pavement and pressed it into her hands. "We need to go. Those guards won't stay down forever."

A little coordination with Eddie and a quick climb down to another glass walkway brought them to the same window washer basket. When Talia dropped down onto the walkway roof, she teetered.

Finn caught her. "Easy there. I've got ya." He had his hands around her waist.

Talia had grabbed his biceps for support. They might as well have been steel cables. She let go and pushed his hands away. "I'm fine. I can handle myself."

Finn frowned. "All right. I didn't mean anything by it."

As soon as he turned away, Talia dropped the defiance from her expression and threw out her arms for balance. She felt like collapsing onto the glass—crawling the rest of the way. But she held it together. She even refused his help a second time when she climbed down into the window washer basket.

The descent took an agonizingly slow ninety seconds. "Where's Bert the Window Washer King?" Talia asked as they reached the bottom.

"Gone." Tyler hopped out of the basket. "We're blown."

Eddie confirmed it. "Your friends from the penthouse reported in. I'm getting tons of chatter on the security net. They have men at the front entrance. More are headed your way."

"Understood." Tyler pushed through the service exit, out into the rain, and led them east, quickstepping along a raised pedestrian plaza.

There were voices from behind. Talia glanced over her shoulder as a pack of guards appeared at the top of the escalators, most of Arab descent. "Here they come."

All three broke into a run. "Eddie, what's the status of our contingency?"

"It's Red Leader."

"Eddie!"

"The contingency option is ready, and I'm locked on to your GPS. I'll guide you from here."

Without an earpiece of his own, Finn was only getting half the conversation. "What contingency? What've you two drongos gotten me into?"

Talia felt like asking the same question, although she had no idea what a drongo was. It didn't matter, she couldn't get a word in between Eddie's directions.

"Take a right—no, a left . . . Yes. Left . . . *Now* right . . . Okay, straight. Doing fine."

They entered a low tunnel. It looked like a good escape route until Eddie turned them left once more and they found their path blocked by an iron gate. Talia skidded to a stop between Tyler and Finn. "This is not fine, Eddie. This is a dead end."

The Shard security men turned the corner and slowed, raising their weapons as they advanced. "You there! Don't move!"

"Look around," Eddie said. "Help is nigh."

"What help?"

Tyler answered for the geek. "Darcy Emile."

At his cue, a young black woman stepped out of the shadows to Talia's right, pulling back the hood of a red sweatshirt. She accepted an earpiece from Tyler and gestured at the floor. "*Bonjour, mes amies.* Please step to the center of the circle."

Talia had not noticed before, but the four of them all stood within a circle of some dark metal, laid out on the concrete floor. Darcy spread her hands and scrunched the three of them together at the center.

"I said don't move!" The lead guard stopped a few feet from

the strip with his men behind. "Hands." He poked the air between them with his gun. "Show us your hands."

"Do not move. Show you the hands." The French chemist made a *tsk* sound with her tongue. "Which is it? Make up your mind, yes?"

Her challenge confused the man. "I . . . You . . ."

"You . . . I . . ." Darcy mimicked his stammering. "Forget it." She pressed the earpiece into her ear. "Red Leader, it is time, no?"

"Red Leader," Eddie sighed into the comms. "I love the way you say that. Welcome to the team. Stand by for detonation in three, two . . ."

A red warning flag went up in Talia's mind. *"Detona—"*

" . . . one."

A rapid series of explosions drowned out the remainder of her question.

FORTY-THREE

PEDESTRIAN COMPLEX EAST OF THE SHARD
LONDON, UNITED KINGDOM

THE NOISE AND A CLOUD OF DUST forced the security team back as the floor dropped beneath Talia's feet. The circle of concrete slammed into another circle of concrete, and then another, still falling, with Talia and the others fighting for balance. The three stacked pieces finally smashed down on rusty tracks. Finn caught Talia's arm to keep her from tumbling off.

The dust cleared, revealing an underground train tunnel lit by work lights. A black SUV sat idling beside the tracks. Talia hobbled down from the slabs on shaky legs. Finn gave her a hand. "Bet you didn't know the Shard sat on top of the London Bridge Train Station."

Darcy stepped down as if stepping off an elevator and started toward the SUV. "Mr. Lukon—"

"Lukon!" The other three cut her off in unison.

"Just . . . Lukon," Tyler finished.

She looked back at them like they were all insane. "Yes. Okay. Whatever. Do we argue about the saying of the names, or do we get in the car?"

"Car." Tyler brushed the dust off his arms. "I'm driving."

MAC HAD THE GULFSTREAM warmed up and ready at the airfield. Tyler spent the first few minutes of the flight changing out of his gear and then handed the bedroom off to Talia to do the same. As he walked forward through the main cabin, Finn and Darcy were arguing over why she got an earpiece and the Aussie didn't.

"It is a matter of position." The chemist held the device close to her eye, appraising it like a diamond. "A matter of one's importance. I am a specialist. My work depends on split-second timing."

Finn's jaw dropped. "And mine doesn't?"

"*Evidemment*, yes? Else Lukon would have given you one." She held the earpiece out, only to snatch it away as he reached for it. "You do not need an earpiece because you are—how do you say?—a grunt. A *minion*."

"You're insane."

"Everyone says that. But I do not see it."

Tyler let the conversation fade as he entered the flight deck. He tapped Mac on the shoulder. "I'll take over for a while."

The big pilot half turned in his seat, expression dour. "You didn't bring me on the job. You won't let me fly. What did you hire me for, any—"

A sharp look ended his complaint.

"Right." Mac punched the autopilot like a giant pouting teen and squeezed himself out from behind the controls. "All yours, then."

The deep contusions from the guard's bullets stabbed at Tyler's spine as he lowered himself into the seat. He prayed the damage was not too extensive. Bulletproof vests were not well-named. *Bullet-resistant* would be more accurate. Focused shockwaves still penetrated the body, chipping bones and bruising organs. He didn't let the pain show on his face. "Try not to clean out the galley stores. The rest of us get hungry too. And, Mr. Plucket"—he glanced over his shoulder—"send Finn up. I need to speak with him."

Tyler needed to maintain a tight hold on that one. Outside of Talia, Plucket was his biggest wild card. Val, he understood, for the most part. Eddie was loyal to a fault. Darcy's insanity made her strangely predictable. But Plucket? Tyler shook his head. The Scotsman would always have one foot out the door and one hand in the till. Without the right balance of carrot and stick, he could betray the team at any moment.

Finn rapped the bulkhead with a knuckle. "You wanted something?"

"Close the door." Tyler waited for the kid to take the copilot seat, then rested an elbow on his armrest and leaned close, lowering his voice to a growl. "What I want is exactly what I asked you for. Did you get it?"

"As requested. Found it in Boyd's desk drawer after you and the girl took your tumble." Finn pulled a thumb drive from a pocket and held it between them. "Good show slipping the job offer into my pocket on the glacier. I didn't find it for an hour—thought I'd gotten the best of ya."

"We'll have to do a rematch sometime." Tyler took the thumb drive and tucked it away. "You played your part well in the penthouse. There'll be a bonus for you in the end."

The Aussie sat back, putting one foot up on the padding at the base of the instrument panel. "We could have called it even if you'd let me have the Fabergé."

"I couldn't do that." Tyler slapped his leg down. "Feet off the leather. Were you raised in a barn?"

"Melbourne. Close enough." Finn laid his head back against the headrest and rolled it over to look at Tyler. "What's the deal with the girl? Why bring a mark on a heist?"

"Talia is no mark."

"Could've fooled me."

"She's our *in*. That's all you need to know." Tyler intended to make that the end of the conversation, but the thief kept watching him. He sighed. "You have something else to say?"

221

"She's a bright girl, that one. She'll figure out the game soon enough. And when that happens, you'll have a hard choice to make." His eyes turned grave. "You saved her from the guard's bullets. Good on ya, mate. But when she looks behind the curtain and sees you for who you really are, who's gonna save her from yours?"

FORTY-FOUR

SOMEWHERE OVER FRANCE

TALIA KEPT HER DISTANCE from the others during the return to Switzerland. How had she gotten there, trapped in an aluminum tube with a French bomber, a Scottish enforcer, and an egomaniacal Australian cat burglar with a clear death wish? Not to mention the man at the helm, a questionably former assassin who had made cameos in her nightmares.

Jordan had once warned Talia that a CIA operations officer might often find herself in a den of thieves. Talia had pictured an unsavory pub, not a Gulfstream flying over the Ardennes. The private jet was plush and clean, but a smoky, back-alley dive seemed safer. In her imagination, there had always been a door marked EXIT—one she could use at any time.

The group reached the chateau in the wee hours of the morning. Eddie met them at the door, and Talia tried to signal him with a *something's not right* look, but he only had eyes for Darcy. He followed the chemist into the great room, chattering away.

Darcy dropped her bag beside the fireplace, looking utterly confused. "Wait. *You* are the Red Leader?"

"Yes—" Eddie coughed, dropping his voice to an ill-fitting baritone. "Yes I am."

"But you are so small and . . ." Darcy repeatedly snapped her fingers. "What is the word?"

"Weak," Mac offered.

"Yes. Weak." She poked Eddie's arms as if inspecting a life-size doll. "Weak is precisely the word."

If Eddie hadn't ignored her when the group walked in, Talia would have felt sorry for him. He stood there as the chemist removed his glasses, looked backward through the lenses, and then returned them to his face, somewhat askew. She made a *pbbt* sound with her lips and threw a hand in the air. "I am exhausted. I must sleep."

"Of course, madam." Conrad shot Talia and Tyler a cross-eyed glance as he bent to pick up Darcy's bag. "Please follow me to your room. May I take your coat and . . . any explosive or incendiary devices you may be carrying?"

Talia did not see where she pulled it from, but Darcy slapped a gray cylinder with wires protruding from both ends into his waiting hand.

"I suggest we *all* sleep," Tyler said, stepping to the center of the room. "We'll reconvene for a late brunch."

Eddie wouldn't sleep. Talia knew that. He had likely slept a good bit already while the rest of them were riding home on the jet. She gave the others half an hour to settle in before she crept down the hallway to his room and lightly pounded on the door. "Eddie?"

He opened it an inch. Talia pushed inside and closed the door behind her. She wrapped him in a hug. Despite his buffoonery with Darcy, Eddie was the only person within a thousand miles she could trust. She laid her head on his shoulder and let out a breath as if she'd been holding it since London.

"Um . . . ," Eddie said. "This is new." He pried himself away. "If this is about Darcy, I swear I won't let my relationship with her affect our friendship." He cocked his head, narrowing one eye as if something else had just occurred to him. "And if this is about *competition* with Darcy"—Eddie stretched his lips back in a *this is awkward* grimace—"we've known each other a long time and I've only recently come to grips with the fact we're—"

"Eddie!" Talia punched him in the chest before he said anything that would haunt her eidetic memory forever. "This is not about Darcy."

Glancing around, she found a pen and pad on the nightstand and wrote a quick note, holding it low between them.

Sweep for bugs and cameras

He lifted a puzzled gaze to Talia. She twisted her features into a *Just do it already* frown.

If there were any cameras in the room, they got quite a show. Eddie launched into a terrible mix of pantomime and forced conversation as he opened an app on his smartphone and began wandering around the room. "Thanks for dropping by, Talia," he said with mechanical rhythm, waving the phone across the wall. "How about that Gulfstream?" He bent backward, limbo-style, to scan a bedside lamp. "Pretty cool, right?"

Shakespeare, he was not. But—Eddie's performance aside—the scanning app hadn't picked up any bugs. He showed her the green check marks on the screen. "No transmitters. No cameras. We're in the clear. What's this about? Why am I scanning a room in Tyler's house?"

"Because Tyler is not who we think he is." The dam burst. All the thoughts and fears she had been suppressing since London came flooding out—her nightmares, the vision she had when she crashed into the pool. "Tyler was there, Eddie, at my dad's accident."

The validation she wanted—needed—never appeared in his expression. Eddie retreated to his bed. "Talia, the mind is a funny thing. New images blend with the old. Remember what we learned about interrogation pitfalls at the Farm. Memories get mixed up all the time."

"Not mine. I saw him, Eddie. Tyler was involved in my father's death. And I think he may have orchestrated the attack on Avantec too."

She expected Eddie to write that theory off as well, but he looked up at her, nodding. "You found an extra bruise when you were checking his back." He shrugged off Talia's look of surprise. "I heard your conversation over the comms. I can read between the lines."

"Yes. On his right shoulder." The old pain in Talia's side began to ache, and she suddenly felt as if her legs would not support her. She pulled the chair out from under the room's small desk and sat down. "I shot the man who killed Ella Visser. I heard the grunt when I hit him."

"And the placement of the wound, the development of the bruise—it all works out with your shot and the timing, assuming the killer had been wearing a bulletproof vest, correct?"

She nodded.

"It's thin."

"I know." Talia didn't say anything else for a while. There was something safe about leaving the implications of it all in the realm of mere theory. But theory wasn't what she had trained for. She rubbed at that annoying ache in her side and took the first step down the road before her. "We need more intel—hard evidence. Start with my dad's accident."

"Talia . . ."

"I'm serious. If Tyler was involved, then the Agency was too. Dig into the records. See what you can find."

Eddie looked down at his fingers, fidgeting. "That's against policy."

"Not if we can tie it to the active mission. Solving one mystery may lead us to answers for the other." It was a long shot. But Talia pushed her friend. "Eddie, I need this."

"Okay. I'll see what I can find. In the meantime, get some rest."

Get some rest. An easy thing for a concerned friend to advise. A harder thing to execute when bedtime arrived in that surreal stretch between *way too late* and dawn.

Talia's mind wouldn't stop grinding on the vision of Tyler. She rolled over in bed, flipped on the lamp, and reached for her worn copy of *The Cat in the Hat,* but then she noticed the Bible resting beside it on the bedside table. What had Tyler told her? *Look into a man named Saul of Tarsus. He was the one looking after the coats.*

Talia knew enough to look for Paul, instead of Saul. The translation was readable, not one of those old-English King James versions, and it had an index at the back. The list of entries led her to the seventh chapter of Acts. A man named Stephen gave an impassioned sermon amid his own trial, and at the end he accused the men before him of murdering "the Righteous One." They stoned him for it. Such a brutal execution must have been sweaty work, because—as Tyler had said—they laid their coats at the feet of a man named Saul.

Talia read on into the next chapter and found the next mention of the man. *Saul began to destroy the church. Going from house to house, he dragged off both men and women and put them in prison.* The image that came to her reminded her of the Nazis, dragging innocents from their homes. She closed the book. She knew the rest of the story. On the Damascus road, during his purge of the new church, Saul met Jesus in the form of a voice and a blinding light. He became Paul, one of the most powerful and zealous leaders of early Christianity.

What had Tyler meant to accomplish by directing her to Paul's story? She had an inkling. Paul had watched the stoning of Stephen with approval. He had stormed homes like a Nazi to drag off early Christians. Yet God had forgiven him. Maybe Tyler saw himself that way, an assassin who met with his own light on a Damascus road. His actions at the Shard, throwing his body between her and the guard's bullets, spoke of a man so reformed. But Talia's suspicions about his involvement in Dr. Visser's murder spoke of someone else entirely.

And how did Tyler fit into her father's accident?

Talia winced as the pain in her side flared. She tossed back a pair of painkillers and rolled over again, letting her worries dissolve into chaotic dreams.

CHAPTER FORTY-FIVE

THE CHATEAU HAD FILLED UP. Talia awoke to the sounds of her new team of elite thieves stirring in the halls, murmuring in an array of accents. She showered and dressed in slacks and a blouse, having no intention of appearing downstairs in her jammies despite the warm scents of cinnamon and tarragon luring her from her room.

When she finally poked her head through the kitchen doorway, Conrad was pulling a pan of pastries out of the oven. "Would you like some *potica*? Half are walnut and apple, the other half are filled with feta and"—he held up a thumb and forefinger—"the thinnest layer of ground sausage. Try one of each. You won't regret it."

"I'll never regret trying your creations, Conrad." *Except the next time I step on a scale.* She accepted a plate with two pastries and turned to see Tyler and Val entering from the garage. "Val? Shouldn't you be in Milan with Ivanov?"

Val's shirt was half untucked from her skirt, and several hairs had escaped the confines of her ponytail. She gave Talia a frustrated smile. "I have less than an hour before I need to get back. So maybe we could skip the whole little-girl-asking-obvious-questions bit?"

Tyler stole Talia's plate and set it aside. "Brunch can wait. Gather the troops. We have a problem."

Conrad, perhaps as a form of resistance to the affront of Tyler confiscating Talia's pastries, carried the full brunch spread up to Mission Control while Talia collected the thieves. Val did not touch a bite of food, and only gave cursory responses to Finn and Darcy when they introduced themselves. She sat next to Eddie at the conference table, tapping a foot against the bottom rung of her stool and checking her watch every few seconds.

"Could we?" she asked as Tyler came through the door.

Tyler gave Eddie a nod. "Let's hear it, *Red Leader*." The way he used Eddie's nom de guerre was not complimentary.

Eddie avoided his gaze and addressed the group. "I . . . missed a small detail in my evaluation of Gryphon's security."

Val grumbled something under her breath.

Eddie blushed. "Okay. I missed a *big* detail."

For the sake of their newest recruits, Eddie rehashed the overall plan. He explained the need to steal the Mark Seven so Mac could fly it up to the mesosphere, giving them direct access to the hypersonic plans stored on Gryphon. "Valkyrie is working Ivanov for the voiceprint ID that will get us past the ship's security protocols, but . . ." He hesitated, looking down.

Val slapped him on the back. "Spit it out."

"But the designs for Gryphon I obtained were outdated. There was a late addendum." He looked to Talia with an apologetic gaze. "Ivanov changed the layer of security at Gryphon's pressure seal. Instead of a ten-digit cypher code, we need a key."

"You mean a keyword?" Mac asked, mouth filled with pastry.

"No. I mean a physical key." Eddie lifted a hand, holding the imaginary object. "A half-inch-diameter stick of synthetic quartz. It should look something like the data crystals used in Superman's fortress of solitude."

Mac and Finn exchanged a glance.

Talia closed her eyes and shook her head. "Eddie, a lot of people don't know what that means."

"Then *a lot of people* need to rent the movie."

Tyler sat forward on the couch, still scowling. "Can't you just put it on the screen?"

Eddie gave him a shrug. "I could make something up, but I don't have the exact design."

"Which means we can't make our own without stealing the original." Val laid a conference badge and a hotel key card on the table. "I brought these for Finn. The quartz key is probably in Ivanov's room. When I give the all clear, Finn can go in and—"

"Finn won't be going in," Tyler said. "He'll be at the airfield, scoping out the security measures for the Mark Seven with Mr. Plucket and me. You're the better choice, anyway. The hotel staff already knows you."

"Can't do it. Ivanov wants me at his side whenever he leaves his room. I was only able to get away this time because he had a late night and he's still asleep."

"Then we give him a reason to leave you behind."

"And how do we do that?"

Tyler turned to Talia.

She stared right back at him. "Why are you looking at me?"

"Set up a meeting, Talia. Today. Tell him it's urgent. You flew in to give him a security update."

Val backed him up. "Yes. Perfect. Ivanov is sure to leave me behind if he's going off to see Talia. He's a typical Eastern European playboy. He won't want two of his imaginary fillies meeting face-to-face." She let out a flat laugh. "Talia knows what I mean. Horrendous flirt. *Exhausting*. Right, Talia?"

The hurt welling up in Talia's chest must have shown on her face, because Val took on a look of mock surprise. "Oh. I'm sorry, darling. Did you think you were special?"

"Pavel is not a flirt. Maybe you're getting the wrong signals."

"Yeah . . . Signals are kind of my thing." Val picked up the key card again, pointing it at her before shoving it in her purse. "Set up the meeting. I'll search the room." She flicked Tyler's arm on her way to the door. "Keep an eye on your girl. She's too emotionally invested."

When the others filed out, Eddie walked over to the door and pushed it closed. "I have something for you."

He had his fidget spinner out. He was nervous. A cold, tingling feeling washed over Talia, and she sat down on one of the conference table stools. "Something about my dad?"

"Sorry. I'm still working on that."

"Oh." The tingling went away. "Then why did you wait until we were alone?"

"Because this is about Tyler's extra bruise, and the idea he might actually *be—*"

"Lukon?" It was the first time Talia had made the association out loud, and she found she didn't want to hear it, even from her own lips. Whatever Tyler's involvement in her father's accident, she didn't want to believe he would betray her.

Eddie returned to the conference table and started working the keyboard with one hand, bouncing the spinner from one finger to the next in the other. "One aspect of this whole operation fell out of focus while we were hiring our thieves."

"And what's that?"

"The real Lukon should be trying to hire them too, right?" He called a series of black web windows up on the big screen. One had grotesque zombies in the sidebar. In another, fire-breathing dragons flew and fought between columns of gray text. "With that in mind, I set traps on the Dark Web. Any mention of our candidates or their code names sends an alert straight to my phone."

"*Annnd* . . ." Talia cocked her head.

"*Annd* the alerts have been coming in on three—Darcy, Finn, and the big ugly Scottish gorilla."

"Mac."

"Yeah. Him. The real Lukon is out there, still trying to make contact with our thieves." He lowered his chin, looking at Talia over his glasses. "Talia, Tyler is legit."

She skimmed the messages. There were vague references to money and jobs. Nothing concrete. No locations. "Tell me you started a trace."

"I put Franklin on it, but keep in mind, these message boards are designed to prevent traces."

Text that had magically appeared within the caves and dungeons of the Dark Web did not prove much. The internet was untrustworthy by definition. So was Tyler. He and Val had started talking about grifting on the way down to the Milan airport. And Val had shared the first three rules of a con, raising a finger with each.

One—make your marks work for every step. Two—keep them busy so they never have time to look behind the curtain. And three—never tell a lie when the truth will do.

Posting fake messages on the Dark Web to hold Talia and Eddie's focus, and getting them to run near-impossible traces certainly fit those first two rules.

Talia let out a breath. "I'm still on the fence. Tyler could have sent those messages himself." She let her stool rotate, narrowing her eyes at Eddie. "The whole crew will be in Milan the rest of the day, Tyler included. You'll be alone in the house with Conrad."

"So?" The geek shrank back a few inches.

"So . . ." Talia gently stopped his fidget spinner. "While Val is searching Ivanov's room, I want *you* to search Tyler's."

CHAPTER FORTY-SIX

EDDIE WAS A SPECIALIZED SKILLS OFFICER. An SSO. A hacker—in his own mind, at least. On the net, he wielded Java-Script and Python the way a superhero wielded eye-lasers and seismic blasts. The less virtual forms of espionage, however, were not his forte.

The crew split into two teams, guys versus gals. Darcy and Talia left for Milan immediately, taking the Tesla. The chemist had insisted on making a few purchases in the city before Talia's meeting. The guys lingered, laying out their recon plan on the kitchen table.

Eddie could feel Tyler-slash-possibly-Lukon watching him, like Tallmadge watching Benedict Arnold. Eddie stood, kicking his chair back with a grinding *squeak*, sweat glands working overtime. "I have . . . things to work on. Hacker stuff." He ran up the stairs and sequestered himself in Mission Control, listening for the telltale *kerchunk* of the front door closing. He heard it twenty minutes later. That left only Conrad in the house.

Potika and blintzes. Cacciatore and coq au vin. Eddie had enjoyed it all, but none of Conrad's offerings fooled him in the slightest. Any killer might be well trained in the culinary arts. If action movies were any guide, they had a propensity for it.

Conrad was no exception. Eddie could see it in the way he chopped his carrots.

Mustering his courage, Eddie peeked out into the hall. No Conrad. He was probably still in the kitchen, a butcher-knife's throw from Tyler's quarters.

They were all supposed to be on the same team, but Tyler clearly had things to hide, perhaps related to the mission, perhaps not. Either way, if Conrad caught Eddie snooping around his boss's quarters . . . As he crept down the stairs, Eddie glanced down at his fingers. They looked a lot like carrots.

Pots clanked in the kitchen. The cook hummed a sea shanty, slipping in the occasional "haul away" or "eventide, my darling." Eddie listened from the bottom step of the main stair for several seconds, and then hurried past the big stone fireplace to the double doors of Tyler's room. He placed a hand on the lever.

The humming and clanking in the kitchen stopped. Eddie let go and glanced over his shoulder.

No butcher knife came flying.

The shanty started up again, and he breathed a sigh of relief and pushed down the lever.

"Eddie?"

He spun around to find Tyler staring at him. "Mr. Tyler?" How long had he been there? Eddie tried to play it cool, leaning a hand against the door, which fell open with an obnoxious *creak*. Eddie yanked it closed again and stuffed both hands into his armpits. "I was just looking for you."

Tyler glared long enough for Eddie to wonder whether the former assassin would do his own throat-slitting or leave it to his cook. Finally he lowered his voice to something between a whisper and a growl. "It's *Lukon*. Remember? Keep it straight in Milan."

"I'm . . . not . . . going to Milan."

"Yes. You are. Mac and Finn gassed up the van. They're waiting for us. Let's go."

In that moment, Tyler, whom Eddie had been so drawn to when they first met, looked like a spider saying *Step into my parlor*. Eddie didn't want to be the fly. "But I always stay in Mission Control."

"Not this time." Tyler turned to go, then stopped and looked back.

Eddie swallowed. "Anything . . . else?"

"Your drone—Susan, Cindy, Sybil—"

"Sibby?"

"That's the one. Bring her along. She may be useful."

The four men took a switchback path of ancient stone down to the street level, where a black panel van sat idling. Mac stuck his head out the driver's window. "Are you two ready to go, or should I take her for another spin around the lake?"

The door behind him slid open and Finn beckoned for Eddie and Tyler to climb aboard. "Mac feels slighted at having to drive anything with less performance than a Lamborghini."

"I'm well aware." Tyler buckled himself into the passenger seat and pointed to the road ahead. "Quit pouting and get moving, Mr. Plucket. We have work to do."

Eddie found with delight that the van was less of a transport vehicle and more of a mobile command center. He took his place in the swiveling chair at the main workstation and read the steel plaque mounted above the screen. GROND: GROUND REMOTE OPERATIONS NODE. There was a black wolf's head beside the text. "Nice. I like the nod to Tolkien, boss. But what's up with this chrome bar in front of the keyboard?" He tried it out, resting his forearms on the bar and attempting to type. He had seen better ergonomics in Brennan's office.

"That's for operational security." Tyler glanced over his shoulder from the front passenger seat, face deadpan. "In case I ever need to chain a hacker to the primary workstation."

Eddie slowly lifted his forearms off the bar. "Ha-ha. Th-that's hilarious."

Tyler wasn't laughing.

The aerospace expo had taken over Linate Airfield on the east side of Milan, the site of one of the few landlocked seaplane runways in the world. A trio of military speedboats raced down the strip of blue-green water as Mac turned GROND onto a nearby agricultural road.

Eddie bounced in his workstation chair as Mac left the gravel and drove up the slope of a rolling wheat field. "Is this absolutely necessary?"

"It is if we wanna see anythin', Wee Man."

"I asked you to call me Red Leader."

"I prefer Wee Man."

"Or you can call me Eddie."

"Wee Man it is, then." Mac pointed through the windscreen. "Thar she is, lads." He parked on a hilltop perch a quarter mile east of the asphalt runway.

Finn slid open the door, handing Eddie a monocular. "If you catch someone looking our way, it means they're getting a glint off the lens. Drop this like a hot potato. Got it?"

"Got it." Again, Tyler had not gone cheap with the tech. The scope focused automatically as soon as Eddie held it steady at his eye. Preparations for the demonstration days at the end of the week were in full swing. Small packs of conference staff watched over the contractors as they set up displays of helicopters, armed drones, and boxy command vehicles.

Shifting to midfield, Eddie found the Avantec tent, one of the largest, with a big elevated display platform in front of the entrance. Ivanov's men were setting up stands there with missile bodies and engines of various sizes.

"The Mark Seven will be under the tent," Tyler said from behind him. "Can you see inside?"

"Too dark. Sorry." Eddie focused instead on a pair of cylindrical devices on either side of the entrance, guarding the tent flap like Chinese lions guarding a palace. They reminded him of the

R-series astromechs from *Star Wars*. He frowned, lowering the scope. "It looks like Ivanov has his own droids. That is so unfair."

"I think those are trash cans." Finn was looking through a scope of his own. "Moving on to perimeter security, I see a standard twelve-foot fence with concertina wire . . . gravel strip at the base. That means an infrared trip wire . . . Ooo." Finn clicked his tongue, lowering the scope. "We've got a couple of German shepherds in the northern guard shack. Can't afford any barking on the night of the job. We'll have to take Fido and friend out of commission."

"No!" The outburst came from Mac. "I winna hurt no dogs."

Finn lowered the scope and cocked his head. "You're an enforcer, you beat people up for a living. But dogs . . . You draw the line at dogs?"

"I prefer flyin'. An' no dog ever owed nobody money. All they do is give."

"We'll use a sleeping agent," Tyler said. "And we'll put it in the finest steaks, okay?"

This seemed to placate the Scotsman.

"Good. Now, we still need a look inside that tent. Time to bring out your pet, Red Leader."

Eddie had almost forgotten about Sibby. He pulled her case out of the van and popped it open on the running board. The two halves of the ball-shaped drone lay snuggly packed in foam. "Give me a sec to sync her to the tablet. What about the girls? Any word?"

"Nothing yet." Tyler glanced at the clock on the van's dashboard. "Ivanov should be arriving for his meeting with Talia any moment now."

CHAPTER
FORTY-SEVEN

DARCY PICKED THE SPOT for the meet, insisting on the refectory of a five-hundred-year-old convent. Talia didn't argue. Geographically the convent was well suited to the mission, far enough from the Excelsior to give Val time to search Ivanov's room. But the art-obsessed chemist had picked the spot for an entirely different reason.

Talia gazed up at the mural filling the interior north wall, stunned by the weight of its significance. The Christ figure sat at the center of his disciples, arms spread wide. "Da Vinci's *The Last Supper*. I didn't realize it was here. Are you religious, Darcy?"

"Not particularly, though my grandfather was." The inflections of her French accent came through crisp and clear on the comm link. "But this is Milan, yes? Why pass up such an opportunity? Consider what lies before your eyes, the master stroke of an incredible creator—the mark he left for all humanity."

"Or she could get on with the job." Val broke into the conversation. Her voice was muted, subdued. "The target left fifteen minutes ago. I'm entering his room now."

"Copy," Talia said, also eager to get the morning's operation over with. "I'm ready."

Darcy seemed to take offense at their tones. "And what does that mean? I am not ready? Are you saying I cannot be ready and discuss a master work of art at the same time?"

"Yes." Val sounded as if she were only half paying attention. Talia heard a drawer open and close. "Now be quiet. I'm working."

"You be quiet. I am already quiet, no?"

Thieves. Talia would have dropped her head into her palm, but Ivanov chose that moment to walk through the refectory door. "Both of you shut up. He's here." She walked out into the light.

"Talia." Ivanov took her hand and gave it a kiss.

The gesture didn't give her heart the same flutter it had in Tiraspol. Val's assessment of the man had dulled the chemistry between them, at least on Talia's part. She tried not to let it show. "Pavel. Thank you for coming."

"How could I resist." He turned to look at the painting and bumped her shoulder with his, tilting his lips close to her ear. "You know how I appreciate beauty."

Flirting. A week before, Talia would have taken it as a compliment. Now she wasn't so sure.

Ivanov nodded toward the mural. "This whole piece is a grand mistake. Did you know? Da Vinci's experimental paints could not withstand the test of time. Yet his artistry is so valued that five hundred years later, the world still fights daily to preserve it." Ivanov glanced her way. "One could only dream of leaving such an indelible impression on history."

"You're doing well." Val was still shifting things around. "Keep him talking. I haven't found the key yet."

Talia didn't need Val's coaching. She knew how to work a target. She had lured Ivanov away from the Excelsior with the promise of a security update, but the plan was thin at best. She steered him toward an easier topic. "So. How is the expo so far?"

"Excellent. In only a day and a half, we have garnered great

interest in the Gryphon project. And I expect much more interest after our demonstration of the Mark Seven tomorrow." His
smile went flat. "But there is this . . . woman."

"Oh?" A little of the lost flutter returned. "What woman?"

"An aide, assigned to me by the conference. She is so needy.
She always wants my attention."

"Really." Talia risked a walk behind Ivanov, tracing a hand
along his back as she maneuvered to his other shoulder. Her
earpiece had been on the wrong side. She wanted Val to hear
this. "This *aide* is *needy*, you say?"

The sound of shifting and shuffling items stopped. Val's voice
grew a little louder. "What's this?"

"You have no idea." Ivanov's expression soured. "Her mode
of dress is evocative, and she pouts if I do not compliment her
at least twice an hour. It's exhausting."

"What are you doing?" Val asked. "Never discuss a crew
member with the mark."

Darcy chimed in, amusement in her tone. "I do not think
that is a rule. You told her to keep him talking, no?"

Talia gave Ivanov a verbal nudge. "I imagine she's a little older
too."

"Oh yes. Fifteen years my senior."

"Ten!" The grifter shouted it so loud that Talia was afraid
Ivanov would hear. Val coughed, switching to an earnest whisper. "Ten. Not a day more. And most men say I look ten years
younger than that."

Talia snickered. "They're lying."

"Who is lying?" Ivanov suddenly looked at her, eyes narrowing.

"Women," she said, covering. "Like your aide. They're lying
to themselves. You know, clinging to youth."

Ivanov watched her for a moment, then nodded, looking at
the painting again. "Yes. Just so."

"He's projecting." Val was still in denial. "He wants to impress

241

you and look like a saint, so he's projecting his own sliminess on me. It's a classic move."

Talia leaned away long enough to tap her earpiece, making a loud *thock* to shut Val up. Ivanov shot her a glance, and she dropped her hand. She gave him a sympathetic smile. "I recently met a woman like that. Sad. It's like I can hear the desperation in her voice even as we speak."

Val growled at her through the comms. "Wait until I get my hands around your scrawny little neck. We'll see who's desperate then." Talia heard the *thump* of a pillow hitting a mattress. "The key isn't here. This whole exercise is a bust."

FORTY-EIGHT

A QUARTER MILE EAST OF LINATE AIRFIELD
MILAN, ITALY

SIBBY'S GREEN LED BLINKED TO LIFE and Eddie's face appeared on the tablet screen, captured by her wide-angle camera. "Hey there, girl. Time to go to work."

Tyler and his two thieves waited outside, waist-deep in wheat stalks, discussing the airfield's security arrangements. They had identified a roving patrol and clocked a shift change at the guard shack. "I expect the next change in four to six hours," Finn was saying as Eddie walked up. "We may be here awhile."

Mac snapped off a wheat stalk, placing it between his teeth. "Then our Wee Man'll have to go find us some food, won't he?"

Eddie hated bullies, so he did what he had done with all the many bullies in his life. He steered clear. He walked around the group to Finn, who stood farthest from Mac, and offered him Sibby. "Ever throw a baseball?"

"Yeah. 'Course, mate. We've had baseball in Australia since the eighteen hundreds." He accepted the drone, tossing it up and catching it overhand. "We had a little setback when the

243

first league manager scarpered with the cashbox, but the game survived."

"Typical Australian," Mac muttered. "Bunch o' thieves."

They all looked his way.

Finn sighed and returned his gaze to Eddie. "You want me to chuck her toward the airfield."

"As hard as you can. I'll do the rest. But"—Eddie reached out a hand as Finn prepared for the throw—"treat her nice. She's kind of my baby."

"Right. Chuck her nicely. Got it." Despite all the talk of baseball, Finn made a running start like a cricket bowler and flung Sibby out over the wheat field.

Working the tablet, Eddie used Sibby's internal gyros to stabilize her flight path, extending the range of Finn's throw.

"Look at that." The Aussie nudged Tyler as he watched it fly, oblivious to Eddie's technological helping hand. "A real ripper."

Eddie waited for Sibby to reach the apex of her flight and then kicked in the rotors, leveling her out and maintaining her vector toward the airfield. The others gathered around to watch over his shoulder. Using simple arrow controls, Eddie brought her down far enough to see into Avantec's tent. He enhanced the image with infrared. "There's the Mark Seven."

"Keep your distance," Tyler said. "Hang back and look closer with zoom only. Defense expos are notorious hotbeds of corporate spying. If Sibby gets spotted, some bored private security consultant is likely to follow her back to the source."

"The boss makes a good point," Mac said. "Maybe I should fly. I *am* the pilot."

That didn't sound good. Eddie wanted to move out of Mac's reach, but Finn and Tyler had boxed him in, still watching the video. "That's . . . not necessary. Really. Sibby's on a modified autopilot profile."

Mac wasn't having it. "Ya might know yer ones and zeros,

Wee Man. But ya don' know flyin'." He grabbed the tablet. "Give it here."

Bullies had taken things from Eddie before—lunch money, hats, calculators, laptops. He had survived the prison-yard atmosphere of grade school and high school by maintaining a strict policy of *let go and live*. This time, however, he couldn't let go. He looked to Tyler. "A little help, please?"

"Mac," Tyler said, not offering much help at all.

Eddie was on his own.

The Scotsman jerked and tugged at the tablet, giant thumbs whacking away at the screen. And through it all, Eddie held on. At one point, both feet left the ground.

"Ah. Thar's the button I'm lookin' fer. Manual control."

"Don't! You'll crash her."

"Quit yer whingin'. I've got it."

He didn't have it.

Eddie watched in horror as Sibby dropped from the sky in front of the Avantec tent. She smashed into the platform. Ivanov's men converged. Eddie couldn't let them have a piece of CIA tech. With a heart-wrenching flick of his finger, he hit the self-destruct.

Zzzzt crack! The sound came to them more than a second after the bright yellow flash of the explosion. By then, nothing remained of Sibby but a lingering puff of smoke.

Mac let go of the tablet, jaw hanging. "Well, that was . . ."

"Excessive," Finn said.

Eddie sat down in the wheat, tablet in his lap, chin resting on his chest. *Bullies.*

"Get up." Tyler yanked him to his feet. "Get on the SATCOM. Warn the girls."

"Of what? They're on the other side of town."

Tyler shoved a monocular into his hand and pointed at the airfield. "Look."

Conference workers and uniformed guards converged on the

site of the blast. One of the Avantec men crouched near the tent's entrance, examining a piece of Sibby's debris and talking into a handheld radio.

Tyler jerked the monocular away and shoved Eddie toward the van. "Warn them! Val is searching Ivanov's room. Talia is meeting with the man himself. And he's about to get a phone call."

CHAPTER
FORTY-NINE

TALIA AND IVANOV STEPPED OUT of the dark convent onto a brick sidewalk bathed in the deep gold of the late afternoon sun. Val had come up empty-handed, and Talia was about to make excuses for a departure when Eddie broke onto the SATCOM link. "We've had an incident at the airfield. There may be fallout."

"What kind of incident?" Val asked, still bumping around in Ivanov's room.

"Sibby's down." Eddie sounded tearful. "And . . . I had to blow her up in front of the Avantec tent."

"Val, pack up and get out." The voice from the van was now Tyler's—calm and professional. "Darcy, be prepared to step in. Talia, expect an interruption. Deflect his questions and disengage."

Talia realized too late that Ivanov had been speaking at the same time. The two strolled together over weathered pavers, looking up at the columned portico surrounding the convent dome. She gave him an apologetic smile. "I'm sorry. What did you say?"

"The security update. You asked me here to tell me something—about Lukon, I presume—but I am afraid I have monopolized the conversation."

"Yes. The update." *Keep it vague, but include specifics that hide the fact you're keeping it vague.* That was the only advice Tyler had given her. Talia had planned to tell Ivanov she had found a record of an online purchase of the sedative used to take out his guards during the botched heist. "We have a new lead. Lukon—"

A black sedan screeched to a stop at the curb. Bazin was at the wheel, red-faced and breathing heavy. "Dr. Ivanov!"

The rank smell of the Russian told Talia that Bazin had been enjoying a smoke break when the call came in, forcing him to run back to wherever he'd left the car. He spoke to Ivanov in rapid Romanian. The CEO absorbed it all with confusion, then understanding, and then turned to Talia.

She couldn't go with the original story. Not now. It was too conveniently oblique. What was Val's third rule of the con? *Never tell a lie when the truth will do.*

"Gryphon." Talia fought to maintain a look of surprise at Bazin's sudden appearance. "According to my intelligence, Lukon believes Gryphon is operational, and that it's where you're storing the plans for some super-weapon." She redirected the inquest, questioning him instead. "Is it, Pavel? Is Gryphon more than just a concept you're selling at the expo? If it is, Lukon is coming after it, and he's coming hard."

Val shouted at her through the comms. "No, Talia. What are you do—" Her question was cut short by something between a squeal and a gasp, followed by the sound of breaking glass.

CHAPTER FIFTY

SANTA MARIA DELLE GRAZIE CONVENT
MILAN, ITALY

A SPACE OF SILENCE followed the crash on the comms. Darcy spoke first. "This sound. It is bad, yes?"

Both Tyler and Val answered at the same time. "Yes."

"I knocked a vase off the mantel," Val said, then added, "a vase filled with flowers. And water."

Either due to her insanity, or simply to poke the bear, Darcy followed up with another question. "I see. And why would you do this?"

"Oh, I don't know. Maybe I was shocked to hear our precious point girl Talia betraying us to the mark."

Talia could not respond to the accusation. Ivanov seemed ready to answer her pointed question about Gryphon, then suddenly closed his mouth and quickstepped to the sedan, opening the rear door. "I am sorry. I must return to the expo to deal with an incident." To Talia's surprise, he stepped aside and motioned for her to get in. "If I could impose on you for a few minutes more, I would like to discuss this further. Please. Ride with me to the hotel."

"Disengage," Tyler said. "Walk away."

Talia agreed. The whole op was going downhill fast. Her affection for Ivanov was beginning to fail. What if he was as dirty

249

as Tyler claimed? She had just told him she knew too much. Getting into that sedan would be like jumping into the back of a windowless van with a man who offered her candy. She backed away. "Oh no. You seem very busy and I have a flight to catch."

A phone rang in the car. Bazin answered, covered the receiver, and spoke urgently to Ivanov. Ivanov barked back at him in Romanian, shutting him up. The CEO turned to Talia, jaw tense. "I see. Well, I am . . . disappointed."

He looked upset, but there was nothing sinister in the way he said *disappointed*. Talia held her distance and asked the question she could feel he wanted her to ask. "How so?"

"I told myself you had concocted a reason to see me again." Ivanov curled one side of his mouth into a sheepish smile. "I thought perhaps in truth you had tracked me down because of our connection."

"You mean our shared background—that we were both orphans."

"Yes, but also . . . our chemistry."

"Ooh," Darcy said. "Chemistry. There are sparks here, no?"

Great. There was nothing like holding an intimate relationship conversation with a potential arms dealer while a pack of thieves and Talia's best friend were listening over a SATCOM link.

Val was probably loving this.

Talia waited for the inevitable sarcastic comment from the grifter. Instead, Val muttered into the comms, "He's an orphan. *That's it.*" She raised her voice. "Talia, ride with him. Get in the car."

Tyler immediately countered the command. "Negative. I told you to disengage."

"Trust me," Val said. "Ivanov is an orphan. I should have seen it before. The key we need is not in his room. He's carrying it on his person."

Ivanov was waiting, holding open the door. "Please, Talia. Indulge me."

"Um. Let me check the boarding time on that flight, okay?" She opened a travel application on her phone, taking her time with the menus.

Val pushed her assertion about the key. "Former orphans spend their lives recapturing the control they lost as a child. They focus their resentment of that loss into an object, like a talisman."

"Talia?" Ivanov asked.

She held up a finger. "One sec."

"For men," Val continued, taking her time, "the talisman shifts—pocketknives, power tools, the keys to a luxury condo or car. Women carry the same talisman their whole lives. Talia, you *know* what I'm talking about. You know I'm right."

No I don't, Talia wanted to say, but her hand moved unconsciously from her phone to her father's dog tag, hidden beneath her blouse.

"I'm telling you, Talia. The Gryphon key is Ivanov's latest talisman. He'll keep it close, probably in his breast pocket. *You* have to steal it."

Tyler attempted to regain command. "Disengage. We'll go after the key another day."

They wouldn't get another day. She put the phone away and gave Ivanov a thin smile. "Plenty of time. Of course I'll go with you." She let him help her into the car.

There was a *bang* on the link, the sound of Tyler pounding his fist against the side of the van. "I guess we're doing things Valkyrie's way now."

There were three more bangs, a sigh, and then Tyler's professionalism returned. "Okay, team. Listen up. The mark is now en route to the hotel with Talia in tow. If he sees his room has been searched, Talia's part in this will be obvious. Oh, and did I mention his bodyguard is an unforgiving former Spetsnaz operator that carries a hand-cannon under his jacket?"

"ETA?" Val asked.

"We have Talia's GPS track. Eddie estimates three minutes to the hotel and another two for Ivanov to reach the room."

A blow-dryer kicked on in the background. "Not enough time. I can pick up the glass, but the carpet is soaked. I need eight minutes, give or take."

"Fine. Execute the contingency plan."

The contingency plan. In the sedan, watching Bazin grumble and growl as he waited for an opening in the traffic, Talia cringed. Tyler had unleashed the mad bomber.

And the mad bomber was overjoyed. "*Merveilleux, mon patron!* I thought you would never ask."

Once he had found an opening and pulled into traffic, Bazin reached back between the seats, waving a phone. "Dr. Ivanov, you must call director of conference. He is waiting."

Ivanov accepted the phone and laid it on the leather between himself and Talia, expression darkening. "I am afraid both the director and our chemistry must wait. There are more pressing matters. What can you tell me about Lukon and Gryphon?"

"Try not to give away the rest of the plan," Val said.

Too late. Talia had already started down a path of truth. Veering off now would raise Ivanov's suspicions. She took a gamble. "We believe Lukon will go after the Mark Seven during the expo and use it to reach Gryphon."

"Aaannd CIA girl gives up the goods," Val said, blow-dryer still running. "Well done, Ta—"

"No." Tyler cut the grifter off. "She made a good call. When forced to surrender information to maintain a cover, give the enemy a morsel easily deduced from the data they already have, thus building trust."

He had quoted a Farm manual, word for word. Talia knew because she had seen the same quote in her eidetic mind before she made the gamble. Tyler was letting his Agency background show.

It worked. Ivanov picked up the phone, tapping it on his

knee. "You may be right. We caught a nano-drone spying on our preparations for Friday's aerial demonstration. The operator destroyed the device before my men could grab it. Thanks to the explosion, the conference director is treating this as a terrorist act, but I believe it was Lukon." He let out a breath, dialing. "Anything else—some bread crumb I can offer the director?"

Talia shook her head. "I'm sorry. And don't tell the conference director anything. Let him run with the terrorist idea. Bringing up Lukon will only complicate things for you."

"Thatta girl," Tyler interjected. "Good damage control. Way to coach the mark."

As he finished dialing, Ivanov gave Talia a grim smile that said the two of them were in sync. He raised the phone to his ear. "*Ah, Portia. Questo è il Dottor Ivanov di Avantec. Direttore della conferenza, per favore.*"

"Speaking of *le dommage*," Darcy said. "The curtain is rising. Let the show begin!"

Bazin turned the sedan onto a roundabout near the center of Milan. Two cars ahead, a pillar of steam shot up with a tremendous *boom*, jettisoning a manhole cover high into the air. The Russian stomped on the brakes and shouted out the window.

"Keep your voice down." Ivanov covered the phone. "Deal with this. Find a new route. I must get back to the hotel."

The impending jam left Bazin no choice but to leave the roundabout. He made the first available turn.

Darcy's voice on the link was positively diabolical. "Yes. Now he takes Via Dante. *Très approprié*, no?"

Talia still had to lift the key. Val gave her instructions. "Now is the time. Start by looking with your eyes, not your hands. Look for signs of the key in his breast pocket—the tiniest bulge in his jacket or a wrinkle running opposite the others."

Talia saw it, an odd wrinkle on his left side. Bazin made a

lane change, and Talia used the sway of the car to make a play for the key. She couldn't do it.

She retreated, pretending to look out the passenger window, and whispered through her teeth. "The shoulder restraint is holding his jacket too close to his chest. I can't reach inside."

"Not a problem," Darcy said. "I am here to help. Look to the left and loosen your shoulder strap. Prepare to steal the key on my count."

Talia loosened the strap and bent forward to look out through Ivanov's window. A round object came flipping down between the rooftops—the manhole cover from the roundabout. How quickly Talia had forgotten it. What had Darcy been up to?

The cover smashed through the overhanging wires of a trolley system. Pedestrians screamed and jumped out of the way as it clanged to the ground. The central trolley wire, laden with ceramic coils, collapsed onto the tracks and sent up a fountain of sparks. With a *pop-pop-pop-pop*, small explosive charges flashed beneath all four wheels. The trolley rolled from its place, picking up speed as it coasted downhill to meet the sedan at the next intersection.

"De toute beauté." Darcy clapped loud enough to be heard over the link. "Now make your lift in three, two, one . . ."

Bazin swerved to dodge the cable car, running up onto the sidewalk and smashing through an empty café table. The move sent Talia flying across the rear passenger bench into Ivanov, who dropped his phone and caught her.

By the time Bazin had settled the sedan onto Via Dante once more, Talia was back on her side, fixing her hair with one hand and stuffing the key into her purse with the other. Ivanov searched the floorboard for his phone, and she used the moment to give a report to the others. She covered her mouth and lowered her chin to her shoulder as if coughing. "I've got it. But Darcy missed. We're still heading for the hotel."

"I missed nothing," the chemist said. "Look to your right."

Talia glanced out her window and saw Darcy on a rooftop one street over. The chemist waved both hands side to side and wiggled her hips. She pointed at the street below. Through the gaps between the buildings, Talia saw the trolley, still rolling.

Via Dante ended at a grand piazza—a thousand square meters of centuries-old stone, ending at the steps of an alabaster cathedral with more Gothic spires than Talia cared to count. Bazin had nowhere to go. He hopped the curb, plowing through a steady eruption of pigeons.

"I take shortcut," he said in his butchered English. "I have you hotel in no time." He turned the wheel and set a course for the narrow street south of the cathedral.

Glancing back, Talia saw the trolley emerge from its own street, hop the curb as well, and crash into an ancient lamppost, crushing the attached electrical box. The four lights at the top brightened and exploded. The trolley had stopped, but that was not the end of it. The destruction of the electrical box set off a chain reaction.

The lights of all the lampposts in that row brightened and burst, one after the other, rippling past the sedan like two hot rods in a drag race. The last lamp went off moments before Bazin crossed in front of it on his way to the side street. The post dropped like a felled tree and smashed down into the hood, bringing the sedan to a screeching halt.

"What have you done?" Ivanov punched the back of Bazin's seat.

The Russian tried to answer, but the airbag—a little delayed—went off in his face.

On the comms, Darcy made a popping sound with her lips. "*Voilà. Très magnifique!* That, my friends, is art."

PIAZZA DEL DUOMO
MILAN, ITALY

THE TEAM MET a short distance from the cathedral, on the rooftop level of a parking garage where Val and Mac had parked the Tesla and the van nose to nose. Down in the piazza the shadows of evening crept in on all sides while mystified workmen lifted the lamppost back up onto its marble pedestal, likely wondering how all its bolts had managed to shear at the same moment. Bazin and Ivanov stood trapped beside the ruined sedan, arguing with a pair of policemen. The Russian crumpled up a ticket and threw it to the ground.

Escaping had not been a problem for Talia after the accident. "Looks like you have a lot to deal with," she had said to Ivanov, and retreated to the nearest underground train station, only to resurface on the other side and make her way to the garage.

Tyler had a scope video of Sibby's explosion and Darcy's video of the sedan getting crushed replaying in a loop on GROND's main screen. "Sloppy work, ladies and gentlemen. This is sloppy work."

Darcy drew a sharp breath. "Sloppy? What is sloppy? Not *my* work!"

"You could have killed me." Talia thrust a hand toward the

screen. "You could have killed a lot of people with that manhole cover and the runaway trolley. You turned Milan into a giant Rube Goldberg device."

"With glorious precision, no? You are privileged. Today you experienced *beauté en action*." Darcy pushed out a bottom lip. "It is only a shame that the world will not see. *Monsieur* Lukon will not allow me to post the video."

Tyler lowered his forehead to his hand, rubbing his temples. "Lukon. It's just Lukon."

"Yes. Whatever. And if not for me, we could not have stolen that." Darcy tilted her head toward the quartz key, which Eddie had placed in a portable 3-D scanner.

"Sloppy or not, we got the job done," Val said, glancing north toward the hotel, a few blocks away. "Eddie will duplicate the conductive crystal and digital code from the key, and I can return the original to Ivanov. He'll never know it was gone." She gave Talia a nod. "Solid lift. And you handled a tough situation well. I'm sorry I gave you a hard time."

Talia bit her lip, lowering her eyes. "And I'm . . . sorry I goaded him into calling you old. That was uncalled for."

Finn waved his hands. "Whoa, whoa, whoa. I'm glad we're all friends again, but aren't we forgetting the explosion at the airfield? The key won't do us any good if we can't get to the Mark Seven."

"He's right," Tyler said, "which brings us back to the sloppy work. Eddie, break it down for them."

The geek glanced up at the video of Sibby's demise. "As you can see, I was forced to destroy Sibby, thanks to that big oaf over there."

"Who ya callin' an oaf, Wee Man?" Mac took a menacing step toward Eddie.

Darcy stopped him with a kick to the shin. "Leave him alone. You crashed his toy."

"Why, you crazy—"

"Hey!" Tyler ended the confrontation with a single clap. "Pay attention. Both of you."

Eddie let his scowl linger on Mac for a moment, then tilted his head toward the video. "I've been monitoring calls in and out of the expo's main office at the Excelsior. The organizers are on high alert. They now think their big gathering of defense contractors is a terrorist target."

"Which means they'll be bringing in extra security tonight," Val said. "And I expect some of the defense contractors will bring in more of their own. The French have already pulled up stakes and left."

Consciously or unconsciously, they all turned to look at Darcy. She shrugged. "Yes. That sounds correct."

"The point," Finn said, "is that short of a frontal assault with a platoon of Marines, we'll never get to the Mark Seven. Management is turning their little airfield expo into an open-air Fort Knox. We're done." He brushed his hands together and held them up. "I'm out. I'm not getting nicked for this."

"You're out?" Val turned on him, scowling. "Well, aren't you a fair-weather thief?"

"At least I *am* a proper thief. Look at the mess you made of a simple break and enter. You grifters are all talk and no skill."

Val's jaw dropped. "All talk?"

"Nothing but hot air. And don't blame me. Talk to the gorilla and the geek. They're the ones who dropped the drone."

The discussion turned into a shouting match with everyone pointing fingers at everyone else. Talia was about to lose her thieves, along with what little control she still held over the mission. In the crucible of need and pressure, an idea came to her. She shouted it out before it had fully formed in her mind. "A balloon!"

The shouting stopped. They all looked at her, and Talia struggled to flesh out the solution, gears turning as she spoke. "We don't *need* the Mark Seven. All we need is access to Gryphon."

"A beast who lives in the deadly domain o' the mesosphere," Mac said. "And in case you've forgotten, no other craft can get us up there."

"Yes there is . . . I think." Talia bit her lip, gauging their reactions. Mac was against her. Finn was coming around. Eddie just looked confused. "Listen. We don't need some high-tech rocket-jet. All we need is a balloon. Finn uses them all the time. I've seen it. Twice. He could jump to Gryphon the way he jumped down to the Shard penthouse."

The burglar seemed to consider the idea. "Most of those balloons peak in the stratosphere. I'd need a special version to get all the way to the mesosphere."

"Do mesospheric balloons even exist?" Tyler asked.

"A couple. Maybe. I've heard rumors of two or three groups building rigs to break the BASE jumping altitude record. To do it, they'll have to go at least that high."

"On it." Eddie's confusion dropped away and he turned to his workstation. Search engine windows came up, and a few seconds later, a satellite image zoomed in on the Alps. "Found one. They call themselves XPC, for Extreme Para-corps. They have a hangar in Lauterbrunnen Valley, three hours north of the chateau." He spun his chair around, grinning and rubbing his hands together. "Who's up for another road trip?"

CHAPTER
FIFTY-TWO

TALIA WATCHED CONRAD push a cart with prime rib warming over hot coals across the stone floor of the great room. He had guilted Tyler into allowing the team a hasty supper before departing for their nighttime mission to Lauterbrunnen, lest his afternoon's work go to waste.

The cook stopped beside Talia's chair, sliced off a piece, and laid it on a plate, adding diced rutabaga and a dab of some mint-green concoction. "The first portion goes to the cook's favorite. The dip is a creamy horseradish with a touch of dill, for both zest and color. It sounds sharp, my dear, but trust me. The effect is mild enough to let the natural flavors of the rib retain primacy."

How could she refuse? Talia accepted the plate and balanced it on her knee. "Thank you. But where is—" She stopped. In that moment, Talia could not bring herself to say *Lukon* in reference to Tyler. "Where is our host?"

Conrad pressed on with his cart, making a subtle tilt of his head toward the foyer.

Tyler shuffled in backward, followed by Finn, both grunting with the weight of a large heavy-duty case. They set it down at the center of the great room.

"What've ya got there, lads?" Mac asked, while at the same time nudging Conrad in a silent demand for an extra slice of meat.

"Weapons." Tyler pressed a latch, and the case cracked open with a hiss. The lid rose on its own. Six submachine guns with helical magazines lay inside, nestled in gray foam.

The Scotsman set his plate on the floor and drew out one of the guns. "Now yer speakin' mah language." He checked the action as Tyler addressed the team.

"Don't let the word *balloon* fool you, ladies and gentlemen. Tonight we're stealing a large and complex aircraft—so large we have to bring a box truck in addition to GROND."

"And XPC is unlikely to give it up without a fight." Finn let out an embarrassed chuckle. "Let's face it. These are my people. They live for late nights, Red Bull, and near-death experiences. That makes them unpredictable. We have no choice but to go in armed."

When he pulled out the helical magazine, Mac's face turned sour. He removed a bullet and held it up. "What's this? A clay round?"

"Nonlethals," Tyler said with a nod. "To the uninitiated, a clay round feels like the real thing. One shot to the chest and a target will think he's dying. If he's wearing a thin shirt, he'll bleed too." He walked around the room, passing a weapon each to Talia and Darcy. "Avoid head shots. Those can kill."

"Cool." Eddie sat forward out of the lounger to grab one for himself, but Finn slapped the lid closed, nearly catching his fingers. Eddie jerked his hand back. "I don't get a gun?"

"You'll be staying in the van." Tyler paused in his walk around the great room, standing next to Mac, who did not look happy. "Problem, Mr. Plucket?"

The Scotsman laid his weapon on the arm of the couch. "How can *you* be the Lukon we've all heard aboot? Am I to believe you've become the world's most merciful assassin?"

Tyler's voice went flat. "Believe what you will. But we do this my way."

"An' what if I per-fer to carry a real gun?"

Talia watched the Scotsman, wary of his tone. She saw his hand, behind the arm of the couch and out of Tyler's view, moving to his waistband. She dropped her plate. "Look out!"

Conrad had Tyler covered. With unnatural quickness for his age, he flung his carving knife across the room.

Tyler caught it inches from Mac's chest and let the momentum spin the blade up under the Scotsman's chin. He moved behind and locked his other arm across Mac's forehead. The knife, smeared with juice from the prime rib, rested against the man's jugular. "Don't move, unless you truly want to meet the assassin you so admire. He's always here, beneath the surface."

Mac froze, eyes seething.

Tyler bent close to his ear. "If you ever thought life was precious, think how much more so it is for the man who knows a thousand ways to end it." He pressed inward with the blade, making Mac draw an involuntary breath. "I remember every kill. I mourn for their loved ones, and mourn even more for those who had none to love. Do not be so eager for such an existence. My job. My weapons. Understood?"

Mac gave him more of a quiver than a nod, afraid of the razor's edge of Conrad's carving knife.

"Good." Tyler reached down to confiscate the pistol at Mac's back. Once he had it, he released the brute and tossed the knife back to Conrad, who caught it with an expert hand. "Enjoy your meal, then put on something black. We leave in two hours."

CHAPTER
FIFTY-THREE

THE INCIDENT WITH MAC cast a pall over the meal. The Scotsman, humiliated, retreated upstairs, although he took an extra helping of prime rib with him.

Tyler's reaction to the near betrayal had reminded all the thieves of who was in charge and why. For Talia, though, his actions brought troubling questions to the forefront of her mind. Perhaps Tyler had channeled the dormant assassin within to keep the Lukon illusion alive. Or perhaps his actions had revealed he and Lukon were one and the same.

The thought sent a chill down Talia's spine. And that made her jumpy.

Talia thought she heard murmuring from the walls as she picked up a black Lycra top. She wrote it off, but once she had the shirt halfway on, one arm in a sleeve and the neckline caught beneath the bridge of her nose, she heard the definite jiggling of a door lever—her door lever.

Someone was coming in.

Perfect timing.

Talia yanked the shirt on and spun out through the bathroom door.

When the intruder came through, he found himself nose-to-barrel with her Glock. Talia scrunched up her features. "Eddie?"

The geek, clutching a tablet to his chest, closed the door with a foot and used one finger to press his glasses into place. "Um . . . Hi."

"Ever try knocking?"

"I didn't want the others to hear." Eddie took himself out of the line of fire, walking deeper into the room. "I have new info. I whispered at the door, but you didn't answer."

"So you picked the lock."

"It seemed like the right move at the time."

"*Ugh!*" Talia hooked his arm and sat him down in her desk chair, taking the edge of the bed for herself. "What info, Eddie? Did Franklin get back to you?"

"Yes. He did." Eddie turned the tablet around.

The CIA's Hispanic double-amputee tech guru waved from the screen. "*Hola*, chica."

Talia gave him a lift of her chin. "Hey, Franklin. What've you got for me?"

"I completed the trace on Lukon's Dark Web posts. They all originated from the same location." Franklin disappeared and a global satellite map came up on the screen, zooming in on the mountains of Romania. "The IP address indicates a coffeehouse Wi-Fi hub in a village called Bran, at the heart of the Transylvanian Alps."

"Transylvania." Talia let out a huff. "Fitting. Any cameras?"

"Lukon is too smart for the café cameras to matter." The map went away. Franklin returned to the tablet screen. "Chances are, he linked to the hub from the street outside."

"So we're still no closer to finding out who he is."

"Correct." Eddie gave Talia a questioning look, and she nodded. He came over to sit beside her on the bed so they could both see the screen, although he kept one foot on the floor. "But you're missing the point. Franklin's trace tells us who Lukon *isn't*." He moved Franklin's window to one side and brought up another with several lines of text. "The traces identify the origin of each post in both space and *time*. Look at the time/date stamps."

Talia read the numbers. "That's three days ago."

"When you were in Venice. With Tyler."

"It's not him."

"Your guy is legit," Franklin said from his tablet window. "And with all the coin Mr. Tyler has laid out for this op, I think he deserves a medal, not your suspicion. Just sayin'."

Talia had to agree. She owed Tyler an apology. She sighed as Eddie made Franklin's window fill the screen again. "Anything else, Franklin?"

"Yeah. Maybe you should sit down."

"I am sitting down."

Eddie tilted the screen to show him Talia's knees.

"Oh. I'll go ahead, then." He had turned serious. All the playful crazy-uncle-ness had vanished. What remained was a Marine, the kind who had seen comrades ripped apart and lived to tell their families. That frightened Talia. So did his words. "This part is about your dad."

Now she knew why he had wanted her to sit down.

Franklin sent a document to the screen, an old mailer advertising discount exterminator services, the sort of junk mail usually addressed to *Current Resident*. Between the lines of text, however, were handwritten phrases. Talia recognized the format, an old-school message coded within the text of an annoying mailer anyone but the intended recipient would throw away.

"I won't insult your intelligence with a summary," Franklin said from behind the image. "You can read it for yourself."

She already had. And her whole body had gone numb.

Contract for Lukon via Archangel

Fee: Standard

Timing: ASAP

Target: Nicolai Inger

"Dad." Talia could barely get the word out. Her throat felt as if it were closing. Pain swelled in her side and she doubled over.

"Talia!" Eddie took her hand.

"I'm all right. I just need a minute, okay? My old pain. It flares up when I'm stressed."

"Yeah. Sure."

Talia breathed in and out. As if from a distance, she heard Eddie and Franklin still talking.

"I'll take it from here. Thanks for the help."

"You got it, *mano*. Make sure to tell her the rest. *Comprende?*"

The rest? What more could there be?

The names. There had been two code names in the letter. Lukon. Archangel. Talia pulled her hand from Eddie's and pushed herself up again. "Lukon was there, at the accident." Her eyes darkened. "At my father's murder. But in the memory, I saw Tyler."

"Maybe not." Eddie gave her his *hear me out* face. "I think your mind was filling in a gap. Memory insertion. I mentioned it before, but you shut me down."

They had learned about memory insertion at the Farm, a key pitfall in intelligence gathering and interrogation. The mind routinely fills memory gaps with whatever spackle it finds lying around the subconscious. With the right phrase, a good spy can make a subject remember her presence at an event she never attended, or replace a mental image of her with the image of someone else.

One caring instructor had taken Talia aside to warn her that those with eidetic memories were just as susceptible to memory insertion as everyone else. Had her mind blotted out her only image of her father's killer and replaced it with Tyler? Was life really so cruel? In Talia's experience, it was. She grunted against the pain in her side.

Eddie touched her knee. "Don't worry. Franklin can't let go of a mystery. He'll run down Lukon and Archangel. We'll find them."

"But why?" Talia held her voice steady, but she couldn't stop the tears from welling in her eyes. She wiped them away. "Why would these people come after Dad?"

"He was an Army Ranger, right?"

"The army gave him his citizenship. They recruited him through a program in Eastern Europe."

"Maybe there was more to it. Think about the time period. The wall had fallen. New opportunities were opening in the intelligence arena."

Talia could feel Eddie leading her toward a conclusion, and before she could ask another question, she saw it. "That's why he moved to Washington. It wasn't because of Mom's death."

Talia's mother had died in childbirth, and shortly after, her father had been assigned to a liaison job in the nation's capital. She had always thought they sent him there to recover from his grief, but in the next seven years, he had never been reassigned to the main Ranger battalions. Grief or not, no army posting ever lasted that long. How had Talia missed it?

Nicolai Inger had been CIA. Just like his daughter.

CHAPTER FIFTY-FOUR

CHATEAU TICINO HANGAR
CAMPIONE D'ITALIA, SWITZERLAND

TALIA AND EDDIE ARRIVED at the hangar to find Mac and Darcy covering the sides of a box truck with black tarps. The artwork they were hiding was a black-and-gold Formula One racer with luciano grand premio painted beneath. Tyler and Finn were loading the last of several portable fuel tanks into the back, also bearing Luciano's logo.

"With these, we can avoid stopping at gas stations along the way," Finn said as he and Tyler slid the last tank into place. "No pesky cameras."

Talia peeked around the two men, counting the tanks. "Looks like you packed a lot more than we'll need."

"Better safe than sorry." Tyler closed the rolling door, cutting off her view.

Mac drove GROND, while Tyler took command of the box truck. Finn attempted to climb into the box truck cab, but Talia yanked him down by the belt. "Nope." She pointed at GROND. "You're in the van. This seat's taken."

Finn stared her down, and the two did a joint pirouette as Talia maneuvered herself between him and the cab. "All right," he said, backing off. "I guess I can put up with Mac's smell for a couple of hours." Finn snapped his fingers and pointed at her. "But you owe me."

The hangar door swung open to the night and Tyler kicked the truck into gear. "Suddenly I feel like the popular kid."

"Don't read too much into it." Talia clicked her seat belt into place and settled in for the ride.

The long drive time had more to do with winding roads and slow climbs through alpine passes than distance. Talia passed the first hour in thought, only partially aware of the occasional flash of brake lights from the van ahead or the glinting of the moon on a stream beside the road. The constant throbbing in her side deepened the mental haze. Her old pain no longer stabbed at her, but it had not gone away after the conversation with Franklin.

"Penny for your thoughts," Tyler asked as they emerged from one mountain tunnel only to be swallowed by the next. When Talia didn't answer, he raised his bid. "Okay. How about a nickel?"

"Always the businessman," she said, watching the van ahead cut through the darkness.

"Always."

Talia didn't want to be forced into talking about her dad's murder just because Tyler was bored. She chose a different topic. "I read up on Saul of Tarsus, the man who became Paul."

"Oh? I'm impressed."

"Don't be." She glanced at him across the cracked vinyl of the old bench seat. "Help me understand. You discovered God through a man you killed, and you believe God then redeemed you, the way he redeemed Paul."

"Through the sacrifice of Christ, his Son." Tyler downshifted for the descent into another valley.

Talia didn't get the correlation. "I went to Sunday school. Paul was a missionary. He sacrificed everything to serve God after his conversion. But you . . . what? Stopped killing people?"

She waved her hands in the air in mock celebration. "Yay, you. This supposed conversion didn't stop you from spending all that blood money."

Tyler went quiet for a long time, and Talia thought she had him. She at least expected him to justify his actions. Instead, he threw them aside completely. "My redemption, and Paul's, are not about what we did. Redemption is about what Christ did. Paul's actions are an outgrowth of his newfound faith. He served out of love and gratefulness."

"And you show your gratefulness by spending dirty money."

"No. For the record, when I quit the Agency, they booted me out of my home. I hung on to the money for a while, but I couldn't spend it. It sat in a couple of offshore accounts until, bit by bit, it all went to charity."

"Yet, somehow, you live like Bruce Wayne."

"What can I say? I have some useful skillsets and a knack for negotiation." The tires bumped in steady rhythm over the steel joiners of a suspension bridge. Tyler waited until they were across to continue. "It started with odd jobs for allied governments. Legal work, meeting a niche demand. I became known for organizing diverse groups to accomplish unique objectives. My first big break came while working for Hungary, I brought down a crime syndicate with several large caches of weapons. The Hungarians wanted nothing to do with the guns."

"So you sold them?"

"Stripped and melted them, actually—all by hand in a low-rent warehouse on the outskirts of Budapest. You'd be surprised at the volume of preprocessed, high-value materials you can get from a bunch of weapons and ammunition."

"Import . . . export." Talia let out a quiet chuckle.

"Now you're catching on. A great many countries are looking to rid themselves of old weapons, and they'll sell cheap when the buyer is not a cartel. Some can be repurposed into nonlethals."

All his money was legitimate. Talia shook her head.

"Something else on your mind?"

"No." She touched her side, hoping he wouldn't notice. "Not really."

They parked the vehicles on a ridge road that looked down into the Lauterbrunnen Valley, a four-mile-long topographic wonder with sheer sides reaching as high as 3,500 feet above the pristine sheep pastures of its floor.

Finn led them to a drop-off called an *exit point*. "Come closer," he said, reaching back for Talia. "You can't beat the view."

"Yeah . . ." She took a step back. "No thanks. I'm good."

"Don't be a baby." Finn finished his work and caught her hand, pulling her to the edge. A few pebbles spilled over. Talia expected to hear them clicking against the cliffside, but she never did. Her knees weakened. She threw an arm around his waist and held on.

"You don't have to squeeze so hard." Finn gave her a wink. "I'm not going anywhere."

"Oh, shut up."

He wasn't wrong about the view. Finn pointed out a pair of pencil-thin waterfalls descending from the opposite wall, dropping so far and so straight they evaporated into mist before reaching the bottom. "There are seventy-two waterfalls along the valley. I've flown through all of them. This is my Jerusalem, my Mecca, the true nirvana."

"Wow." Eddie snorted as the two left their perch. "How many religions can you offend with one statement?"

Talia could see he was trying to fit in with the Aussie by ribbing him—the geek trying to be cool with the jock. It didn't work. Finn looked back with a scowl. "What do you know, eh?"

"But he is correct, no?" Darcy leaned against GROND's open panel door. "My grandfather immigrated to France from Kenya, where he says Ngai resides on Mount Kirinyaga. In his stories, it is the creator's presence that makes the mountain holy. You want to make this one holy by climbing up, only to jump off and climb up again." She made a *pbbt* sound and gestured at the view. "It is pretty, yes? But your mountain is empty."

Finn stared at her for a moment, then shook his head and ducked into the van.

"Thanks for standing up for me." Eddie touched her arm. "Here and back in Milan."

The chemist gave him a smile. "Of course. You and I, we are in different fields. But those fields have some common math, yes?"

"Uh. Yeah. They do."

Talia thought she saw him blush.

"Also you are very small, no? You need the help."

Eddie turned and walked away.

No less than sixteen parachute rigging and tour companies occupied the long stretch of pastureland a mile south of Lauterbrunnen's village, most in ugly prefab buildings. "The daredevils and townspeople don't mix," Finn said. "To be fair, the wingsuits make a buzzing noise that scares the sheep, and the schoolchildren here have seen more violent death than some combat veterans."

Tyler squinted at the burglar across the moonlit road. "And you think Darcy's crazy?"

Thanks to the BASE jumpers' love for self-aggrandizing videos, the valley was filled with high-definition webcams. Eddie hacked the various feeds from the van's control center, and looking at the buildings, it was clear XPC were the kings of Lauterbrunnen. Their fenced-in compound sat on a grassy outcropping, high above the competition, complete with a helipad, an equipment shed, and a log-cabin dormitory for tour groups of trust-fund thrill seekers.

Finn tapped the live image of the shed. "They'll keep the rig here. Three hundred thousand euros' worth of record-breaking engineering protected by nothing but a two-thousand-euro aluminum shed." He let out a disbelieving laugh. "Some people just don't get it."

"Yeah." Talia looked sideways at the thief criticizing the law-abiding citizens he was about to rob. "Some people."

An hour of patient surveillance told them XPC and their clients had retired to the dormitory for the night. Eddie stayed with GROND on the ridge to keep a bird's-eye view of the operation, and the others rode down into the valley. Mac idled the box truck at the base of XPC's outcropping while the others piled out of the back and climbed the hillside on foot. At the top, Finn handed Tyler a set of heavy wire-cutters.

"For cutting through the fence?" Talia asked.

Finn gave her a smug chuckle. "I cut through windows on skyscrapers. I never cut through fences." He turned and sprinted toward the back corner of the fence line, where it ran closest to the valley wall. Without breaking stride, he ran diagonally up the cliff face and did a twisting layout over the barbed wire, landing in a somersault that brought him back to his feet.

Tyler heaved the cutters over the fence.

Finn caught them with one hand and pointed them at Talia. "You're impressed. Don't try to hide it. I can see it on your face. That flip was—"

"Do you mind?" Tyler glanced at his watch. "We're on a schedule. Go let Darcy in."

The lights on the perimeter dimmed one by one a heartbeat before Finn passed beneath them, courtesy of a gadget he wore on his wrist. With barely a *clink* of the cutters, he clipped the padlock on the gate's control box and motored it open for Darcy and her duffel full of surprises. The two ran crouching toward the dorm. They had preparations to make, leaving Talia and Tyler to watch and wait.

Tyler offered one of his nonlethal submachine guns to Talia. She winced as she pulled the sling over her head.

"You okay?" He checked his magazine, seeming only half interested in the question.

"I'm fine. An old pain, that's all. No big deal."

"That's not what I was talking about. You've been on edge the whole night. Do you have something to say about the way Conrad and I handled Mr. Plucket at dinner?"

"No. It's just . . ." Talia sighed. She didn't want to talk about her father, but the night was dragging on, and she didn't have enough brain bytes left to make something up. "My dad. I had Eddie and an Agency friend dig into his death. I always thought he had died in an accident. I blamed God for taking him from me. Turns out God had a little help. Dad was murdered."

Tyler froze at the word *murdered*. He looked up at her as he clicked the weapon's magazine home again, eyes searching her face. "Murdered?"

"We found a file. Dad worked for the Agency, and Lukon took him out, made it look like an accident. He almost killed me too." She winced again, bending into the pain. All this talking was making it worse.

Tyler watched her for a moment, then returned to his inspection. He held the weapon up and looked through the sights, tracking Finn's movements. "Did you ever think your chronic pain might be more emotional than physical?"

"Meaning what?"

"Meaning you've been mad at God for a long time." Tyler lowered the gun as Finn disappeared behind the shed. "Now this new information has given you an additional target for your anger. Is it really a coincidence that your pain is flaring up at the same time?"

As if to lend support to his argument, the pain stabbed at her, but Talia refused to buy into his psychobabble. "You're talking about correlation, not causation. The wound flares up when I'm stressed, no doubt. But the reason for that stress is irrelevant."

"Mindless denial doesn't suit you." Tyler let his weapon fall to his side and nodded at hers. "Check your mag. Go safety off."

She glared at him, but went to work.

As she did, Tyler kept prodding. "Let go, Talia. Let God in

and forgive the man who wronged you—even though what he did is unforgivable. You might be surprised at the result."

"Forgive him?" Talia shoved her magazine back into place. Her finger slid unconsciously around the trigger. "Not a chance. When we find Lukon, I'm going to make him pay."

With one hand, Tyler pressed the machine gun down to her side. He placed the other on her shoulder. There was such sadness in his voice. "I'm sorry to hear that, but it's your choice. You *will* find Lukon before this is over. And if you still feel that way, I'll help you put a bullet in his brain."

A light flashed near the shed. Tyler let go of her. "There's Finn's signal. Time to go to work."

CHAPTER FIFTY-FIVE

"Red Leader, I'm up on comms and starting Phase Two." Talia shoved an earpiece in as she and Tyler ran through the gate. "Send Wheels."

"On his way."

Mac grumbled at them over the link. "I told ya before. Don' call me Wheels."

In the background of his complaint, Talia could hear the rumbling of the box truck. A few seconds later, her ears picked up the same rumble on the night air. And if she could hear it, the daredevils in the dormitory would hear it too, soon enough, and that would mean trouble.

Talia placed a hand on Tyler's back, letting him lead her in the run to the shed while she kept her eyes on the buildings. "Darcy's solution had better work," she whispered as they reached the shed's rear door. "I saw what she had in that duffel. Where did it all come from?"

"I had a few odds and ends lying around." Tyler lightly knocked on the door. "You know, leftovers from my day job." The door opened and Finn stuck his head out. Tyler scrunched up his brow. "What took you so long?"

"The rig is in pieces. It took some doing, but we got it sorted."

Finn and Darcy had been hard at work inside the shed. The balloon, its air system, and the space-capsule-style gondola were neatly piled onto a pair of shipping pallets.

"It'll take all four of us," Finn said. "With two on each pallet, we can make it in one trip."

"We'd better." Tyler killed the interior lights. "Wheels, what's the holdup?"

"Ya think you can do better? *You* try drivin' a box truck back'ards up a mountain rood!"

Tyler sighed. "He'll . . . be here in a minute. Red Leader, you have the count."

"Copy," Eddie said. "I have the count."

Shuffling in the dark, Finn and Darcy positioned themselves on either end of the first pallet with Talia and Tyler taking the other.

The noise of the truck grew louder. "I see the gate," Mac said. "Last curve."

Talia pictured the Scotsman rounding the final bend. The rumble ramped up to a howl as he pushed the box truck's reverse gear to the limit on the straightaway.

"Stand by, team," Eddie said. "Here we go in three, two, one . . ."

With a *bang* and a flash, a section of the shed's north wall blew out and fell. Talia looked out past the other three and saw the box truck sail backward through the gate, veer off the road, and trundle across the grass, making a beeline for the opening.

"Go!" Tyler shouted, and the four of them lifted their burdens.

Finn and Darcy went first. As Talia followed, carrying the front end of her and Tyler's pallet at her back, she shot a glance at the dormitory. Lights blinked on. Silhouettes appeared at the windows. That was expected, and Darcy was supposed to have set something up to lock them down, but nothing was happening. "Darcy? What's the holdup?"

"It is not a holdup," the chemist called, two steps ahead of her on the rear end of the other pallet. "I gave them time to waken, yes? What is art if no one is there to see it?"

"*We're* here to see it!"

"And so you shall!"

Lines of blue fire suddenly lit the doorframes of the dormitory, dripping molten metal and welding the doors shut. Men pounded and shouted from the other side. More silhouettes gathered at the windows. Several sets of hands tried to lift the glass, but charges blew behind the cabin's open snow shutters, slamming them closed. Blue flames sealed those as well.

Darcy looked back at Talia while they jogged across the grass with their burdens. "*Voilà!*"

The box truck stopped inches from Finn, and he laid his end on the lip of the open cargo bay. He hopped inside to drag the pallet forward. "I wish we had that on video."

"Red Leader is taking care of that, yes?" Darcy grunted, shoving from her end.

Eddie chuckled into the comms. "Oh yes." But then he started shouting. "Movement! I have movement at the main office. Someone's coming!"

Darcy hadn't sealed the office.

Talia set her end of the pallet on the back of the truck and looked toward the building, only to see a man stumbling across the lawn.

"*Wer ist das? Was machen Sie?*" He sounded German. And drunk.

"Deal with him." Tyler shouldered Talia away as she tried to help him push the remainder of the pallet into the truck.

Talia didn't want to *deal with him*. The German was just some guy defending his business. But the criminals were watching, and strangely enough, they were all depending on her.

"*Hör auf! Das ist unser!*" The man stopped thirty feet away, tilted his head back to chug down half a beer, crushed the still-dripping can against the side of his head, and let it fall. Apparently that was his method of waking himself up to fight intruders. He raised a mountaineer's ice axe and charged.

"Stop!" Talia leveled her machine gun. "Don't make me shoot you."

He kept coming, though not precisely in a straight line.

Maybe he didn't speak English. "*Halt!*" Talia's German wasn't that good. What was *please*? "*Bitte?*"

"*Ich werde dich töten, Dieb!*"

She knew the word *töten*—to kill. Now he was a serious threat. "Sorry, buddy." Talia pulled the trigger, capping off the guy's future hangover with a three-round burst to the chest.

"Nice!" She could hear Eddie slap the worktable in the van. "That is so going on your greatest hits reel. You dropped him like—"

"Like a drunk guy hit with three clay rounds traveling at four hundred feet per second?" Tyler caught Talia's hand and hauled her up into the truck.

Finn yanked a strap tight, securing the second pallet, and Tyler pounded on the front wall of the bay. "We're all inside, Wheels. Go!"

CHAPTER FIFTY-SIX

MAC DROVE THE TRUCK to a lakeside intersection in the next valley over to rendezvous with Eddie. The thieves jumped out of the box truck, laughing and joking. But when Tyler shouted at them, "All of you, shut up and get over here!" the team went silent.

Talia could see the rebuke ready on his lips as they all gathered around. She knew why. Eddie had failed to account for all the personnel in the compound. Thus, Darcy had done nothing to block the office door, allowing a drunken brute with an ice axe to come after them. To cap it off, Talia had hesitated, waiting too long to put the man down.

Tyler scowled at the group. "After Milan, I wasn't sure this group could work as a team. After tonight, I know"—his frown cracked into a smile and he pulled a cooler out of the bay—"you *are* a team." Tyler tossed them each a bottle of Socata, the same citrus drink he kept on his Gulfstream. He raised one in toast. "To small victories, ladies and gentlemen. Let's hope the final heist goes as smooth."

It took a moment for Talia and the others to catch on, and

then Finn popped the cap of his bottle and held it high. "Hear, hear!"

Soda bottles clinked. "Hear, hear!"

Finn and Darcy chuckled over the fireworks on the dormitory exits. Mac commended Eddie for his work watching over them.

"I did good, right?" The geek balanced his fidget spinner on his index finger.

"Yeah, you did." Mac clapped him on the back hard enough to knock the spinner into the grass. "That'll do, Wee Man. That'll do."

Talia stood apart from the thieves, quiet. Tyler came over to join her. "Something wrong?"

"No. That's just it. I had . . . fun."

"And that's bad?"

She shrugged, lowering her voice so the others wouldn't hear. "Maybe. It should be bad if I'm having fun while committing a crime." She bit her lip. "The man I shot. He'll be okay, right?"

"He'll be fine." Tyler finished his drink, set the bottle down in the grass, and popped open another. "So will his buddies. And you can bet Brennan will approve an anonymous donation that covers their loss. With interest." He paused to watch Mac entertaining the others with a reenactment of his backward driving. "Sometimes the moral ambiguities of covert work are hard. We do the job with the legal blessing of one government, acting against the laws of another."

Talia pursed her lips. "Yeah. I took those classes at the Farm. We serve the greater good. That's fine, but the instructors were never too clear on a full definition of the term."

"In that case, you *should* feel bad, or perhaps concerned. Never serve something you can't define, Talia. Personally, I don't bother with the greater good."

I don't bother with the greater good. The statement sounded positively villainous. Talia tried to laugh it off, bumping his shoulder. "Look, if you're about to tell me to embrace the dark side, I—" Her voice fell away. Tyler was looking at her without one hint of sarcasm in his eyes. "Um . . . Okay. Why would I *not* serve the greater good?"

"The greater good is malleable." He turned his eyes to the thieves again, tipping his bottle toward the Scotsman. "Mac's greater good is money. Our chemist's greater good is art and political self-righteousness. Finn's is the thrill of the heist." Tyler shrugged. "To the Supreme Leader of Iran, the greater good involves wiping Israel off the map. If you don't believe me, check his Twitter account. The *greater good* is shifting sand. You can't trust it."

"So how is a spy supposed to know what's right or wrong?"

"I told you when we first met." Tyler returned to his drink, giving her nothing else.

Talia searched her memory and read the words of their first conversation as if they were text. Tyler had quoted Jefferson. *I know but one code of morality for men.* "God," she said slowly. "To Jefferson, morals were not malleable. They were absolute, and they came from one source."

Tyler affirmed her answer with a single nod. "Don't focus on the greater good. Focus on a higher power—*the* higher power. That's how we put what we do to a moral test."

Over by the truck, the celebration was winding down. Finn and Mac climbed into the bay and began securing the equipment for the long drive home.

"What's left?" Talia asked.

"Only one thing." Tyler picked up his empty bottle and dropped it into a plastic bag. He collected hers as well, raising his voice so the others could hear. "We're down to the final step. Val has to get Gryphon's voiceprint ID from Ivanov. She says she's close."

Finn poked his head out from the cargo bay. "How long?"

"Less than twenty-four hours. Tomorrow, Ivanov presents

the Mark Seven and the Gryphon concept to the expo. That's when we make our play."

Talia rode home in GROND, with Mac at the wheel and Eddie at his station, while Tyler and Finn hung back to refuel the truck. She didn't wait up for them at the chateau. The team still had preparations to make, but her body would not let her stay awake another minute. She would nap for a few hours, and then get back to work.

After a yawning good night to Eddie, she kicked off her shoes and climbed into bed. Sleep came on quickly, perhaps thanks to Franklin's information. Her dad's murder and history with the Agency were a shock, but they were answers—real answers. She found solace there. Tyler would help her through the rest. She had misjudged him.

WHEN TALIA NEXT AWOKE, she found the late morning sun pouring through the break in her curtains. How long had she slept? She had no idea. The room had no clock, and she hadn't checked the time on her phone before passing out. After a quick shower, she walked down the hall to knock on Eddie's door.

No answer.

She pushed in, one hand covering her eyes. "Eddie, if you're in the shower, say something. Quick." But she heard no running water from the bathroom. She dropped her hand. "He's probably in Mission Control."

In no particular hurry, Talia tromped down the stairs to the next floor and rounded the corner into the big media room. "Eddie, you should have—"

Empty.

Downstairs, the great room was empty as well. The fireplace was cold. "Where is everybody?" Looking past the fireplace, she saw the double doors to Tyler's master suite hanging open and walked in. "Hey! Tyler! Are you in here?"

A shaft of light shone in from the balcony, spilling across the carpet. The bed was made. The bathroom door was open. She turned in a slow circle until her gaze fell on the largest of Tyler's Orthodox oil paintings, hanging on the wall above his desk. The scene depicted a wolf and lamb lying peacefully in a deep green valley underneath a quote in gold Cyrillic lettering.

A blinking green light beneath the painting caught Talia's eye. Tyler had left his laptop open on the desk, with a thumb drive active. Talia walked over. Maybe the last thing Tyler had been working on would tell her where everyone had gone, assuming she could guess his password.

"Oh, Tyler. Really?" There was no password. She frowned at his poor security as the screen came to life. There was only one file in the thumb drive folder, one with a file extension Talia didn't recognize. She tried clicking on it. A document full of garbled symbols opened.

A fraction of a second later, the computer ran an automatic decryption program. Line by line the symbols resolved into names and numbers. The column headings were BIDDER, RE-SERVE, and ACCOUNT NUMBER, and the center column of every line read $250,000. This was an auctioneer's list of buyers, with their earnest money stored in separate escrow accounts.

Scrolling down, Talia found the auction notes.

ITEM FOR SALE: DETAILED DESIGN FOR AIR-BREATHING HYPERSONIC MISSILE

BROKER: THE ENGLISHMAN, STANDARD FEE

BIDDING TO COMMENCE FOLLOWING PROOF-OF-CONCEPT DEMONSTRATION

It looked like Tyler had found a list of Lukon's buyers, compiled by the Englishman, the third-party broker referenced in the Dark Web post he had shown her back in Tiraspol. It was a serious lead. Why hadn't he shared it with her?

Talia lifted her eyes from the laptop to the wolf and lamb painting. She focused on the Cyrillic, a scripture reference in archaic Russian—something about a wolf dwelling with a lamb. The word for "wolf" gave her trouble. In her language studies, Talia had learned that older Russian and Cyrillic often borrowed words and letters from Greek. She sounded out the phonetics in her head. What she came up with made her world tilt on edge.

LUKON.

CHAPTER FIFTY-SEVEN

LUKON.

The name filled Talia's mind, slamming piece after piece of the puzzle into place until she let out a scream. She swept the laptop off the desk, stumbling across the floor until she grabbed the high back of an upholstered armchair to keep from collapsing to the carpet.

Lukon. Tyler. The Wolf.

They were one and the same. Tyler had played her. After all his talk of God and forgiveness, Tyler had turned out to be the sociopath she had always thought him to be. But Franklin and Eddie had traced Lukon's messages. Tyler could not have sent them. Talia herself was his alibi.

"An accomplice," she said to the empty room. "He must have used an accomplice." With Tyler's connections, that could mean almost anyone. She let the accomplice's identity rest for the time being and let her conclusions roll onward.

If Tyler was Lukon, then he had spread rumors of his own impending heist across the Dark Web and used them as false intelligence to manipulate Brennan and the CIA. Talia and Eddie had been unwitting tools, helping him case Avantec security protocols and access their servers. And when the task of stealing the hypersonic designs proved more daunting than he had first thought, he had tricked them into helping him put together the team of elite thieves he needed.

So he could stay on schedule. To blow up Washington, DC.

But Talia was not some random patsy. Tyler had targeted her. He had arranged to work with her out of some sick fascination with her family. Tyler was Lukon. He had assassinated her father.

She stared at the painting again, at the green eyes of the wolf, rimmed with the same gold. Talia's memories had not been wrong. Tyler *had* been present at her father's death. And that was where he'd become fascinated with her. That was how he knew the way she liked her coffee, her favorite soda. How long had he been following her? Fifteen years?

Another scream. Talia chucked her phone at the painting with all her might, ripping a hole through the canvas between the wolf and lamb. She dropped to her knees and cried.

"EDDIE!" TALIA RAN TO THE CENTER of the great room, shouting for the geek. While they had slept, Tyler and the thieves had set off to launch their attack on Gryphon, gaining a head start of several hours. Before leaving for the previous night's job, Tyler had asked Eddie to arrange a no-questions-asked cargo flight to get the balloon into its launch position beside the Black Sea. A simple phone call could have changed the timing of the flight.

Talia and Eddie had one play if they wanted to stop the heist. The stolen balloon had to launch from the Black Sea, close to Gryphon, but Ivanov could fly the Mark Seven straight to the airship from Milan. She had to bring him into the loop.

"Eddie!" Talia called again, jogging down the steps to the kitchen.

She stopped at the bottom.

Conrad stood at the range top, calmly stirring a pan of plain scrambled eggs. "Your friend is not here. He left with Finn and the others hours ago."

"He left with them?" Talia advanced toward the island, watching the cook and kicking herself for leaving her Glock in her room. "Or was he dragged away kicking and screaming?"

"Ehh." Conrad bobbled his head as he lifted the pan from the fire. "I don't recall any screaming. But our Scottish friend is fairly adept at keeping a man quiet."

So they had taken Eddie. Tyler still needed his skills. Talia tracked every movement of Conrad's hands, wary. The carving knife stood within his reach, and she had seen how accurately he could throw it. "Are you going to kill me?"

"Don't be absurd, my dear. I'm going to feed you." He slid the eggs onto a plate, added a fork, and set them in front of her.

Talia didn't move a muscle. "They're poisoned."

"Far from it." Conrad removed his apron and kept talking as if it were any other morning. "You row, correct? Did Adam ever tell you I rowed in school, as well?"

She didn't answer.

"Wooden shells and waxed runners. Nothing so fast as your team at Georgetown, but we had our victories. We had our losses too." He hung the apron on a hook and turned to face her, shoving his fingers into the pockets of his slacks and casting a pointed glance at the eggs. "After a hard day on the water, my grandmother would always cook for me, something warm. When your world comes crashing down, a little warmth makes all the difference."

Who was this guy? A friend? An enemy? Something oddly neutral like their Swiss surroundings? Talia didn't know how to process his kindness. Tears brimmed in her eyes. "Why me, Conrad? I get that Tyler wanted to con the Agency into putting this heist together, but why me? Why, after all this time, after what he did to my father, did he crawl back into my life?"

In answer the cook laid a silver chain across the edge of her plate. Threaded at its end were a cross made of bronze nails and a dog tag that matched the one Talia still wore around her neck.

She stared at them in shock. If Tyler was the chief suspect in her father's assassination, then the dog tag and cross were the smoking gun. "Those belonged to my father."

"Adam is sorry, my dear. He is sorry for all of it."

"*Sorry?*" She snatched up the chain and shoved the dog tag in his face, with the cross below. "Look at that name. Read it! Nicolai Inger. Tyler killed my father. And he's sorry? He's a murderer, Conrad. How does *that* fit in with his faith?"

"Sin. Forgiveness. Redemption. Your father's murder did not fit in with our faith. Everything that followed does. We forgive because Christ forgave. Forgiveness belongs to him, Talia. One debt paid for all."

Talia hung the chain around her neck and tucked the two emblems under her shirt, reuniting them with the dog tag she had carried for fifteen years. "I'm bringing him down. And when I'm done, I'm coming back for you."

THE TESLA FLEW DOWN THE ROAD south to Milan, weirdly silent despite its speed. Talia had never touched the eggs. Conrad had protested, urging her to eat before she left, but he had done nothing to stop her from taking the car.

She punched on the autopilot and picked up her phone, hands shaking so much she could hardly dial. The line rang once, twice. "Pick up, Pavel." It went to voice mail. She slapped the wheel. "Dr. Ivanov. This is Natalia. Call me when you get this."

Talia hung up and dialed again. A man at the Langley switchboard answered, his voice tinny and hollow. "Identify."

"Inger, Talia. Emergency call. Badge number 29753."

"Verified. What section?"

"Ops Directorate. Russia Eastern European Division." Talia closed her eyes and sighed. "*Other*. Get me Frank Brennan."

There was a long, static-filled pause on the line. "I'm sorry. Mr. Brennan is out of the country inspecting a station attached to his section."

"Then forward the call."

"Unable. He's currently in transit—a commercial flight from Bucharest to Frankfurt."

It took several heartbeats for the implications of that first city to sink in. "Repeat that please."

"Mr. Brennan is on a commercial flight from Bucharest to Frankfurt. We can't connect to his sat phone because of interference from the aircraft comm systems."

She didn't hear most of the last part. *Bucharest. Romania.* Franklin had told her the Lukon messages were traced to a café in Bran, Romania. And to get her on this assignment, Tyler must have had an inside man. Talia almost didn't want to ask the next question. "How long was Frank in Romania?"

"Stand by, please."

Another long pause.

"Several days, ma'am."

"Thank you." She hung up and let the phone drop into her lap. Her own boss was Tyler's accomplice. Talia had been right to suspect him way back in her first week. Jordan should have listened.

CHAPTER
FIFTY-EIGHT

TALIA DROVE straight to the aerospace expo. She had to find Ivanov before his Mark Seven demonstration. Finn had not been wrong about the increased security measures that followed the incident with Sibby. The expo organizers had brought in multiple contractors to cover the gaps.

Paramilitary vehicles with a variety of logos were parked in the grass. Guards walking the fence line eyed the Tesla as Talia drove by. And there were more—lots more—crowded around the queue of impatient guests at the gate, putting purses and briefcases through portable X-ray machines.

Talia winced as she pulled into the lot and saw the guard at the front of the line scanning badges. The expo was a closed event. She had no badge, and Eddie was not there to whip something up. She would have to improvise.

She parked at the back of the lot and waited.

A prime candidate left the gate a few minutes later—high heels, nice and unstable, eyes buried in her phone. Perfect. Talia left the Tesla and jinked over an aisle, lining up her approach. She hit the woman at half speed and spun her off balance.

"I'm sorry. So sorry." Talia caught the poor woman's arm

to keep her from falling across the hood of a BMW, and then attempted to help her lift the strap of her purse back up to her shoulder.

"*Guarda dove stai andando, tu klutz!*" The woman batted Talia's hand away and stomped off, wobbling a bit on her right heel.

Talia watched her go, then headed for the gate. "I really am sorry . . . *Gianna*," she whispered, reading the badge she had stolen before clipping it to her blouse. "But you didn't have to go all *Jersey Shore* on me."

The guy scanning badges didn't give Talia a second look. And the metal detector failed to sense the Glock tucked into the small of her back with its three remaining ceramic bullets. Three bullets, that was all Talia would get. Three chances to take out her father's killer.

She left the gate behind and steeled herself for her next obstacle. In all likelihood, one other member of Tyler's team had been left behind.

Valkyrie.

Talia narrowed her eyes with no small measure of malice as she searched the booths and displays for Ivanov and his fake aide, hoping for the chance to knock the con woman flat on her rear end. But she didn't see either of them.

The general flow of conference-goers moved toward the big tents between the runways. A crowd was gathering near the one with Avantec's three-rocket logo. Ivanov's demonstration. Talia checked the clock on her phone. He wasn't supposed to speak until the afternoon. Were they starting early?

She quickened her pace, ignoring the gripes and complaints of the guests she bumped and jostled. "Dr. Ivanov! Pavel!"

Again, she didn't see him.

Several Avantec employees stood on the black platform in front of the tent. Bazin was among them, which meant Ivanov couldn't be far away. Bazin was locked in a heated discussion with a distressed and sweaty Italian in a pinstripe suit. She took him to be one of the expo's organizers. The Russian bear growled. The Italian answered with wild gestures, pointing at the tent. Something was wrong.

"Hey! Bazin!"

He didn't answer. The Italian had his full attention.

The crowd pressed against her more than before, and Talia glanced over her shoulder to see a six-pack of uniformed officers marching through—men on a mission. These were not contract security guards. They were bona fide *polizia*. She saw her chance.

She pushed back through the mass of people and maneuvered in behind the cops, falling into step. A no-nonsense look and a rapid flash of Gianna-the-*Jersey-Shore*-Girl's badge got her past the Avantec men at the platform steps. Once through, she held back a pace and listened.

The lead police officer rattled off something in Italian.

Bazin frowned. "English, please. Unless you speaks Russian."

Apparently, he didn't speak either. He rattled off something else, and the sweating suit from the expo translated. "*Ispettore* Diolo demands to see the body."

What had Valkyrie done? Talia no longer had the patience to wait on the sidelines. "Bazin!"

Their eyes met, recognition set in, and the Russian's countenance fell—the face a man makes when he feels a headache coming on. He nodded at two of his men and they closed in, blocking Talia's view.

"Wait! I have information about what happened to Dr. Ivanov!"

A grumble in Romanian. The two muscly minions stepped aside like two halves of a heavy curtain, and Bazin gave her a flat look. "What information?"

Meanwhile, the Italian police officer kept peppering away at the suit from the expo, becoming more and more agitated. The suit forced himself between Talia and Bazin. "I am sorry, but the *ispettore* insists on seeing the body."

"It's . . . there." Talia pointed at the tent's entrance, where two men in thick glasses and jackets marked POLIZIA MORTU-ARIA had emerged with a gurney, transporting a body bag. They pushed it toward the platform ramp.

Talia did not wait for an invitation. She shoved her way around the suit and Bazin. "Stop. You there. Hang on."

The men let the gurney roll to a halt and backed up, giving her room. Hesitantly, needing to know but afraid of who she would find, Talia pulled back the zipper and put a hand to her lips, breathing out the name as a whisper. "Val?"

The grifter's lips were blue beneath a thin layer of artificial color. Talia passed a hand over the open eyelids, and by some measure of grace, they stayed shut.

"*Scusi, signora. É necessaria un'autopsia immediata.*" The older of the two men, perhaps the local medical examiner, would wait no longer. He zipped up the bag and the two started for the ramp again.

The *ispettore* walked beside them, shouting, clearly upset they had disturbed his crime scene, but the medical examiner waved him off.

"She came at me with a gun."

Surprised by a voice she had never expected to hear again, Talia turned to see Pavel Ivanov wearing the metallic-mesh pressure suit he used when flying his experimental aircraft. She wrapped him in a hug. "I thought you were dead. They were talking about a body, and I didn't see you. I assumed the worst."

Ivanov pushed her away, looking down at his pressure suit, wet with water and blood. He seemed dazed. "I cannot get the stain out."

The policemen were still following the body. Bazin was busy arguing with the sweaty suit. For a moment that would not last long, Talia had Ivanov to herself. She pulled him into the tent, into the shadow of the Mark Seven's composite wing. "What happened? What do you mean, she came at you with a gun?"

"There was so much blood." His eyes stared right through her. Talia wasn't sure he even recognized her.

"Pavel. It's Talia."

That seemed to do it. His pupils tightened in focus. "Talia?"

"Yes. I'm here. I have urgent information about the threat to you and Avantec, but first tell me what's going on."

He nodded. "My aide. I don't think she really worked for the expo. I was preparing for a dry run of the demonstration in the tent's back office, when that"—he glanced at the platform, the spot where Talia had stopped the gurney—"woman interrupted me. She drew a gun and demanded I give her the voiceprint code for Gryphon. She told me she was out of time. She . . ." His voice trailed off, eyes drifting.

Talia caught his chin and reeled him back in. "And you gave her the code."

"No. I refused. She came at me. I made a grab for the gun. It went off." He looked down at the stain on his suit. "So much blood."

There were voices on the platform. The *ispettore* had given up on the medical examiner and returned. He would want to interview Ivanov, and under no circumstances would he let him leave. Talia was out of options.

"Is the Mark Seven fueled and ready?"

Ivanov squinted at her. "What?"

She grabbed his shoulders. "Focus, Pavel. The Mark Seven. Is it fueled up and ready to fly?"

"Yes. Of course."

"Good. It's time for your demonstration." Talia pinched the metal mesh at his bicep, assessing the elasticity. It could work. "And . . . I'm going to need your spare suit."

CHAPTER
FIFTY-NINE

GROND THE VAN
LOCATION UNKNOWN

EDDIE JERKED AGAINST THE SHACKLES that confined him to GROND's workstation. Tyler had been a little too honest during the airfield surveillance trip when he had joked about chaining a hacker to the computer.

"Stop, please." Darcy glanced back from the driver's seat. "You will only damage your little wrists, yes?"

Why did she have to hurt him like that?

"They're not 'little wrists.'" Eddie considered the validity of his argument for a heartbeat, then sighed. "Okay, maybe they *are* little. And maybe I like *Star Wars* and fantasy role-playing games, and maybe I have an unhealthy collection of fidget spinners, but I'm still a real man. I can do things with digital code your mindless ogre friend Mac never dreamed of."

"Mac was in Europe's astronaut program."

Eddie couldn't even win on the brains front. He let out a guttural "Aaaaggh!" and thrashed against the shackles.

"Okay. Okay. I do think of you as a *real* man. I always have. Happy?"

He settled down and dropped his head onto his knuckles. "No."

The two were alone in the van. Eddie knew this from sound, not sight. He had woken up chained to the workstation and wearing a blindfold, but he could not hear Finn's obnoxious accent or smell Mac's sasquatch breathing.

The last thing Eddie remembered was Mac's ugly face hovering over him in the darkness of his bedroom. He had felt the prick of a needle and heard Tyler's voice as the blindfold went over his eyes. That traitor had told him to be thankful it wasn't a bag.

It irked Eddie to realize he *was* thankful it wasn't a bag. Bags were stinking, musty breeding grounds for mold and fungus. Gross.

Okay, maybe he wasn't a real man.

The motion of the psychotic yet undeniably cute Frenchwoman's driving felt unnatural. Maybe it was an effect of the drugs, and maybe not, but Eddie had vertigo. And the engine noise was all wrong—too loud, too droning. "Are we in a plane, Darcy?"

She didn't answer.

She didn't have to.

The cargo plane. Before Lauterbrunnen, Tyler had asked Eddie to find air transport for GROND and the balloon truck from Milan to the Black Sea. Eddie had put out a request, and a little Albanian outfit with a propeller-driven Antonov AN-70 cargo plane had been happy to oblige. No questions. Cash only.

Eddie's ears popped. They were descending. Beneath his sneakers, he felt the grind of the gear coming down, followed far too closely by the jarring bump of the landing. Minutes later, light filtered in through the blindfold, and he heard the *bang* of metal hitting concrete behind them. Darcy backed GROND down a ramp and stopped.

A man came to the window and conversed with her in French. Eddie heard the *flip-flip* of paper currency changing hands. Moments later, the ramp motored up and the thunderous growl of the propellers receded, leaving the two of them in relative silence.

The blindfold came off.

From behind his chair, Darcy placed Eddie's glasses on his nose at an awkward angle, and he immediately looked around. Through the tinted rear windows he could see a broken tarmac with crops of weeds growing in the cracks. Out the front windscreen, he saw nothing but deep blue water.

Darcy settled her chin on his shoulder. "You know. I kind of like you this way, *Red Leader*, all chained up so I can do whatever I want." She rose up again and flicked his ear.

"Don't do that. It's cruel."

"Perhaps." Darcy made a popping sound with her lips and flicked his other ear. "But I think you like it, no?"

He did. A little. That was so wrong. Pouting, Eddie tried to cross his arms, but the shackles caught him. He sighed. "I hate you."

"No you don't." Darcy opened the door, dragged out a pair of bulky duffel bags, and slid it closed again.

He glanced over his shoulder. She was gone.

"You might think about rolling down a window!"

Eddie took a deep breath to put her out of his mind and surveyed the workstation. Cursors blinked on every monitor. All the CPUs were humming, and the shackles gave him enough freedom of movement to work the keyboard. Darcy had left him there with several teraflops of computing power and a SATCOM antenna linked to the CIA mainframe. She might as well have left him with a machine gun in one hand and a nuclear missile in the other.

"This might be fun." Eddie rolled his wrists in the shackles, cracked his knuckles, and let his fingers hover over the keyboard. "Okay. Here we go."

"Oops!" Darcy flung open the van door, flooding his monitors with daylight. "I almost forgot." She reached in and flicked a lighted switch on the floor, about six inches beyond Eddie's reach. The monitors blinked off. The CPUs spun down. She gave him a wink. "I will be back, yes? Do not run away." The door slammed closed again.

"Aaaaggh!" Eddie cried again. "I hate you!"

She pounded on the door and he heard her muted, melodic voice from outside. "No you don't!"

Eddie let his chin drop to his chest. "No. No I don't."

FINN LOOKED UP from his work in the back of the box truck to see Darcy lugging a pair of duffels across the desolate Black Sea airbase. Crumbling buildings, crumbling bunkers, all on a peninsula of sun-bleached concrete jutting out into the Black Sea. And then there were the rows and rows of rusted, forgotten aircraft. He found the sight of them depressing. Lukon had sent them to a kind of post-apocalyptic purgatory—once a Soviet naval airbase, later a military storage facility called a boneyard, and now abandoned to decay.

"You have the capsule ready?" Darcy let the bags drop to the concrete.

Those bags were filled with explosives. "Please don't do that."

"Do what?"

He traded a screwdriver for a wrench, adjusting one of the four small reaction control jets used for positioning the balloon in flight. "Nothing."

A few minutes later, the two carried the capsule to a helicopter pad at the water's edge. After using a pneumatic gun to anchor the launch clamps to the concrete, Finn hooked up the balloon to a hose running from more than a dozen hydrogen tanks and began the long process of inflation.

He lifted his hand off the valve. "Watch this while I change into my pressure suit. Do *not* let it fill too fast. This hydrogen gas is mixing with the oxygen inside the balloon. One little rip, a spark of static, and boom." He spread his hands to form a mushroom cloud. "*Comprendez-vous?*"

Darcy made an incredulous *pbbt* sound. "Your French is atrocious. I am a chemist. You think I do not know how to safely handle hydrogen?"

"Yeah. Well"—Finn glanced at the bags of rockets and explosives she had dropped onto the concrete—"safety really isn't your thing."

A few minutes later, Finn emerged from the truck wearing a formfitting pressure suit and an aerodynamic back shell filled with his chute and equipment. With the high-pressure hydrogen pouring in, the polyethylene balloon had already stretched to the height of a small skyscraper.

He strolled over and checked the gauge, casting a glance at Darcy.

Darcy unzipped one of her duffels. "I told you. I know what I'm doing. Now come here, yes? It is time to strap on your wings."

She called them wings, but in reality, they were packs of three rockets each, fueled with Darcy's own special blend of insanity. She strapped the first set to his right ankle, then moved on to his left. "You must use rockets because a wingsuit will not work in the mesosphere."

"And neither will a parachute." Finn raised his arms so she could secure a control box to his waist. "I remember the briefing. The chute in my shell pack is a streamer. It won't inflate. The air is too thin up there."

"Correct. The streamer stabilizes your flight, nothing more." She handed him a trigger wired to the control box. "Acceleration, deceleration—you do it all with rockets. *Comprenez-vous?*"

"So that's how you say it."

"Shut up and get in the capsule."

Capsule was a strong word. Finn climbed aboard XPC's conical jumping platform. It might have been stitched together from soda cans. The thing had barely enough structural integrity to survive the ascent, let alone any positioning maneuvers with its RCS thrusters. And it had no door, leaving him exposed to rapid drops in temperature and pressure.

Heating elements laced into the metallic mesh of his pressure suit would counteract the cold, but the batteries had limited life. Finn would have to wait until the brink of hypothermia before activating the system. He turned around and knelt inside the glorified aluminum can. "I can't believe Lukon talked me into this."

"You did not need to be talked into anything." Darcy turned the valve to shut down the hydrogen and began disconnecting the hose. "All you needed was the opportunity."

She had a point. Finn's entire life had been a search for the status of *legendary*. Jumping from target to target within the mesosphere would earn him that title for sure.

"The last mountain was empty," she said, bringing him his helmet. "Now you climb a new mountain to seek a new god, yes?"

"No." Finn jerked the helmet from her hands. "I don't know. Maybe." He put it on and pressurized the seal. When he tried to speak again, his voice bounced back at him, muted by the polycarbonate face mask. "Head over to the van. Let's do a SATCOM check before I launch."

Darcy held a hand to her ear and scrunched up her nose. "Launch? Okay, if you think you are ready." She laid a hand on the actuator that would unlock the anchor clamps.

Finn waved his hands. "No, no, no! That's not what I said!"

"*Au revoir.*" She pulled the lever.

CHAPTER
SIXTY

As Talia ran out from the dressing area at the back of the tent, she saw Avantec workers ripping away the entire face of the expo tent. Bazin the bear danced back and forth on the platform out front, arms spread wide, herding the *ispettore* and his men down the ramp.

She saw Ivanov as well, through the angular canopy of the Mark Seven's flight deck, taking his place at the controls. He revved the engines and rotated the aircraft to face the crowd. She took a last look around and ran up the moving hatch steps to join him.

Ivanov occupied the left seat in the cockpit. Talia took the right. She set her helmet on her knee. The spare suit, with its highly stretchable mesh, had a one-size-fits-all feel. "Ready for takeoff?"

"Yes." He flicked a toggle, and the hatch motored up behind them. "So, Miss Talia, where to?"

"Gryphon," she said, pulling her restraints down over her shoulders. "Lukon and his band of thieves are already on their way."

302

"Then we must head them off at the pass, as you Americans say. Hold on to something. This first stage is a little rough."

The Mark Seven rose into a hover, ghosting out toward the safe zone of the water runway. As soon as the whole craft had cleared the cheering crowd, Ivanov canted her forward and jammed the throttles to the stop. The aircraft leaped into the sky.

Talia fought against the G-forces to look down at the expo. Every head had ducked against the spray of water kicked up by the jets. Now the onlookers all peeked out from under their arms to watch the Mark Seven rocket away. "Oh, I think they'll remember this."

The climb was fast and violent, nothing like the gradual ascent of a conventional airplane. In short order, the altitude reading projected on the canopy in front of her rolled through twenty-five thousand feet.

"We did not get a proper clearance." Ivanov fixed his gaze on the sky above them. "Watch out for commercial airliners. We would not want to split one in half."

She laughed.

He didn't.

"Oh. Right." Talia looked up through the glass.

By sixty thousand feet, where the daytime sky grew dark, their climb rate had slowed to a shallow angle. Ivanov made a check of his systems and set the autopilot. "Helmets on."

Talia watched him lock his helmet into the rigid collar of the suit and tried unsuccessfully to mimic the procedure.

Ivanov smiled at her efforts. He flicked a switch on his collar, activating a microphone, and leaned over to help. "Like this." She heard a *hiss* and a sharp *thock* as he locked her helmet in place.

She didn't feel any different, other than a sudden urge to scratch her nose. She activated her microphone. "Shouldn't I feel something?"

"Not unless the Mark Seven loses cabin pressure. Gryphon is pressurized as well. The suits are a mere precaution. Should we lose pressure on the airship, we run the risk of exposure to a near-vacuum."

"You mean the kind where blood literally boils?"

"No, no." The microphone added a layer of static to Ivanov's laugh. "The air in the lower mesosphere is still a thousand times thicker than the thermosphere, the true edge of space. Although, without the suits, the more readily available moisture in our bodies would, indeed, flash boil. The water on our eyeballs, for instance."

Talia grimaced at the image of moisture boiling away from her eyeballs.

"The rest comes with time. After thirty seconds we would experience"—he paused as if searching for the right word—"*bloating*. Yes, bloating in the soft tissues like you have never imagined. Only then, after our subsequent deaths, might our blood begin to boil."

If Ivanov was trying to offer her comfort, he had failed. "Thanks. That description was very reassuring."

Ivanov glanced at her, confused by her tone, then returned his attention to his readouts. "We have some time. The Mark Seven travels at Mach 2, but Gryphon is still an hour away."

Talia looked out through the windscreen, searching the sky as if she might see Finn's weather balloon way out in front. She knew she wouldn't. And yet she could feel it climbing toward the goal. "Mach 2 may not be enough. This race will be close."

CHAPTER
SIXTY-ONE

EDDIE HAD A PLAN.

It lasted all of ten seconds.

Darcy reappeared and flicked the main switch, activating GROND's computers, and the moment Eddie had a cursor, he started typing. His fingers flew over the keyboard, trying to get a message to Langley.

She slapped his hands away. "Stop that. You think I do not know what you are trying to do?"

He locked eyes with her, knuckles smarting. "Is that all you've got?"

"Eddie . . ."

He tried again.

She slapped his hands.

Back and forth they went, typing and slapping, typing and slapping, with little more than gobbledygook showing up on the monitors.

Finn's voice came over the SATCOM. "Oi! What're you two doing down there?"

They both stopped. Eddie checked the radio. In the struggle,

Darcy had hit the hot-mic switch. He shut it off and pressed the transmit key. "Nothing. We're . . . just . . ." He glanced at Darcy.

She shrugged.

". . . checking our systems." Eddie didn't know why he felt guilty. These two were the enemy. He was supposed to be mad at them. He *was* mad at them. At least, that's what he told himself.

"Focus," Finn said. "I'm riding up into the atmosphere's most electrically active zone under a big bag of explosive gas. I need to feel like I'm going to survive."

"Yeah. Okay. Stand by." Eddie switched to an internet screen and brought up a weather readout for the Black Sea region. He saw a chance for a little psychological revenge. He sweetened his tone. "Don't worry. Those mesospheric explosions only occur above bad weather. And I see only one patch of storms on the scope."

"Yeah. I see it too—a sea squall building to the east." Finn went quiet for a moment, and Eddie could hear the wheels turning. "So, which direction will I be jumping?"

"East." Eddie grinned at the mic, letting that sink in, then added, "I hope you get fried by a red elf and swallowed by a big blue sprite."

"Why, you little—"

Darcy switched off the SATCOM. "What are you doing?"

"I'm sorry." Eddie raised his hands as far as he could, rattling his chains. "Were you expecting me to cheer him on?"

She pursed her lips. "I get it. You are upset at how we treated you, yes? But that is no reason to curse the man to death. Jumpers are very superstitious, and Finn is in a delicate place right now. You must show sensitivity."

"I don't care. Why should I help you people?"

Her answer surprised him. "For your friend. Talia. Her life depends on Finn's success."

That was news to Eddie. "You're lying. Talia is safe, we left her back at the chateau."

"Not true. She is on her way to Gryphon as we speak, and Finn must get there first, or she will die."

Eddie looked from one of Darcy's deep brown eyes to the other.

She nodded, and all her insanity seemed to fall away for just a moment. *"Fais-moi confiance."*

He didn't know what *fais-moi confiance* meant, other than that Darcy was telling the truth. "Okay. You win."

"Good." Darcy switched on the radio. "Now tell Finn he will be all right."

"What? No."

"Do it."

Eddie sighed and pressed transmit. "Finn?"

"Yes?"

"You're going to be okay."

A long pause. "Thank you."

While they waited for the balloon to climb, Darcy had Eddie hack into Gryphon's encrypted GPS beacon. Finn needed pinpoint accuracy for the type of target-to-target jump he had planned. Eddie finished the hack, passed the coordinates to Darcy to calculate his trajectory, and gave Finn an altitude check. "I have you passing one hundred forty thousand now."

"My gauge reads the same. We're in sync."

"How does it look up there?"

"Like the edge of space, Red Leader. Thanks for the support. True blue. I know this isn't easy for you."

Finn had never called him Red Leader before, and Eddie could swear he heard a quiver in the Aussie's voice. He squinted at Darcy. "Is he getting emotional?"

"No. He is getting cold." Darcy leaned over him and keyed the mic. "Finn, the cold is penetrating your suit, yes? Switch on your heaters."

"No worries. I can wait a little longer."

They heard his teeth chattering. "Hypothermia," Darcy said.

"He has waited too long. The cold is affecting his thinking." She tried again. "Finn, listen to me. Turn your heaters on."

There were several seconds of static. "I'm telling you. I'm fine."

Eddie gave it a try. "Finn . . . this is Ed—er . . . *Red Leader*. I'm looking at your battery readout." Eddie had no such thing. "You've got plenty of juice. Go ahead and turn those heaters on for me."

"Yeah, all right, Red Leader. If you insist."

Darcy patted Eddie's shoulder. "See? He needs you. With your help, he will make it."

Eddie stared at his screen for a long moment. "No. He won't."

He brought Darcy's targeting plot over to the main monitor. A split display showed the lateral and vertical paths from the balloon to the airship, with real-time updates accounting for the balloon's wind readouts. The updating vertical path gradually dipped below the airship. "The winds are stronger than forecast up there. He's going to fall short."

"That cannot be right." Darcy pulled his keyboard over and began typing.

"Can't he get closer? I thought the balloon had an RCS."

She kept working, occasionally drawing in the air with her finger, doing math in her head. "He has had the RCS on since launch, pushing him east over the water, but it is not very strong. It was designed for station-keeping only."

"What about going higher?"

"We are already pushing the balloon to its limit. At higher altitude, it may burst." Darcy entered several more calculations before finally sitting back in triumph. On the display, she had aligned the vertical path with the airship again. "There. A little extra speed—a longer burn from my rockets—and *voilà*, he will make it."

"You forgot the need for deceleration."

Darcy scowled at him. "I did not. I can do the math. Finn has time to slow down for the landing."

"I can do the math too." Eddie pointed to a line of data below the display, jerking his wrist against his shackle. "He has the time, but not the fuel. His rockets will burn out before he slows down enough, and he'll skip right off the top of Gryphon. Darcy, if Finn attempts this jump, he's going to die."

Her eyes widened. Darcy smashed her hand down on the transmitter. "Finn! Do not jump!"

"Have to. N-no other option. No p-p-parachute, remember?" His teeth were still chattering.

"The heaters aren't enough," Eddie said. "He's still hypothermic. He's not in his right mind."

Darcy keyed the mic again. "The hydrogen will dissipate. The balloon will descend. Stay on board. We'll find you."

"B-balloon won't last that long. S-seeing flashes of electric act-tivity. P-p-purples. R-reds."

Eddie checked the weather screen. "That can't be right. The storm's too far away. You're seeing things."

"I c-can see the airship in the flashes. She's the size of a f-football stadium. I c-c-can't miss."

"You won't miss." Eddie laid his hand on top of Darcy's, pressing the transmitter down with her. "You'll hit the top and skip off. Do you understand? You don't have enough fuel to slow down. Finn, this is Red Leader. Stand down!"

"Balloon has m-maxed out at a hundred s-seventy-five thousand. Starting to d-descend. C-c-can't wait any longer. I'm out the door."

"Finn!"

BLUE SPRITES. That's what the geek had called them. Finn watched the strange bulbs of lightning flash at regular intervals all around the massive airship. He had to stick the landing. That was all. Use the conductive key at the hatch and get inside. Gryphon would have heat for its servers, and the rigid composites made it impervious to the electrical storms—a safe haven in a deadly realm.

Frost obscured the edges of Finn's mask. With a shaking hand, he pressed Darcy's trigger, firing the rockets.

Tumbling.

Turning.

Bedlam.

He had forgotten the streamer.

Straining against the forces acting on his body, Finn reached down to his waist and pulled the rip cord. The nylon streamer slapped against his legs and then, with a tremendous jerk, it straightened him out. He bobbled for several seconds, working the rockets to find his line, searching for the airship. In a rippling flash of purple sprites, he found it.

He could do this.

"I'm on c-c-course, Red Leader." Darcy had warned him that the force of his fall through the charged air would kill the signal, but he transmitted anyway. Ahead, he saw another round of flashes, blue this time. Gorgeous, but deadly. "You should s-see it up here. It's—"

A burst of red shocked him into silence. A thousand feet above him—two thousand at most—a rapidly expanding disc of red plasma swallowed the sky. Finn looked back in time to see it split the balloon in half. The trapped hydrogen and oxygen ignited in an explosion of brilliant yellow, made humongous by the low pressure.

So Darcy's contingency plan—skip the jump and ride it out in the balloon—had not been such a great option after all.

Gryphon grew larger. Finn had his course wired. He set his aim past the airship's far end, burned on that line for another second to make room for deceleration, tucked his knees, and pushed his legs out front, reversing his thrust. A few seconds later—far too early—his rockets sputtered out.

The ship came up fast. A round of blue sprites flashed all

around, reflecting off the composite surface as Finn's boots made contact. His body slammed into the deck. His helmet bounced. The impact set his head to ringing, but he kept enough mental acuity to roll himself over. His streamer still flew behind him, straps whipping his shoulders. He tried digging in with his gloves to slow himself down, but the surface was impossibly smooth.

He never got the chance to look back.

Finn knew he had reached the end of the envelope when his boots lost contact. He grabbed wildly for the streamer, the only thing within reach that his gloves could grip.

And then his body pitched over the side.

CHAPTER SIXTY-TWO

THE MARK SEVEN'S CLIMB had steadily degraded. The four jet engines clawed for every foot in the thinning atmosphere. Ivanov pointed this out to Talia, showing her the correct read-out in her heads-up display, and then began flipping switches—a long line of them on the dashboard.

"What are those?"

"We're passing eighty thousand, entering the transition zone between aerodynamic and astrodynamic flight. The Mark Seven's turbojets are almost useless here. I'm activating the APS, the Alternative Propulsion System."

She eyed the line of switches. "What sort of alternative propulsion?"

"Rockets."

He punched a red button. The Mark Seven surged upward, shaking so much Talia thought it might break apart.

"These are thrust oscillations! The dampeners will settle it out momentarily!" By the time Ivanov had finished the statement, the dampeners had done their job, ending the quaking. The roar of the rockets diminished as well. He lowered his voice to a normal level. "The faster we ascend, the less the rockets have to work to hold our speed. That is the nature of physics."

She could tell he was enjoying the science of the flight as much as the exhilaration of the rockets, perhaps more. Talia watched the control wheel tilt and rock under the influence of the autopilot. She pressed her helmet against the glass to her right and looked down. A gray-white exhaust trail fell below them, drawing a line toward the earth. She could see the entirety of the Black Sea, along with a growing storm near its eastern shore. "Incredible. I—"

A gun barrel dug into her back between the shoulder blades. Was this Ivanov's idea of a joke?

Talia lifted both hands and slowly turned away from the canopy. "Pavel, what are you doing?"

But Ivanov had his hands up as well. Mac, sporting a pressure suit of his own, stood behind the pilot seat with a machine gun leveled at the CEO's head. She kept her slow turn going, and a second man came into view. "Lukon."

The eyes behind the polycarbonate shield—eyes that had haunted her nightmares—were grieved. He stepped back and lowered his barrel. "With you, I prefer Tyler."

"Is there a difference?"

"Yes. A great deal of difference."

"How—" Ivanov looked from one to the other. "Where—"

"We stowed away in the shaft for the docking hatch." Tyler glanced back at the shaft and nodded. "Good job on that, by the way. Surprisingly roomy and comfortable."

"But what are you doing on my ship?"

"I should think that was obvious." Mac waved the machine gun back and forth. "We're hijackin' it."

Tyler touched the Scotsman's arm in a gesture that said, *Try to act like a professional.* "We needed a ride up to Gryphon. You don't mind. Do you?"

Ivanov made a grab for the controls.

Mac was too fast for him. The Scotsman let his gun hang from its strap and caught the CEO under the arms. He dragged Ivanov out of the pilot seat and tossed him to the floor at Tyler's feet.

Ivanov came up swinging, but Tyler raised his weapon. "Ah, ah, ah. Behave."

The last time Talia had seen those guns, they were loaded with clay rounds. And her Glock, with its three very-lethal bullets, was tucked into the right-leg cargo pocket of her suit. She could take them, but she would have to pick her moment.

"What about Finn and the weather balloon?" she asked, staying cooperative, hoping they would drop their guard. "Was that whole escapade robbing XPC an act for my benefit?"

Tyler's expression hardened, becoming unreadable. "No. But on occasion, contingencies must be enacted."

Contingencies did not sound good. Something had gone wrong. Talia swallowed. "And . . . Eddie?"

"Eddie's fine."

"Ha!" Mac climbed into the pilot seat while Tyler kept watch over the others. "Wee Man is more'n fine. He's havin' the time of his life, held captive by his dream girl."

Tyler shoved Ivanov to Talia's side of the cockpit. The barrel of his machine gun tracked the CEO at all times, never Talia. He didn't seem to consider her much of a threat. His mistake.

"She's on autopilot," Mac said. "But I need to get a feel for the controls before we reach the target. It'll be rough for a bit."

"I understand. Go ahead."

Rough sounded good to Talia. Mac punched off the autopilot. The Mark Seven bucked, disrupting Tyler's balance. Talia launched herself out of the seat.

She got one foot planted on the deck and stopped. Her cargo pocket was empty.

Mac steadied the aircraft.

Tyler found his balance. "Looking for this?" He held up Talia's gun and turned it over and back before sliding it into the pocket on his own leg.

The gun pressed into Talia's neck moments before had been a distraction, keeping her eyes faced away and her focus on the feel of the cold barrel against her skin. That way, she hadn't noticed the Glock leaving its place. Tyler was a true thief.

Of course, he was much worse than that. "You're a monster."

"I was. But not anymore." He gestured at Ivanov with his gun. "Dr. Ivanov is the monster these days. I know this looks bad, but Ivanov is still the one attempting to sell the hypersonic designs, not me. And he is the one with a missile pointed at Washington, DC."

"Wait." Mac shot a glance over his shoulder, frowning. "We're *not* sellin' the plans?" Apparently this was news to him.

Tyler motioned toward the controls with his gun. "Keep flying. You'll still get paid."

Talia wasn't buying any of it. "You tried to blame Ivanov before, in Tiraspol. I didn't believe you then, and I don't believe you now. You have no proof." Her hand went to the dog tags beneath her suit. "But I do. You're a murderer, Tyler. I can prove you killed my dad. Give me time and I'll prove you killed Dr. Visser too!"

"Dr. Visser *was* my proof. I didn't kill her. Ivanov did."

"Lies!" Ivanov took an angry step out of his corner, but a twitch of Tyler's trigger finger cowed him. "Lies," he said again, a little softer. "Ella was my partner."

"Ella was your prisoner," Tyler countered. He glanced at Talia. "Dr. Visser passed a note to me not long after I first gained Ivanov's confidence. The advances in hypersonics belonged to her, not him. But Ivanov kept her prisoner at Avantec, threatening her sister and her nephews to keep her from leaving."

Ivanov leaned closer to Talia. "This man is a criminal. He is a trickster, a liar. Do not believe a word he says."

She didn't want to. But Tyler's explanation had logic to it.

Talia remembered the day she had met the Dutch scientist. She remembered the nervous glances. "So your attack on the compound was what? A rescue?"

"She wouldn't leave without her designs. She knew how lethal they were. But the job went bad. I didn't know about Gryphon." Tyler thrust his chin toward Ivanov. "His system isolated the data by sending it to the airship, and he shot Ella before I could get her out of the building."

"Another lie," Ivanov said. "I didn't even have a gun. *You* shot Ella."

"Did I?" Tyler raised the machine gun to his shoulder, and fired.

Both Talia and Ivanov ducked away from the shots. When she looked up again, she expected to see the CEO crumpling to the deck. But he was fine—shaken, but fine. Tyler made a subtle nod toward the titanium wall. His shots had left three gray marks, similar in appearance to the marks she had found in Ivanov's lab. Tyler had been carrying the same type of weapon that night. He couldn't have killed Visser.

Ivanov saw the marks as well. Realization washed over his face. "That weapon is nonlethal."

The tensing of his jaw, his shoulders, told Talia he had come to a snap decision.

Tyler seemed to recognize the same signs. He let the machine gun fall against his hip and drew Talia's Glock. "Don't, Pavel. I don't want to use this, but I will."

The CEO backed down.

Tyler switched the Glock to his right hand and fished around in his cargo pocket. After a few seconds, he tossed a small metal object to Talia—a spent bullet, split like a flower at the tip. "I pulled that from Visser's ashes. I had to break into the morgue and steal it after Ivanov had the body destroyed."

He left the implications unsaid, but Talia understood. The spent round was too small to have come from Bazin's Desert

Eagle. Her gaze drifted up to Ivanov. She held up the bullet. "Did you do this? Did you kill Ella Visser?" Her trust in both of them was shaken. Who was telling the truth?

There was a cough from the pilot seat. "I hate to interrupt, but you'd all better hang on. Things might get a wee bit bumpy."

"What do you mean, *bumpy*?" Talia kept her eyes locked on Ivanov.

Mac rapped her arm with his knuckles and pointed out through the windscreen. She tore her eyes away from the killer and turned. The altitude readout in her heads-up display was rolling through one hundred sixty thousand. Blue and purple spheres, trailing tentacles of lightning, flashed above them. And in those flashes, she saw a massive black form.

Gryphon.

The rockets went quiet for a moment, then thundered at near full power to hold the Mark Seven in a hover a few feet below the airship. Red, yellow, and green arrows blinked on the lower fuselage, directing him to the correct position for docking.

Tyler pushed a hand against the ceiling for balance and shouted at him over the roar. "Keep her steady!"

"Easy ta say! Harder ta execute! It's not just the Mark Seven that's bouncin' around, is it? That Gryphon don' want to be tamed. She's a movin' target!"

"Let me do it!" Ivanov looked sincerely worried. "You'll damage her!" He turned to Tyler, who tracked him with the Glock despite all the jostling. "Consider a child's balloon caught in turbulent waters. That is Gryphon in the mesospheric currents." The aircraft bounced again and he caught himself on Talia's seat. "I don't know who this mindless brute of yours thinks he is, but he'll never manage to dock!"

A *clank* echoed through the hull. The rockets went silent.

Mac let go of the controls and crossed his arms, glowering at Ivanov. "You were sayin'?"

Despite the eerie silence, the turbulence continued. Talia held on to her seat as Gryphon's clamps drew the Mark Seven up the last few inches to the docking port. She heard a ripple of clinks and a hiss. The arrows above them changed to green circles.

"You." Tyler motioned to Ivanov with the Glock. "Go first. Open the hatch."

Ivanov scowled, but complied, stepping into the vertical shaft beneath the docking port. He steadied himself against the rail of the integrated ladder, but he made no move to unlock the hatch a few inches above his head.

"Open it," Tyler said.

"I will. Stop barking orders at me." Ivanov produced the same quartz key Talia had stolen, Eddie had cloned, and Val had returned. What had been the purpose of that exercise? Or of Val's subsequent death? She and Talia had not exactly been friends, but it had still hurt to see the grifter lying on that gurney, a cold and empty shell.

Ivanov pressed the key into a hexagonal keyhole and turned it until the quartz lit up green. With a heavy *clunk*, the exposed bolts slid back, and he eased the hatch open. A red glow illuminated the shaft beyond and ladder beyond. Ivanov immediately pressed a button in the upper shaft and laid a hand on the lever, glancing down at Talia.

The look on his face—the slight widening of those gray eyes—was almost regretful, a man about to toss away a favored possession. He wrapped an arm around the rail, and in that moment, Talia understood.

"Stop him! He's trying to blow the seal!"

CHAPTER SIXTY-THREE

MARK SEVEN EXPERIMENTAL AIRCRAFT
LOWER MESOSPHERE

TALIA HAD NOTHING USEFUL to grab on to. As she watched Ivanov crank the lever down, she prepared herself to be ejected into the extremes of Earth's upper atmosphere.

"Not today, mate."

A hand appeared from above, catching Ivanov's wrist in an iron grip and pulling the lever back into the safe position. Finn stuck his head down into the shaft and gave Talia a wink. "Welcome to Gryphon, your luxury accommodations in the sky."

LUXURY WAS A GROSS OVERSTATEMENT. Aesthetics had played no part in the design of Gryphon's flight deck. Exposed carbon fiber ribs arced low over a rubber panel floor. Data servers, stacked between the portal windows, took up the entirety of the side and rear bulkheads, while the forward bulkhead held the ship's scant controls and a booth marked emergency pressure chamber.

Finn looked like he'd run into some trouble breaking into the airship. Black streaks marred the front of his suit, and there were scorch marks on his calves. His helmet, hanging from a clip on his belt, had a chip in the shield.

Talia raised an eyebrow. "Rough day?"

"You've no idea. But I'm all right. Nine lives and all." He thrust his chin at Ivanov. "Oi. You. I left a streamer hanging from the front of your ship. Banged her up a bit as well—mostly with my face. If the insurance won't cover it, send me the bill."

Ivanov glared at him, seething. "Oh, I will do so much more."

It was a side of him Talia was only just beginning to recognize. She had been blinded by her affection for him, but Tyler's spent bullet had cracked open a door in her mind. And Ivanov's attempt to blow the pressure seal had flung that door wide. Tyler had set him up. By allowing Ivanov to go first up the ladder, Tyler had given him the opportunity to show his true colors. Finn had been waiting there as a safety net. But now Talia was faced with a choice between helping the man who killed her father and helping a man who might be planning to fire a hypersonic weapon at the US capital.

The electrical storm flashed outside, adding purples and reds to the antiseptic white of the overhead lights. Every flash came with a bump or roll that kept her constantly fighting for balance.

First Mac and then Tyler removed their helmets, clipping them to their belts as Finn had done. Talia struggled to do the same. Hers was stuck.

Finn came over to help. "Hang on," he said after a failed attempt to release the lock. "Something's not right." He checked the back of her neck, then glared at Ivanov. "Did you do this?"

Ivanov looked away.

"Brace yourself, Talia." Finn gave the helmet a forceful twist, and it came free. He let it drop to the floor.

"Hey. Don't I need that?"

"Not anymore. Looks like Ivanov tore the main valve from your collar. The gap's so big, you'd never hear the leak. Your suit is useless."

Talia had heard a *thock* when Ivanov helped her with the helmet. His never made that sound. She should have guessed. But an hour ago, she had still trusted him.

Finn nodded at a panel on her left arm, covered by a Velcro flap. "Check your gauge."

She ripped the flap back. The oxygen readout showed zero.

"If he'd blown the seal, you'd have died, whether you managed to stay on the Mark Seven or not." He gave her a wink. "Good thing I was here."

"One more offense for Mr. Ivanov's trial." Tyler laid a firm hand on the back of Ivanov's neck and steered him across the deck to the control section—a pair of terminals, each with a monitor and fold-down keyboard. He positioned Ivanov in front of the starboard terminal and folded the keyboard down to expose a flush microphone and a pair of lighted buttons. "Before we lock you up, we need some information. Use your voice ID pass code. Unlock the data vault."

"No."

"How aboot a little motivation, eh?" Mac raised his machine gun. "Let me give him a once-over with these fancy clay roonds."

"You're not helping." Tyler waved the Scotsman off, earning a sour look. "Pass code, Pavel. Now."

"Never." Ivanov ducked out of Tyler's grasp and backed away. "I will not help you steal my designs. You will fail, as that woman masquerading as my aide failed. She died in vain."

"No. She didn't." Tyler produced a smartphone and tapped the screen with his thumb. A recording of Ivanov's voice came through crystal clear in the quiet of the airship.

"Portia, Aria, Natasha."

Talia blanched at the way Ivanov's recorded self spoke each name. "Women? Really, Pavel?" She remembered Val's assessment of the man. She should have listened

Ivanov looked stricken. "I never gave your con woman my code words."

321

"You did." Tyler tapped the screen again, watching Ivanov's reaction.

"Portia, Natasha, Aria."

"And what's even better, you wanted to."

Finn coughed, reclining against a rack of servers on the other side of the deck. "You see, Dr. Ivanov, passwords are an aberration, a collision between human nature and the digital age. Our minds don't *want* to keep secrets. But today, we keep so many secrets in the form of passwords that our minds have become overloaded."

"It's true." Tyler waggled the smartphone at Ivanov. "Phones, apps, bank accounts, work accounts—we've created such a mental logjam that our subconscious selves yearn to be unburdened. With a little directed conversation, Val unburdened yours."

"She wasted her time." Ivanov crossed his arms. "You may have the names, but you do not have the correct order for the voice identification. There are six possible combinations. Two failed attempts and Gryphon will lock down the system."

"Four combinations, actually," Tyler said, punching a button on the panel with the barrel of his Glock. "I've played two of them so far, and your reactions told me all I needed to know."

Mac held up two fingers. "That's a two-in-four chance—fefty-fefty." Talia glanced at him, and he shrugged, bobbing his weapon. "I was always good at the maths."

Finn just rolled his eyes.

An LED on the panel turned yellow, and Tyler played the next combination.

"Natasha, Portia, Aria."

The LED turned red and a feminine digital voice answered back in Romanian—probably a warning that another wrong pass code would lock down Gryphon's servers.

Ivanov smiled. "Now it is one chance in three. Your odds are shrinking."

"An acceptable risk." Tyler played the next combination.

"Natasha, Aria—"

"Stop!" Ivanov shouted over his own voice, interrupting the code.

They all went quiet. Talia held her breath, waiting for the LED to turn red.

It never changed.

Finn strolled across the flight deck, slowly clapping. "We have a winner."

"What is happening?" Ivanov stumbled to the side as the Aussie brushed past him. "Why isn't Gryphon locking down?"

The Aussie ripped the entire voice ID panel off the bulkhead. There was a matching panel underneath with small pieces of hastily applied Velcro in each corner. Finn lightly rapped Ivanov's face shield with the piece he had torn off. "Fake panel. Did you think I came up here early just for the view?"

Talia laughed. They had conned Ivanov into revealing the correct order of the code words.

"Thanks for your cooperation." The Aussie tossed the fake panel aside. "Worst-case scenario, we'd have eliminated all but two combinations. That's two combos for two chances, which is . . ."

Mac raised a hand. "A one hundred percent certainty."

Finn winked at Ivanov. "He's good at the maths."

"Hilarious." Tyler punched the button on the real voice ID panel. "Keep him quiet this time. We can't have him fouling up the voiceprint." He waited for Mac and Finn to drag the CEO away and played the same recording over.

"Natasha, Aria, Portia."

"No!" Ivanov screamed, but Finn had covered the speaker on the collar of his suit.

The LED turned green. The monitor flickered on, showing the Gryphon logo set against a sky-blue background. Tyler plugged a thick, rubber-coated antenna into the keyboard's data port. "Red Leader, she's all yours."

Red Leader. Eddie. Tyler was using an earpiece, talking through the team's SATCOM net. Talia took an involuntary step forward. "Eddie?"

Finn held her back. "Your boy's all right. He heard you. Says he's okay. Turns out he really shines when the pressure's on."

"He does," Talia said with a little laugh. "I never really thought about it before, but he sure does."

The logo disappeared and a command prompt came up. Lines of code flew across the screen as if typed by a ghost. The ghost hit enter, and reams of data flowed.

Tyler nodded. "We've got it."

As he spoke, the storm outside intensified. There was an enormous *crack*. Blinding purple light filled every portal. Gryphon's deck dropped beneath their feet.

Everyone on board stumbled, but Ivanov used the momentum of his fall to fling himself at Tyler. Both men fell to the deck. The Glock skittered across the floor.

CHAPTER
SIXTY-FOUR

GRYPHON DATA VAULT
LOWER MESOSPHERE

TALIA MADE A RUN for the Glock—*her* Glock—but Ivanov got to it first. He scrambled to his feet, leveling it at her chest.

Tyler raised his machine gun, glaring down the sights at the CEO, and Mac followed his lead.

"Lower your weapons." Ivanov shifted his aim to Tyler to stop an advance, then back to Talia. "Your shots may cripple me for a moment, but my shots will surely end her life."

Tyler held his aim for a few seconds longer, then signaled to Mac. Both men lowered their guns.

"Good. Now stop the transfer."

"Can't," Tyler said. "It's done." He cast a glance at the monitor. "Red Leader, final protocol. Now."

A new line of code appeared on the screen. In sequence, the lights of every server in Gryphon flashed red, then extinguished. The monitor went blank.

"Aaagggh!" Ivanov cried out, pressing the Glock toward Talia, finger tight around the trigger. Mac moved to flank him, but Ivanov moved as well. He stepped around Talia in an arc, working his way toward the docking hatch. "You have not stopped me. I still have the prototype. My buyers will see its power. They will bid. The winner will pay."

325

Tyler tracked him with his sights. "We wiped the servers. You have no designs to give them."

"You know nothing."

"Why, Pavel?" Talia tried to distract him with the question, to help the others move in. Gryphon could not make a controlled descent out of the mesosphere without the Mark Seven to act as tug. If Ivanov reached the docking hatch, he could strand them all. "Thousands of people in Washington, DC. Will you kill them for a quick payday?"

He snorted. "You do not see the bigger picture. To be fair, neither did I until a high-level operative in the CIA brought me the plan."

Talia must have flinched at the mention of the Agency, because Ivanov's expression changed. "Oh, I see." He laughed, turning the Glock over and back. "Now it makes sense. *You* are from the CIA. How did I not see this? My commendations on a part well played. And since you and my contact share an employer, perhaps you will like what you're about to hear."

Mac took another step toward the hatch.

So did Ivanov. He pointed the Glock at the Scotsman to stop his movement. "Don't. I see what you are doing." He returned his aim to Talia. "The United States has fallen behind in the hypersonic arms race. My contact, a true believer and patriot familiar with Visser's work, would gladly sacrifice a few thousand in your capital to save hundreds of millions more."

"I don't understand." Talia risked another step. She would be within arm's reach in two more paces.

"Don't you? My prototype will hit Washington, DC, anonymous and unclaimed. The United States will have no choice but to dump their defense budget into hypersonic development."

Tyler closed as well. "And your friend in the CIA promised you the contracts, is that it?" The four of them—Talia, Tyler, Mac, and Finn—had cinched the net down to a few meters.

"Just so. We are talking about years at the crest of a new arms race. My contact wants to save your country from itself." Ivanov shrugged one shoulder. "I just want the money."

Mac lowered his barrel a few degrees. "How *much* money?"

"What?" Ivanov asked.

"Come again?" Tyler asked at the same time.

Mac turned his weapon on Tyler, sidestepping closer to Ivanov. He glanced at the CEO. "How much money? Gev me a figure, lad. And hurry up."

A grin spread across Ivanov's face. "Billions. How would you like to have an annual salary that rivals the gross domestic product of Liechtenstein?"

Mac let out a gruff laugh. "I'd like that very much."

"I'll hunt you down," Tyler growled. "Remember who you're dealing with."

"A man gone soft, that's what I see. Also"—he shrugged—"a man we're about to leave for dead on a glorified hot air balloon." Mac gave a head tilt toward Ivanov. "No offense."

"None taken."

The Scotsman raised his eyebrows at Tyler. "You should've told me the whole plan from the start."

"You wouldn't have come."

"Too true."

"Mac, please," Talia said. "Think about this. That missile has the explosive yield of a ten-kiloton nuclear weapon. Thousands will die."

Ivanov backed toward the vertical shaft of the docking port. His right heel hung over the edge. "His bank account will ease his conscience, I assure you."

"No it won't." Tyler ignored the CEO, keeping his focus on the Scotsman. "Ask yourself what kind of man you want to be, Mac. Because once you cross that line, no comfort this world can provide will ease the burden on your soul."

Talia stared at Tyler, both hearing and seeing the burden

he spoke of. *No comfort this world can provide.* When her gaze returned to Mac, his eyes were distant. Tyler had gotten to him.

The Scotsman blinked and shook his head, grip tightening on his weapon.

"Good," Ivanov said. "Now, it is time to leave. You and I have a missile to launch." He switched hands with the Glock to keep Talia covered and stepped down onto the ladder.

Tyler cocked his head, a deep warning in his tone. "Mac . . ."

The Scotsman gritted his teeth, scrunched up his nose, and then turned on Ivanov and fired.

Tyler fired as well. Ivanov screamed in pain, but he stayed upright through the hail of projectiles, eyes fierce.

Talia lunged for the Glock.

The CEO pulled the trigger, and Mac went down. Finn ran to help him.

Talia's hands closed around Ivanov's wrist and forearm before he could shift his aim to Tyler. His next two shots flew wild and then the Glock clicked. He kept pulling the trigger. *Click, click, click.*

"It's empty!" Talia fought to keep hold of his arm. "Give up!"

Ivanov stopped flailing.

With the exception of Mac's groans, the deck went quiet.

Ivanov looked Talia in the eye and let his feet slip from the ladder, so that gravity overcame Talia's grip. He dropped through the shaft. On the way down, he caught the emergency release handle and blew the seal.

CHAPTER SIXTY-FIVE

GRYPHON DATA VAULT
LOWER MESOSPHERE

A FORCE like none she had ever experienced sucked the air out of Talia's lungs.

The same force tried to yank her through the hatch, but an opposing power held her fast in a strange tug-of-war. She gasped for air in empty hiccups she could not control. Her tongue felt dry and effervescent at the same time. Her eyes went as cold as ice in a tearless blur. There were bangs, crashes, and shouts, but they all seemed far away.

The opposing force won the tug-of-war and dragged her across the deck, still gasping with those horrible empty hiccups. A door slammed. A misty flood of pressure threatened to collapse her eardrums. In tiny but growing victories, her gasps pulled air into her lungs.

Tears returned to Talia's eyes. She blinked them away to find herself trapped behind the polycarbonate door of Gryphon's emergency pressure chamber. Tyler stood on the other side, hands flat against the pane. His face was drawn, eyes vacant. His helmet hung useless from his belt. He had not taken the time to put it on before shoving her into the pressure chamber, and now she feared he no longer had the cognizance to use it.

Talia jerked at the handle, but the pressure-locked door wouldn't budge. "Tyler!"

At the sound of her voice, his lips, thin and blue, spread into a flat smile, and he collapsed.

"Tyler! Tyler!" Talia pounded on the door, crying for this man she had sworn to kill.

Finn appeared, wearing his chipped mask. He knelt beside Tyler, and in short order he had the helmet in place. Talia wondered if it would matter. He had to get Tyler's lungs working again. She slapped the polycarbonate. "Finn! Overpressure! Turn his air on full blast. Force it into his lungs."

The Aussie nodded his understanding and grabbed Tyler's forearm. He tapped furiously at the suit's control pad. "Got it! Air's flowing."

"Good. Now tilt his head back and open his airway."

Finn complied, but frost was forming on the inside of her door, making it hard for Talia to see. She rubbed it away with her sleeve and waited. "Is it working?"

"Give it a moment."

They both watched for some sign of breathing. The quiet seemed to last forever.

Finn shook his head. "It's been too long. I'm starting CPR." He centered his palms on Tyler's ribs and rose up in preparation for the first hard pump.

Tyler threw him clear with a punch to the chest. He bolted upright, sucking in a deep breath. "What are you trying to do, break my ribs?"

"You weren't . . . breathing, . . . mate." Finn rolled onto his side and clutched his chest where Tyler had struck him.

Tyler stood, yanking Finn to his feet at the same time, and held up his suit's control pad. He swiped the screen. A digital heart flashed on the next page, with big red numbers rising through ninety-seven. "Next time, check for a pulse."

"Don't worry boot me, lads. I'm fine." Mac had managed to

get his helmet on, but blood darkened the left leg of his suit. A trail of vapor rose from the hole. "Traded a billion dollars for a gunshot wound, that's all."

"I saw the hit when it happened." Finn laid his hardened-shell backpack down beside the Scotsman and began fishing around inside. "The shot went clean through—wrong side of the leg for the artery. I'm less worried about the hole in your leg as I am the hole in your suit." He pulled out a roll of duct tape. "I shouldn't help you, mate. You were ready to sell us out."

"It was quite a lot of mooney, lad, but I couldn't shake what Lukon said aboot the burden on my soul."

"That's good news, mate." Finn finished his work and patted the wound, making the Scotsman wince. "Sounds like you've turned a corner."

Through the whole exchange, Tyler kept his gaze locked on Talia. His eyes asked, *Are we okay?* They weren't, not as far as she was concerned, but at that moment, she needed him to help her stop Ivanov. She gave him a subtle nod.

Tyler nodded and went to the second control station, flipped down a keyboard, and pulled an extension with a full-size joystick out from the compartment behind it. He pointed at Finn. "Get Mr. Plucket up. He's got a ship to fly."

"All she has are reaction control jets." Finn took Mac's hand and leaned his weight back.

The Scotsman used the leverage to rise on his good leg. "That'll have ta do." With Finn's help, he hobbled over to the control station and began tapping at the keyboard. "First we've got ta vent some o' this hydrogen." Flight data appeared on the monitor. Mac frowned. "Oh."

"Oh?" Talia didn't like the way he said it.

The other three followed Mac's gaze as he turned toward the hole where the docking hatch used to be. Wires and ragged strings of rubber flooring hung down into the empty space below.

"Our Dr. Ivanov did some real damage when he blew that seal, din'ee?" Mac turned back to his data, punching more keys. "Debris from the dockin' clamps must've punched through the envelope. We're venting gas, so the good news is we're comin' doon."

Talia, still trapped in her pressure cage, stood on tiptoe to peer over his shoulder at the screen. "What's the bad news?"

He glanced back at her, expression grave. "We're comin' doon way too fast."

SIXTY-SIX

ABANDONED SOVIET BONEYARD
BLACK SEA COAST, UKRAINE

EDDIE WATCHED THE STORM over the Black Sea grow into a churning gray mass, filling the windscreen of the van. His shackles were gone. Darcy had removed them the moment Ivanov had shown his true colors.

The two had heard every word spoken on Gryphon through the comms. Now the airship was falling out of the sky, straight into the storm, with Eddie's best friend trapped on board in a pressure-sealed polycarbonate booth. To keep her company in this dire hour, she had the assassin who had murdered her father, the new world record holder for high-altitude jumps, and a marginally loyal Scotsman. Life had become far more surreal than Eddie had ever imagined, and that was saying a lot for a kid that grew up in Bombay, New Jersey.

"Mac is pushing her close to shore with the RCS," Tyler said through the comms. "He's aiming for your position. But the hydrogen is gone. Our fall is accelerating. How bad will it get?"

"Stand by." Eddie switched off the microphone and looked up at Darcy, whose fingers rapidly worked the screen of a tablet. "Anything?"

"Hold on. These equations are not so simple, yes?" She stopped tapping, shook her head, and swiped something away as if crumpling a sheet of paper. "We must be precise. Call up Gryphon's aerodynamic data."

Eddie dug the numbers out of the files they had stolen from Avantec and put them up on the screen.

Darcy set to work on the tablet again, then pushed out her bottom lip. "So . . . the news is not fantastic. They will decelerate in the lower atmosphere, but not enough. They will hit the water at thirty-five meters per second, give or take."

"That's almost eighty miles per hour."

She shrugged. "I said it was not fantastic, no?"

Eddie switched on the microphone. "Um . . . Yeah . . . Mr. Tyler, by our calculations you might hit the water a little fast."

"How fast?"

Eddie gave Darcy his *Should I tell him?* shrug, and she answered with a *Not on your life* shake of her head. He winced. "Uh . . . you know . . . pretty fast. But we're developing a solution."

"That's good to hear. Get back to us soon."

Darcy reached over him and switched off the mic, scrunching up her nose. "What solution? You did not tell me you had a solution."

"I don't."

Their assets were not promising. Eddie removed his glasses and rubbed his temples. "With the computing power on this vehicle, I can retask satellites, divert airliners, or launch rescue missions from a dozen nations. But I can't stop Gryphon from crashing into the sea." He swiveled his chair toward the open panel door, putting his glasses back on, and Darcy's duffel bags came into focus. "Um . . . Exactly how much explosive did you bring?"

"Hard to say. A little of this, a little of that." Darcy made her *pbbt* sound. "One must come prepared for anything, yes?"

"Yes." Eddie glanced from the bags to a line of derelict boats lying upside down on the tarmac outside. "Anything."

ACCORDING TO MAC, the airship's free fall had topped out at over two hundred miles per hour. That's when Talia's feet had left the deck, and she had hung there for the last several minutes, hovering in her booth. "It's like zero gravity," she said, watching Finn zoom across the cabin.

"On the contrary." Tyler held on to a server rack, keeping himself firmly planted on the rubber floor. "*Too much* gravity is our biggest problem."

Finn slowly tumbled back and forth. Mac's feet rose behind him while he worked the RCS to drive them closer to Eddie and Darcy. The rush of air was like white noise from a sleep app. It felt strange. Peaceful.

Tyler closed his eyes and Talia could see he was praying. A big part of her wanted to pray with him, but how could she kneel beside a man she hated and pray to a God she had despised for most of her life? The words appeared in her mind, just the same. *Dear God, don't let Ivanov hurt all those people. Please protect Jenni and the rest of those families who took me in.*

Her families. Talia had not thought of any of her foster parents in that way for years.

Peace and prayer did not last long enough. Once the airship fell into the storm clouds, mayhem took over.

Dense air and updrafts slowed the ship's fall, dropping them all to the deck. Gryphon rocked and pitched like a raft in a typhoon. The smooth rush of wind became a terrifying racket as hail pelted the cabin. A chunk flew up through the hole in the floor and ricocheted off the ceiling. Finn shielded his face to fend it off, shouting at the top of his lungs. "Gryphon's special hull will protect us from the lightning, right?"

"It should!" Tyler knelt beside Talia's door, using the butt of his machine gun to chip away the ice that had formed along the seal. "Too bad it won't protect us from the crash waiting at the—"

Tyler stopped working and furrowed his brow, as if listening to the comms through his earpiece. A moment later, he glanced at Finn, who was shaking his head.

"What is it?" Talia shouted.

"That was Eddie!" Tyler started chipping the ice again. "He and Darcy are going to blow up a boat!"

"Wait! I've heard this one!" Using the bulkhead and server stacks for balance, Finn crossed the deck so they could hear him better. "It's like that guy who fell out of a B-17 in World War II! The blast of his own bombs cushioned his fall!"

The turbulence worsened as they fell, but the racket of the hail stopped. Talia wedged her hands into the corners of her booth to keep from getting tossed around. "That's just a myth."

"For a human, yes," Tyler said, "but this airship is wider than a football stadium and made of ultralight materials. Darcy's blast will catch it like an airbag."

"That's fifteen thousand." Mac was still furiously working the joystick. "The air is breathable."

Talia jammed a shoulder against her door, cracking through the remainder of the ice. With help from Tyler, she stepped out onto the deck. She was free, for all the good it did her.

"Ninety seconds!" Mac called. "Brace yerselves!"

Finn laid his body flat on the deck. When Talia and Tyler gave him incredulous looks, he motioned for them to do the same. "Trust me!"

What did they have to lose? Talia lay down.

Tyler lay down beside her. "I'm sorry."

She met his eyes for a long time, feeling the rumble of the ship beneath them. "I know."

EDDIE MOTORED a sputtering old Russian gunboat back toward the boneyard. By Gryphon's GPS signal, the airship would soon be coming down right on top of them. He and Darcy needed to get out of the way.

Rain pattered down from the dying storm. The waves brimmed at the rails of a leaky skiff they had loaded up with Darcy's explosives and anchored offshore.

"She's sinking." Eddie coasted the gunboat in beside the abandoned helipad. "Will the C4 work wet?"

"Oh yes. Not a problem." Darcy helped him up onto the platform and pointed at the sky. "There they are!"

A massive black form broke through the hanging mists of a dissolving rain cloud, catching a fresh ray of sunlight. Eddie knew Gryphon's dimensions by heart, but he was not prepared for the sight. It looked like the Death Star falling into the sea. "Now?"

"Not yet. We must be exact!" Darcy held her tablet, tracking the airship's fall with its camera and reading real-time data from the screen. "Too early and they will have time to speed up again. Too late and they will not slow down enough."

The heart of Gryphon's shadow engulfed the sinking skiff so Eddie could no longer see it. The sheer size of the airship made it seem closer to the water than it was. He couldn't bear it. "Now?"

"Not yet."

"Darcy, they're going to hit!"

"A little more . . ."

"Darcy!"

"Now!" She mashed down on a remote trigger, and both ducked at the sight of the explosion. The *boom* and the blast wave passed over them first, followed by a drenching shower.

Eddie wiped his eyes and blinked to find the Black Sea had reached up like a giant hand to catch their friends. Gryphon splashed down, banged up and broken by the storm and the explosion. "Come on, Talia." Eddie watched the surrounding waves. He felt a hand in his and glanced down.

Darcy squeezed his fingers and repeated the plea. "Come on. All of you."

A hand appeared above the froth, holding a helmet high.

Then a head appeared, and another. Finn and Mac bobbed side by side as the thief helped the wounded pilot swim.

But Tyler and Talia were not with them.

"Please, Talia. Where are you?" Eddie heard a shout—maybe. His ears were still ringing from the blast. He shielded his eyes and looked farther north. At first he thought they might be a mirage, a trick of the sunlight reflected on the water. But then Talia and Tyler both waved. He waved back, jumping up and down. "We did it!"

Darcy jumped beside him, still holding his hand. When the two of them stopped, they stared into each other's widened eyes, and then crashed together in a passionate kiss.

OUT IN THE WATER, with Gryphon sinking behind him, Finn watched the pair embrace. "The geek and the psychopath. That's not gonna end well."

"Yeah." Mac held on to Finn's shoulder and kicked with his one good leg to keep his head above the waves. "That's quite a kiss, though. Ya think they'll simmer down long enough ta get in that boat o' theirs and come get us?"

SIXTY-SEVEN

ABANDONED SOVIET BONEYARD
BLACK SEA COAST, UKRAINE

"TELL ME YOU GOT A LOCATION on that missile." Tyler stood bare-chested, partially hidden by GROND's driver-side door, changing out of his pressure suit. "If I know Ivanov, he went straight for it."

Eddie brought up a map on his main screen. "I tracked him with the beacon you left on the Mark Seven. He flew to an island in the Black Sea, forty-eight miles away."

"You left a tracker on the Mark Seven?" Talia asked, watching the map zoom in on the island.

"Contingencies." Tyler emerged from behind the door wearing cargo pants and a tactical vest. "Like I told you before."

She nodded, then shifted her gaze to Finn and Mac. The Scotsman sat on the back of the box truck while Finn tended his leg wound. Each had also exchanged his pressure suit for tactical gear. "You thought of all these *potentialities*." Talia returned her gaze to Tyler. "And yet you still failed to bring me a change of clothes. I look like a half-drowned comic book hero."

He shrugged, offering a half smile. "I'll take note of that for next time."

Mac hobbled over to the van, aided by Finn. "I heard Wee

Man sayin' he found the Mark Seven." He squinted at Eddie's screen as he approached, frowning. "I don't see it."

"This is old imagery," Eddie said, with a hint of *you're a brainless Neanderthal* in his tone. "Although . . ." He created a green box around the island, a hunk of brown rock half the size of the airfield where they were parked. "We might be able to get a real-time look."

Darcy laid a hand on his shoulder. "You told me before that you could retask satellites, no?"

"Yes."

"And was that true, or were you trying to impress me?"

"Both." Eddie got to work, and soon the telemetry data for a reconnaissance satellite appeared on his secondary monitor.

Darcy leaned down, putting her cheek next to his. "You are a genius."

"No," he countered, giving her a peck on the cheek without breaking the pace of his typing. "*You* are a genius."

"Yeah . . ." Finn closed his eyes and shook his head. "This will get old fast."

Talia didn't care about Eddie's budding romance. She was worried about the ramifications of hacking a satellite. "I don't think the Agency wants us tapping into the US reconnaissance constellation. This could bring a lot of heat down on Brennan."

"It's not a problem." Eddie waved off her concerns with the flick of his hand. "I didn't hack a US satellite. I hacked a Russian one."

In short order, he had live video of the same brown rock up on the main screen. Eddie pointed at some shading on the eastern side. "That shadow is too uniform to be natural." He pressed his nose closer to the image and then let out a laugh and tapped the keys. "Oh, I see you now. You can't hide from me."

That section of the island grew bigger and the clarity resolved. Talia could make out a man-made structure—brown-painted concrete merging with the surrounding rocks. A rectangular section near the center was angled upward at twenty degrees. "There it is," she said, "our launch facility."

"And the Mark Seven." Eddie lifted his hands from the keys in triumph. He circled a finger over a large object on the north end of the picture, covered with camouflage netting, and looked up at Talia. "We've got him."

"We haven't got a thing. Ivanov can launch at any time."

"Actually, he's on a schedule," Tyler said. "His promised demonstration is still more than two hours away. And he's in no hurry. He thinks we're all dead." He crouched down beside Eddie. "You can hack a satellite. Can you hack the island?"

"Already working on it. I'm targeting the facility's network using our satellite's UHF transmitters. And . . . I'm in." A schematic of the island popped up on the screen. Eddie zoomed in and the view shifted to a large, angled hangar next to a stacked control room.

Talia knelt down at his other shoulder. "And the missile?"

"I can see the hangar. But I've got no access to the hardware. Ivanov is smart. The island's key systems—locks, security, the missile systems—they are all isolated in closed loops. Without hooking in a wireless receiver, I can't touch them. Not yet, anyway."

While Eddie kept trying, the rest of the crew stepped out onto the tarmac to survey their options. Tyler nudged Darcy and thrust his chin at the gunboat she and Eddie had used to tow their explosives into position. "What about your boat? How fast will it go?"

"Ten knots. Assuming she can sustain it. You heard her engine, no? We barely got her back to shore after picking you up."

Finn turned to Talia. "You're an American operative. Call in reinforcements?"

"Already have," Eddie said from the van. "When Ivanov escaped, I alerted an Agency asset embedded with a Special Tactics Team at Incirlik. They'll be wheels up in thirty, plus three hours' flight time."

"More than an hour too long," Tyler said. "And we can't ask the Russians for help. They'll haggle for some kind of recompense like Abu Dhabi carpet dealers. There's no time for that kind of negotiation."

Darcy made her *pbbt* sound. "Then it seems we need a better boat, no?"

"No. Not a boat, per se." Talia's eyes had settled on a bunker at the end of a man-made inlet. "We need that."

The nose of a Soviet beast of legend was poking out of the bunker, a monster long at rest. She could just see its eight jet engines placed like gills on the forward canards. Tubes for anti-ship missiles rose from its back like the spines of a sea dragon. The Soviets had called it an *ekranoplan*—a half ship, half aircraft designed to fly mere feet above the waves at over three hundred knots. She nodded in the beast's direction. "All we have to do is get it started, and that thing will get us to the island with time to spare."

SIXTY-EIGHT

ABANDONED SOVIET BONEYARD
BLACK SEA COAST, UKRAINE

"WE'LL NEVER GET THIS THING STARTED," Finn said. The team had driven both vehicles to the corner of the marine hangar. The Soviet sea monster's armored hull rested in a floodable track with a foot of stinking, bloodred canal water pooled at the bottom. "For all we know, she's rusted in place."

Mac pushed himself down out of the box truck. "I don' think so. If she's Russian, then her hull is titanium—rust resistant. And look." He pointed to cracked vinyl slips protecting each engine. "The engines're covered, and there're no oil stains beneath. They've been properly drained. This great beastie was once some Soviet crew chief's wee babe. He took great care when he put her to bed for the last time."

"Then maybe we can wake her up." Tyler clapped his hands at his crew. "Get to work. We need her running in an hour."

While Finn and Tyler scavenged fuel and oil from the graveyard derelicts, Darcy and Eddie jury-rigged the truck battery into the electrical system. That left the avionics to Mac and Talia.

"She's not really that old." Talia rubbed away the dust with a rag from GROND's toolkit. "At least, she's not as old as the other relics in this boneyard. The big ekranoplans were the final extravagance of the Soviet war machine. This one was probably brand new when the wall came down."

Mac caressed the controls. "Oh, she'll fly. Won't you, beastie?"

In answer, the lights in the dash came on. Eddie shouted at them from below. "Battery's in!"

It took all hands to filter the muck from the gas and oil. Talia imagined the loving crew chief who had cared so much for the monster would have a shoe-throwing hissy fit worthy of Khrushchev if he saw the foul-smelling sludge they were feeding her. But the ekranoplan had to run for only twenty minutes. To boost the monster's chances, they added fresh diesel from the spare barrels in the box truck, which Tyler had been saving for a drive out of there. Mac said it was as good as any military jet fuel.

Far too many minutes later, Tyler secured the fuel panel door atop the right wing and kicked the last barrel over the side. "We have to go! Ivanov will launch in approximately fifty minutes. What's left?"

"The floodgate." Mac hobbled in from the mouth of the hangar, having fashioned a crutch out of a helicopter gear strut and half a tire. "The gears are rusted solid. It won't budge."

"Not to worry. Darcy has taken care of this, yes?" Darcy appeared behind him, holding up a remote trigger. Without warning, she pressed the button, and with an echoing *boom* the floodgate blew out in a cloud of rust and mist.

The team ducked in surprise. When Talia looked up again, canal water was pouring into the track. "I thought you used up all the explosives to slow Gryphon's fall."

"I did. But when I was searching the plane for tools, I found a cabinet of miniature depth charges."

Finn interrupted with a chuckle. "Three cheers for Soviet inefficiency, yeah? Mama Crew Chief put her baby to bed nice, but Daddy Munitions Officer failed to empty the weapons diaper."

Depth charges. Talia glanced up at the missile launchers on the beast's spine and saw mortar tubes poking out at right angles from the base of each. She had read about the Soviet obsession with them, long after the rest of the world had moved on. "How *many* depth charges?"

"Twelve. Ten kilos each. I used one to blow the floodgate."

"Okay. So that's a hundred ten kilos of—"

The ekranoplan groaned, demanding the whole team's attention. Water had been surging around the hull since Darcy had blown the gate. Now the craft listed hard, banging a wingtip pontoon on the concrete deck. Tyler, still riding on top, had to grab a missile tube for balance.

"Come on, lass," Mac said. "Wake up."

The pontoon bounced once, but not again. The wings settled. The monster rose in her track in a gentle bob.

"Oh yeah." Mack laid a hand on her hull. "I'm gonna enjoy flyin' this un."

Tyler vaulted down from the wing. "You're not flying anything. You're wounded. And Finn's cleanup job won't be enough to save that leg. As soon as we're gone, Eddie is taking you to the nearest medical facility."

"No. You don' understand."

"Mac . . ."

"I hafta go, all right? If not for me, Ivanov never would've escaped. You told me to ask m'self what kinda man I wanna be. Well, it's not the kind that lets thousands die because of a selfish mistake."

Tyler hesitated, then gave him a single nod. "Okay. But if you end up with a peg leg because you were so bent on flying this pirate ship that you skipped proper medical attention, that's on you."

With less than forty minutes to go, the team climbed on board, leaving Eddie in his usual position at GROND's computers, still in control of his Russian satellite.

"Comm check." Tyler handed Talia an earpiece and shoved his own into place.

"Red Leader is up," Eddie answered from the van, and the rest followed suit.

Mac cranked the turbines using the truck battery wired into the electrics. "She has an emergency start system, designed ta fire all six engines at once. That's our best bet if we're ta have any chance." He flexed his hand on the throttle, preparing for ignition. "Seems like somebody oughta say somethin' memorable b'fore I give 'er a go."

"Um . . . ," Eddie said into the comms. "How about *Release the Kraken!*"

Mac laughed. "That'll do nicely." He pushed the throttles over the hump. "C'mon, beastie. Show me yer fire."

There was a horrible gassy smell, and then a tremendous *foomp* as the engines caught. Growling and wailing, the ekranoplan emerged from her cave.

SIXTY-NINE

**THE BLACK SEA
SOUTHEAST OF UKRAINE**

MAC'S KRAKEN PLOWED through the chop, slowly rising out of the water. "Eighty knots!"

Tyler and Finn sat beside him in the other two forward crew seats, while Talia sat at the weapons station. She had sent Darcy to the back for a quick project.

"Thirty-five minutes to launch." Finn winced as the monster crashed into a wave, shaking the hull. "And we have to factor in time to breach the facility. I hate to say it, but we *must* go faster."

Tyler rapped a gauge with his knuckle, watching the needle bounce. "Engine temps are holding. Keep pushing her, Mac. Either she'll fly or she won't. We have to risk it."

"Twist my arm!" The Scotsman pushed the craft past one hundred knots and eased back on the yoke, lifting her bulbous nose. An instant later, the rough ride settled out.

Finn laughed. "We're up."

"And now we can go even faster. But carefully." Talia had read about the ekranoplans in her Russian studies. They took advantage of ground effect, a cushion of air created by a wing passing close to the earth's surface. Highly efficient. Highly

347

dangerous. Fly two feet high and the craft would stall. Touch the waves at high speed, and she would cartwheel.

The Scotsman worked the yoke with smooth, even motions. "You're in good hands, lass. This beastie and I—we've got an understandin'."

"One sixty." Tyler tracked the speed. "One eighty. Two hundred. Two twenty."

Talia left her station, crouching between Mac's and Tyler's seats to look out at the rushing sea. The island would be in sight in moments. "We're going to do this," she said to herself. The thought brought a sudden pang of regret. With luck, and maybe some of Tyler's prayer, this oddball team might finish the job they started. But not all of them. "I wish Val were here."

"That can be arranged," Tyler said in a matter-of-fact tone.

"Excuse me?"

He slapped Finn on the arm with the back of his hand. "Show her."

In turn, Finn passed an order to Eddie over the SATCOM. "Red Leader, transfer the signal." A moment later he showed Talia a picture of Val on the screen of a smartphone. Except it wasn't a picture. It was video—live video of Val seated on the couch in Mission Control. Conrad sat to her left, and to her right sat a pair of men in the same blue jackets worn by the Italian medical examiners Talia had seen at the expo.

Without the hats and glasses, or the older man's apparently fake white hair, Talia recognized the two. "Luciano?"

"And son." Val glanced at the men as both touched their temples in salute. "Did you really think a grifter like me could get shot with her own gun?"

"Yes."

"You're precious."

Talia frowned. "Eddie, you knew about this?"

"It's Red Leader, and to be fair, nobody ever told me Val was dead in the first place." He sighed into the comms. "Nobody ever tells me anything."

Talia returned to her station, flumping down into her seat. "But why?"

"Access." Finn turned the phone so Talia could still see the screen.

Val shrugged one shoulder. "And to see the look on your face. But yes, mostly for access. It all started with Mac crashing Eddie's drone."

Mac lifted a hand from the controls. "My first bit of actin'. Not bad, eh? Not long after he told me you were CIA, Lukon . . . er . . . Mr. Tyler confessed that we were connin' ya"—he shot a look at Tyler—"'cept he didn't tell me the *rest* o' the story."

Tyler smacked his arm. "Hands on the wheel, Mac. And eyes on the road."

Val continued her explanation. "We knew Eddie would activate Sibby's self-destruct, forcing the expo to hire on more security and giving Tyler an excuse to steal the XPC balloon for Finn."

Beside her, Luciano said something cheery in Italian and turned his medical examiner jacket inside out. The other side read EUROPROTECT, INC.

The ekranoplan hopped in the air, bouncing them all in their seats. Mac raised another hand. "It's all right. I've got her."

Tyler growled at him. "Hands . . . on the wheel."

"Is everything okay?" Val asked.

Talia flopped her fingers at the phone. "It's fine. Go on. Something about security?"

"Right. Tyler, Mac, and the Lucianos gained access as security contractors amid the flood of local help. Once inside, they flipped the jackets around, and my little stunt with Ivanov got them into the tent. Four medical examiners went in. Two came out."

Tyler glanced over his shoulder. "Mac and I stowed away

on the Mark Seven, and you came along right on schedule to convince Ivanov to fly her up to Gryphon."

"Because you needed him to put the voice ID pass code in order."

Tyler touched his nose.

Talia took a moment to process the whole plan. "But the balloon was *my* idea."

"Are you sure?" On the smartphone screen, Val shrugged. "It's called neurolinguistic programming. Thieves and magicians use it as a matter of routine. Think back to the argument on that garage rooftop in Milan—when Finn and I got heated. What words did we use?"

Finn raised a hand. "Hot air."

"And fair weather," Talia said, half to herself. "I get it."

Val walked up to the camera. "Weather. Hot air. Your brain went straight to balloon. What's the first rule of the con?"

"Make the mark work for every step."

"And a good grifter makes her marks think all that work was their idea in the first place."

"I hate to interrupt," Eddie said through the SATCOM, "but by my calculations, you're less than five minutes out."

"Copy that." Talia left her seat, heading back to retrieve Darcy for the crash landing. She hoped the chemist had finished her assignment. If not, they'd have little chance to stop Ivanov.

SEVENTY

THE BLACK SEA
SOUTHEAST OF UKRAINE

"Two minutes out," Eddie called as Talia and Darcy strapped themselves in.

The island, initially a brown mass, took form in the windscreen. Tyler raised a monocular to his eye. "There's fence along the shore, Mac. We'll have to carry enough momentum to break through."

"Yeah. Momentum's not gonna be a problem, boss."

"And there's something else." Tyler leaned forward, laying a hand on the dash. "Red Leader, what are those cylinders on the north and south points of the island?"

"Droids," Eddie replied.

"Come again?"

"Sorry. That's what I thought when I saw them at the Expo." Eddie went quiet for a moment, and Talia could hear him clicking his keyboard in the background. "Although, now I see them in their natural environment, they look a lot more like knockoffs of the Phalanx point defense system than a pair of astromechs."

"I followed less than half of that." Finn squinted at the island. "Point defense system—what's that supposed to mean?"

Seated between them, Tyler grabbed both Finn and Mac by the shoulders and yanked them down. "It means duck!"

Talia saw the spurts of fire from both ends of the island just before she threw her head down below the level of the dashboard. With a series of pings, spits, and crashes, high-velocity rounds peppered the hull and smashed through the windscreen. Glass flew into the cockpit. The leftmost engine burst into flames, and the whole craft yawed.

"I've got her!" Mac straightened her out, now flying on the ship's antiquated instruments because he couldn't lift his head above the dash.

"Do something, Eddie!" Talia shouted.

"I told you. I can't hack the island's security without a receiver in place."

Another set of rounds strafed the craft. Mac fought the controls. Tyler growled into the comms. "Give me something, Eddie."

"Uh . . . Okay, I can see the specs. They have a min range for safety."

"Another engine's on fire." Mac pulled all six throttles back. "Gotta set her doon."

"No!" Talia stretched a hand forward to catch his fist. She pushed it forward again.

"She's right," Tyler said. "Keep your speed."

"One more engine and she's comin' doon whether ya like it or not." Mac fought the yoke with both hands, letting Talia control the throttles. "If we hit the water too fast, we're done for."

The third volley from Eddie's droids ended after only a few rounds, and Talia jerked the throttles back. "*Min range for safety*. That's what Eddie said. Now that we're close, they can't shoot us."

"Of course . . ." Finn peeked over the dash. "That also means we're extremely close to the shore."

Talia sat up and saw the fence and rocks coming on fast. Mac saw them too. He dumped the nose and splashed down. The seawater extinguished the engine fires and the cushioned impact slowed their speed, but not enough. The craft bounced on the surf.

"Brace for impact!" The Scotsman cinched his harness down and frowned at Tyler. "Ya know life has taken a right awful turn when ya have ta say that twice in one day."

The *screech* of rocks against titanium came first, followed quickly by the fence. It left a band of concertina wire lodged in the broken windscreens, barely a foot from the faces of the three men in the front seats. A low ridge split the beach. Hitting it turned the craft. The monster's nose went right, causing the pontoon to dig in and wrench the whole craft forty-five degrees. With a final groan, the tail—the section where Darcy had left her newfound explosives—rocked up into the air and slammed back down into the rocks.

Everyone cringed.

Nothing exploded.

"Out!" Tyler shouted.

"Watch it," Eddie added. "Company's on the way."

Talia bent down to look through a portal at the beach to their right. "I see them. Five men coming over the rise at the south end of the beach. All armed."

"Six, actually," Eddie said. "One is a little pudgy. He's lagging behind."

Tyler helped Talia jump down from the open hatch as machine gun rounds smacked into the opposite side. He pressed her back against the hull beside the others. "We don't have time for this, Red Leader. What can you do?"

"Talk to Finn. He's got my receiver."

The Aussie removed a black antenna from his tactical vest, furrowing his brow. But then he seemed to understand and took off toward the ridge at a run. "Right. Cover me!"

"With what?" Mac balanced himself against the craft and waved his crutch at the burglar. "Where's he goin'?"

Talia didn't take the time to answer. She had caught on to Eddie's idea. "Darcy, did you hold any TNT back?"

"Two charges. Half a kilo each."

"Use them."

"But—"

Bullets kicked up dust on the ridge, pinning Finn down. He couldn't get any higher than the wing of the ekranoplan.

"Use them!"

Darcy removed two squares that looked like caramel fudge from her vest, crammed a short metal tube into each, and with the attitude of a teenager forced to wear a blouse she despised, lobbed them over the wreckage. She did not flinch at either *bang*, or at the resulting shower of gravel. "There was no elegance to that, no panache."

"There will be." Talia rushed to the tail section to get a look at the security team. They were all running for cover. The pudgy one puffed and stumbled behind the rest. "Finn, go!"

He was already over the ridge, breathing hard on the comms. "I see a junction box, Red Leader. The lock is child's play."

"Good, find a cable that looks like a network line."

"Will do."

Talia cast a knowing glance at Tyler.

He nodded and caught Mac's arm, leading him toward the place where the nose met the ridge. "You're with me. Let's have a little fun."

On the comms, Finn was running again. "You're in, Red Leader. Go!"

"One second . . ." Keys clicked, and Eddie talked to himself. "Where are you? Where are you? Aha! These *are* the droids I'm looking for."

"Eddie . . . ," Tyler said.

"I have control of the point defense guns. Removing safeties. And . . ." A stream of heavy rounds rocked the ekranoplan.

Talia covered her head. "Eddie!"

"Sorry. Sorry about that. My fault. Just getting the hang of things."

Talia checked on their attackers. Seeing no further explosives, and perhaps emboldened by Eddie's accidental cover fire, they had emerged from the rocks, advancing on the craft.

The next set of rounds from the defense guns pelted the ground behind them. They started running. Pudgy tripped and fell.

Eddie laughed. "That's right, monkeys. Dance."

"Drive them toward the nose," Talia said. "We need those weapons."

"Copy that."

As Talia looked on from the tail section, Eddie steered his fire. All the guards except Pudgy ran halfway up the ridge and around the nose. They were too scared and confused to see what waited on the other side.

Mac met the first two with a front and back swing of his crutch, and the third caught a fist in the nose. He tried to get up, but Tyler grabbed him by the collar and smacked his head against the hull. Four and five came reeling to a stop, face to barrel with their comrades' machine guns, now in Mac's and Tyler's hands. The security men dropped their weapons.

Finn rejoined the group and used the guards' own zip ties to bind their hands and feet while Talia and Tyler checked on Pudgy.

"What should we do about him?" she asked as the lone guard raised his head to look their way.

Eddie unleashed a hail of artillery to make him duck again. "I've got him."

"Let him go," Tyler said. "Ten minutes to launch. We're running out of time."

The artillery ceased. Pudgy left his gun in the dirt and made a break for the hills.

While Tyler distributed the confiscated weapons, Talia briefed the team on her plan. She sent Finn, Mac, and Darcy over the rocks toward the island's center while she and Tyler made for a bunker entrance fifty meters away. When they reached the shadow of its overhang, he offered her a familiar set of sunglasses. "Here. I saved these for you."

The lenses faded to pale blue as she accepted them. "Franklin's glasses."

"I lifted them before we left the chateau this morning."

"To limit my communication options?"

"To keep them safe." Tyler nodded down at the device. "Put them on." As he spoke, the bunker door swung open. "Thanks, Eddie."

"You're welcome. But that's all I've got. The entrances were tied in to the same net as the defense guns. The interior doors are out of my reach."

With a series of lefts and rights he guided them to the upper level of the missile control room. They encountered two guards at the final corner, and Talia shot both on instinct. A chill swept through her as she watched them fall. She had never shot anyone before, not for real.

Moaning, one of the guards tried to rise. Tyler rushed ahead and smashed him in the forehead with the butt of his gun, catching the other one in the temple when he sat up as well. "Vests," he said, pulling down the second guard's collar as Talia came up beside him. "In this world, if you really have to kill a man, aim for the head."

One final door with a six-digit key code barred their path to the missile control room. "He's in there," Talia said. "And we have maybe eight minutes before the launch. How do we get through? Eddie?"

"I told you. The interior doors are out of my reach. But Finn has the skills to hot-wire that pad."

"True . . . blue." The cat burglar puffed into the comms. "But I can't . . . reach you in time."

"This one is on you, Talia." Tyler positioned her in front of the pad. "You can do it."

Six digits. An impossible number of combinations. Talia had bypassed locked doors at the Farm, but not under this level of pressure. When she was faced with key codes and passwords, her training had taught her to consider the organization—or in cases like this, consider the man. After a few more seconds, she let out a laugh. "Aria, Natasha . . ." She pictured the letters of a telephone keypad and tapped in the code. "P-O-R-T-I-A."

The numbers flashed. The lock clicked.

CHAPTER SEVENTY-ONE

"WATCH OUT. Ivanov has cameras," Eddie said. "One above the door and another in the corner to your right. He knows you're coming."

Tyler took a step back and blew the camera above the door off its mount.

Talia caught his intent. She turned and took care of the one in the corner. "Let's not give them any more awareness than they already have." She pointed to Tyler and directed two fingers at the floor, indicating he should go low. Then she tapped her chest and pointed to the door.

He nodded, pressing close to the wall. Tyler fired a burst the moment she opened the door, and kept firing, crouching low and sidestepping in a wide angle. "One guard, headed for the stairs," he said, and pushed inside.

The floor beyond the threshold was steel plate. Talia advanced, keeping the barrel of her confiscated MP-5 above Tyler's stooping shoulder, and experienced a faint sense of déjà vu. Looking down past the rail, she could see the two other levels of the stacked control room, reminding her of the Sanctum and her failed final exam. Ivanov and at least one guard waited

358

for her below. She could hear Jordan's voice in her head. *The high ground is everything. You get an edge and you keep it!* She should have held back one of Darcy's spare bits of TNT for this moment, but she hadn't. Was she about to fail the same test she had before?

Talia felt the old ache in her side.

Her eyes strayed to the hangar, visible from each level through a Lexan window. Three missiles, not one, sat on long metal rails, angled up at twenty degrees toward a broad rectangular door. Ivanov was using an electric rail-launch system—no blast for early warning sensors to detect. She fired at the nearest missile, but the Lexan deflected the rounds.

"Watch it!" Tyler backed into the corner at the top of the stairs as more bullets plinked the platform. He returned fire.

Talia raised her weapon to join him, and felt an arm wrap around her neck from behind. "Ty—"

The arm choked off her cry. Talia elbowed her attacker in the gut, ducked out of the chokehold, and turned. "Pudgy?"

He bristled at the term. She didn't care. She punched him in the trachea and his eyes bulged. Pudgy's hands went instinctively to his throat. Talia caught his right sleeve, spun him sideways, and swept his left leg, using his weight and his own forearm to pinch off his left carotid. The blade of her wrist took care of the right. Pudgy's pupils rolled back.

Talia let him fall and bound him with the zip ties from his utility belt. She pulled a Taser from his vest pocket and patted his cheek. "This may not be the right career for you."

"You done?" Tyler asked, still trading fire with the guard below.

"You could've helped."

"I was busy." He tilted his head toward a countdown clock on the hangar wall. Less than four minutes remained. "It's time to get serious."

Eddie saw it too, through Talia's glasses. She heard him

clicking madly at his keyboard. "That's . . . That's not what I calculated. We're short."

"Yeah, well, that happens." Tyler kept shooting. "Finn, say your status."

"We're in place, but the door is heavy steel—hinges on the inside. We can neither open nor jam it."

"Not an issue."

"It *is* an issue," Eddie countered. "That door uses high-speed actuators, like the bomb bay doors on the F-22, designed to minimize exposure of the interior."

"So?" Talia rested her back against the wall. Pudgy stirred. She hit him with the Taser. He flopped around a bit and went limp again.

"So Ivanov's missiles will be heading up the rails *before* the door opens. Our plan won't work!"

The gunfire ceased.

The clock read two minutes and fifty-six seconds.

Talia heard a slow clapping from the bottom level. "Mr. Tyler. Miss Natalia. I am impressed! Surviving the fall of Gryphon is quite an achievement. I am so moved that part of me wishes to reward your efforts by stopping the launch." He let the clock count down three more seconds before continuing. "Alas, it is only a very small part."

Talia thought of rushing down the stairs with Tyler, guns blazing. But abandoning caution had caused her fiasco at the Sanctum. This was no test. Thousands of lives depended on her getting it right. She needed help. "Keep him talking," she whispered to Tyler, backing up against the wall beside him. "Eddie, get me Val."

"Already up." The grifter's voice came through calm and even. "Did you think I would miss this?"

"We're out of brute force options. I need to *talk* Ivanov into stopping the launch. That's your department." Talia rolled her head left for a look at the clock. "Not to rush you, but we have two minutes and twenty-five seconds before this goes horribly south." She waited.

Val said nothing.

"Twenty-three . . . Twenty-two."

"Hush, darling. I'm thinking."

From the top of the stairs, Tyler interlaced one-round pot-shots with verbal pokes at Ivanov. He was conserving ammo, and that meant he was running low. "Three missiles?" he shouted, lowering the gun for a moment. "Since when do you have multiple prototypes, Pavel?"

"Did I not say you knew nothing?" Ivanov waited for his guard to take a shot of his own, a stream of bullets that chipped away at the cinder block wall above Tyler's head. "*One* prototype system, that is true. But that system has *three* kinetic missiles. Each strikes in geometric harmony with the others, amplifying the blast to match the destruction of Hiroshima." The guard fired again and Ivanov chuckled. "Trust me. If I hold one back to reverse engineer Visser's design, the remaining two will supply enough death to impress my buyers."

Two minutes remained.

Talia prodded the grifter. "Val?"

"Okay. A good con builds on mutual goals, right? What is it that you and Ivanov both want?"

Talia frowned at the thought, as if Val could see her face. "Ivanov wants to destroy Washington, DC. I want to stop him. Our goals are *mutually* exclusive."

"Yes, but there must be something in between—an intermediate step."

An intermediate step. A light dawned in Talia's mind. "I've got it. Stand by, Val. Tyler, cover me."

With Tyler shooting measured bursts to keep the guard pinned, Talia crawled forward to the edge of the walkway, enough to see Ivanov's control panels. She checked the clock. One minute seven seconds.

Val kept coaching. "Good. Now, this next bit is subtle. Use a slightly lower register in your voice to—"

"I said I've got it." Talia opened fire in full auto. She sprayed the Lexan above the control panel, aiming high for fear of causing an early launch. The move had the desired effect. Talia couldn't identify the door control, but Ivanov didn't know that.

"She's trying to jam the door!" He stepped into view below, firing a pistol to drive her back. She feigned compliance, and saw him crank down on a black-and-yellow lever. The hangar door flashed down. Daylight flooded the bay. "You cannot stop this!"

"Oh, but I already have, Pavel."

"I don't get it," Val said.

"Your mutual goal. Ivanov wants to fire the missiles. I want to stop him. But we both needed the same intermediate step— opening the hangar door. I just got him to open it early." Talia shifted her gaze to the hangar windows. "Now, Finn!"

With forty-three seconds on the clock, Finn appeared at one corner of the hangar door. Mac, supported by Darcy, appeared at the other. Both men heaved bulging duffel bags into the hangar, and all three dove out of view. The bags slid down the canted floor, coming to rest beneath the missiles.

Ivanov shouted something.

The ensuing blast covered his words.

Darcy's salvaged TNT shattered the Lexan windows. Dust and flame flew into the control room. An instant later, the fuel cells of the missiles blew. The rails collapsed. The walls of the hangar burned. A sprinkler system kicked on.

Ears ringing, face stinging as if from the worst sunburn, Talia pushed herself to her feet and stumbled to the rail, remembering too late to raise her gun. It didn't matter. Ivanov, along with not one but three guards, was dead. The other two had been hiding. If she and Tyler had rushed the lower level, they would surely have been killed, and Ivanov would have destroyed DC's National Mall.

Talia had kept the high ground. She let out a pained laugh. "Thanks, Jordan." She turned the empty corner where Tyler had been. "Tyler?"

"Down here." His voice was weak, barely audible in the gentle patter of the sprinklers. He was lying on the stairs, a few steps below the upper platform. Tyler used the rail to pull himself up to his knees. Blood ran from his ears, mixing with the water. His gun had fallen to the landing below. He swallowed, looking up at her. "It's over."

Talia kept her machine gun leveled. She still had half a magazine. "No, Tyler. It isn't."

CHAPTER
SEVENTY-TWO

"UH, TALIA?" EDDIE SAID. "What are we doing?"

She ripped off the glasses and flung them across the room. The earpiece came next. Talia ground it under her heel and nodded to Tyler. "Yours too."

"Right. Sure." Tyler pulled the device from his ear and tossed it over his shoulder. He gave her a thin smile, squinting against the spray from the sprinklers. "Now we're alone. Before we go on, I'd like to say you did well today. From the moment you saw the ekranoplan, you became our strategist. You helped Darcy come up with the TNT charges, fought off a guard well enough to make Mac proud, and unlocked a door that neither our burglar nor our hacker could breach." He made a face. "I'd have to say your final grift was a little brutish, but it did the trick."

"Enough." Talia walked down a step, bringing the gun closer to his head. "Why, Tyler?"

"I told you in Milan. Your dad was my final hit."

"And you were just following orders. That's not an excuse."

"No. It's merely the reason. I questioned those orders, but when pressed, I took the wrong action. I should have waited." Tyler dropped his eyes. "God forgive me. I should have waited."

Talia snorted. "You think he'll forgive you?"

"He has. I know that. But you haven't." Tyler sat back on his heels and gestured at the disaster area surrounding them, a blend of fire, water, and smoke. "That's what all this has been about. The mission. Our time together. Do you understand? I wanted you to know me before we came to this moment, the way that only those who've fought side by side can know each other."

"*Know you?*" Talia couldn't believe Tyler's gall. "How can I know you? You've been lying to me since we met. You told me you would help me kill Lukon."

"I didn't lie about that." With speed that Talia could not counter, Tyler caught her weapon in both hands. She resisted, but he overpowered her and jerked the barrel up against his own skull. "I told you that if you still wanted it, I would help you put a bullet in Lukon's brain. Here I am."

The strength of his voice, the fierceness in those eyes that had haunted her nightmares for so long, took Talia's breath away. She tried to pull the weapon back. Tyler held it fast.

"That's why you risked your life for me, isn't it? It's why you put us in harm's way in the first place." Tears that Talia didn't want fell down her cheeks. "The bullet you took at the Shard. That stunt on Gryphon, shoving me into the pressure chamber before putting your helmet on. You wanted to die. You wanted to die for me."

"A life for a life." Tyler let out a rueful huff. "A life for two lives. I took your father's life and destroyed yours. For fifteen years, this hate has devoured you. If my death helps you let go— if it gives you a chance to rediscover the God I found through your pain—then it's worth it. Greater love hath no man than this, that he lay down his life for his friends." Tyler spread his arms and leaned forward, letting the barrel of Talia's gun take his weight. "This is a debt I'm willing to pay."

Greater love. The debt paid. Talia's eidetic memory returned to Conrad, wearing that ridiculous apron. *Forgiveness belongs to him, Talia. One debt paid for all.*

Her finger tightened around the trigger. She looked up and screamed into artificial rain, then threw the gun aside and dropped to her knees, wrapping Tyler in an embrace. "I forgive you! I forgive you!" She sobbed into his shoulder, and her voice dropped to a whisper. "I forgive you."

SEVENTY-THREE

THE POTOMAC RIVER
WEST OF THE GEORGETOWN BOATHOUSE

THE RACING SHELL cut an even furrow through the black waters of the Potomac. The low morning mist swirled above the eddies left by two big oars—one Talia's, one Jenni's.

The pain Talia had learned to live with, a pain she had come to expect with every pull of an oar, was gone. A few times since she and Jenni had left the dock that morning, she had caught herself searching for that pain, perhaps even missing it. But those moments had quickly passed.

"Are you sure . . . you don't mind . . . hitting the water this early?" Talia worked the question into her breathing cycle, using the recoveries between strokes.

Jenni did the same with her answer. "Totally . . . In fact . . . we should make this . . . our thing."

Talia glanced over her shoulder, giving Jenni a smile and checking their heading. They were nearing the deep water east of the Three Sisters, where they had capsized on their last row. But they had found a good rhythm this time. Despite the challenge of balancing the two staggered oars of the sweep-style pair, Talia had no fear of flipping over again. "Let's pick it up!" she said and dug in with her next pull.

The Special Tactics Team from Incirlik Air Base had raided Ivanov's island an hour after Darcy's TNT destroyed the hangar. By that time, Tyler and his thieves had found an Avantec runabout and made their escape, leaving Talia with only Pudgy for company. He had started shouting in angry Moldovan the moment the soldiers hit the beach. One of them, whom Talia suspected was the Agency asset embedded with the team, shot Pudgy with a tranquilizer dart to shut him up.

The road home, traveled mostly in cramped economy-class seats on regional airlines she had never heard of, gave Talia a good deal of time to think. It also gave her time to pray. She prayed more than she had in her entire life. She told God she forgave him for the loss of her father, admitted she had no right to be angry with him in the first place, and asked him to forgive her for the unforgiveness she had harbored for so long.

Talia still wasn't entirely sure where to go from there, but when she had landed at Dulles—as if in answer to all those prayers—there had been a message waiting from Jenni.

The two rowed on past the Sisters, pushing the workout. Neither of the girls had enough spare breath to continue the conversation until they let up at Fletcher's Cove.

"Dinner," Jenni panted, dragging an oar in the water to turn the boat.

Talia wasn't sure she'd heard correctly, or maybe part of her was afraid she had. "What was that?"

"Dinner . . . Tonight . . . My place."

"You mean your parents' place."

"*Our* parents' place."

They steadied the boat to let the current take them, and Talia glanced over her shoulder. Jenni cocked her head, biting her lip, waiting.

They had talked about it briefly on the phone, with Talia crying outside the ladies' room at the Dulles baggage claim. The words had come pouring out of her. Each of her foster fathers had been faced with an impossible task, a gap impossible to fill. And whether they tried or not, Talia had punished them for it, getting angrier with each passing year. Jenni's father, Bill—Talia's last foster father—had answered that immense challenge with love, pure and simple.

In the pattern of unforgiveness she had clung to, Talia had created anger where none belonged. She had placed it squarely between her and Bill and let it fester so long. She didn't know if she could face him. "There's so much I have to say."

"All the more reason to start saying it."

The islands passed them by. Talia dipped her oar to navigate the river bend and sighed. "I . . . I can't."

"Oh." Jenni sounded so disappointed. "Okay."

"I can't tonight, I mean. I have a prior engagement. How about tomorrow night?"

She could hear the smile return in Jenni's voice. "Well . . . tomorrow night is Bible study night at the church. Sometimes we chitter-chatter too long on the back end, so the timing is hard to pin down. But if you came with me, we could do a late dinner at the house afterward."

Talia laughed. "Sounds like I don't have a choice."

"No. You don't."

The boathouse came into view. Talia balanced her oar and leaned back to stretch, and Jenni trapped her in a one-armed hug. "Welcome home!"

THE SMELL OF ROASTED COLOMBIAN BLEND drew Talia into a detour on her way to the Directorate's Russia Eastern European Division.

Luanne showed no surprise at her reappearance after the two-week absence. "Back to the grind, huh, rookie?" she asked after Talia ordered a venti semi-diet morning dessert. Luanne glanced at the tip jar as she turned to the machines. "Another day, another *dollar?*"

"You're right." Talia slipped a bill into the jar. "I'm glad to be home safe and sound with my overbearing boss."

"Mm-*hm.*"

Talia watched her work for a few seconds, then added a second dollar to the jar. "You know what? Make me a Frank Special as well, please."

"Will do. But just so we're clear, you orderin' that 'cause you wanna make him happy, or 'cause you wanna kill him?"

"A little of both."

BRENNAN ACCEPTED THE COFFEE without a thank-you. He took a swig and set it down beside his donut. "Our man at Incirlik says you made quite an impression on the boys in his unit. After the mess you made of Ivanov's island, they're calling you Nyx."

Talia scrunched up her brow. "Nyx?"

"The Greek goddess of night, daughter of Chaos." Brennan shrugged. "There's a lot of Hellenistic influence in Incirlik's operations area."

"I had help with the chaos."

"They know that. But guys like that prefer legends to facts."

Talia hesitated at his desk. There was a conversation she wanted to have, and she decided it was best to have it before Eddie showed up.

"Something else on your mind?"

"How much did you know?"

"More than you. Even now." Brennan took a bite of his donut and kept talking as if he hadn't. "And before you say anything else, you need to understand that I'm not under duress, here. Tyler may have pushed me regarding your involvement, but he's an old friend. And there's a bigger picture beyond the two of you and your dysfunctional past."

He had wasted no time in coming to the heart of her concerns. Talia had seen Brennan's edited version of the after action. A key line was missing from the part she had written. "You're talking about the Agency conspirator Ivanov mentioned." She hit him with the question on her mind point-blank. "Was it you?"

"Would I have helped you and Tyler take Ivanov down if it was?"

"Then why remove the reference from my report."

"Simple. We can't risk alerting the real traitor, the one Tyler suspects of being Archangel."

Archangel. The name hit Talia hard. She had let her anger go, but this was still the person who had ordered her father's murder. And after-action reports from REED's various sections stayed in house. That meant Brennan suspected someone inside their little corner of the Clandestine Service.

He finished the donut, licking the powdered sugar off his fingers and wiping them on a well-worn napkin. "Now that we understand each other, we can work together on this. The operation you just completed was the first step in a long sting—or maybe a long con, as your new friend Valkyrie would put it."

How could stopping a missile attack be the first step in a con?

Talia blinked. "The data from Gryphon."

Brennan touched his nose, exactly as Tyler had done on the ekranoplan. "After Visser's kidnapping, Tyler came to me with the suspicion that Ivanov had a contact within the Agency— even had a notion as to who. Once a bad seed, always a bad seed, even after fifteen years." Brennan looked down at the lonely crumpled napkin in the space where his donut had been. He frowned. "It'll take weeks to mine through all that data from Gryphon and from Avantec's other servers, but somewhere in those files are links that will help us build a sting to take the traitor down."

"Why not tell me all of this from the beginning?"

"Need-to-know." In the absence of another donut, Brennan turned his attention to his deadly coffee. He took a long drink and wiped the drips from his mustache. "Sometimes, in the greater plan, we only get the information needed to help us do our part the way we're meant to."

Talia folded her arms and frowned. He was starting to sound like Conrad.

Brennan leaned back in his chair. "That's how life works, kid. Might as well get used to it."

She couldn't argue with him. Talia sighed. "That leaves the Russian—Bazin. He can't be innocent in all this. It's a shame he got away."

"Give him time. He'll turn up. Bad rubles always do."

There was a knock at the door, and the knob was already turning as Brennan called, "Enter!"

Mary Jordan stepped into the small office, keeping her arms close to her body, as if a brush against any surface might contaminate her clothes.

"Chief," Brennan said, not bothering to stand. "Funny you should show up. We were just talking about you."

CHAPTER
SEVENTY-FOUR

BRENNAN'S GLANCE SPOKE VOLUMES, enough to knock Talia back a step—away from Mary Jordan. *We were just talking about you.* Talia struggled to maintain a neutral expression. Archangel?

"*You.*" Jordan ignored Talia and headed straight for Brennan's desk. "You took a new recruit—my recruit—and used her to subvert my authority."

Brennan spread his hands. "Why, Chief, whatever do you mean?"

"Don't play that game with me. You authorized a dozen outlandish expenditures that should have come across my desk. You sent an operative beyond Other Branch's area of responsibility, causing police incidents and terror task force responses in no less than three allied nations. And you deployed a US special operations team on foreign soil without notification to *any* authority, let alone the *proper* authority."

"Actually"—Talia raised a tentative hand—"Mr. Brennan had nothing to do with the special ops team. Our man on-site notified the unit commander of a threat to the US, and the commander made his own decision." That earned her a glare.

Talia tucked the hand behind her back and cleared her throat. "As to the larger expenditures, it is my understanding that the civilian liaison for this mission covered them out of his own pocket and has not asked for compensation."

"You mean Tyler. This is all him, isn't it?" Jordan let out an angry chuckle. "Don't be fooled, sweetie. You have no idea what kind of man he is."

"What kind is that?"

"The kind a rookie like you shouldn't be conspiring with, if you know what's good for you." Jordan gave her a look that said *Pipe down, the grown-ups are still talking* and then returned her attention to Brennan. "You and I are not finished. There will be repercussions."

"Like sticking me in a broom-closet office for the rest of my career?"

"Oh, Frank. You want to play it like that? Fine. How about I start by removing the best young operative you've ever had from your command?" She turned to Talia. "You stopped a major attack. I can push that with the higher-ups to get your career back on the fast track. Your penance in Other is done. Report to the Russian Ops desk first thing in the morning." She left them both and headed for the door. "Starting tomorrow, Talia works directly for me."

Russian Ops. It was a major step up, one small leap away from Moscow Station. But how could Talia do that to Brennan? Her hand came up in protest, but a sharp glance from Brennan shut her down. He *wanted* her to take the job. Why? Talia could only assume he wanted her to keep a closer eye on Jordan. The *broom-closet* remark had been a calculated push. Brennan had just played his boss like a mark—as well as Tyler or Val ever could have. Talia gave him a subtle nod to let him know she understood, then made an additional gamble. "Wait!"

Jordan turned in the doorway. "Excuse me?"

"Could . . . Eddie come too? He worked as hard on this op as I did."

"Ah. Yes, what a wonderful idea." Jordan gave Brennan a thin but triumphant smile, as if she had won another small victory, stealing another good operative. "Gupta can join us as well."

Brennan raised his coffee in mock salute. "Good riddance. That kid eats all my donuts anyway."

His unruffled response didn't help Jordan's mood. She held him with a glare for two more heartbeats and then stormed out of the room.

Poor Eddie arrived at precisely the wrong moment. He had to throw himself flat against the wall to avoid the flying door and the angry division chief. He sidestepped across the threshold and looked to Talia. "What did I miss?"

Jordan answered from the hallway. "You work for me now, geek. That's what you missed." There was a slight pause, followed by "And lay off those donuts!"

THAT EVENING, Talia and Eddie ventured far beyond the confines of the DC metroplex to a place both had heard rumors about but never seen.

The mansions scattered among the islands of Chesapeake Bay were the stuff of legend. Some said they were the summer homes of politicians and movie stars. Talia subscribed to a different but popular theory—that several belonged to the big defense corporations, whose CEOs needed comfortable places to camp while lobbying Congress for bigger contracts. Most of these estates could not be easily reached by car, so Tyler had made other arrangements for his two friends.

Mac met them at a marina near Londontowne with a midsize runabout.

"I see he's still got you driving stuff other than planes." Talia let the Scotsman help her down into the boat. "I thought this sort of thing wasn't in your job description . . . Wheels."

"One more time." Mac pushed up the throttle and started out into the darkening bay. "And only for you, lass. Let's not make a habit o' this."

In place of a dock, the house across the bay had a long rectangular inlet lined with stone walls and boxwood hedges, lit by gas lanterns. *A cozy little place I'm watching for a friend.* That's what Tyler had called it. "Cozy. Right." Talia counted the lighted windows as Mac coasted in. She estimated over twenty rooms.

Conrad met them at the door and took Talia's bag. She had not brought much. They were only staying the one night. Tyler had something special planned.

"Where is he?" Eddie asked as they followed the cook up a grand central stairway.

"I'm afraid he hasn't arrived. But he requests your presence at breakfast in the eastern sitting room. Five thirty sharp."

Talia waited until Mac and Conrad had gone, then slipped into Eddie's room and closed the door.

Eddie spun around, shirt up under his armpits. "What are you—" He jerked the shirt down to his beltline. "That's not okay, Talia. Just because I'm a guy doesn't mean you don't have to knock."

"I know. I'm sorry. But I wanted to talk." She sat down on a cushioned bench in Eddie's window. "Tyler didn't give me any details. What are we doing here?"

Eddie pulled the copper fidget spinner from his pocket and twirled it, balancing the center point on his thumb. "I don't know . . . exactly."

He was acting nervous. She crossed the room and snatched the spinner away. "You know *something*. What is it?"

"Okay. Don't be mad."

That was never a great phrase to hear. "Don't be mad about what?"

"I made a copy of the Gryphon data before turning it over to the Agency. Tyler asked me to. And before you freak out, Brennan knows. He's on board. With everything."

That much Talia could have guessed from her conversation with Brennan. "Okay. What else?"

"Tyler had other data, a thumb drive full of number strings. I don't know where he got it, but I found a similar set in the Gryphon files and we merged the two. The combined numbers formed the pass codes for the escrow accounts from Ivanov's auction." Eddie shrugged one shoulder. "We . . . emptied them."

"You robbed a bunch of terrorists?" Talia backed up, sitting down on the bench again. She had so much trouble wrapping her brain around the thought that she almost started twirling the fidget spinner herself. Where were the lines in this world of spies?

"Actually, we repurposed funds the terrorists had already spent. Ivanov wasn't going to use them, and the US couldn't confiscate them without acknowledging events that officially never happened. We put part of the money into an account to pay the fees Tyler promised each of our thieves. He's brought them here to this meeting to collect their paychecks."

Talia frowned. Old worries—old accusations—were cropping up in her mind. "And I suppose the rest went into Tyler's bank account."

"Not a dime. The rest went to an organization that feeds and educates kids all over the world."

Talia tossed him his spinner. "How much?"

Eddie made his *You wouldn't believe me if I told you* face.

TALIA RETIRED TO HER ROOM to read her worn copy of *The Cat in the Hat*, keeping to her pre-sleep tradition for a new place. She started a new tradition as well, adding a chapter of scripture. A ribbon in the Bible she found by the bedside had marked Ephesians chapter four. And at the bottom of the page was a verse about thieves stealing no more, and doing honest labor so they could give to those in need. She fell asleep wondering if Tyler had made that very thing his mission.

Morning came early. Talia tromped down the stairs at twenty after five to find the rest of the team seated beside a crackling fire, with the dim blue of twilight gathering on the water outside the sitting room's picture window.

Tyler entered from an adjoining hallway with Conrad. The cook carried a tray of small plates, each with a pair of pastries. Tyler carried a tray of steaming mugs and teacups. "Welcome. All of you. We have tea, coffee, and hot chocolate. Your choice."

"Why are we doing this so early?" Val took one of the coffees and tucked it close to her oversize sweater.

Darcy chose a mug of chocolate. "Because he is a sadist, no?"

"No," Tyler said. "We're here at this hour because dawn is a special time of day."

Eddie bit into a pastry, eyes half closed. "For sleep, you mean."

Tyler ignored the hacker's remark and took up a position by the fireplace mantel. "In the past, I have put teams together for onetime operations, disbanding them afterward. But this team is different." He glanced around at their faces. "I don't think any of you can deny that we work well together. You all have unique talents. And last week you used them to save lives."

Mac raised a finger. "And to get paid."

"Yes. You'll get the money I promised. But I'm asking you to look at the bigger picture. I know you can, Mac, because I watched you make the same choice on Gryphon."

The Scotsman opened his mouth to reply, then closed it again and looked down into his coffee.

Tyler looked to the rest of them. "I'm asking you all to make that choice. Work with me. In the past you used your talents to enrich yourselves. Now use them to make the world a better and safer place."

The first rays of sunlight filtered in through the windows, painting the room in rosy hues, and six sets of eyes darted around, questioning one another. They all finally settled on Tyler.

Talia gave him a nod. "You know Eddie and I are in."

"Me too," Val said, "although I have very specific travel and housing requirements."

The others made similar comments—all in the affirmative, with small addendums.

That was enough for Tyler. "Excellent. Then I believe a toast is in order." He raised his mug toward the rising sun. "To a job well done, to good friends, and to new horizons."

THE STORY CONTINUES IN
**CHASING
THE WHITE LION**
AVAILABLE SPRING 2020

READ ON FOR A SNEAK PEEK . . .

CHAPTER ONE

VOLGOGRAD, RUSSIA
WHARF DISTRICT
PRESENT DAY

THE CAB DRIVER cast a nervous glance down the alley at the unlit streetlamps and iron bars guarding blacked-out windows. An old man in a mud-stained coat stumbled out of the darkness and passed through the headlights, talking to himself in the singsong voice of the permanently delirious.

The cabbie honked his horn at the bum and turned in his seat with a wrinkled brow. "*Vot? Ty unveren?*" *Here? Are you sure?*

Talia Inger smiled, answering him in flawless Russian, refined at the Central Intelligence Agency by America's top accent coaches. "Oh yes, my friend. This is exactly where I want to be."

She climbed out and paid him, slipping in an extra five thousand rubles because he hadn't wanted to drive to that side of town in the first place.

The driver thumbed through the money and smiled up at her—a soft, worried smile, as if his next words might be the last she'd ever hear. "You are a nice lady," he said in his native tongue. "I will stop at St. Peter's and light a candle for you."

She reached through the open window and squeezed his forearm. "*Spasibo,*" she said, thanking him, then took in a deep

383

breath as he drove away. The night air stank of drizzle and old fish.

Glorious.

The entrance to the *Som*—the Catfish—lay at the bottom of a steep set of stairs halfway down the alley. Like many of the most interesting places in the world, the Catfish could only be found by those who already knew where it was. It had no webpage, no Instagram feed, no neon sign, just three Cyrillic letters scratched into the hunk of black-painted iron that served as its door. Talia pulled it open, absorbing a blast of heat, noise, and cigarette smoke, and waltzed past the bouncer like she owned the place.

Several sets of eyes turned her way. Most of the men seated at the bar or tucked into the dark booths were murderers and thieves. Talia didn't fit the profile, but she didn't care. She could handle them. She picked the beefiest patron looking her way and met his eyes with a disgusted glare. *"Na chto ty smotrish', izvrashchenets?" What are you staring at, pervert?*

He growled and went back to his drink.

The others laughed.

A wooden table near the back sat empty, lit by nothing more than the faint red glow of the liquor shelves behind the bar. Talia pulled out a three-legged chair and checked the clock on her phone. The man she intended to turn would be along at any moment. In the meantime, she was content to sit and wait—to soak it all in. Volgograd, still known to most Americans as Stalingrad, was Cold War Russia trapped in time. For Talia, this was all the preconceived images gained during her studies and training.

A seedy bar filled with the refuse of Siberia's prisons.

A rendezvous with a potential agent.

A shot at several years' worth of vital counterterrorism intelligence.

Talia had envisioned Russian dives like the *Som* when Jordan first recruited her to the Clandestine Service, officially *the Directorate*. Like she'd told the cabbie, this place—this dank, smoky, dangerous place—was exactly where she wanted to be.

Her fish entered the bar a few minutes later. Oleg Zverev remained true to his file photo, down to the blue leather motorcycle jacket. Talia guessed he thought the padding in its shoulders made him look bigger. It had the opposite effect. Compared to the gorillas and grizzly bears at the bar, Oleg looked like a rat wrapped in a blue leather blanket.

The gorilla at the door stepped in front of him, folding his arms, and for a moment, Talia worried she might have a problem. The rat answered with a sour look. The gorilla chuckled and stepped aside.

"Vera Novak." Oleg spotted Talia at the table and greeted her with the cover name she'd given him. She stood to take his hand, and he held her fingers far too long while his eyes passed up and down her form. "What a *pleasure* to finally meet you in person."

What mass delusion made men from every culture think women enjoyed leers and innuendo? Talia slipped her fingers from his grasp. A little sweat. A little hair product. Gross. She took her chair again and wiped her hand on her jeans under the table. "You can speak Russian, Oleg. I'm fluent."

"I want to practice my English. Besides, it is safer for us. These overgrown morons can barely speak their own language, let alone another."

The music blaring from behind the bar—some Russian knock-off of nineties American metal—would cover their conversation, but Talia didn't argue. "Suit yourself."

"I will. First round is on me. What do you want?"

"I'm here for business. Not a date."

The corners of his mouth turned up on either side of his rat nose as he walked away. "Why can it not be both, eh?"

Oleg returned from the bar with an entire bottle of vodka

and two tumblers, which he filled well past the customary level. "*Pahyekahlee.*" He tossed his drink back in one gulp.

Talia slid hers aside with the back of her hand. "Nice place you picked, Oleg. A lot of . . . atmosphere. What kind of name is Catfish for a bar?"

"It is good name. In Volga River—mother river of Russia— the catfish is king, top of food chain, up to five meters long and three hundred fifty kilograms." The rat took her tumbler, swallowed its contents, and poured two more. When Talia's flat expression didn't change, he spread his hands. "*Three hundred fifty kilograms,* Vera. The *Som,* the Volga Catfish, is bigger than mako shark!"

"The Mako. Now *that* is a good name for a bar."

"You Americans have no imagination." Oleg slid the tumbler in front of her.

Talia pushed it aside again.

He frowned. "Fine. Business it is. You wanted to meet best forger in Russia? Here I am. What do you want?"

"To make your bank account grow." Talia produced an envelope, fat with cash, and the flaring of Oleg's nostrils told her she had his full attention.

"I am listening." He leaned across the pocked wood of the tabletop, bringing with him the stench of vodka breath and perfumed hair, and reached for the cash. But his fist closed on air as Talia snatched the envelope away.

"Not so fast. This is one hundred thousand US, a good-faith payment to show my employer is serious about this relationship. I want to know you're serious as well."

"What sort of relationship?"

"The profitable kind."

Oleg sat back and let his eyes drift around the bar in poorly feigned disinterest. "I have many such relationships. My identities are best in Russia." He pressed his thumb and forefinger together in the primo sign. "Best in all of eastern hemisphere. I am not copy-shop hack making fake passports. I build *complete* identities. Documents. Digital histories. Life stories." Oleg gestured at the envelope. "I can do this for your boss. A hundred thousand will buy him five identities." He laughed and raised his chin. "Ten with new customer discount."

"You mean a hundred thousand will buy *her* ten," Talia said. "My boss is a woman."

The rat raised an eyebrow. "How modern. I cannot wait to meet her."

"You never will. And she doesn't want new identities for her organization. She wants copies of the new identities you create for others."

The leer dropped from Oleg's face. "Perhaps my English now fail me. It sound like you want me to betray my other clients."

"Not me. My boss. And don't think of it as betrayal." Talia lifted her hand, revealing the full thickness of the envelope—the weight of all that money, and watched Oleg lick his lips. She had the rat salivating now. "Think of it as a bonus. Knowledge is power, and she'll pay handsomely for it."

His fingers crept across the table, eyes seeking her permission.

She owned him. "Go ahead, Oleg. The money's yours."

Talia let her new pet rat pick up the envelope, watching his Adam's apple dip as he swallowed.

"My boss wins, your clients win, and best of all, you win. Think about it, Oleg. You'll get paid twice for every identity you create."

He drew back the lapel of that obnoxious blue leather jacket and tucked the envelope away. "It sound like good deal, yes?" Then his eyes snapped into focus. He raised his voice above the music. "But tell your boss I pass."

As if the statement were a command, all the grizzlies and gorillas at the bar swiveled on their stools and glared at Talia. Others emerged from the booths like tigers from a forest.

Oleg laughed, zipped up the jacket, and patted the envelope inside. "Did you think I would not find out who you were, Miss *C-I-A*? Identities are my business, and Vera Novak does not exist." He slapped both hands down on the table. "Like I said. You Americans. *No imagination.*"

Talia tensed, hands inching toward the Glock in her waistband. "How?"

"Keep asking yourself that question. How did little Oleg Zverev outsmart the brilliant CIA agent?" Oleg stood and backed away, taking the vodka bottle with him. He took a swig and grinned. "Let it be the last thought that ever crosses your mind."

CHAPTER
TWO

TALIA LEAPED UP from her chair, leveling her Glock.

In the same instant, a meaty hand wrapped the barrel and tore it from her fingers. A Russian gorilla stepped out from behind her and handed the weapon to Oleg.

The rat laughed and spread his arms, holding Talia's Glock in one hand and the vodka bottle in the other. "Nice try. But you cannot save yourself. This was your last mission, Miss CIA Agent."

"You mean, 'CIA *officer*.'" The correction came from a man at the bar, the only one who hadn't turned at Oleg's command.

The rat lowered his arms and looked his way. "What did you say?"

"The term is *officer*, not agent." The man kept his face buried in an untouched drink. "If you must to resort melodrama, at least get your phrasing right. My friend here is a CIA case officer. She was trying to turn *you* into an agent."

Talia knew the voice, despite the fake Russian accent. "Adam Tyler. What are you doing here?"

He swiveled the stool, bringing his face into view. The accent vanished. "Looking after you."

"I don't need looking after."

"Hey!" Oleg waved the bottle and gun in the air. "What goes on here? Who is this guy?"

Tyler ignored him. "Are you sure? I count fourteen hostiles. One of them already has your weapon."

"Fifteen. You're slipping. And I can handle them."

Tyler glanced at Oleg. The two shared an incredulous look and asked the same question in unison. "Oh, really?"

"Yes. Really."

With a grunt, Talia lifted the little table and launched the two vodka tumblers. She swatted one with an open hand, sending it flying at Oleg to shatter on the bridge of his rat nose.

At the same time, Tyler left the stool to bring a closed fist down on Oleg's forearm.

The Glock fell. The rat clutched his bleeding face and ran for the door. "Kill them, you idiots! Kill them both!"

The gorillas and jaguars converged. Talia's world descended into hairy, smoke-scented mayhem.

Her first target, the man who had torn the Glock from her hand, caught a knee in the groin, followed by an uppercut that met his face as he doubled over.

Another Russian dived for the Glock, but Tyler soccer-kicked him in the temple, and the weapon slid into the dark space under a booth. Talia had no chance to go after it. A gorilla arm caught her in a choke hold. She clawed at his skin, fingernails slipping on hair and sweat.

As she fought for breath, a figure swept in from her left, swinging a bottle. Talia cringed, but the bottle connected with her attacker's head, not hers. The sweaty arm went limp.

She grabbed the bottle-swinger by his lapels, jerking his face into the light. "Finn?"

Michael Finn—Tyler's forever-shadow and daredevil cat-burglar—pumped his dirty blond eyebrows.

Talia pushed him away. "I should have known."

The Australian gave her a self-assured smolder, the one she never knew whether to love or despise. "The count was fourteen. Not fifteen. You included me. So—" He paused to level an oncoming attacker with his elbow.

"So Tyler was right, and I was wrong. Yeah, I get it. Do you really have to be here?"

"Someone's gotta look out for Tyler while he's looking out for you, right?"

One of the Russians pinned Talia's arms with a bear hug. She drove her heel repeatedly into the man's instep, shouting with each stomp. *"I don't . . . need . . . looking . . . after!"* The hold loosened. She ducked out and shoved the Russian back over an empty chair. He fell at Tyler's feet and got a face full of boot.

The three fought their way through the bar, laying out their attackers with chair legs and liquor bottles, until Talia reached the gorilla at the door—the biggest of them all. He crossed his arms and growled, "Where *you* going . . . *little girl?*"

Behind her, Tyler knocked out his last opponent, raised a gun, and fired three rounds into the ceiling.

The gorilla stepped out of their way.

Tyler walked past, slapping the weapon into Talia's hand as he started up the steps to the alley. Her Glock. He must have dug it out from under the booth while she was talking to Finn.

She checked the mag. Plenty of rounds. "You couldn't have used this earlier?"

"What? And skip all the fun of a full-on bar brawl?"

With Tyler in the lead, they headed for a Toyota Hilux pickup across the street, where a third member of his team waited. The big Scottish pilot, Mac Plucket, stood next to the cab, holding Oleg by the collar of his blue leather jacket. Oleg's kicking feet were a good six inches off the pavement. "Evenin', lass. Your wee friend here offered me a hundred thousand ta let him go."

Talia and the other two climbed into the back of the truck. "And what did you say?"

Mac produced the envelope. "I accept."

"You forgot the *let me go* part." Oleg swung his fists at Mac, never connecting.

"Good point, lad. My mistake."

"That's our Mac." Talia held Oleg in the Glock's sights as Mac heaved him into the truck bed. "Talk." She shoved the gun closer. "There's no way a little rat like you broke through my cover. Who tipped you off?"

In place of an answer, blood spurted from the rat's lips as bullets riddled his body. More rounds plinked off the Hilux. A black sedan raced up the street with a shooter hanging out the passenger window. The bouncer must have called in reinforcements.

Finn lifted Oleg's body as a shield. Tyler pulled Talia down and pounded on the bed. "Mac, get us out of here!"

The trees of Volgograd weren't large, but they were everywhere, lining even the busiest streets. They grew in the empty lots and the train yards, gradually turning a gray former Soviet city into Sherwood Forest. Now the forest whipped past while gunfire splintered every trunk.

Talia rolled over to yell at Tyler. "A pickup truck? This is what you chose for an urban rescue?" They both lay on the bed, keeping their heads below the cover of the tailgate and the dead forger. Talia raised herself on an elbow, emptied the Glock, and dropped down again to change magazines. "Poor turning radius. Limited cover. Limited speed." She slammed her spare mag home and chambered a round, passing the weapon to Tyler. "Why bring a four-by-four when a lighter, faster vehicle will do?"

The next volley hit the trees to their right. Tyler raised the Glock with one arm and fired blind. Glass shattered. Tires squealed. Talia stole a glance over the tailgate and saw the sedan back off four car lengths, one headlight shot out.

How did he do that?

Using the Glock, he gestured at the road ahead. "That's why we needed a four-by-four."

The end of the street came on fast, and beyond it, nothing but a mile-wide stretch of the Volga river. Mac hit the curb at full speed, bouncing Oleg up into the air. The body landed next to Talia with an ugly *thud*.

She gave Finn a look.

He shrugged. "Sorry, princess. I didn't have as good a grip as I thought."

The truck barreled over rough ground, and it took all Talia's strength and coordination to avoid smacking her head repeatedly into the bed. She could barely speak. "You slowed them... down... but they're still... coming. Your plan... didn't work."

"Oh, it'll work," Finn said. "Trust us."

A sharp bend in the river loomed ahead. Mac adjusted course to line up with a dirt berm. The engine surged.

"Mac?" Talia shouted.

"Hang on!" Finn shouted at the same time.

The Hilux roared up the berm and sailed out over the river. Talia went weightless, floating in space with the dead Oleg.

The truck splashed down with water flying high on all sides. Talia groaned and pressed up to her knees and saw Mac climb out through the driver's window just as the river began pouring in. He cast a sour look at Tyler. "Ya said I'd get to fly on this partic'lar job. Ya didn't say I'd be flyin' a truck."

A motorboat pulled alongside them, piloted by a young black woman, Darcy Emile, Tyler's chemist and demolitions expert. She helped Mac into the boat first and gave him the wheel before helping the others into the back. "Nice of you all to *drop in*, yes?" she said to Talia a singsong French accent, handing her a towel.

"Hilarious." Wiping the river from her eyes, Talia looked warily back at the berm. Where Darcy went, explosives were sure to follow. Something was about to go boom.

She hoped.

Before following the rest of the team, Tyler took the time to strap Oleg into the sinking truck with a set of tie-downs.

"What are you doing?" Talia asked.

"Keeping options open."

The Russians had carried enough momentum to drive the sedan to the top but not over. Five men piled out, all armed with submachine guns. Talia pulled Tyler into the boat. "You've given them the high ground. If you've got another trick up your sleeve, now's the time."

"Oh ye of little faith." He pulled a wet handkerchief from his rear pocket and scrubbed at a spot of Oleg's blood staining his jacket. "Darcy, you're on."

"Wait." The French woman watched the pack of thugs with interest, as if watching lemurs at the zoo. "I want to see their smiling faces, yes?"

A fusillade of bullets peppered the water, and more than a few poked holes in the fiberglass at the back. Mac revved the engines. Everyone but Tyler shouted at the chemist.

"Darcy!"

"Yes, okay. Here goes."

With a tremendous *foomp*, an entire section of the berm rose skyward. Five thugs and one car went flying on a cushion of dirt.

Finn poked Talia in the shoulder and laughed. "I told you it would work."

ACKNOWLEDGMENTS

IT IS NOT trite to give God top billing in the thanks department. It is appropriate and correct. I thank him for life, for salvation, for every day on Earth, and for the doors he has opened that allowed me to be here.

Now to everyone else . . .

I don't know how many authors can say their spouses read every single chapter the moment it's finished. But I can. I've said it before. Cindy is my first-line editor, my cheerleader, and my shoulder to cry on. Without her, my books would not be possible. She keeps me sane. And she feeds me.

I am so thrilled to join the team at Revell. Andrea Doering, Barb Barnes, Michele Misiak, Gayle Raymer, and the rest are a blessing. I am also grateful to my agent, Harvey Klinger, for his guidance and support on this project. He helped me turn this idea into what it is today.

Three others made significant contributions to this work. Two are men I go to routinely for spiritual guidance. The third God put in my path, presumably to demonstrate his providence. Dr. Gary C. Huckabay and Dr. Jeremy Evans both provided invaluable advice and guidance concerning forgiveness. In addition,

God placed me on a flight deck with Captain Philippe de Chambrier, an expert in counseling victims of trauma and helping them learn to forgive. Thank you to all of you.

Secret places and secret people do exist in this world. I've had the pleasure of seeing some of the former and know a few of the latter. Thus, there are a few individuals whose help I can neither confirm nor deny I received. You know who you are, and you know I'm grateful. Also, I apologize for ignoring certain truths and details. I do, after all, write escapist fiction. You understand.

A few authors deserve thanks—professionals who've given their time to critique and hone my craft. You'll find their names in the cover blurbs.

And finally, there is the growing cast of characters—and they are characters—who help me with every project. They aid my work with critiques, encouragement, instruction, and advice. They are Todd and Susie, John and Nancy, Chris and Melinda, Seth and Gavin, Danika and Dennis, Rachel and Katie, James and Ashton, Nancy and Dan, Steve and Tawnya, Randy and Hulda, and the Barons. God has blessed me through all of you, and I am grateful both to you and to him. I love you all.

JAMES R. HANNIBAL is no stranger to secrets and adventure. A former stealth pilot from Houston, Texas, he has been shot at, locked up with surface-to-air missiles, and chased down a winding German road by an armed terrorist. He is a two-time Silver Falchion Award winner for his Section 13 mysteries for kids and a Thriller Award nominee for his Nick Baron covert ops series for adults. James is a rare multi-sense synesthete, meaning all of his senses intersect. He sees and feels sounds and smells and hears flashes of light. If he tells you the chocolate cake you offered smells blue and sticky, take it as a compliment.

CONNECT WITH
James Hannibal

f JamesRHannibal   **◎** JamesRHannibal
𝕏 JamesRHannibal   **g** James R. Hannibal